By Dean Murray

Endless

Dean Murray

Copyright © 2014 by Dean Murray

Published by Fir'shan Publishing

ISBN 978-1-9393635-3-4

www.FirshanPublishing.com

First Edition

For Randy

Thank you for telling me that I exceeded your expectations both on the river and off.

Hearing that was a real confidence booster at a time when I needed exactly that.

Chapter 1

Not even the world's most gorgeous lightning storm could distract me from the fact that the guy I was sitting next to no longer trusted me.

Don't get me wrong, the storm was the kind of thing that most people never got a chance to see. Saying it was spectacular wouldn't have begun to do it credit, but the damage I'd done to my relationship with Jace wasn't the kind of thing I could push to the back of my mind—not even for a little while. Which was too bad, since that was the whole reason we'd come out here.

Jace had been the one to suggest the outing. He'd seen the clouds far off in the distance starting to light up and convinced me to leave the house so we could spend some time away from the pressures inherent in cramming six very stubborn people into one house—even a house as big as the one Jace and Kat had purchased when they'd moved to Cold Springs.

Leaving the house and wandering more than a mile away wasn't usually a good idea right before a storm this size blew in, but it wasn't a big deal for us. Even running through the forest, jumping over trees and all, it took us less than three minutes to cover the distance between the house and the top of the hill behind it. That kind of mind-shattering speed becomes commonplace when you're a demigod capable of amping your systems up to superhuman levels.

When we'd first arrived I'd been convinced that the whole trip had been a mistake. Standing on the top of the hill meant we had an unobstructed view of the destruction left from when Jace, Kat and I had faced off against Mephistoles and Sandra, and what we'd left behind wasn't pretty.

There was a reason that the Greeks had considered us gods and claimed that we'd been descended from powerful giants. The ground looked like it had been torn up by impossibly strong beings. Patches of the terrain had been scorched by fire, others had been blasted by lightning, and there was only one section that had any surviving plant life. We'd nearly lost—we would have lost if not for Kyles' help.

Yay for Kyle! He'd been the hero of the hour—or at least he would have been if not for the fact that he also happened to be Jace's brother and sworn enemy. Neither of the two liked each other, but they both wanted to date me. Actually, where Kyle was concerned, it was almost more like he wanted to possess me.

Kat, my best friend from before I'd been killed during my last incarnation, thought I was out of my mind for even thinking about dating Kyle, but I just couldn't seem to help myself. He'd come so far from where he'd been, but it was more even than that. I'd read an account written in my own handwriting from the last time we'd been together and it sounded like we'd been perfectly happy. That wasn't the kind of thing that was easy to dismiss.

Jace was frustrated by the fact that I hadn't started reading the journals he'd been saving for me. He had a point. It had to feel like I was stringing him along. I'd told him that I couldn't make a decision until after I'd had a chance to read through my later journals—the ones from when I'd been with him—and then I'd promptly spent the next two weeks not reading them.

I wasn't trying to lead him on. Reading more of my journals was terrifying. I did want to read them. I just wanted to make sure that I got everything I still remembered about my most recent incarnation down before I started into another project.

Yeah, the fine print in the metaphorical contract we all signed was a real killer. We could kill people with a look or make ourselves stronger than any three power lifters, but all of that power came at a price.

Every time we used our ability we lost some of our memories. Maybe only a few seconds, maybe months—it all depended on what we were doing. That would have been bad enough, but there was another gotcha. Our memories were the raw fuel that our abilities needed to function, but in order to make any given effect work we also had to be in the grip of a strong emotion.

If one of us Awakened wanted to be more powerful then we had to cultivate even stronger emotional extremes. It turned out that when a strong emotion was entered into willingly it had a little less power to influence your words and actions. That was good, but it wasn't the same thing as having *no* ability to influence you.

All of which went a long way towards explaining some of the craziness that is a recurring theme in basically every mythology known to man. Greek, Norse, Aztec...they were all stories about beings who were too powerful for their own good, people who reacted on an emotional basis far too often, people who sometimes couldn't even remember who their real enemies were.

I wouldn't have chosen the life of an Awakened for myself, but it wasn't like I ever had a choice. Luckily there were a few offsetting advantages to being an Awakened. Kat was one of them. What girl would willingly turn down a chance to have a friend who'd known them for more than three hundred years?

Of course I didn't remember any of that friendship and Kat remembered less than a hundred years, but things like that happened when you got killed and were reborn into another incarnation. Even so, Kat knew me better than almost anyone else.

I'd been a different person back then, with different experiences altogether, but after being reborn I still had the same basic personality. I still liked the same kinds of things and I still hated Sandra. All of which meant that Kat sometimes knew me better than I knew myself, which was occasionally unsettling, but usually just what the doctor ordered.

Up until recently, the other huge benefit was Jace, but me kissing his brother while I'd been trapped in Kyle's hidden bunker had soured things there. Jace still wanted to make things work, but there wasn't any denying the fact that things were different now.

All of which brought me back to the fact that I was sitting at the top of a hill watching the world's biggest thunderstorm head our way. I'd seen my share of thunderstorms, but this was the first time I'd seen the lightning striking behind such a large bank of clouds.

It was nearly dark, but there still just enough light for me to see that the cloud front stretched for dozens of miles in either direction, and every second or two vast sections of the approaching storm lit up with a gorgeous blue light. I was used to thinking of a lightning storm being nothing but cerulean forks briefly connecting the ground and sky, but this was something else altogether. This was like fireworks.

As the storm got closer to us, the frequency of the lightning strikes picked up to the point where there were often multiple strikes in any given second. It would have been a nightmare to endure outside, exposed to the elements, but seen from a distance it was the kind of thing I wished I could never forget.

"So, how was your day?"

Jace's question was nothing more than a weak attempt at breaking the ice. Given that we shared every class at school he already knew everything there was to know about my day, but I still loved him for making the attempt. We both wanted things to work, we just needed to find a way around our respective issues.

"Not bad. I got most of my homework done last night before dropping off for a full three hours of sleep, so I was able to get more written in my journal than I was expecting to."

That was another advantage to being an Awakened. I only needed two or three hours of sleep a night. It meant I had a lot more free time to do whatever I wanted. I had a suspicion that it would start to feel more like a curse than a blessing as the centuries rolled by, but Jace and Kat maintained that it wasn't bad as long as I could come up with an enjoyable hobby.

"I'm glad. I'm sure that you'll feel a lot better once you get it all down and know that it isn't just going to evaporate on you the next time you get pulled into a big fight."

"What about you? What have you been working on?"

Jace shrugged. "A little of this, a little of that. Between getting moved into our new place, and all of the craziness that took place immediately after we met you, I fell behind on my journaling too. I'm just about caught up though, so last night I spent a good chunk of time looking back through your research journals."

I knew that he didn't mean that as a reproach, but I couldn't help but flinch. When Jace and Kat said that endless nights wouldn't be that bad as long as I had a hobby to distract me, what they really meant was that I should spend all of that extra time researching new and exciting ways to kill other Awakened.

I wasn't just any old Awakened chick, I was one of my race's star researchers. Who knew that geeks in lab coats would be the most desired individuals in a world of demigods?

"I'm sorry, Jace. I've been meaning to get to those too…"

He flashed one of his trademark crooked smiles. "I wasn't trying to make you feel bad, Selene. I know you've been busy. I wouldn't have said anything, but you asked me what I've been working on, so I told you."

Maybe he hadn't meant to make me feel bad, but it was hard to just shrug his statement off. We were stronger numbers-wise than we'd been since Kyle had split off from our pantheon, but we were still far from the largest pantheon around, which meant that our continued survival was heavily dependent on me getting back up to speed with the research I'd been pioneering when I'd been killed the last time.

Jace and Kat seemed confident that it was just a matter of *when* rather than a matter of *if*. I wasn't quite so sure. I wouldn't say that I hated math—not exactly—but we weren't really on a first-name basis. Based on what I'd seen in Kyle's lab when I'd been stuck inside his bunker, research involved a lot of math. Complicated math.

"So what are you working on right now—research-wise, I mean?"

"I've pretty much cherry-picked as much of your findings as I can. I was hoping that one more pass would reveal something else useful, but it's not looking that way."

I wanted to curl up in a little ball and start crying, but I put on the bravest face I could. "So it's all just a big waste of time, then? All those years of research and I wasn't actually accomplishing anything?"

It wasn't like anyone could blame me for what my last incarnation had been up to, but it did speak to my underlying character. If I'd wasted my time back then it was only reasonable for

Jace and Kat to worry that I would do the same thing this time around.

They wouldn't kick me to the curb for that—I was still an Awakened, I still represented power that our little pantheon needed in order to avoid being destroyed by rival groups of Awakened—but it might change how willing Jace was to put up with my crap. I didn't think so—Jace had never seemed like the kind of guy who was only interested in what I could do for him—but there was still a chance and even just a shadow of a chance would have been enough to make me worry.

"No, that's not what I'm saying at all. Your journals aren't as straightforward as some kind of recipe book. Partly that was because you were writing them for yourself rather than someone else, but mostly it's because you didn't want anything you'd been working on to end up in the wrong hands. You wanted anyone who managed to get their hands on your journals to really work in order to unlock their secrets. You've got hints as to what you were working on, but the end result isn't something that you actually came right out and discussed even in your most private journals.

"Anyone who wants to take advantage of your work—including me—is going to have to be bright enough to work through all your math and understand the potential applications of what you discovered."

"Awesome. Yet more math. Why does everything have to involve so much math?"

That actually made Jace chuckle. I'd missed hearing him laugh—there hadn't been much laughter since I'd returned from Kyle's bunker.

"Math is the only way to really describe anything."

"Not true. I can point to the lightning and tell you right now that it's blue and jagged."

"Sure, but you can't tell me how long it lasts or the speed that it's moving at, or the strength of the current without resorting to numbers. Math is the language that we all resort to when we try to describe the world in enough detail to be able to work effects."

"Not all effects."

"No, not all effects—at least not the weaker forms of the effects in question—but if you want to work anything really powerful you have to understand its true nature. Otherwise you're just burning peak memories and forcing ridiculous amounts of power into a crude tool and getting a really inefficient result out the other end."

"Okay, math is necessary. It's still evil, but it's a necessary evil."

That drew another smile out of Jace. He was so gorgeous that it made my chest ache. It wasn't just the outside package either. Jace had wavy blond hair that always looked like it had just been prepped for a photo shoot, a square jaw that even plastic surgery couldn't bestow on someone, and the kind of muscles that you didn't get without serious time in a gym, but that was just the start of his attractiveness.

Jace was a genuinely good guy, one who helped people simply because it was the right thing to do, who was honest and kind, and who seemed to understand me on levels I hadn't even realized existed. I'd screwed things up and I didn't know how to fix them—at least not as long as I was still trying to hold onto the possibility of Kyle turning out as something other than an evil overlord who was bent on world domination.

"What did I say this time?"

Jace cocked his head to one side. "Worried I'm secretly laughing at you?"

"Not at all. I'm just desperate to find out how I made you happy—even temporarily. That's been a pretty rare occurrence lately and I'd like to know how to make it happen more often."

Even as I said the words I knew they weren't the right thing to say. I half expected Jace to retreat back inside his shell, but this time he didn't. He just met my gaze with a smile that was slightly sadder than the one from a moment earlier.

"You just reminded me of another conversation we all had a long time ago. Back then it was Kat complaining about all of the math and you telling her why it was so necessary. It's just funny the way that we all end up behaving so similarly. It makes me wonder if a couple of incarnations from now it will be Kat who's the ace researcher and me who's complaining about how hard all of the math is."

I felt myself start to shake deep down inside wherever it was that tears started before they could work themselves up out to a person's eyes. I didn't want to cry, didn't want to manipulate Jace into taking me back by letting my emotions run wild, but I wasn't sure that I was going to manage to keep the tears from overflowing.

Jace looked away, maybe uncomfortable with where the discussion had been headed, or maybe just trying to give me time to gather myself again. Either way, it was what I needed. I turned away and looked back out at the storm.

The lightning had moved close enough now that it wasn't all shrouded behind layers of clouds. A fair percentage of the strikes were still lighting up the sky, sometimes in unexpected ways as a cloud bank blocked a portion of the light and let other pieces through, but now some of the strikes were out where we could see them.

The lightning was bright enough and close enough that I expected the thunder to make my entire body vibrate, but it was strangely hushed. The first few drops landed on my upturned face and I pulled my windbreaker closed. If it was going to rain then it was probably time for us to go back home, but I didn't want to leave. I wanted to stay out there—risking death by electrocution if necessary—until we resolved things. Only that wasn't possible until I figured out what—who—I actually wanted.

"I'm so sorry, Jace. I didn't mean to ruin everything..."

"I know, Selene. I always knew something like this was going to happen sooner or later. Kat kept telling me that I should lock you down as soon as possible, make you fall in love with me and get you to marry me before you found out about Kyle, but I knew that would just lead to more heartbreak eventually. It's not possible to just ignore that kind of history."

"I did fall in love with you—I'm still in love with you."

"You just can't let go of what might have been. I know, it's the same thing you struggled with right after the two of you broke up the last time, and you were the one who broke things off then. It's hardly surprising that it's a challenge this time around, not when Kyle so obviously wants you now."

"Does he? You could have fooled me. He threw down an ultimatum, refused to let me have my journal, and then proceeded to tell me the next time I saw him things would be different—not in a good way."

Jace looked pained. I was such an idiot. Talking about the other guy you were interested in was basically engraved in the list of top ten things you didn't do with a guy you were hoping to make fall madly in love with you. Asking him if the other guy really liked you just made things a hundred times worse.

I opened my mouth to apologize—even though I knew it would be too little too late—but Jace responded before I could get the words out.

"Yes. He does want you. He's changed a lot since he broke away from us a couple hundred years ago, but that hasn't changed. He never stopped wanting you, he just hid all of that behind other urges. He's just really out of practice when it comes to dealing with other people and he doesn't like the idea of needing you, of anyone having any kind of power over him."

"You didn't need to answer that, Jace. I'm sorry, I didn't mean to ask—my head is still spinning and I don't feel like I have anything to hold onto with everything that's happened in the last few weeks."

"I know. I don't like talking about Kyle, but if that's what it takes to have you spend time with me I'll do it."

"But you said—"

"I know what I said, but back in the day I spent decades following you and Kyle around, decades trying not to feel for you. This can't be any worse than that. I want to be here for you right now, Selene, it's just hard for me. It's hard to be around you and wonder if each second is going to be my last with you.

"I don't think we can go back to how things were the first time around. Kyle and I are too different now. Whoever doesn't get picked is going to end up running as far and as fast in the other direction as they can. We won't be able to help ourselves."

The pain shining out of his eyes was the kind of thing I couldn't have ignored even if I'd wanted to—but I didn't. I was confused and stupid, but I cared about Jace. I didn't want to see him hurting.

I could only think of one thing to do to take away the pain, but even that wasn't a permanent solution. We were long past the point where I could just make everything better by kissing him, but that didn't stop me from leaning in. Even knowing that this could just make things harder in the long run wasn't enough to stop me from inching closer to him.

Maybe I was just kidding myself. Maybe this wasn't about Jace, maybe it was just about me and my need to touch him. Whatever the real cause was, I seemed to be powerless to stop myself from reaching up to cradle the side of his face.

He hadn't shaved yet today, and the hint of stubble I could feel on my palm was like coming home. I wanted him like I'd only ever wanted one other person—but I refused to let myself think of Jace's brother right then.

I leaned in until we were almost touching and then lost my nerve. I wanted to go all the way in, but my second thoughts were starting to get the better of me. I held the distance between us down to something measured in millimeters, and then right as I started to pull back Jace reached out and pulled me the rest of the way in.

There was a need to his touch that I didn't remember being there before. It wasn't bottled lust like I'd expected, it was a need to know that I still wanted him, that I still craved his touch the same way that he craved mine.

Despite the exterior package, Jace wasn't some unsure teenager. He was hundreds of years old, and even if he only remembered the last hundred and twenty years he still understood what he brought to the table.

He was sexy and desirable, and he knew it. He was bottled confidence when it came to working effects or negotiating multi-million dollar deals, but there was one tiny chink in his armor. He didn't know if all of that was good enough for me.

I'd never felt that kind of power where a guy was concerned, and the combination of vulnerability and raw confidence was a heady mixture. I couldn't have pulled away even if I'd wanted to. I needed him in ways that I couldn't describe, on levels that were deeper even than I'd realized.

His lips against mine completed me in ways that I'd been needing my whole life. I'd gone more than seventeen years feeling like something important was missing. The entire time I'd been missing him but I'd had no way of knowing it until he'd found me.

Some of the urgency dissipated from his touch as he grabbed my waist and pulled me close enough that I was almost sitting in his lap. That didn't do anything to bank the fire I could feel building between the two of us, it just meant that we'd both been reassured and were connecting in different ways.

Jace's fingers moved to my neck and I felt myself tremble. He knew exactly where to touch me. Part of me wanted to break away and tell him it was too much, too soon, but a bigger part of me wanted to beg for more, wanted to tell him that I only wanted him.

The temptation to throw myself at him and promise my undying love was almost over-powering, but I knew that wouldn't be fair—especially not to him.

I would have liked to be able to say that I managed to do the right thing and pull back, but I didn't get the chance because right then we were interrupted by the arrival of a bloody, dying man who I'd never seen before.

Chapter 2

I wouldn't have said that anything could put out the desire I was feeling in that moment, but I would have been wrong. I cooled down faster than if I'd had a bucket of ice water dumped on me.

Our new arrival dropped to his knees less than five feet from us and then fell face first onto the forest floor. I had a split second to take in the fact that he had curly dark hair, and that he looked like he was in his mid to late thirties, and then Jace was pulling me over to the man.

It probably would have made more sense to just leave me back where we'd been sitting originally. I'd only been working effects for a few weeks, which wasn't even close to enough time to begin learning how to heal people. I was apparently some kind of savant when it comes to picking up new effects, but nobody was that good.

ENDLESS

Even as the thought crossed my mind I realized it wasn't true. I'd healed Jace after the fight with Mephistoles, I just didn't know how I'd done it. Jace and Kat both had theories about what was going on. They thought I'd somehow managed to carry bits of knowledge forward from my last incarnation...only that was impossible and we all knew it.

I'd died, and not the fifteen-minutes-of-zero-brain-activity-before-popping-back-up-with-crazy-stories-about-the-afterlife kind of death. I'd died, left behind a body that had been buried, and then been reborn as an infant. I shouldn't have been able to bring anything forward other than my core personality, and even that should have been heavily influenced by my formative years.

It was a mystery that none of us had any way of solving, a mystery that none of us were even quite sure was important, but it had been on my mind a lot lately.

Jace flipped the man onto his back and put his hands on the massive cut that ran from his right hip up to the bottom of his ribs on the other side. I felt a warm tingle as Jace tapped into the positive emotions that he used as a lens for his effects, and then watched as the gash disappeared.

"I've repaired all of the vascular damage and stabilized the affected organs. I also kick started the process of replacing the blood he's lost."

Jace's voice had a semi-detached sound to it, the kind of tone you heard out of world-class doctors who were in the middle of a complicated procedure that might or might not be sufficient to save a patient. Under other circumstances I probably would have just sat back and enjoyed seeing Jace do what he'd been born to do, but this time I was too freaked out to appreciate the show.

"I don't know what that means. Is he going to make it?"

Jace had his hand on the side of the guy's neck. He waited several seconds before responding. "I'm not sure. I think I've got his blood pressure up enough, but I won't know for sure until we get him back to the house where I can hook him up to real equipment."

"Can't you just make more blood?"

"It doesn't work like that, Selene. Unless I want to burn multiple peak memories I've got to have *something* to work with. This guy was so close to the edge that it's a miracle he made it this far. He's dehydrated and he's burned through most of his spare body fat. I could start trying to convert muscle and bone to blood, but that's incredibly dangerous."

"Okay, so what do we do then?"

"We amp ourselves up and get him back to the house as quickly as possible. Once he's back in the house I can run a drip. That will help with his blood pressure and if his hematocrit level is too low I can transmute it to more blood."

"Kind of crazy to think that there are some things that modern technology does better than Awakened effects."

Jace shrugged as he bent down and picked the man up. He was strong enough that he didn't have to amp himself up to do that, but even Jace couldn't carry someone at a pace of thirty miles per hour for more than a mile without giving his body a little something extra.

"Our abilities are capable of miraculous things, but we aren't actually gods, Selene. We're still constrained by the rules of physics, we just use loopholes that modern science hasn't discovered yet."

I nodded as I reached out for the pulse of our surroundings. The approaching wall of water made it easy. I honed in on the sound of the rain hitting the ground and dialed it back at the same time that I tapped into the reserve of happiness I'd been laboriously building up and forced my system into overdrive.

I only amped myself up to three times normal speed, but even so I felt a burst of memories flow out through the center of my forehead as Jace took off like a bullet. I threw myself after him, pacing him with a grace and ease that I never could have managed without my abilities. Now that the effect was up and running, keeping my system amped up wasn't requiring as much of an expenditure of memories, but there was still an ongoing drain. As I jumped over one fallen log and then ran along another, I wondered what I would end up losing.

I'd started out terrified of losing my memories. I still was in a lot of ways, but I'd finally started to come to terms with the fact that there wasn't any way to avoid using my abilities, not if I wanted to keep my friends and family safe.

We covered the mile from the hill to the house in just over three minutes, and I managed to remember to drop my strength and speed amp before I tried to open the sliding door. Things like opening doors got tricky when you were amped—I'd already broken several things over the last two weeks by accident. Getting stuff replaced wasn't a big deal from a cost perspective—money was basically a non-issue when you could transmute sand or clay into precious metals—but none of us really wanted a bunch of strangers inside the house repairing fixtures because I'd been too stupid to remember that I needed to let my effects expire before I tried to open a door.

I thought about yelling for help, but as soon as I got the door open Jace blasted past me at better than twenty miles per hour. I followed him at my best speed and found him in the triage area attached to the gym at the back of the house.

It was starting to make a lot more sense why Jace and Kat left most of the doors inside the house propped open. It meant that some of the internal security features weren't operating as intended, but it also meant that they didn't have to slow down and wait for doors to open with glacial slowness when they were in a hurry.

I heard drawers banging shut as I finally caught up to Jace, and he'd managed to start an IV by the time I made it to his side and he flickered back to normal speed.

"Okay, that should do it. I'll go ahead and hook up the monitoring equipment, but once the IV has had a chance to empty into his system he should be out of the woods."

"What do you want me to do?"

"Could you go get Kat and the others? They need to know that we've got someone else in the house. Kat knows how to lock down the interior, which she should go ahead and do, but I don't expect it to make much of a difference, not against another Awakened."

"Wait, you mean he's one of us?"

Even as I said it I reached out with my mind in an attempt to sense him. It took a second. That was partly because I was so unpracticed at sensing other Awakened, but mostly it was just because his presence was so weak as to be virtually undetectable.

"How is that even possible? He's unconscious, so he's not actively masking his presence, and even if he was I didn't know it was possible to mask yourself so completely."

"It isn't, but if you push yourself close enough to the edge you can come close. Based on the state he appears to be in, his emotional reservoir is empty and he's pushed his body to the point of collapse. We've got about twelve hours to figure out who he is and what he wants. After that, he'll start recharging his reserves enough that he'll be a danger."

Chapter 3

Jace's revelation wasn't reassuring. So far my experiences with other Awakened hadn't exactly been positive. Mephistoles had almost managed to kill me, Sandra had been more than happy to stab my dad before throwing herself at me in an effort to make sure that I breathed my last breath, and Kyle had turned my entire world upside down. In fairness, that last one had been as much my fault as it had been his.

This guy might be the nicest person in the world, but I seriously doubted it. It was a lot more likely that he was going to try to slit all of our throats while we were sleeping.

I found Kat and my dad sitting awkwardly by themselves in the media room. I wasn't sure which of them had suggested that particular idea, but even I could have told them that it was a terrible one. My dad hadn't been out on a date in five years, and it had been almost two decades since he'd gone out with anyone other than my mom.

Kat liked movies, but I knew her well enough to know that she really just wanted a chance to sit down and talk to him. A movie wasn't going to provide that—all it was going to do was make things weird between the two of them.

I sighed as I flipped the lights on and pointed back towards the triage area. "We've got a visitor. Jace wants everyone back in the medical room so we can decide what to do with him."

I tried not to notice just how relieved both of them looked at the interruption, but it was obvious that neither of them was comfortable with how their date had been progressing. I didn't wait around to listen to them try to convince each other that they'd been having a good time.

Ari was outside in the garage. By herself. I was worried about her, but I wasn't sure what to do about it. It had been my dad who'd spent several days as Mephistoles' prisoner, not her. Still, being locked away downstairs in the vault while Jace and Kat had gone looking for me had taken a toll on her. She was still my little sister, but she was different.

As nearly as I could tell she'd pulled away from her friends at school, and she seemed to have given up on the crush she'd been feeling for Jace. I wasn't sure if that was because she was uneasy around him now that she knew he and I had a history together that was literally longer than our country had existed, or if she was still just in shock that Jace, Kat and I had been keeping such a big secret from her.

Whatever the reason, she'd changed. She came inside the house to eat and to sleep, but she wasn't doing enough of either. She spent every waking moment working on my car. She'd pulled my engine out and removed all of the body panels, which meant it was no longer drivable, but that didn't matter since we were riding into school with Kat and Jace.

Kat had given Ari a credit card that didn't seem to have a limit, and she'd been using it to buy car parts. Turbos, new rims, new exhaust systems, she'd purchased at least one of just about everything under the sun.

When she finally finished up with her project my car was going to look brand new and completely unrecognizable, but it didn't really matter. I already had more than five million dollars' worth of platinum stockpiled inside of my room. Once I got a chance to turn some of that into cash, it would be the easiest thing in the world to replace my old clunker with any car I wanted.

After watching the slow transformation of my car over the last couple of weeks, I was actually kind of curious to see what it was going to look like once she was done, but at the same time I was scared to death of that day arriving. I wasn't sure what Ari would do once she no longer had that distraction to keep her from facing her demons.

"Hey, Ari. Jace and I found a guy out in the forest and Jace wants everyone to meet inside the house and discuss what we do next. He's in the triage area off the exercise facilities."

"Can't you just call an ambulance and let someone else worry about him?"

"No, he's an Awakened. That means he could be dangerous."

"Okay, I'll be in shortly. I just need to finish tightening down these bolts."

All of that drifted out from underneath the car—she didn't bother rolling out to where I could see her. I stood there for several seconds wishing I knew what to say, that I had the words to fix whatever was bothering her, but I didn't. In the end I just turned around and walked back inside.

There was only one other person I needed to hunt down, and she was the person I was least excited to see. It took me another five minutes, but I eventually found Sandra in the main basement level, sketching in one of the black-bound journals that Jace had given her.

She didn't look up as I walked into the large sitting room. I watched her from across the vast expanse of carpet for several seconds before finally clearing my throat.

"Jace has asked everyone to meet upstairs. Another Awakened practically tripped over us while we were out in the forest. He's hurt, so he's not a threat right now, but we're going to have to decide what to do with him before he wakes up."

She continued drawing without acknowledging my presence and I had to suppress a rising tide of anger. This kind of anger would have been bad enough for a normal person to deal with. It was twice as bad for me because the anger meant that I was that much closer to working an effect.

I started across the room, all but shaking from anger. "Did you hear me, Sandra?"

"Yeah, blah, blah, go upstairs and listen to everyone else make decisions that I have absolutely no input into. Blah, blah, a new one of us has arrived so I'm even less important than I was before, blah, blah."

I pulled up short, my mind reeling. "Really? That's how you're going to behave after everything that Jace and Kat have done for you?"

"What, you mean like not killing me? Yeah, I get it, I'm a massive bi-otch who nearly killed your dad. I deserve to have my pretty little head chopped off, but you're all so wonderful that you decided to save me despite all of that."

"I didn't say anything about that."

"You don't have to, Selene. It's there underlying everything any of you say or do. Here's the thing though, I don't remember any of that. All I have is your word as to what happened, and I can't seem to get past the fact that I hate your guts with an intensity that should scare me, but doesn't."

"I don't know what to tell you, Sandra. You've hated me for as long as I can remember, but I've never done anything to deserve your hatred."

"Yeah, I got the memo on that too, but that doesn't change how I feel. From everything you've all been saying, I shouldn't remember anything more complicated than how to walk or use a fork, and I can't—not really—but I can't get away from the feeling that you stole something from me, something that you didn't even want."

She was talking about Jace, but I wasn't sure how to respond. I didn't remember any of that—I hadn't even read my journals from back then yet. All I knew was what Jace and Kat had told me.

"Look, I'm going to level with you, Sandra. This all happened way before either of our current incarnations, but my understanding is that you and Jace used to be an item. For a while it was you, him and Kyle, but then Kat and I happened along and the guys threw their lot in with me. You didn't handle that very well. It was ultimately the reason why you ended up joining forces with Mephistoles the first time around. I don't know anything more than that—I promise."

"You must be loving this."

"What do you mean?"

"I mean you got everything. Jace and Kyle are fighting over you, you have the clothes and the money—everything you could possibly want—and I'm sitting here in borrowed clothes with a memory that covers only the last two weeks. You've got superpowers, and I do too, but nobody is willing to teach me how to use them because none of you trust me. I apparently have a dad, but I'm not allowed to go see him, and he must be freaking out about me, but there isn't anything I can do about it other than just sit here wondering when I'll be something other than a slave."

"You aren't a slave. You have the run of nearly the entire house, and the only reason you're stuck here is that you're not capable of protecting yourself right now. If we let you run around by yourself you'd end up captured or killed by one of the other pantheons. Believe me when I say that either one of those options would be a ton worse than what you're going through right now."

"Then teach me how to defend myself. Show me a little trust for once."

I forced myself not to grind my teeth. "It's not about trust, Sandra. You don't have enough memories to power any worthwhile effects. Knowing how to create effects is addictive. Once you know how to do them, it's nearly impossible to avoid using them. If we taught you right now, you'd just wipe away what few memories you have left and you'd be back to where you were two weeks ago.

"Give it some time. In five or six years you'll have enough baseline memory built up for us to begin teaching you how to defend yourself. After that, you can go off and do whatever you want."

"Whatever. I'll believe it when I see it."

"Fine. Stay down here for all I care, but don't go whining to everyone that you don't have a say in what's going on if you're not willing to come up and participate in the discussions where the decisions are made."

I turned and walked away from her without looking back. A second later her pencil went spinning through the air past my head. It slammed into the wall next to the stairs, but I never even flinched. I'd had much worse things thrown at me lately.

Chapter 4

Everyone but Sandra made it up to the triage room by the time the new guy woke up. I was surprised that he was conscious so soon after nearly dying, but I shouldn't have been—Jace did good work.

Most healers could save someone if they were on death's doorstep, but it was a rare individual who had a light enough touch to save someone without throwing the rest of their systems off so badly that they would have to spend several days in bed recovering.

The new guy opened his eyes and then shut them immediately. Jace looked up obviously planning on asking one of us to darken the windows, but Ari was already on it. She turned the dial on the wall while the rest of us were still looking around trying to locate it. The windows slowly polarized, bringing the light level down to where our visitor could open his eyes with a minimal amount of squinting.

"I guess you're as good as they say you are, Jace."

I half expected Jace to shake the guy's hand and pat him on the back, but instead Jace produced a knife from somewhere and stood between the new guy and the rest of us.

"Who are you, and how did you find us?"

"My name is Byron. I'm part of the Helena pantheon."

Kat had put on a hard facade too. "Nice try. There isn't any pantheon in Helena."

"That's what we wanted everyone to think. The truth is that we've been there for the better part of the last sixty years, we just keep a very low profile."

Jace shook his head. "Nobody keeps that low a profile. Even the best of us can't manage to drop completely out of sight for that long. Five years? Sure. Ten years? Maybe. Sixty? Not on your life."

"It's possible. You just have to cut off all contact with the fae and avoid using your abilities. If you can live like a normal human for a year or so, your presence starts shrinking down. After eighteen months it becomes possible to hide your signature from anyone not right on top of you."

Ari and Dad didn't seem to understand the significance of what we'd just been told, but

Jace, Kat and I were all reeling. It seemed too impossible to believe that there was really a way to bow out of the eternal fighting that seemed to go hand-in-hand with being one of the Awakened. I was so shocked that it took me a second to realize the importance of the first half of his comment.

"Wait, are you trying to say that we can't trust even the Seelie court?"

Byron gave me a once-over, eyes stopping on Bethany, who'd landed on my shoulder as I'd climbed back up the stairs from talking to Sandra, and then nodded.

"You must be Genevieve's latest incarnation. Yes, contact with the fae always causes nothing but problems. I'm a big fan of your work, by the way."

Bethany took off from my shoulder like she was planning on dive-bombing Byron, but then realized that she was still much too small to be a match for him, even in his weakened state.

"Take it back! I would never do anything to bring harm to Selene or her friends."

Byron shrugged. "That may be the truth. It probably is given that you're so newly created and Selene is so close to Genevieve, but that's not the case with all of the fae."

I was glad that Kregor wasn't around. He was still relatively weak for a fae, but he was big enough to be dangerous under the right circumstances.

"So we're fine. We limit our contact with the Seelie court to just Bethany and Kregor, stop using our abilities, and then in a year or so we'll manage to drop out of sight and live normal lives."

Byron shook his head. "I've spent the better part of the last five hundred years learning how to disappear. I figured out how to make my signature disappear more than four hundred years ago. I thought I had the answer I was looking for back then, but then I spent the next two hundred years running from one pantheon or another. It wasn't until my friends and I cut ties with both courts completely that we were able to get under the radar."

Jace was considering Byron's words. In another life I would have been the one matching up what he was telling us with all of the theories our pantheon had put together regarding how the world worked, but I wasn't that person anymore. It was possible that Jace was right about my capability to one day become a star researcher again, but for now I didn't even begin to have the background knowledge needed to evaluate what we were being told.

"So what happened?"

"A lot of things. Sometimes our familiars got frustrated by the fact that we weren't burning memories anymore, sometimes one of the Unseelie Court happened along unexpectedly and we ended up having to defend ourselves, sometimes we got flushed out of hiding by stuff that seemed like freak accidents."

"But you're not convinced?"

"Nope. I'd like to think otherwise, but the freak accidents all stopped happening when it was just us Awakened."

"What's your working theory?"

"I'm not sure. The courts both operate giant intelligence networks. It's possible that the Lady was keeping tabs on us for some benign reason and she just has a leak somewhere in her organization, but I think that the courts can sense each other."

We all turned to Bethany, who I could feel shifting around from foot to foot.

"Don't look at me like that. I can't sense anyone but Selene."

I reached up and patted her on the backs of her legs. "Nobody is saying that you're going to betray us, Bethany. It could be any number of things that made it so the Helena pantheon was able to drop out of sight after they stopped interacting with the fae. My bet is that one or more of the other pantheons have figured out how to sense the presence of members of either court."

Byron shrugged. "It's a possibility. I wondered as much myself, but not using my abilities for the last few decades has pretty much precluded any useful research in that area."

Jace hadn't put away his knife. He wasn't being overtly threatening, but it was obvious that he still didn't trust our visitor.

"You still haven't explained why you're here or how you found us."

"I'm here because my entire pantheon is dead—everyone but me."

You could have heard a pin drop in that instant. Back in the day it hadn't been unheard of for one pantheon to completely destroy another, but that had been before it had been so easy to cover vast distances in just hours or days. Now it was uncommon for an entire pantheon to be destroyed unless they were caught by surprise and totally outclassed.

"How many of you were there?"

Even as the words tumbled out of my mouth something told me that I didn't want to hear the answer. He'd just told us all that Shangri-La really existed, and then turned around and announced its destruction in the same breath.

"Twenty-five."

Kat pushed past Jace and grabbed Byron's arm. "How did your group get to be so big? That's the biggest pantheon in recorded history. Some of the ancient groups managed to get nearly that big, but that was all a function of large human populations to draw on and some kind of natural barrier or societal advantage that kept the barbarians outside the gates."

"We've been recruiting for a long time. Not everyone, just people who'd been in their current incarnation for long enough that we felt confident they would fit into our group. People who default to positive emotions mostly."

Kat pulled back like she'd been slapped. My dad and Ari looked confused, but I understood what had just happened. Kat had just realized the cost of her choice in default emotions. Byron continued on before I could comfort her.

"Your pantheon has been on our radar for quite a while, Jace especially. We figured he would make a perfect addition to our group, but some of our members weren't so excited about the rest of you. You're both powered by anger and several of us weren't so sure that Kyle would let...Selene drop out of sight."

Jace looked like a man who was trying very hard to remain objective, a man who wanted to believe, but who knew that there was a chance that we were just being told what we wanted to hear because it was the best way to get close to us.

"You're awfully well-informed about our group."

"We had to be. One bad recruit had the potential to ruin things for all of us."

"How did you manage it? How did it work?"

"Manage what? Gathering intelligence?"

Byron looked legitimately unsure of what Jace wanted to hear, but part of me—a suspicious, jaded part that felt too old and cynical to have come from anywhere other than my last incarnation—wondered if he was just buying himself time to come up with a believable lie.

Jace stepped closer, trying to intimidate Byron and throw him off his game.

"I want to know everything. How you gathered information, how you went about recruiting people, and most of all how you found us. Don't jerk us around or I'll bury your body myself."

"I'd say I'm surprised to hear that from you, Jace, but your history shows that you're extremely protective of the members of your pantheon."

"We're still waiting."

Byron slid further back on the table so that he wasn't quite so close to Jace. "We can't use our abilities without risking discovery, so by and large we've had to develop other methods of information-gathering. We've got some of the world's best hackers in our ranks. It turns out that the attributes that make a good researcher tend to translate well into cyber-security and most of our people have had the benefit of being around since before the dawn of the computer age."

He was right, a hundred years was a long time to spend learning all the ins and outs of hacking a computer system, and when you threw in the fact that his pantheon wasn't forgetting any of the stuff they were learning, it turned into a recipe for hacker domination.

"At this point we have backdoors into every major intelligence agency in the world and we use that to make sure that we're as informed about the movements of the other pantheons as possible. We've been running facial recognition programs on every form of social media since before even the NSA started doing it."

Jace shrugged. "We've been doing that too. It only works if you've got a decent picture of the person you're looking for."

"Not exactly. We've got pictures of some of the different Awakened out there courtesy of the intelligence agencies, but recently we've been scanning for instances where large numbers of people with very similar appearances show up in different locations. Most of those people will be mimics, but it's letting us generate a pictorial database of other Awakened. Sooner or later the humans we've identified will age enough to remove themselves from the running and we'll be able to track all of the Awakened."

He was painting a picture of a world that I wasn't sure I wanted to be a part of. It was the logical extension of what Jace and Kat had already done to find me, but it was still chilling. The idea of being tracked wherever I went, of having someone always looking over my shoulder, waiting for the perfect moment to strike, was going to give me nightmares.

Jace stepped even closer. "How did you know that we were here?"

"This was considered a hot spot because we'd registered the possibility of two new incarnations. We've been watching land purchases for a while and this house showed up as the perfect base for any Awakened who decided to stay in the area. The shell company you used to purchase it was quite good. None of us had been able to track ownership back to any known Awakened, but I had a hunch that it was you and Kat. If somebody else had shown up for Selene or the other one they would have just grabbed them and kept moving. You and Kat are the only ones who would care about trying to minimize disruptions to Selene's normal life."

He had a point there. Everyone else would have either just killed me so that I wouldn't be a threat for another twenty years, or kidnapped me and brainwashed me into working for them similarly to what Mephistoles had done with Sandra. Of course she'd been more than willing to sign onto anything that resulted in her being able to take a swing at me.

"As for how we recruit, we spend decades watching potential allies. Sooner or later they at least partially fall off the radar on their own and we approach them with an offer to provide them with sanctuary for a trial period. Coming up with a way to keep them out of sight for long enough for their signature to shrink down took some doing, but eventually we decided to just hide them out in plain sight."

Kat closed her eyes and shook her head. "You guys are the ones responsible for Camelot, aren't you? I knew that there was more going on in New Mexico than anyone suspected"

Byron smiled like Kat was an exceptionally bright student who'd just managed to surprise him. Jace looked poleaxed; the rest of us just looked confused. I finally broke the silence.

"Wasn't Camelot in England?"

Kat waved me off like she was too frustrated to speak, but Jace pulled himself together enough to respond.

"Yeah, the first one was in England. Arthur was actually one of us, by the way, as were most of his knights and a few of their ladies. It was an odd time. Some of us were still claiming to be gods, but Arthur wanted to create a different society, one where the Awakened weren't worshiped, but rather respected for their knowledge and wisdom. Several nearby pantheons ended up getting together and wiping out Camelot, but shortly after the New World was discovered legends started circulating among the fae and the Awakened that a new Camelot would be constructed somewhere in the western half of the continent.

"A little while ago one of the most powerful wards anyone had ever seen flared into existence down in New Mexico. Everyone has spent the last hundred years or so wondering who was behind it, but nobody has managed to catch anyone coming in or out. People started claiming that whoever created the ward had gone crazy from all the isolation and killed themselves."

I realized I was rubbing the side of my head and forced my hands back down to my side. "If it's really as big as what you're describing then it's got to be easy to find. Why hasn't anyone taken it down?"

Byron smiled. "Nobody has taken it down because nobody is willing to invest the time and effort it would require. None of the fae are strong enough to do it yet, and none of the pantheons have been willing to collectively invest the centuries' worth of memory that would be required to bring it down."

I looked over at Jace and shook my head. "So why didn't Kyle just do something like that rather than hiding his wards behind weaker wards?"

"Because Camelot is the single biggest target for both courts. It represents more collected power than they could hope to find anywhere else. The courts are both in an arms race. Whoever manages to become strong enough to feed off of that ward first will grow at an incredible rate. They will end up with a clear advantage and finally have a chance at wiping the other side out of existence."

I turned back to Byron. "So why not run there instead of coming to us? Your group has obviously been cycling people through Camelot, leaving them there for a year or two until their signatures shrink to the point where it's safe for them to join the rest of you. If your pantheon was destroyed, wouldn't it make a lot more sense for you to go hide in the one place nobody else could touch you?"

"Yeah, that would make a lot of sense, other than the fact that sooner or later Kyle is going to break down the ward surrounding Camelot and then I'll be back to dealing with the same problem—just without any possibility of getting help from anyone else."

I gave him another confused look, but this time I wasn't the only one. Jace and Kat looked just as unsure of where Byron was headed.

"I don't understand. What does Kyle have to do with anything?"

"Kyle is the one who destroyed my pantheon. He and his lackeys took down more than twenty of the oldest, strongest Awakened alive and sooner or later he'll be coming here for a repeat performance."

Chapter 5

I felt like I'd been spun around so many times that I no longer knew which way was up. Once Byron finished answering all of our questions, we left him in one of the spare bedrooms and retired to the basement where the wards would prevent anyone from listening in using unconventional methods.

Sandra didn't want to talk, but Jace didn't give her a choice. Jace was the one person Sandra seemed to listen to. Normally I would have dismissed that as no big deal, but given the fact that her feelings toward me had survived the transition from one incarnation to another, it wasn't entirely beyond the realm of belief to think that her feelings toward Jace might have done the same.

I knew that Jace wasn't interested in her—Kat had told me several times that he'd never expressed the slightest interest in going back to her over the several hundred years that he'd known me—but I couldn't stop myself from worrying that he would change his mind. There weren't very many guys who'd be willing to wait even just a year or two for a girl. Jace had just finished waiting for me for eighteen years and before that he'd sat around for more than a century pining for me while I'd been married to his brother.

Jace was the next best thing to an honest-to-goodness saint, but even he had his limits and, despite our kiss a few hours earlier, I couldn't help but worry that he was starting to approach the end of his.

Once Sandra joined us, the discussion about what to do in response to Byron's news ran fast and furious. Kat wanted Byron to take us to Camelot and let us hide in their equivalent to Kyle's bunker.

Ari thought we should recruit an army and take the fight to Kyle—not that she had any idea of what that would take—and my dad seemed to just be concerned with getting his daughters out of the line of fire. Saying that he was disappointed to find out that I'd already worked way too many effects for my signature to go unnoticed would have been a profound understatement.

Sandra basically said that she would do whatever Jace thought was best—which wasn't a surprise—and that just left Jace and me. I tried to get him to go first, but he refused, so I ended up telling everyone that despite being scared to death of what was coming, I didn't think it was right to just put our heads in the ground and pretend like nothing was happening.

Jace considered everyone's comments in silence for several seconds before stating that he thought it was too early to be making any significant decisions. He felt like we needed to do our homework and substantiate as much of what Byron had told us as possible before we started planning out our future.

It was the logical answer—the right answer—but it still left me feeling like the meeting had been a whole lot of wasted time. Our group wasn't organized like a military unit, so Jace couldn't just order everyone around, but I still felt like it would have been better if he'd kept the discussion more tightly focused.

Then again, part of my resentment probably had to do with the fact that my dad had called in sick to work so that he could be there for the meeting. In theory my dad didn't need to work anymore, but I didn't actually have the cash in hand that I'd need to make the mortgage payment and given the bomb we'd just had dropped on us, it was possible that I might not have that kind of cash for a while.

All of that meant I didn't feel like there was much I could do to stop my dad from feeling stressed at missing a day of work. I'd thought that my being an Awakened would finally mean my dad wouldn't have to keep working at the tile factory, scrimping for every penny, constantly worried he was going to piss off Sandra's dad and get fired. Silly me; I should have known that being an Awakened would just mean things would get worse.

The money situation wasn't any better and now he had to worry about psychopaths like Mephistoles kidnapping him, Ari or me. Actually, kidnapping was probably the best-case scenario.

As Jace laid out his proposed course of action—which sounded like a lot of waiting around while Kregor visited other Seelie Court fae—I could see the stress building inside of my dad. When the meeting finally broke up Dad left without saying a word. Dad was nothing if not polite. Acting like that was a sure sign he was approaching his personal breaking point.

I hurried after him and caught up to him in the bedroom that Kat had offered him two weeks ago when she'd told him that it wasn't safe for me to be living at home anymore. The room was much smaller than the paired master suites upstairs where Jace and Kat slept, but it was still bigger than any of our rooms back home and the furnishings were just as lavish as everything else in the house.

I hadn't been inside Dad's room here since I'd helped him carry in his suitcases. As I followed him inside I was struck by the fact that he hadn't unpacked. His closets were empty; it looked like he was still living out of his suitcases.

"I'm sorry you had to take the day off of work, Dad. I'll talk to Jace about that. There wasn't any reason that you had to be there for that meeting—not when we weren't going to decide anything anyway."

Dad opened his mouth, but I talked over the top of him. "I've been wanting to talk to you about money, Dad. I know you don't want to accept anything from Kat and Jace, but the very first thing I learned how to do was transmute sand into platinum.

"I've already got millions of dollars' worth of platinum transmuted. Things are a little tricky right now because I'm not sure when Kat will be taking me into Denver to sell my metals, but there really isn't any reason for you to keep working. I can pay off the house and make sure that you and Ari are taken care of regardless of what might happen to me. I hate knowing that you're still always worrying about money. I just really, really want you to be happy."

Dad kind of deflated right before my eyes. He'd been looking older and more careworn for a while now, but this was nothing like that. He seemed to be aging before my eyes and it scared me in ways that I wasn't prepared to face. I'd already lost my mom, and it was recently enough that it felt like it had just happened yesterday.

Now that I knew I was an Awakened, there wasn't any getting around the fact that I was going to watch everyone I knew—everyone but Kat and Jace—age and die while I still looked seventeen, but I wasn't ready for my dad to get old—not yet, not while there was still so many years where I was going to need his advice and want to be able to make memories that involved him.

"Dad, are you okay? I'm sorry, I didn't mean to make you feel like you weren't needed or something. You're so much more important to Ari and me than just someone who provides for us."

"I know, sweetie. I appreciate your offer. I would tell you that I didn't want you to use memories taking care of me—not when that's supposed to be my job—but I know you're going to do it anyway. Besides, you've already got the platinum. It's not like my refusing to take the money would bring those memories back."

"So you'll let me help out?"

"I don't think I really have any other alternative."

I'd known that this conversation had the potential of being difficult, but I hadn't expected it to leave me feeling like I'd just kicked a puppy.

"What's going on, Dad? This is a good thing. You can stop stressing about money for once. We'll get all of the bills paid and never have to worry about money ever again."

He reached over and took my hand in his. "I know, Selene. I'm grateful that you're willing to help out your old man, but the truth is that missing work today is towards the very bottom of my worries. The three of us have basically been living here for the last two weeks, which means that our food bill is non-existent and our utilities bill will be a fraction of what it is normally. I could miss three more days this month and still probably make the mortgage payment without too much of a problem."

"That's a good thing, Dad. You deserve to have some breathing room."

He gave me an absent-minded smile. "Do you know that I tried to pay Jace for our room and board? Jace told me that it was too soon to discuss anything like that—that we didn't even know if I still had my job at the tile factory. I knew he was just putting me off, but I didn't know what to do about it. I should have just left things there, but instead I talked to Kat."

"I'll bet she all but tore your head off."

"Yeah. She told me in no uncertain terms that if I ever made an offer like that again she would pay off all my debts and start a trust fund in my name that would make the Conners look like paupers."

"I knew there was a reason I liked Kat. If it had been me I probably would have just done all of those things and not even asked you."

"Well then, I guess I should be grateful that Kat isn't more like you when it comes to money and dealing with old men."

There was something in his voice that told me we were finally starting to get to the heart of the matter. I needed to pick my next words carefully.

"You're not old, Dad. You just turned forty this year. You still have half of your life ahead of you."

"Do I? It doesn't feel like it. It feels like I've wasted most of my life working at the factory and I don't have anything to show for it. The really scary thing though, is that I don't know what to do with myself if I don't have to go into work every day. For the last twenty years I've defined myself as a husband, a father, and an employee. Piece by piece that is all being taken away from me. First your mom died, now I'm not going to need to work, and it won't be that much longer before you and your sister will be graduating and leaving the nest."

"We aren't going anywhere for years, Dad. Besides, you're so much more than any of that, you—"

"Am I, Selene? Let's ignore for a moment that you, Jace and Kat could end up leaving at any moment and just focus on the heart of the matter. I don't know what to do with myself. I don't have any hobbies and I'm not interested in whiling away the time I have left playing golf or painting furniture. All I know is taking care of the two of you and that factory. That's all I have left in this world, all I love."

"I'm sorry that Mom is gone, Dad. It's hard for Ari and me, but she and I should do a better job remembering that it's even worse for you. Is this about Kat?"

"No. Yes—I don't know. All of that other stuff is true. I feel like a fool to have given most of the best years of my life to that factory, but it would be easier to deal with that right now if I wasn't also trying to get my head around this thing with Kat."

"What's to get your head around, Dad? She likes you and you like her. It's basically the oldest story in existence."

"No, this is far from a regular boy-meets-girl story and you know it, sweetie. She looks like she's young enough to be my daughter."

"She's not. In fact, if anyone is robbing the cradle it's her."

"Yeah, my head knows that, but I'm having a hard time getting my emotions on the same page."

I tried to put myself in my dad's shoes, but this was just so far outside of anything I'd experienced that I didn't even know where to start.

"Are you worried about what everyone else will think?"

"I'd like to say no, but I'm sure that's part of it. I know there's this whole thing about older, rich guys dating girls decades younger than them, but that's not me. My friends—what friends I still have—aren't members of that crowd. Under other circumstances maybe I could ignore all of that, but if I'm not going to be working any more, then what else am I going to do with my time but hang out with people who aren't going to understand that Kat is actually several hundred years old?"

I shrugged. "I don't have any real answers for you, Dad, but nobody is saying you can't work. If you want to work that's fine, but the key thing is that you won't *have* to work anymore. You can set your own hours and terms. You can learn something else if you want to. You could become a doctor or an accountant if that would make you happy—there isn't anything stopping you from doing whatever you want."

"Okay, that's a fair point."

"Great. As for the other, I know you're probably feeling guilty on lots of levels, but you being miserable isn't going to bring Mom back. I never thought that I would ever be telling you to date one of my friends, but I actually think that you would be good for each other. Kat needs someone in her life to help remind her that life isn't all just darkness and sadness. She needs a good person to help her reach the potential she's spent so long hiding from and I can't think of anyone I know who's a better person than you."

"It's happening already."

"What's happening? Did you do that thing where you change the topic of conversation without telling me?"

"No. I was just realizing that you've already grown up to the point where you're smarter than your old man."

"Not in six lifetimes, Dad."

"I sure love you, Selene."

"I love you too, Dad."

Journal Entry
December 12, 1797

I can't remember any time when I've ever been happier than I am now. Kat would tell me that's just a dodge, but the truth is that even my journal entries from my time with Kyle weren't like this.

I still miss Kyle. Researching without him isn't the same. I miss having him to bounce ideas off of and challenge my theories. I'm sure that my progress these last several decades hasn't been as fast as it would have been with him at my side, but I'm finally coming to realize that there is more to life than just my work.

It's funny. I told myself that I was going to do better after Kyle lost himself, but I didn't really change until after he left us. I still thought somehow that advancing the frontiers of my knowledge, mastering some new effect that Jace and Kat wouldn't be ready to learn for another few decades, would somehow fill in the hole that had been carved out of my chest when I lost Kyle.

Jace was the one who showed me there is more to life than just an endless battle. All of our work wasn't enough to save Kyle, and I've finally come to understand that I'll never be able to guarantee the safety of the people I care most about.

ENDLESS

I actually feel more productive over these last few years since I finally let go of my need to control everything. It's probably an illusion, but I'm trying not to look too closely at it.

My understanding of the nature of crystals seems to be coming together in leaps and bounds. I so wish that I could tell Jace and Kat about what I'm doing right now, but they wouldn't understand. It's hard to blame them for their disinterest though. This is all foundational work—even I am not sure exactly how it will pave the way for what I'm eventually hoping to do.

Jace took me out to the opera last night. It was incredible. I spent so long after we arrived here convinced that this wretched continent would never be anything but a brutal wilderness. I can't say how glad I am that I was wrong. Jace was right to insist that we fight against the king. Ever since then it is as though the wheels of progress have sped up with each passing year. We live better now than we ever did back in England and do so on half the expense.

The soprano was absolutely marvelous—a young lady from Italy who was barely more than a girl. I would try to describe her performance, but I would never do it justice here on cold, unfeeling paper.

Kat was gone for the night, and Jace sent the servants home, so we had the entire house to ourselves. Our bedroom was carpeted in rose petals when we returned—I finally understood why Jace was so anxious for me to spend the afternoon with Kat. I'm pretty sure my attire for the evening scandalized half of New York society, but I would do it all over again if I had the choice.

Lying there in Jace's arms last night was a defining moment for me. I shouldn't compare him to Kyle, but I do. I wouldn't even put this down on paper but for the fact that Jace comes out on top in any comparison. I thought that things were perfect with Kyle, thought that I loved how driven he was, but the truth is that he didn't value me like Jace does.

Kyle appreciated me, but Jace spent more than a hundred years wanting me, a hundred years desperately fighting against his feelings for me, and that adds something to a relationship, something more wonderful than I can even begin to describe.

I think in some ways that my being with Kyle made him a better person, but what I've come to realize is that Jace makes me a better person. I've never been so balanced, so in tune with who I want to be, as I am right in this moment.

With Jace I never feel like there is any need for me to be anything other than who I am, but somehow that leads me to be so much more than I ever thought I could be. I'm a better friend and a better wife around him than I ever was with Kyle.

Kyle saved me—saved all of us—back in London, but Jace is the one who made me worth saving. It's hard to explain, even to myself. I owe Kyle so much and I still wish every day that I could bring him back to us, but in a competition between Jace and Kyle as he is now, Jace wins hands down.

Chapter 6

I'd finally done it. I'd started reading my journals. I'd been hoping that doing so would make my choice clear. The passage from the night that Jace and I had spent at the opera should have decided me in Jace's favor, but something in the back of my mind refused to let me tell Jace that I'd picked him, that I would never again think about Kyle as anything other than my enemy.

It was crazy, but I just couldn't seem to get past it. Maybe there was something wrong with me. Kat certainly thought so, but that hadn't stopped her from agreeing to run me into Denver to exchange some of my metal for cash.

She agreed to go, but that didn't mean that there wasn't any awkwardness between us on the way there. We passed nearly the entire drive in silence, but I decided to try and restart the conversation as we hit the outskirts of the city.

"Thank you again for taking me, Kat. I know you'd rather be with my dad right now. I just need you to show me the ropes this once and then I'll take care of it on my own from here on out."

She shook her head. "There isn't going to be another time, Selene."

"What do you mean?"

"I mean we're starting to get a trickle of information from the Seelie Court through Kregor. They haven't been able to confirm the fact that there was a huge pantheon taken out in Helena, but they agree that Kyle is on the move and he's targeting anyone he thinks could cause him problems."

My stomach dropped. "So it's not going to be safe for me to leave the house."

"Yeah. Honestly, it's not safe for the two of us to be out and about today, but I told Jace to shove it when he tried to tell me that. You and your dad need cash and he's not going to take it if he thinks it's just a gift from me."

My knees were bouncing around from the adrenaline that had started trickling into my system, but I tried to play it off as nothing more than boredom-induced fidgeting.

"How many places do you think we'll have to hit up in order to move everything I brought?"

"There isn't any way to know for sure. It all depends on how much cash the buyers in the city have on hand. At least four or five—maybe as many as ten."

I patted the heavy steel briefcase resting on my lap and said a silent prayer to whoever might be listening that we wouldn't have to drive all over the city. We needed to get in, get the money, and get out.

"I guess I owe you an even bigger favor than I thought."

"No, we're square. Your dad told me about your conversation with him yesterday. I appreciate that—I know this has to be weird for you. It was weird enough back in the day anytime I started to fall for a human, but at least back then it wasn't your dad. By the time you and I met the first time around, your parents were both safely in the ground where I couldn't get to them."

"Stop that, Kat. You're not some kind of pedophile. My dad is a grown man and if the two of you make each other happy I'm the last person who is going to get in your way. My dad is important to me, but you are too. I know how crazy it probably sounds, but I don't feel like we've only known each other for three weeks. I feel like you're the long-lost friend I've been missing my entire life. I want you to be happy."

Her eyes were shiny with unshed tears when she finally looked away from the road. "Thanks, Selene, that means a lot."

"Okay, so I still owe you for this trip and we're square where my dad is concerned?"

That earned me an eye roll. "We're square on all counts. You don't owe me for anything."

After that the conversation went much more smoothly and almost before I knew it we were pulling into a parking garage in the older part of town.

Kat pulled a silver briefcase of her own out of the trunk and then we started off towards the first place Kat had identified online. We'd been walking for less than a minute when Bethany came streaking out of the sky and landed on my shoulder.

"You should have told me that you were leaving, Selene!"

"Sorry, you've been gone a lot lately with Kregor and I didn't want to hold Kat up when she said she could go today."

Bethany frowned at me. "I don't like you going places without me. The last time that happened the results weren't pretty."

"Okay, Nanny Bethany. I'll try to keep you more in the loop about what I'm planning, but if you're really worried about me leaving the house without you, you'll have to do a better job of staying close."

Even as I said it, I couldn't help but wonder how much of her concern was genuine and how much of it was her keeping tabs on me for the Seelie Court. If Byron had been sent to us solely to make us doubt each other, he was succeeding. Despite my best efforts I now trusted Bethany less than I had before. She'd already admitted that her first loyalty wasn't to me—at least not this version of me—so it wasn't that much of a jump to suspect that other people might also stand higher in her estimation.

I really hated all of this double- and triple-think. I would have made a terrible spy.

Our walk over to the first place went without any problem. Kat looked around for a few minutes, and then walked over to the guy behind the counter who dazzled the two of us with a brilliant smile.

"My name is Rog. What can I do for you ladies?"

"I need to see your rates for buying precious metals."

Rog nodded and grabbed a small whiteboard that had been resting on the counter. Kat accepted it without angling it to where I could see it.

"Don't waste my time. Platinum hasn't been this low ever."

Rog shrugged. "There's a glut on the secondary market right now. New York and LA are practically swimming in it. You're lucky that my boss is willing to buy it from you even at that rate."

Kat handed back the whiteboard and then pulled out her phone. It took her less than a minute to confirm that platinum—and every other precious metal—had recently taken a precipitous dive. She'd walked over to the far end of the store while checking the prices and I wasn't sure what I was supposed to be doing, so I followed along behind her.

Kat looked up from her phone with a sigh and pulled me in close enough that we would be able to whisper.

"This is bad, Selene. Platinum prices are down more than thirty percent. Under normal circum-stances I wouldn't even bother trying to negotiate with these guys, but he's actually quoting us a decent price given where the market is trading right now."

"I don't get it. Is it normal for the price of metals to drop like that?"

"Nope—especially not without some kind of severe shock to the market. It took me less than five seconds to confirm the price he was quoting was legit. I spent the rest of the time trying to come up with a reason for the price to plummet like that. Usually this would be attributed to a new mine opening up."

"What did you find?"

"Nothing. Everyone else is just as stymied. All of the talking heads are saying that the change is purely from the secondary market, which probably means that it's coming from other Awakened."

I took a deep breath, but even that didn't entirely manage to stop me from freaking out. My heart rate was through the roof, but my voice still sounded mostly normal.

"Kyle. Kyle and the rest of his group are dumping metals."

"Yeah, and based on the drop we're seeing he isn't doing a pound here and a pound there like we are planning to do today, he organized some kind of massive sale. Based on the volumes being reported, the only reason the price hasn't dropped even further is the fact that everyone is betting this is just a blip—that the price is going to bounce back up to normal levels within a few weeks."

"He really is gearing up for a war—it's just like Byron told us."

"Probably. There's a chance that this is still someone else, or even that Byron is part of a group that dumped a ton of metal to freak all of the various pantheons out, but I'm starting to believe that this is really Kyle making a move to weaken his enemies by making it so they can't liquidate their stores."

"So what do we do?"

"We liquidate everything we brought and if necessary we make a trip to somewhere we can get more raw material to transmute and we clean out every place like this in the entire city. If things are really headed the way it sounds like they are headed, then we're going to want all of the cash we can get our hands on—regardless of how low the price is. Are you okay with that?"

"Yeah, whatever you think is best works for me."

"Okay. We should have brought bigger briefcases. At least Bethany is here."

"Wait, what's Bethany going to do?"

Bethany had been hovering in front of a big-screen TV, but her hearing must have been even more amazing than I'd realized, because she shot back over to us before my question was all the way out of my mouth.

"I can shift items over to the unseen realm—not an infinite amount of stuff, so it's good that cash is light—but I can make it disappear and then once we're back to the house I can bring it back."

My head was spinning again. It was a good thing that I wasn't going to get old and die any time soon. I was starting to suspect that it was going to take me at least the next hundred years getting caught up on all of the basic stuff I didn't know yet.

"Wow, I take back implying that you were spending too much time with Kregor lately. If he's teaching you how to move money around like that, then it's time well spent. What do we do if another fae shows up and steals it?"

Bethany blew a raspberry at me. "Kregor didn't teach me that, I already knew all about it. As for someone else stealing something I've moved to the unseen realm, that's impossible. Only the fairy who moved stuff can bring it back."

"Hmm, I should have you shift a few thousand dollars and a change of clothes away for me once we get back home. You're like the ultimate emergency preparedness kit."

"I'm not your personal carryon bag, Selene. I'll help you out this one time, but it's not like towing stuff around behind me in the unseen world is pleasant. Someone like the Lady could basically hide an SUV, but I'm only good for a few more pounds."

Kat nodded. "Thanks, Bethany. If nothing else, maybe you can make some trips back and forth from here to the house."

Bethany looked like she was going to protest, but I gave her my best puppy-dog eyes. "Please, Bethany? I'll be your best friend…"

"You're already my best friend."

"I'll use some of the proceeds to buy a bigger TV for your room."

"Okay, throw in a hundred DVD's of my choice and you've got a deal, but only if we can't come up with another option for moving the cash around. If things are really as bad as they sound, I'm not going to want to be running around on my own much anymore. If I get disembodied that's the end for me and you'll never get your cash back."

I blew her a kiss. "Thanks, Bethany. None of us want that—and for the record you're much more important than the money."

Kat nodded and headed back to the counter. "I've got some high-value items. Is the owner around?"

"No, but I can help you out with whatever you need."

Kat gave him a cold smile. "Sorry, I don't have any time to waste today. Call your boss. The business I'm looking to do will be well above your weekly limit."

The guy behind the counter looked back and forth between Kat and the silver case in her hand several times before running a hand over his shaved scalp. "Not happening. If you want me to call in my boss then you're going to have to prove that you're on the level."

Even I could tell that he wanted Kat to open up the cases and let him see what it was that we were carrying, but Kat shook her head. "I'm not opening up this case for you. Your boss wouldn't like that."

I thought Rog was going to kick us out right then and there, but Kat fished out a stack of hundred-dollar bills and slapped them down on the glass.

"Trust me, we're on the level."

"Okay, I'll call the boss, but you better be legit. If I call him in for no reason, he's going to be pissed."

Given the heavy tattoos Rog was sporting, I had a sneaking suspicion that the fact we were girls wouldn't be enough to save us from a beating, but Kat didn't seem concerned. Then again, the more I thought about it, the more I realized that I didn't need to be worried either. No normal human had a chance against us.

Kat gestured me closer and whispered into my ear. "Keep an eye on him. He should make one call. No more than that. And tell me if he starts texting on his phone."

"Okay, what are you going to do?"

"I'm going to start making some calls. Given the number of places we're going to have to hit up today I'm going to see if I can find out which shops are going to have the owners around."

I nodded and walked back over to the counter as Rog finished up his call and hung up the landline.

"Okay, he'll be here in fifteen minutes."

I nodded without taking my eyes off of his cell phone.

"So what's your name?"

I almost told him, but at the last second I realized that the less information I gave out the less he'd have to go on if he decided to try to track me down later.

"Sammy. You can call me Sammy."

"I can call you Sammy, but that's not your real name?" Even as he said it he reached for his cell. Without thinking, I amped my strength up to twice what it normally was and grabbed his arm.

"Let's just leave the phone right there, Rog. My friend and I are feeling a little jumpy right now."

I'd grabbed him harder than I meant to. He was probably going to have a hand-shaped bruise wrapped around his arm, but there wasn't much I could do about that now. Instead, I just looked him in the eye and refused to back down.

"Fine, fine. You want me to maintain radio silence, then I'll keep radio silence."

A short time later the owner, a heavyset guy with dark hair who looked like he was in his fifties, walked in and showed Kat and me back to his office. I was not at all surprised to see that he had a set of scales in his office, but I was pretty sure that Kat was going to check his weights against the scale inside of her briefcase.

The pawn shop owner—who had introduced himself as Jeb—leaned back in his chair without touching the metal. "That's quite an impressive collection you've managed to pull together. Where did you steal it from?"

Kat didn't even bat an eye at the accusation. "We didn't steal it."

"You can't actually expect me to believe that a couple of teenage girls got their hands on that much gold and silver through legal means."

"Believe whatever you want, Jeb. The gold is here waiting for you to make an offer on it and nobody is going to come around sniffing for it. Make me an offer or we'll go find another buyer."

The next half an hour blew my mind. Kat was one of the best negotiators I'd ever seen, but she wasn't just after the best price per ounce, she was after the biggest single deal she could get Jeb to agree to.

Jeb kept trying to bring the discussion back to the fact that he didn't even know for sure whether the metal was real, but Kat ruthlessly kept the discussion focused on the amount and price that he was willing to accept.

Once that was done, the two of them made sure that their scales were reading the same weight for a given bar of metal, and then Jeb proceeded to weigh out the metal, shaking his head the whole time at Kat's single-mindedness.

"Okay, so we've got a price and a total weight, but I'm still not convinced that any of this metal is the real deal. Frankly, I would have already kicked you to the curb except for the fact that you flashed all of those Benjamins to Rog…"

Kat gave him a humorless smile. "That's okay, I'm assuming that it's going to take you some time to pull all that money together. We'll leave the gold here for you to test and then we'll be back here to collect. We'll take as much cash as you can get your hands on and a cashier's check for the rest."

Up until that moment I would have said that nothing could have surprised Jeb. He was a hard man who worked with desperate people. He had an air about him that said he'd seen it all years ago, but he actually did a double-take at Kat's words.

"You can't be serious."

"Why not, Jeb? You're an honest businessman, aren't you?"

He nodded, but the gesture had the disoriented feel of a punch-drunk prize fighter. "Of course I am, but only a fool would leave more than three hundred thousand dollars' worth of metal here unsupervised."

Kat's expression turned cold. "I'm not a fool, Jeb, and I'm not some child. You're not going to double-cross us because if you do I'll personally make sure that you suffer ten times the value of this metal in losses. Broken legs will be the least of your worries. I'll burn this shop down and then move on to your vehicles and home."

He jumped to his feet—obviously intending on using his size to intimidate her—but I'd felt her amp up her system even before she started talking, and she shoved him into his seat like he was nothing more than a child.

"As long as you deal honestly with me you have nothing to worry about, Jeb, but I don't make idle threats. I'd like to do repeat business with you at some point, but that's only possible if you understand who's holding the whip in this relationship."

There was another flash of energy as Kat burned away a few more seconds' worth of memory, and a tide of fear suddenly crashed over me. It was so powerful that it took me a second to realize that the source of the fear was Kat.

Jeb's fists went white, but he didn't get out of his chair. My opinion of him actually went up by several notches. I had the advantage of understanding what was going on, and I *still* wanted to run screaming out of the room.

I could see the fear fighting with the desire to cash in on the metal purchase Kat was offering.

"It will take me a couple of days to test all of this metal."

Kat shook her head. "No. You can have three hours. That gives you two hours to test it and an hour to get to the bank."

"How am I supposed to test this much metal in that amount of time?"

"I don't actually care how you test it. Melt it down and then test it all at once, or test it individually if you have enough acid to do that. I don't care how much you get tested, but when we get back, anything you don't want to buy is walking back out the doors with us."

Kat gestured for me to follow and a few minutes later we were back at the car and driving towards a home improvement store. Bethany was still on my shoulder, but she kept jumping up in the air and then buzzing back down.

"Wow, Kat. The first trip back home with a stack of cash is on me! I've never seen anything like that."

Kat turned away from the road just enough to give Bethany a wry grin. "You obviously spent most of the last eighteen years with Jace rather than with me. I always prefer to set up longer-term arrangements with potential buyers, but given the fact that we don't know how much longer we're going to be able to liquidate metal, it seemed best to dust off my time in Prague.

"Selene, we're going to have to move quickly if we're going to make it through my list of possible buyers before shops start closing down. Do you mind waiting inside the car and transmuting stuff while I make the arrangements?"

"Not at all. I've never done gold or silver before though. Is it going to cause a problem if I just do nothing but platinum?"

"Maybe, but I don't have time to make sure that you're getting the gold and silver right, so just stick to what you know."

The next three hours went by in a blur. Kat ran into the store and came back out with six bags of decorative white rock. I had my doubts about our ability to actually move the better part of one hundred and twenty pounds of platinum, but transmuting it was easy enough and the price in memories was small enough that Kat apparently figured it was best to over-prepare.

We didn't leave the car behind after that. Instead, I remained with the car at each stop while Kat walked in with both briefcases loaded with precious metal.

Bethany was all aquiver at the idea of seeing Kat intimidate men more than twice her size, so she went inside with Kat and I was left sitting alone in some fairly seedy neighborhoods. It was unnerving to be sitting there changing rocks into tiny bars of platinum, but I just locked the doors and reminded myself that no regular human was going to be able to give me any problems. Even so, that didn't stop me from being thankful that Kat's car had tinted windows.

The first few stops were more pawnshops, but eventually Kat moved on to small and medium-sized jewelry stores. We fell into an easy rhythm. While Kat was inside, I would transmute a briefcase or so worth of rocks and then I'd call two or three establishments from her list and ask to be connected with someone who had the authority to make a large purchase of platinum at below-market prices.

The last two shops we managed to get in and out in less than ten minutes, which frankly blew my mind considering how much time we'd spent at the first place.

"How are you managing that, Kat?"

"I offered a bigger discount on the metal. That's the piece that makes all of this possible. Intimidation and the 'fear me' aura can help tip the balance your direction if you've pushed them too far on the price or the size of the purchase, but mostly it comes down to the fact that they all know they can flip the metal for a ten-percent profit tomorrow."

Kat checked the GPS on her phone and then merged back into the interstate for the short hop that would take us back to the first shop.

"You have to remember that a lot of these guys are borrowing the money to buy this metal. They'll be tapping a line of credit and just about cleaning themselves out to get the cash they need to purchase as big a chunk of what we left behind as possible. That makes people uneasy. Most of them won't have the time to test all of the metal, so they'll test as much as they can and then buy a little more in the hopes that it will turn out to be legit as well."

"Wow, that feels risky."

"Yeah. The smart ones will limit their exposure on the stuff that they haven't tested so that even if it turns out to be worthless they'll still come out flush, but most of them will try to grab all of it. Never underestimate people's capacity to think that they've just found their big break."

"You sound like a con woman."

"It's the same principle, I just don't use it to defraud them."

"But you do put them in a risky spot though. If the prices drop even more they could lose money on this."

"Yeah, but it would have to drop a lot. Here we are. You okay with waiting in the car again while I run in and grab the cash and whatever metal is still left over? Keep your eyes open. If things go south, this is where it's most likely to happen."

I nodded and then watched her walk inside, but I was suddenly not so sure how I felt about this exercise. Maybe I just wasn't cut out for business. I'd headed out this morning thinking that we were looking for a fairly black and white transaction. I never would have guessed that there was that much in the way of gray out there.

Five minutes later Kat was back outside with Bethany floating next to her. She slid the silver briefcase over to me as she put the car into gear.

"He had a hundred thousand in cash on him and managed to get a cashier's check for another hundred and fifty. I got him to throw in a bag—it's in the case—go ahead and throw the metal in the bag, it's worth trying to keep the cash and the metal separate.

"I thought I would get more out of him than that. Hopefully the jewelers are able to come up with more than that or we're going home a lot lighter than I was thinking we would."

The next several stops proved to be more lucrative, but I wasn't sure if that was because they were taking a bigger risk than Jeb had been willing to take, or if it was a function of having access to people they trusted to help test the metal.

As we pulled up to the second-to-last stop, the amount of cash had grown to the point where it wouldn't have all fit in the second briefcase and we had almost twice that amount in cashier's checks. It was a lot less than Kat had been hoping to get—and it was far less than the metal we'd moved was really worth—but it was still a mind-boggling sum, the kind of money that I'd never expected to see all in one place.

"Can I come inside with you on this last one, Kat? I'd really like to see at least one pickup today."

"Yeah, that's fine. This is a decent neighborhood. There's still a chance that somebody is waiting to break into our car in the hopes that we've got some metal sitting here unprotected, but the car will still probably be drivable, so I suppose it doesn't matter all that much if we lose the metal. Just make sure that you grab the briefcase that has all the money."

I nodded and then looked down at the pile of money sitting at my feet. Apparently Kat hadn't realized just how much money hadn't fit inside the briefcase.

"Bethany, would you be willing to make this pile disappear? Just until we make it back to the car?"

"Okay, but you're going to have to carry me around everywhere—this much weight will make me fly slower than a pregnant turkey."

It took everything I had to not roll my eyes at her. I didn't want her to pout and refuse to help me out with the several hundred thousand dollars in cash sitting on the floorboard of Kat's Mercedes.

"I thought turkeys laid eggs like other birds."

Bethany shrugged. "Yeah, probably, but there are plenty of expressions that don't correspond perfectly to the real world."

Kat apparently didn't share my concerns about Bethany refusing to send the cash off into the unseen world.

"Whatever, that's not an expression. You made that up all of five seconds ago."

"So what if I did? All great expressions have to start somewhere. Flying like a pregnant turkey is one of the best expressions ever."

"Just keep telling yourself that."

Bethany dropped down onto the pile of cash in a huff and the first stack of bills disappeared a split second later.

"You just don't get it because you can't fly. Just watch. I'm going to use that expression on Kregor and he'll love it."

Kat rolled her eyes. "Yeah, I'm sure that flying is the best thing ever—that's probably why the Lady walks around with a pair of wings sprouting out of her back and Fenrir flitters around from one spot to the next like some kind of massively overgrown canine butterfly. The truth is that all of you fae ditch the wings as soon as you accrue enough power to shape your forms. Give it another hundred and fifty years and you'll only dust yours off when you need to fly somewhere too far to walk."

"Kregor hasn't done that."

"Yeah, because Kregor is odd even for a fairy."

Bethany had continued to shift stacks of bills away while she and Kat were arguing. As she shifted away the last one, I shook my head at the two of them and pointed to the jewelry store.

"If the two of you are done, can we please go finish this? I'd really like to get back to the house and see Jace and my dad before today turns into tomorrow."

I half expected the jewelry store to still be open, but apparently the owner hadn't trusted his employees around the amount of wealth Kat had left with him. Kat knocked on the door and a few seconds later a short, balding man in his fifties opened the door.

"Can you give me more time? I've been working as fast as I could, but when news of the attack aired on the television it threw me off."

I'd been looking around the store, wondering if I could justify spending a little bit of the money we were about to get on a diamond necklace, but his words tore my attention away from all of the sparkly things.

"What attack?"

"I'm not surprised that you haven't heard. There have been a series of tanker car explosions in the middle of major cities. Washington, Boston, Chicago, and L.A. have all been hit. The authorities have been suppressing news of the incidents, but nobody believes that it was an accident—not given that all four explosions happened in the same way at exactly the same time. It's got to have been some kind of terrorist strike."

ENDLESS

The world was wobbling around me, but Kat had become more focused rather than less.

"How are they suppressing information?"

"Cellular networks have been down for the last half an hour. Internet providers have been instructed to go offline, and every cable and television network has been silent as well, so I can only assume that federal officers are there censoring everything that's being aired.

"I keep a CB radio in my workshop—it's been a hobby of mine for years. Somebody dropped the ball in not jamming the public airwaves. I had a good feeling about you, and all of the metal had tested as good, so I went and grabbed my cashier's check more than an hour ago. I would have left already, but anytime there is a terrorist strike like this people start hoarding precious metals."

Kat ran a hand through her hair. "You're figuring that the price is going to skyrocket over the next couple of days."

"Yes. Maybe I shouldn't have told you, but it just doesn't seem right not to."

Bethany hadn't left my shoulder, but now she moved in closer and whispered. "Here's the honest man you were hoping to find."

I could tell that Kat was about to try to renegotiate the price, but I shook my head at her. We already had more money than we could conceivably spend and given what had just happened, money was going to be less of an issue in the short run simply because everyone would be hoarding food and other basic necessities.

"It's fine, we'll stand by the original price and sell as much gold to you as you'd like to buy from us."

That earned me a frown, but when the jeweler turned to look at Kat she grudgingly nodded. "What she said."

"Would you be willing to accept unset diamonds as partial payment?"

I wasn't sure what Kat was going to say to that. Presumably it was just as easy for us to transmute stones into diamonds as it was for us to transmute them into gold, but given how difficult it had been for me to form my platinum into simple bars I suspected that it was a lot harder to get a diamond to have the right cut as part of the transmutation process.

"Yeah, if they are cut we'd be willing to accept part of the payment that way."

"Very good. Do you have any extra metal that you didn't leave with me?"

I nodded. "I'll go get it while the two of you work out the metal-to-diamond exchange rate."

Bethany was quiet until after I was safely outside. "What does this mean, Selene?"

I shrugged as I pulled out my cell phone and confirmed that it was indeed not getting any bars. "I don't know. I'm pretty sure that Kyle and his friends were the terrorists though, which means that's one more reason to believe Byron. I guess we should probably stop off at a grocery store on our way back home and stock up on as much food as we can fit in the car. I'd say that we should deposit the cashier's checks too while the banks still have some cash on hand, but they're all closed and I'm betting that this will all be common knowledge by the time they open up tomorrow."

Bethany was usually a spunky force of nature, but for once she was subdued. "How many people do you think died?"

"I don't know, but those are pretty big cities and a big enough blast could kill hundreds or even thousands."

"I get why he would go after the Helena pantheon, but why kill a bunch of humans?"

I wished more than anything that I could just tell her I didn't know, but this time I had a pretty good idea.

"Kyle wants to take control of everything. He thinks that the Awakened should rule over the humans and that he should rule the Awakened. I suspect that he's hoping to destabilize the government to the point that people will welcome any form of stability. As long as he can keep it a secret that he's the one creating all of the destruction, people will welcome whatever structure he puts in place to replace the current government."

I had to amp up my strength to lift the remaining platinum, but it took only a few seconds to get it out of the car. The bag wasn't anywhere near strong enough to carry that much weight, but as long as I picked the metal up from below it seemed to be up to the task of keeping everything together in one place.

It meant that my arms were full though, so I had to wait for Kat to come get the door for me. As she pushed it open I saw something odd in her expression.

"What's wrong?"

"I'm not sure. I thought I saw something across the street."

"Something?"

"Yeah. Before you ask, I don't know what it was or I wouldn't have referred to it as just being something."

"Hey, we're on the same side, remember? No need to get snippy with me."

Kat had the grace to look embarrassed. "You're right. This guy wants us to hang around while he finishes testing roughly a million dollars' worth of gold and platinum. Now that I know Kyle has escalated stuff I'm feeling awfully exposed out here. I'd feel a lot better if we were back home and could make a run for our wards if something went wrong."

"You figure it's him too, then?"

"Yeah. The pieces all fit together too well. Jace probably has some kind of confirmation from the Seelie Court by now, but, with all of the phones down, we won't know for sure until we make it back home."

"Well, let's get the metal back to our new friend and see if there's anything we can do to move things along. We may have a million dollars' worth of metal, but there's no way he's got that much in cash and diamonds to trade with."

"Yeah, but at the price we're selling at he's only got to come up with half a million to clean us out. He's down that hall—go ahead, I'll lock the door."

I'd only covered half the distance to the hallway Kat had been pointing at when she swore. "Drop the metal, Selene, we need to get out of here right now!"

I'd turned back expecting to find out that she was having a hard time getting the door to lock again. Seeing that she had the door open and was already headed towards the car at a dead run with a briefcase in one hand threw me for such a loop that I just stood there frozen. Right up to the point where I saw something shadowy and four-legged throw itself at Kat.

If it had been me I would have been killed, but Kat had amped herself before the door even finished swinging closed, and something—maybe a whisper of sound—warned her that she wasn't alone out there.

I was so busy amping myself that I missed the first couple of exchanges, but by the time I was moving at four times normal speed Kat had a pair of knives out and one of them had blood on it.

I sprinted towards the door and hit it hard enough to rip the heavy metal frame free of the anchor points that tied it into the rest of the building. My shoulder was going to be black and blue the next day, but my bone augmentation had kept my bones from shattering, and that was all that mattered.

"Bethany, find me something I can use as a weapon!"

Even as the words left my mouth I realized that I should have stayed silent and tried to sneak up on the Unseelie fae that Kat was desperately fighting. It whirled around and charged toward me with a speed that was still breathtaking even when I was moving at four times normal speed myself.

I threw myself to the right, timing it so that it was too close to adjust its path, but not close enough to catch me in its jaws as it passed. I almost cut it too close; something tugged on my shirt for the briefest of instants before the material tore free.

My attacker was shaped vaguely like a dog. For a split second I was worried that we were up against Fenrir again, but this fae was much too small to be him. Besides, the shape of the head was all wrong, more angular, almost snakelike.

Kat danced back in and cut our opponent across the shoulder before it could spin around and slash her with the odd, talon-like claws at the end of its feet. It was a good strike, but trying to disembody a fae that size just by bleeding it out seemed like it would take forever.

"What about that weapon, Bethany?"

I could feel her swaying on my shoulder, tiny hands wrapped around my hair, wings going like crazy to help her maintain her balance.

"I'm trying but I don't see anything!"

Kat ducked under a slash and shot forward, sinking her knife into the snake-dog's stomach and carving a grisly furrow more than a foot and a half deep, but its counterattack caught her across the back and she reeled away with several bloody slashes showing over her kidney.

We were out of time. I conjured the heat I needed for an offensive effect and scored on the snake-dog with a sun lance that was as thick as one of those fat highlighters Ari was so fond of.

I'd been fighting so many bigger Unseelie fae lately that I'd forgotten just how destructive a properly-executed sun lance really was. I managed to catch our enemy in the side, just forward of its back legs. I'd been expecting the attack to do little more than stagger it—maybe blasting a fist-sized chunk of flesh away. I was completely unprepared for the sun lance to blast cleanly through it and tear a massive, smoking hole in the sidewalk twenty feet away.

I cursed myself for not waiting until I had a better angle, something that would have let my beam hit it lengthwise, but the attack did what it needed to do. It bought Kat time to recover, to catch her balance and jump back into the fight.

Kat managed to land another strike, this one across the snake-dog's nose, but it didn't even slow down. It charged forward with enough speed to knock her back into our car as it brushed past, and I suddenly realized that I was much too close for a fight where I didn't have any kind of weapon in my hands.

The snake-dog was moving just as fast as before, but there was a jerkiness to its movements that was making it harder to time everything. As the distance between us vanished, I realized it was because of the injury I'd done with my sun lance, but by then it was too late.

I dodged to my right, spinning as I went, and slammed the outside edge of my hand into the creature's face in an effort to keep it from biting me. It shouldn't have worked. Even as I was doing it I knew that I was probably going to lose my hand, but I was hoping that it would at least be enough to keep it from getting hold of something more important.

Somehow I managed to score on the snake-dog. The blow was hard enough to leave my bones aching, but even that wasn't enough to put the Unseelie fae down for good. The punch did however impart more spin to me, and I dug in with all of the force I could safely muster out of shoes that had already been subject to titanic forces they'd never been designed to withstand.

I pushed off with both feet and drove my right hand into the fairy's ribs with every ounce of strength I could manage. The dog was less than a third the size of Fenrir, but its bones were still preternaturally strong.

If I'd been a mere human the best possible outcome would have been my shattering all of the bones in my hand. As it was, that was still uncomfortably close to the actual outcome. The ache from my knife-hand blow to the snake-dog's face was nothing compared to the pain from punching it.

Every part of me was amped up, reinforced to the point where I was no longer even close to human, and that was just barely enough. I hit the snake-dog and through the flash of pain as bones and soft tissue were both stressed right up to the edge of what they could take, I felt its rib break.

It probably would have still managed to kill me—a broken rib wasn't lethal even to a normal human—but the force of my blow was sufficient to knock the Unseelie fae away from me. Kat got both of her knives into it this time before being forced to throw herself backwards.

This enemy wasn't as big and strong as Fenrir, but it was marginally faster and Kat almost wasn't quick enough. As she tried to dodge the jaws coming towards her face one of her knives caught on a bone and refused to come free. That robbed her of just enough speed for the snake-dog to slice her across the cheek.

The part of me that was usually in control of my actions was screaming that I needed to get back in there and save her. That was the part of me that had never been anything other than a normal girl, the part that had never needed to worry about anything more dangerous than whether the popular girls in school were going to pick on me after school.

I told that part of me to shut up and followed instincts I shouldn't have had. I spun towards a stop sign less than twenty feet away, shoes groaning in distress as I milked them for every bit of speed my super-charged frame was capable of.

Even as I crossed the distance, I summoned the heat I needed for another sun lance, but this time it was barely more than the heat of a summer afternoon. I was less than five feet away from the sign when the bar of molten gold shot out, no bigger than a needle, and sliced through the base of the sign.

I grabbed the sign as it fell, and then spun around and charged back into the fight. Kat was down to one knife and was backing away for all she was worth. The gashes across her stomach and arms were testament to the fact that she'd only barely managed to keep from being pinned down and killed.

She was retreating, but once she saw me running forward with what amounted to a giant aluminum club, she started circling back in my direction. Everything still felt like it was simultaneously moving in slow motion and much too fast. I felt first my right shoe and then my left come apart from the stresses I'd put on them, and then I was running across the pavement in bare feet, cursing the entire way.

My skin was amped up to the point where I could have probably walked across thumbtacks without having them draw blood, but skin with that level of tensile strength didn't have anywhere near the traction of rubber soles. I wasn't going to be able to stop in time—not if I wanted to save Kat.

In the end I didn't even try, even though I knew that was exactly what our opponent wanted. The snake-dog spun around so that it was heading towards me as I crossed the last few feet separating us, but rather than bringing my club around in an overhand blow like I'd originally been planning, I flipped it around and brought the end with the stop sign still attached to it up with everything I had.

The aluminum pole that the stop sign was mounted to was incredibly strong—it had been designed to shrug off anything other than a direct impact from one-ton vehicles moving at a speed of several miles per hour. Even so, I wasn't sure that it was going to be up to withstanding the forces I was applying to it.

I hit the snake-dog directly in the chest, and I led with the edge of the stop sign in the hopes that it would cut into the evil fairy's chest. I was almost right. The stop sign hit and sank nearly an inch into the snake-dog's chest. It sheared through muscle, but it wasn't up to cutting into the unnaturally hard bones underneath. The sign deformed, rolling up like a scroll, and then tore free of the bolts that had been used to anchor it to the aluminum pole.

If I'd done as I'd originally been intending and hit the snake-dog from above that would have been the end of me. Instead, the force of my club hitting my enemy bled off most of the momentum I'd carried into the blow with me.

The aluminum rod transmitted an incredible shock to my hands, and the vibrations felt like they went on and on, but it was a necessary evil. The upward force I slammed the snake-dog with created an equal and opposite downward force. For the briefest of instants it was as though I weighed more than three times as much as normal and that was the final piece I needed to reverse course.

It was a good thing too. My blow staggered the snake-dog. I heard its breastbone crack, and its front legs came up more than two feet off of the ground, but it lunged forward, pushing off with its back legs, and my desperate evasive maneuvers were just enough to keep me away from its jaws. I took a long set of gashes across my left leg—apparently my skin still wasn't up to withstanding that—as Kat reversed directions again and slammed her remaining knife into the side of the fairy's neck.

Something told me that her attack had gone home perfectly, that it should have killed our enemy. Apparently the wolf-dog's anatomy wasn't the same as a regular dog's anatomy though. The artery or vein she was looking for was somewhere else, and I could tell that she'd put too much into the attack. She'd been so sure that this attack would be lethal that she'd left herself off-balance and vulnerable.

There was a single frozen moment where the Unseelie fairy had the chance to pick its next target. Neither of us was in a position to dodge, whomever it went after next was a dead woman. A second later, a tremendous roar slammed into my ear at the same time that a cloud of buckshot tore into the snake dog.

It was the tiny old jeweler. Moving in what seemed like slow motion, he pumped his shotgun and started bringing the barrel back down towards the snake-dog.

The first shot had done more damage than I would have expected. The flesh over one shoulder was almost completely blasted away, but I knew a second shot wasn't going to be enough to save our rescuer. The snake-dog probably would have been better served to kill Kat or me, but it changed course again and charged the old man.

I could tell that I was only going to get one more hit in. My last blow to the snake-dog's chest had reversed the motion of my improvised club. It felt like an eternity had passed, but in reality it had been barely more than an eye-blink since then. I used the momentum my club already had, spinning the aluminum post over my head with everything I had, and slammed it into the snake-dog, hitting it just in front of its shoulders.

It was a blow that would have felled an ox. It managed to drive the snake-dog into the ground, but I could tell it wasn't going to stop the snake-dog—not permanently. I'd failed. My club was rebounding upwards with too much force for even my augmented muscles to bring it back down in time, and I knew that the old man was a fraction of a second away from death.

Only I was wrong. There wasn't any-thing *I* could do, but Kat darted in before the snake-dog could regain its feet and her knife once again took the Unseelie fairy in the throat. This time she didn't miss the artery she'd been aiming for.

Chapter 7

I wanted nothing quite so much as to just drop to the ground and hyperventilate, but Kat didn't give me a chance. She collected her knives and then grabbed me by the arm.

"No time for that! It was just a scout. There are two Awakened headed our way."

I started to ask her how she knew that, but before I could get the words out I realized that I could feel them too. They were out there at the very edge of my range like an itch, but so faint I didn't notice it until she'd pointed it out to me.

"Get in the car, Selene."

The jeweler looked shocked. "What was that thing?"

Kat spared him half a glance, but she didn't stop in her mad dash toward her car. She slowed just enough to grab the metal briefcase she'd dropped at the beginning of the fight. "Trust me when I say you don't want to know. Call the cops and get your door replaced. Tell them you fought off a gang—by the time they get here that thing will be gone."

"But your money—"

"We don't have time. Keep it—if we survive the catastrophe that's headed this way we'll eventually be back for it."

I'd headed back to get the second brief-case—even though it was empty—before I'd completely understood that we were up against more than just one Unseelie fae. It was a good thing that I was still amped. I slipped past the jeweler, grabbed the empty briefcase and was back at my door fumbling with the latch by the time Kat got the car started.

Now that we were out of immediate danger, my mind was having a hard time functioning. I kept thinking that my body felt wrong, that my shoulder was too light.

It wasn't until I got my door open that I realized what was wrong. I turned around, looking desperately for Bethany, but Kat was still one step ahead of me.

"Bethany, get your butt into the car or I swear I'll leave you to make your way back home by yourself."

Bethany had stayed on my shoulder for the entire fight. It made no sense. She was too small to make any kind of difference. She'd be way safer taking to the sky, but she'd once again showed a strange reluctance to leave me when the crap hit the fan.

ENDLESS

I hadn't even noticed her leave me, but sometime between when Kat had landed her final blow on the snake-dog and when I'd made it to the car, Bethany had flown over to the fallen fairy and landed on its shoulder.

My mind was working better now—I managed to get the door open without looking away from Bethany. "She's right, Bethany, there are two Awakened on their way and who knows how many more Unseelie fae running around here. You need to be in the car now!"

I dropped down into my seat and lowered the window as I shut the door. Bethany zipped over faster than I could have blinked now that my effects had all been dropped. One part of me was trying to remember when I'd let all of my augmentations drop away, but most of me was trying to decide how Bethany was moving so quickly while she had all of that money still shifted over to the unseen realm.

Kat dropped the Mercedes into gear and tore away from the curb like she had demons chasing her—which wasn't all that far from the truth. I managed one last wave urging the jeweler into his store, and then the window was closed and we were turning off onto another road.

"You get your fill before we left?"

Kat asked the question without looking away from the road, so I didn't realize at first that she was talking to Bethany instead of me.

"Yeah, mostly. I could have probably absorbed a little more if we'd had another hour, but I sucked down all of the easy-to-grab stuff. It's still probably not enough to allow me to survive a disembodiment, but between that and what I absorbed from Selene during the fight I'm feeling a lot peppier than I've ever felt before."

I hadn't realized that I'd been channeling any happiness at all. Despite all of my effort, anger still showed up a lot easier and in a lot more force than happiness, but apparently I'd managed to tap in at least a little to the happiness that I'd been trying to nurture. That was good, but the fact that Bethany had retained enough presence of mind to drain away some of the free memories from our having disembodied the Unseelie fae was even better.

There was no use letting them go to waste and, my recent worries about her loyalty notwithstanding, anything that made her stronger made all of us safer.

"What are we going to do, Kat? They're getting closer."

She nodded. "Yeah, I can feel them too. That's why I was headed out of the store. I should have known that thing wasn't working alone—not with them coming in from two different directions like that. In order for them to know where we were, they had to have a spotter."

"The snake-dog."

"Yeah, the snake-dog. It must have seen us stop off at one of the last few places and then gone off to get help. It's just dumb luck that it was able to make it back and attack before we left town."

"Not so dumb considering that we were planning on staying there for a few hours if that was what it took to get the rest of the metal exchanged for diamonds."

"Yeah, you've got a point there. I should have expected something like this. First Mephistoles and then Kyle. It looks like the Unseelie Court has decided to abandon its traditional neutrality where the Awakened are concerned."

"They were neutral?"

"Yeah...or maybe it would be better to say that they hated all of us equally. This is a big deal, Selene. It was bad enough when we just thought it was Kyle and a few other Awakened causing all of this. If the dark court is helping the bad guys out, things are about to get a lot tougher. We can't sense the fae like we can our own kind. That means these kinds of excursions are completely out of the question. One Unseelie fairy will generally leave two Awakened alone, but if they can call in reinforcements who they don't have to worry will steal the excess memories, we won't dare go anywhere unless we're all together."

Kat whipped the steering wheel around and grabbed the parking brake. The back end of the car slid forward until it was almost even with the front wheels and then we were moving at a right angle from the direction we'd been traveling just a second before. Kat had apparently dropped her strength amp, but she was still running with a time amp.

"I wish I'd had time to really get to know Denver. I'm going to have to try to convince them I'm headed somewhere other than where we're actually headed."

"What's the use? They'll know as soon as we change direction."

"Yeah, but I'm not worried about actually losing them right now. I'm just trying to out-think them so that we can get on the interstate without them getting in our way. Once I've got a long straightaway, I should be able to stay ahead of them for long enough to make it back home. Unless they brought something really high-performance."

Kat took another turn still moving at more than twice the posted speed limit, and for a second I thought my lunch was going to come up. I'd survived Kat hot-rodding in Jace's Viper, but this was something else entirely. Then Kat had been driving crazy fast, but she'd been amped so it hadn't been as crazy as it had seemed from the outside. Unlike now, she hadn't been driving like her life depended on employing every bit of speed the car could muster.

This time her driving ability was the only thing between us and a quick death at the hands of two Awakened who were coming into the fight fresh.

The back end of the car hit the curb, and Kat swore. I looked over at her hands and they were shaking.

"It's okay. I thought for a second that I'd messed up the alignment, but everything still seems to be more or less working like it's supposed to. Hold on, we've got another turn coming up."

Kat threw the Mercedes into another turn and I tried to match up our location with my somewhat spotty knowledge of Denver.

"Kat, aren't we headed the wrong way? The closest-on ramp is over there."

"Yes—I'm hoping that this will convince them that home's in the other direction. If they reposition based on that I should be able to get us onto the interstate before they realize that they lined up to ambush us in the wrong spot."

"What if you're wrong?"

"Then they'll be waiting for us on the interstate, one in front of us and one behind. They'll vaporize our car without even having to slow down."

Bethany was on my shoulder again, holding onto my hair for dear life. I told myself that it was probably just my imagination, but she felt heavier than she had before the fight.

Kat looked away from the road just long enough to meet my eyes. "Is your phone still down, Selene?"

I pulled it out and checked. "Yeah, no bars at all."

"Okay, Bethany, you need to shift all of that money back into the car—you're going to need all of the speed you can manage."

Bethany dropped down to my feet and tightly-bound stacks of hundred dollar bills started appearing one right after another.

"You want me to go get Jace?"

"Yeah. Sandra won't be any help, but if Jace thinks that Byron is at all trustworthy now is the time to bring him along."

My stomach started tying itself into knots, which was ironic. I wouldn't have thought that anything could make me more worried than I already was.

"If Byron is at all dirty he'll just wait until Jace's back is turned and kill him."

"Yeah, but that was already a risk from the moment that you and I left. We don't have a choice though—I'm not sure that the three of us will be a match for whoever is back there, not with you and me already running almost depleted from that last fight. By the way, from now on you don't go anywhere without some kind of weapon on you. That fight would have been completely different if both of us had been armed."

"Noted. So you want Bethany to go on ahead of us and have Jace and Byron ambush the guys chasing us?"

Kat spun the wheel to the right and the car screeched onto the on-ramp. I extended my senses, desperately trying to locate the other two Awakened. One was definitely behind us—quite a ways in fact. The other felt like he was…just ahead of us.

I looked over at Kat to ask her if I was interpreting things correctly and saw sweat running down the side of her face. That was all the confirmation I needed. A second later, the road shook and I felt all four tires lose their grip on the road.

Kat swerved, overcorrected, and then a chunk of the overpass we were on dropped away in front of us. I wasn't amped and even if I had been I still wouldn't have been able to dodge the gaping hole we were headed towards, but Kat managed to skirt by the trap, wheels within inches of the concrete that was still falling away.

"Hell, yes!"

I started to ask her what she meant and then realized that I could still feel our pursuers, and both of them were now behind us.

"The second guy was in front of us, but he wasn't on the interstate."

"That's right. I was hoping as much, but I wasn't sure until we were crossing over the top of him."

"How did he make the road collapse like that?"

Kat shrugged. "I'm not sure—I expected them to use something flashier than that, but maybe they're under orders not to make a big scene right now. He probably increased the effect of gravity inside of a small area of space. We're lucky that he didn't have a direct line of sight on us or we would have been squished flat. As it was, all he could do was take his best shot and he wasn't quite strong enough to bring down the entire interstate."

Bethany finished rematerializing the money and hopped up onto the back of my seat so she could watch behind us.

"What do you want me to tell Jace?"

"That depends, how fast are you?"

"I'm faster than Kregor. Over short distances I can do almost two hundred and fifty miles per hour. Over longer distances I can maintain two hundred."

Kat did some quick math in her head and sighed. "I'll be driving with the accelerator all the way to the floor, which means that you're not going to have as big of an advantage over us as I'd like, but that can't be helped. Tell Jace to meet us where the road goes around that big hill before dropping into that canyon. Coming up out of the canyon like that should mean that whoever is behind us will be going slower and be an easier target."

Bethany darted around in front of me and nodded. "You want me to come back and try to find you after I drop off the message?"

"No, it's going to be too dangerous. The Mercedes is pretty fast, but I can feel whoever is behind us gaining already. They'll have caught up with us long before you could possibly get back, and there's no point risking you getting caught in the crossfire."

Kat looked over at me as she lowered the window behind her. "Don't unroll the window, she'll never make it out that way. Count to three and then push your door all the way open. That should flush her out the back corner of the car and give her the best shot of getting clear of the vehicle without hitting anything."

Bethany had moved closer to me as the window came down and the air inside the car got more and more turbulent. She landed on my shoulder and grabbed the side of my face. She'd touched my skin dozens of times before this, but there was something different this time around. It was silly, she was only a year or so older than I was and she'd spent most of that time unable to interact with anyone, but in that moment she felt like an older sister, one with a hundred times more life experience than I'd ever had.

The feel of her tiny hands touching my face sent waves of calm radiating outward. "You can do this, Selene. You just need to hold them off for a little while, just long enough for Kat to get you two to the rendezvous so Jace and Byron can put down whoever is following you."

I hadn't realized that I needed reassuring until that moment, and I was so overcome with gratitude that I couldn't manage to get any words out. I just dropped the metal briefcases on top of the money at my feet before nodding and grabbing my door handle tightly. Bethany seemed to know that I wasn't going to be up to a countdown. She gave me another smile and then repositioned herself to the edge of my seat, grabbing onto the headrest with everything she had.

"Open it!"

I'd never tried to open a door while doing more than a hundred and twenty down an interstate, and for the briefest of seconds I worried I wasn't going to be strong enough, but I threw my shoulder into it and suddenly a gust of wind tore through the car. I caught a flash as Bethany was sucked out of the car, and then she was gone.

Kat rolled her window back up as I closed my door, and then looked over at me. "Go ahead and get as much of that money as possible into the second briefcase. It's probably not going to make any difference, but we might as well give ourselves a fighting chance of coming out of all of this with something to show for our efforts."

I nodded numbly and grabbed the empty silver briefcase. I was pretty sure she was mostly just trying to give me something to do, but she was right. I needed a distraction from the fact that we were still in way over our heads.

By the time all of the loose money was safely stowed away, even I could feel our pursuers getting closer. One was definitely in a faster vehicle than the other, and it wasn't too long before Kat was paying more attention to her mirror than she was to the road in front of us.

"Stop doing that, Kat, we're going too fast for you not to pay attention to where you're going. Tell me what to look for."

"You're looking for the guys chasing us. They'll be the only people on the road moving as fast as us."

Kat bit off another curse as someone switched lanes unexpectedly and she was forced to hit the brakes to avoid rear-ending them. The force of our deceleration slammed me forward against my seatbelt, but before I could even adjust to the change Kat threw us to the right and gunned the car again so she could pass on the inside.

"What do I do once I see them?"

I was proud that my voice came out nearly normal despite how terrified I was. Kat's driving was getting more and more desperate with every minute. We weren't passing on the right because there was an actual lane there, we were passing on the right because Kat figured there was just enough room there to intimidate the person next to us into shifting over enough to let us by. It was like she'd invented a whole new way of playing chicken, and I still wasn't okay with the old way.

"Try to anticipate any attacks they might throw at us so I can try to dodge them."

"What, like sun lances?"

"Yeah, if they stick their hand out the window that's a pretty good sign they're about to take a shot at us."

"What about the gravity attack they used to bring down most of the overpass?"

"I don't have any idea what we're up against there. It's entirely possible that they can throw that from inside their car without ever giving any indication of what's coming."

"That's not very reassuring…"

"We're not in a very reassuring situation. At least an attack like that is tougher to aim."

I considered responding with something snarky, but right then didn't seem like a good time to be giving Kat grief. Instead, I just turned around as far as I could go in my seat. I would have unbuckled my seatbelt, but given the way that Kat was swerving in and out of traffic that was asking to be thrown against a window.

We made it another five minutes before I caught my first glimpse of one of our pursuers. They were in a black sports car that looked like something out of a science-fiction movie. It was low-slung and so fast I was astonished it hadn't managed to catch up with us before then.

"I see the first one, Kat. There's a black sports car behind that group of cars that cut you off."

"Which lane is it in?"

"The left one."

Kat nodded and shot into the left lane, putting several more cars between us and the other Awakened.

"Tell me when you see him change lanes and I'll try to keep something between him and us."

"There's not that much traffic back there right now."

"Yeah. I know."

It took the black car maybe another twenty seconds to work its way around the two cars that had given Kat so many problems, twenty seconds in which Kat managed to stretch out the distance between us a little more, but then our pursuer was in the clear and he surged forward with an abruptness that took my breath away.

"He's coming, Kat!"

Kat was already reckless, but now she stopped using her brakes. We shot through a rapidly-closing gap between two cars like a bat out of hell, but this time I was too freaked out about other things to worry about the possibility of wrecking.

"I'm not going to be able to keep stuff between us for much longer, Selene. Roll down the windows and throw some sun lances back in his direction. If you can hit him that would be phenomenal, but right now I'll be happy if you can just manage to slow him down a little."

I found myself in the back seat with no recollection of having unbuckled myself or of crawling over the center console. The windows came down with a glacial slowness that was my first indication that I'd amped myself up.

It was like someone else was giving the orders inside my own head. I'd amped up my time sense, but left everything else alone. I debated letting the effect drop—I wasn't in a position to waste any of my emotional reserves—but I was only functioning at twice normal speed. Besides, somewhere along the way my terror had transmuted into anger. I tapped into the raging heat inside of me and sent a line of vibrant gold light back at the black car that had just finished darting around the last obstacle between it and us.

My attack was thinner than a pencil. I had no idea if that was going to be enough to cut all the way through a car, but I didn't want to waste any power unnecessarily. Besides, I was very aware of the fact that we weren't the only ones on the road and I didn't want to vaporize some poor soccer mom on her way home from a game.

The sun lance shot out, moving at the speed of light, and lasted for only a split second before I let it go. For less than a heartbeat a thread of molten gold connected my hand to the front corner of the sports car. I nearly cheered until I realized that my attack hadn't managed to hit anything vital.

The Awakened behind us swerved out of the line of fire and a tree behind him started on fire as the last of the energy from my attack was expended against it.

"Change lanes, Kat!"

She didn't question or yell that there wasn't room, but the fact was that she'd just swung out around another car in an attempt at passing them. There wasn't anywhere else for us to go, so Kat took us right up to the edge of the railing that separated us from the other two lanes of oncoming traffic. I snatched my hand back inside just in time to avoid having it shattered against a sign, and then the car was filled with the high-pitched sound of metal ripping into metal. As fast as Kat had reacted, and as completely as she'd thrown herself into the evasive maneuver, she'd still only barely been able to dodge the attack that the other Awakened launched at us.

A bolt of golden light shot through the space the car had occupied less than a second previously and tore a massive gouge in the road ahead of us.

"Crap, our aerodynamics profile is all shot to hell! That's going to make us even slower. You've got to keep him busy or they'll blast us into a million pieces."

I bit off a scathing response about the difficulty of hitting anything while a crazy woman was swerving across the road, and threw myself over to the other side of the car. I stuck my hand outside the window and forced another sun lance into existence. This one was even thinner and shorter-lived than the first one, and it wasn't due to the fact that I could feel my emotional reserves continuing to drain away. I could, but this was more about the fact that the angle wasn't any good and I was worried about my attack blasting through the black car and taking out whoever was behind him.

I was used to aiming sun lances with my hand positioned just in front of me and it was harder than I'd realized to hit something when my hand was dangling outside the car. I still managed to score on my target, but it was just another grazing shot—this time to the back corner of the car.

Now I was the one swearing, and Kat swerved across the road without any prompting necessary on my part just before another sun lance went hissing past us and demolished most of the back half of a minivan less than fifty yards in front of us.

It looked like someone had planted a bomb in the back of the minivan. One second it was driving along normally and then in the next instant shards of metal and glass were flying everywhere.

Even with my time sense amped up to twice normal speed, I still would have plowed the Mercedes into one of the guardrails. There was simply too much debris and no way to avoid it all. Luckily Kat wasn't me—she didn't even try. She just headed for the least dense patch of space and shot through the potentially lethal cloud like it was nothing more than confetti.

ENDLESS

The glass in front of Kat went almost opaque from the white spider web of cracks, but she still somehow guided us past the front half of the minivan, which was still skidding to a stop in a spray of sparks and fire.

"Selene!"

Kat didn't bother turning back to give me the look of reproach I deserved for not keeping our enemies occupied, but that was only because she was focused on trying to keep us on the road. She reached forward with her right hand and I felt an angry prickle of energy a split second before a misty white pulse of force shot away from her hand and blew the front windshield up and away from our car as she grabbed her sunglasses.

It was another desperate move; now there was nothing but some flimsy plastic blocking the blinding wind headed towards her, but I couldn't blame her—the alternative was just a different kind of blindness. It was good though because her action made me realize what it was that I'd been doing wrong.

"I can't hit it hanging out the window like this. Can you blow out the back window for me?"

Kat didn't ask questions and I almost didn't have time to duck before she turned in her seat and let loose with another pulse of power that blasted the glass out of its moorings. I didn't waste any time sticking my head over the seat and shooting another sun lance back at the pursuing car.

I was still using relatively weak attacks, milking my remaining strength for everything I had left, but I managed to connect with an attack that blasted away a big chunk of the passenger side roof.

Kat cheered as the other Awakened darted back behind another vehicle. "Nice, you almost took off his ear that time."

I shook my head—even though I knew she wouldn't see it—as I peeked just over the top of the seats.

"It wasn't good enough. He's still back there and now he has all of the advantage because I can't attack him until he decides to dart back out and attack us."

"At this point I'll take whatever we can get, Selene. Besides, he'll be fighting more wind resistance now too. Even a Ferrari will eventually struggle to break one-ten if you blast enough pieces off of it."

Before I could respond the black car—the Ferrari—swerved back out onto open road and a sun lance that was bigger around than my head shot towards us. It was perfectly aimed—right for the middle of the car—and it should have consumed both Kat and me in a fraction of a second.

My head knew that sun lances moved at the speed of light, that there was no time in which to dodge once the attack actually materialized into existence, but some other part of me felt the attack coming and knew it was going to hit.

As the Ferrari broke to the right, I threw my hand up intending on blasting the other car off of the road, but instead of launching another sun lance as I'd intended, I forced a rippling, clear barrier into existence just behind the car. I would have said that nothing could withstand the ravening forces that had just been thrown my way, but somehow the barrier I'd created managed to hold.

It had been the perfect response. I'd managed to throw it up even before our attacker had forced the sun lance into existence, but nobody had ever taught me how to do anything like that.

"What the—Selene, when did you learn how to create barrier effects?"

Kat cranked the wheel hard to the left as she asked the question, forcing me to grab the seat in front of me or risk being thrown free of our vehicle.

"I haven't. I'm not sure how I just did that."

Kat looked back just long enough for me to see something that looked almost like fear in her eyes, but this time I knew that the fear wasn't because we were being chased by two Awakened who currently outclassed us. This time she was scared of what I represented. She was scared of all of the questions my actions raised, questions that the rest of our kind thought had been settled long ago.

I wanted to explain, tell her that I was still just me, but there wasn't time for that. Besides, actions always spoke louder than words—I was most definitely not just another Awakened girl only seventeen years into her latest incarnation.

I turned back around so I was facing our pursuer and tried to get a good enough angle on him to have a chance of tagging him with another sun lance. I was just about to tell Kat to break to the left again so that I could get off another attack, when whoever the Ferrari was hiding behind finally got over the shock of being caught in the middle of a war zone and veered off to the side of the road.

It was exactly the chance I'd needed. Another finger-sized fusion of light and heat flashed into existence and this time I hit his car lower down, vaporizing big sections of the hood and passenger seat before the beam burrowed into the engine block in the back of the vehicle. The gigantic puff of black smoke was the first real evidence of something going our way and it was immediately followed by a sharp decrease in the speed of the Ferrari.

"I'm such an idiot; take out the road, Selene."

I could barely hear her over the roar of the hundred-mile-per-hour wind pummeling me.

"No way! We'll cause a huge wreck."

ENDLESS

"We're never going to get another chance like this. With everything that's happened over the last few seconds everyone behind him is already slowing down. Don't take it completely out, just cut it down to one lane. That will be enough to slow them down and buy us enough time to make it to the rendezvous."

I took a deep breath and nodded. A split second later a wrist-sized blast of power lashed out and turned the entire left lane into a twisted field of rubble.

Chapter 8

Somewhere along the way the Mercedes had sustained more damage than I'd realized. My bet was that it had happened when the back end of the minivan had exploded and Kat had been forced to drive through a cloud of shrapnel. It shouldn't have taken me by surprise, not given the way that there were holes in the hood where shards of hot metal had burrowed past the thin sheet metal, but somehow I'd thought we were home free once I cut the road behind us down to a single lane of traffic.

I'd been able to feel the distance between us and the two Awakened who'd been trying to kill us stretching back out, but then the Mercedes started running rough. Kat slowed down, trying not to stress the engine, and I went back to sitting on my hands in an attempt to force myself not to bite my nails.

When we finally started back up the climb to the big hill where Jace was supposed to meet us, I wasn't sure that the Mercedes was going to make it, but a few minutes later we crested the hill and pulled over to the side of the road.

Kregor found us a second later. "Jace says that the pair who are following you are at least a few minutes back?"

Kat nodded. "Yeah. They're pushing out their signatures in an effort to make sure they don't lose track of us. Selene wrecked the road, so the second car just barely made it back up to highway speed. I'm guessing both of them are in the same car now. Where's Jace?"

"I'll go get him."

I checked my phone while we were waiting. "The phones are still down. Is that a good thing or a bad thing?"

"Depends. It may mean that our buddies out there haven't been able to call back to Kyle and let him know where we are located. Kyle obviously suspected that we were still in Colorado—that's probably why that Unseelie fairy was hanging out in Denver. I knew it was a mistake not to move after the fight with Mephistoles."

I shook my head at her. "It wasn't just me that wanted to stay. We all talked and agreed that there were risks associated with staying in Cold Springs, but there were risks involved in traveling too. I just didn't see anything like this happening as a result of Kyle knowing where we lived."

Jace stepped out of the darkness and I was surprised that I hadn't noticed him getting closer. "You didn't see it because you're still not used to the idea of thinking of Kyle as the enemy."

I felt like I'd been slapped, but he held a hand up. "That wasn't a criticism. I'm dealing with some of the same issues. He and I haven't seen eye to eye on things for a really long time, but even now I'm having a hard time thinking of him as an active threat."

Jace nodded to Byron. "I thought about leaving when we got news of the Helena pantheon's fate, but I kept thinking that we were safer there at the house where we already had wards set up than dashing out into the world unprepared because of information that might have been provided to us for exactly that purpose."

Kat gave Jace an inquiring look. "So does this mean you trust our new arrival? I assume he's the one who taught you the little trick you just used to sneak up on us?"

"Yeah. Apparently the Helena pantheon managed to come up with a few tricks before they swore off using their abilities. They found a way to suppress a person's signature for a period of time."

Jace grimaced and I suddenly realized that Byron was gritting his teeth. "There's a reason that we never viewed signature suppression as a valid...lifestyle. It burns memories the entire time it's active, and it's unpleasant in the extreme, but it seemed like the perfect way to deal with whoever is back there."

Kat walked around and popped open the trunk of the Mercedes. A few seconds later she had pulled up a false bottom and armed herself with a sword that was almost as big as she was. She tossed me a slightly smaller weapon and then turned back to Jace.

"Okay, so what's the plan? I was thinking that you could meet us out here and that would be enough to convince whoever is out there to back off until we could find a way to drop off their radar, but obviously we've got other options now."

"Yeah. Regardless of what we ultimately end up deciding as far as the house goes, we'll be better off if Kyle has two fewer goons working for him. Byron and I will walk down the road and wait at the top of the climb. The two hostiles will be able to sense you sitting here motionless and they'll assume that your car broke down. As soon as they get within thirty yards of us, Byron and I will take them out."

Jace was looking at Kat the entire time he explained the plan, but there was something about his expression at the end that told me he was trying to pass a message to her. He wanted her to know that he still didn't trust Byron—not completely.

Kat sighed and then nodded as Bethany fluttered over and landed on my shoulder. I half expected Bethany to insist on getting her two cents in, but she just stood there and waited to see what Kat was going to say.

"Understood. Selene and I will wait here for the ball to drop. If the bad guys survive your initial attack we'll be already moving towards the four of you to help out however we can. Just remember we're both running pretty low on juice right now. Selene especially—she was throwing sun lances at the lead car and at one point she even managed a shield effect."

I opened my mouth to tell everyone that I was okay, that I didn't feel as depleted as I expected to, but at the last second something stopped me. Maybe it was the double-take that Jace and Byron both did when they heard that I'd managed a barrier.

It made sense for that to surprise Jace—he knew that I hadn't had a chance to learn that particular effect yet—but I wasn't sure what had thrown Byron for such a loop. That would have been plenty of reason to keep the state of my emotional reserves to myself, but there was something else too. I'd been exhausted just a short time before, wrung out and having a hard time feeling anything other than despondency, but now I seemed to have a reserve of happiness and anger both that was ready and waiting to be tapped.

I told myself that I was keeping quiet because it made sense to keep a few cards up our sleeves in case Byron turned out not to be trustworthy, but I had a sneaking suspicion that I just didn't want another look from Kat like the one she'd given me in the car.

I was already a freak just by virtue of the fact that I was one of the Awakened. If I was unusual even for an Awakened, there wasn't anywhere else I could go in order to feel normal.

"Yeah, I'm pretty tuckered out."

The lie sounded flat even to me, but Jace and Byron just nodded and set out to get into position before the other Awakened arrived. Kat and I watched them get set—I half expected them to both go invisible, but maybe whatever they were doing to suppress their signatures precluded using any other effects.

Kregor looked like he wanted to fly back and forth between us and Jace, but Bethany waved him over to my free shoulder and suddenly my exhausted legs were supporting ten extra pounds. I just forced a smile and worked a slight strength amp—nothing major, just enough to keep my legs from buckling out of sheer exhaustion.

"Just hold on for a few minutes, Selene. Amping lets us function beyond our usual abilities, but it's not without a price. Some of the energy you burned during that fight still came from your muscles. Thanks, by the way. That was pure brilliance to grab that stop sign pole like that."

"Thanks, but it didn't feel like brilliance—it felt like good old-fashioned desperation."

"Yeah, well, necessity is the mother of invention and all that. Really, thanks."

I looked over at her and saw a shadow of what I was feeling in her eyes. I reached over and took her hand. "You're welcome, Kat. Thank you for keeping me from falling apart out there. I don't know how you do it."

"Give it a few decades and you'll have done all of this so many times it will become second nature."

"Wow, that's a loaded statement. If I had a choice, I wouldn't have picked this life. The idea of always having to be on guard is terrifying, but I guess if I have to be on the run for the next few centuries I couldn't be in better company."

"Don't you forget that."

I didn't know what else to say, but as it turned out there wasn't time for any more talking. Even my less-practiced ability to sense others of our kind was telling me that our pursuers were nearly to the top of the grade.

My heart rate sped up, and I found myself reaching out for the pulse of our surroundings and amping my time sense up to four times normal. It meant that the next ten seconds of real time stretched out to something that felt like forever, but it also meant that I had plenty of time to see Byron and Jace stand and unleash their respective attacks at the same time.

Jace opted for a standard sun lance, and his attack hit a split second before Byron's. The destructive beam took both of the Awakened inside the car by complete surprise and between one second and the next, the car flew apart in an explosion of metal and glass that exceeded even what had happened when the minivan had been hit earlier in our flight.

I started to turn away, instinctively trying to shield my eyes from the hail of shrapnel headed our way, but before the debris could travel more than a few feet it all slammed into the ground as though driven there by a massive, invisible hammer.

Jace's attack had been nothing less than spectacular. He'd launched a sun lance that was bigger around than my waist. I couldn't have managed anything like that without resorting to a peak memory, but Jace apparently was practiced enough to power that monstrosity on nothing more than his baseline memories.

The tail end of Jace's attack had slammed into the mountainside on the other side of the road and vaporized something like a hundred cubic meters of solid rock, but that was nothing compared to what Byron had done. Byron had increased the gravity inside an area more than fifty feet in diameter by such an incredible amount that the road sank more than three inches into the ground in a perfect circle.

Kat looked at me with worry in her eyes and I could have predicted what she was going to say with perfect certainty.

"I guess the two guys who were following us aren't the only ones who know how to play with gravity."

Chapter 9

We stripped the car down of anything useful, moved the weapons and the money into Jace's SUV and then headed back to the house. Dad, Ari and Sandra were waiting downstairs in the secure vault, protected by the wards that Jace had put up when he and Kat first moved in.

It was clear to all of us that we needed to come up with a course of action that would keep us alive if Kyle came after us for real, but Kat and I were just too tired to manage it until after we'd slept. Under other circumstances I probably would have just thought it was coincidence that everyone else chose to stay down in the vault with us until after we woke up, but I knew that wasn't the case right now. We were all scared.

I was still a little groggy when Kat and Byron got into the fight that I should have seen coming from miles away.

"We need somewhere safe to lie low while we figure out what to do next. Take us to Camelot and attune the wards to us so we can take shelter there."

"No."

Byron didn't sound combative, but it was obvious—to me at least—that he wasn't going to back down. I shook the sleep out of my head and stepped in before Kat could completely flip her lid.

"I'm sure you have a reason, Byron. Why are you so reluctant to make the facilities your pantheon built available to us?"

"He'd better have a good reason. We took him in and healed him rather than just letting him bleed out like most other pantheons would have done." She poked him in the chest with her index finger. "Don't think that I didn't notice that your go-to attack is the same gravity distortion effect that nearly got us killed when we were trying to get on the interstate. How many Awakened do you think know that particular effect?"

"I don't know, Kat. It was common knowledge inside my pantheon. One of the earliest joiners brought it with him. My impression is that it's very common in various parts of Asia."

"Wow, that's a convenient excuse if I've ever heard one. I thought you guys didn't use your abilities."

Byron held up a hand. "It took us a period of time to hit upon abstinence as a sustainable method of signature suppression. There was a period of decades in which we were still using, still experimenting with new effects, and it was during that time that I became proficient with that particular effect."

"Come on, you two. You don't actually believe his story, do you?"

Jace shrugged. "He didn't try to overpower me while the two of you were gone. That counts for something in my book. When you throw in the fact that he helped destroy the two guys who were after you and Selene, I think there's a pretty compelling case that we can trust him."

"Yeah, he was so helpful—he waited to attack until after you did so that he wouldn't have his friends' blood on his hands!"

"That's enough, Kat."

The words popped out of me without any conscious decision. I had no right to talk to her like that, and I knew it. Maybe the old Selene had been able to get away with that kind of behavior, but I was so far away from being that woman that it wasn't even funny.

Kat's face was usually fairly guarded. She tended to hide her serious emotions behind a screen of unimportant feelings, but this time I saw exactly what she was thinking. The shock of having me order her around was quickly replaced with anger, but I managed to get my response out before she could tear into me.

"I'm sorry, Kat, I don't know where that came from. You didn't deserve that, but it's equally true that Byron hasn't done anything to deserve having you go at him like that. The truth is that we need him. Our little pantheon is vastly stronger with him than it is without him."

"We've got Sandra."

Sandra had been remarkably quiet, so quiet that I'd forgotten she was even around. I half expected Sandra to flip out too, but she looked like she was in a different world. I wondered what had made her so pensive. Jace had probably said something to her while Kat and I were asleep, but there wasn't time right then to figure out the root cause of her atypical behavior.

"Yes, we have Sandra, but it's going to be years before she'll be in a position to defend herself. Sandra is starting from zero. She doesn't know any effects and even if she did, she doesn't have any memories with which to fuel them. If we get into a fight with a group of three or four people she'll be nothing but a liability and I'm only half a step ahead of her. Byron, on the other hand, knows effects that none of the rest of us remember and based on what he's telling us, he's got hundreds of years of memories swimming around inside his head, just waiting to serve as fuel for effects if things get tight."

I'd tried to be as conciliatory as I could, but the look in Kat's eyes told me that she wasn't ready to let it all blow over.

"Sure, because relative power is the only thing that matters. Jace and Byron should run the show for now—just until you get your legs under you and return to being the world's best researcher—and then Sandra and I will hold your coats and salute on command just like the good little cannon fodder we are."

Kat grabbed Sandra's hand and stormed out of the room with the younger girl following along behind her. I was left in a state of near shock. I'd never expected Kat to take Sandra's side against me. I stood up to follow the two of them, but Jace grabbed my hand and my dad shook his head at me.

"Give her some time, sweetie. I'll go talk to her and see if I can calm her down. You need to stay here with Jace and Byron. We can't let ourselves get bogged down with internal drama, not if the situation is as serious as it seems."

Ari looked back and forth between Jace and the door a couple of times and then stood up and headed out of the room. It broke my heart to see the way she was refusing to meet my eyes.

"You don't have to go, Ari. This concerns you too."

"I know I don't have to leave, but to be honest, I'd rather be by myself right now."

"It's not safe for you to be out in the garage right now."

She finally looked directly at me and nodded. "I know. I'll find a quiet corner down here."

She slipped away before I could say anything else and I was left wondering how I'd managed to empty the room so quickly. I looked around and realized that we'd started out two people short.

"Where are Kregor and Bethany?"

Jace gave me a crooked smile that seemed to say that he knew what I was thinking, that he understood the way that my loyalties to my friends and family were being pulled against the injustice represented by Kat's treatment of Byron.

"They went out to get something to eat. Kregor has a field of wildflowers nearby so they should be relatively safe. They are fast enough to run away from any of the more powerful fae who might be hunting in the area."

I nodded absently as I turned back to Byron. "You never got a chance to answer me. Why is it that you're so opposed to the idea of taking us to Camelot?"

Byron sighed as he ran a hand through his hair. "I don't know if any of you are going to understand this, but I've spent the last several hundred years hiding in one way or another. Up in Helena, inside of Camelot, skulking around in the wilderness, it's all the same thing and it's the wrong answer.

"The group in Helena was the single biggest gathering of Awakened I've ever read about, and we were all fueled by positive emotions. At the time, I was just like everyone else there. I wanted some peace, wanted to live life without constantly looking over my shoulder wondering when the next attack would materialize, but that was the most selfish choice we could have made. We should have been out in the world, working together to stop people like Mephistoles and Kyle.

"Maybe if we'd been a force for good we could have stopped all of this from coming. Instead, we just made the forces of good weaker when they needed us most. We recruited away some of our side's best and brightest and left the rest of you to fight our battle for us."

I considered my words carefully, but there just wasn't any way for what needed to be said not to come across potentially sounding harsh.

"So you're saying that you guys screwed up and now you want us to fight the war that you should have been fighting all along?"

"I guess that is one way of looking at it. I prefer to think of this as me stopping you from repeating my mistake, but I can't argue with your point."

I'd been expecting him to bristle at my criticism, but he shook it off with surprising ease. He wasn't perfect—the mistakes he and the rest of the Helena pantheon had made were evidence of that—but there was a quiet confidence to Byron that I'd never encountered anywhere else.

It was the kind of simple self-assurance that I'd seen a couple of times out of an older woman that Mom had taken care of for a while before Mom had gotten sick. I would have said that it was just a function of having lived so long, but Kat was evidence that long life didn't necessarily infuse someone with a Zen-like understanding of themselves.

Jace had it, but even he fell short of what I felt coming off of Byron. All I could figure was that it was some inherent quality that certain people possessed, a quality that only age was able to bring to the surface.

I was still looking at Byron with a contemplative stare when Jace broke in. "I respect your position, and I think there's some validity to the idea of striking back now while there are still enough unaligned Awakened to have a chance of taking Kyle down, but that idea is going to go over a lot better if you at least leave open the possibility of us sheltering inside Camelot for short periods of time."

Byron gave Jace a sad smile. "I'll consider it, but in the meantime we should create a much more powerful set of wards here. We're past the point where we can hope to remain hidden. It will take a while for the wards to reach their full strength, but the sooner we start, the sooner they'll be of sufficient strength to hold out at least some of our enemies."

"Okay, that's a fair point. Any other ideas you want to share while we're at it?"

"I think that you should try to set up a meeting with someone from the Seelie Court. The Lady if you can manage it."

Jace shook his head. "She won't talk to me. We called upon her for help to get Selene out of Kyle's bunker just a few weeks ago. It went well and she was able to disembody Fenrir at least once, but she seems to make a policy of only helping out once per incarnation. I think she doesn't want the Awakened or our side to depend on her too much."

Byron shrugged as he looked back and forth between Jace and me. I was pretty sure it was just my imagination, but it almost seemed like his gaze rested on me for a fraction of a second longer than it had Jace.

"You never know for sure until you petition to talk to her, but you might as well try. You have nothing to lose by asking and you may just be surprised at her response."

Byron turned to walk out of the room, but stopped in the doorway. "Make sure that you tell her that the petition is coming from all of us."

Chapter 10

Kregor took our petition to the Lady, and then returned two hours later with an invitation to visit her at the Seelie Court's compound in Salt Lake City. I half expected us to leave within an hour of Kregor's return, but it took us two more days to get everything in order so that we could leave.

Kat and I made a trip into the bank to deposit the cashier's checks we'd collected in Denver, while Jace created a new set of interlocking wards that were designed to protect the structure of the house without extending so far out that normal people would stumble into them and be killed. Byron offered to help with that, but Jace politely told him that there was no need.

It wasn't until I saw a flash of satisfaction in Kat's eyes that I realized it was a trust issue. Apparently you could tune wards to allow specific people through, and the creator of the wards could even tune them to allow other people to modify access, but there was no way to exclude a ward's creator from the list of allowed individuals.

Kat was positively gleeful on the way to the bank as she explained that any wards Byron put up in our house would always be a security risk because it was always a possibility that he would lock us out of that section of the house. I understood the concern and I thought it was only prudent for Jace to take that particular precaution, but I didn't like how vindictive Kat was being. She was better than that.

Once the money was all split up between half a dozen different banks and the wards were in place, Byron spent a good chunk of the next day teaching Kat and me how to temporarily suppress our signatures. He and Jace had been right, maintaining a suppression effect wasn't a pleasant experience. It only took me a couple of tries to get the hang of creating the effect, but maintaining it was another matter altogether.

It had taken half a dozen attempts before I was able to hold the effect up past the initial flash of pain that assaulted me as soon as I forced the effect into existence. The sensation wasn't like anything else I'd ever experienced. It wasn't exactly a headache, but that was as close a description as I could come up with. A headache would have been bad enough, but there was also an odd vibration going on inside of my head that set my teeth on edge. It felt like my mind was trying to pull itself in two different directions, and it didn't get any less painful with practice.

After learning how to suppress my signature altogether, I moved on to lessons from Jace on how to shrink down my signature through more conventional means. That wasn't as bad, but even it wasn't the kind of thing I would want to do for hour after hour.

There was no effect, no invisible stream of memories shooting out of the center of my forehead, but it still required sustained concentration to tighten down the metaphysical radar inside of my head that was automatically programmed to try to find others of my kind. By the time I'd been at it for a couple of hours, I felt like someone had given me a squishy ball and told me to hold onto it. At first it was no big deal, but the longer I held onto it the more I wanted to just let go so that my hand could go back to a relaxed state.

Jace briefly had me play around with flaring out my signature in an attempt to increase my sensory range, but I could tell maintaining that for hours was going to be just as wearing. The cherry on top of everything was the fact that once we got done I was told to unwind for a while so I would be ready to shrink my signature down for hours while we drove to Salt Lake.

By the time I wandered upstairs and changed into some workout clothes, I just wanted to scream. I did a couple of miles on a treadmill in the hopes that physical exertion would take my mind off of my mental pain, but that just left me aching and sore both inside and out.

We left the next morning as soon as Dad and Ari woke up, since they were the two who needed the most sleep. We could have left before then and let the two of them sleep in the back of the RV, but none of us were in too much of a hurry to get on the road. Realistically we should have probably done all of the signature manipulation stuff as soon as Kregor got back, which would have let us set out a full twenty-four hours earlier, but we all felt a lot better knowing that Jace's new wards had been able to crystalize for an extra day.

They still wouldn't be enough to hold off any kind of determined assault, but between them and the older, more established ward we figured most attackers wouldn't be able to make it into the vault in less than a day and a half. That still wasn't ideal, but unless Kyle tasked a significant force to go after our assets, it meant that our journals would be safe while we drove back from Utah.

The trip to Salt Lake was just as unpleasant as expected. Jace, Kat and Byron took turns flaring out their signature in an attempt to make sure that they would be able to sense any nearby enemies. Meanwhile, the rest of us kept our signatures reduced down to the point that we weren't little metaphysical suns yelling for attention.

The hope was that whoever was flaring their signature would be able to spot the bad guys well before anyone got close enough to detect the rest of us, but that was far from a sure thing, so the rest of us keeping our signatures coiled tightly around us helped buy more time for the scout to detect any nearby signatures.

We made it nearly two hours without any incidents, and Kat got surlier and surlier with every passing minute. Jace had warned me the day before that Kat wasn't a very happy traveler, but I still hadn't expected it to be so bad.

I got why she was unhappy, but it was still all I could do to keep from pointing out that at least she got to switch off between flaring and contracting her signature. I didn't get even that much of a break and by the time we stopped for gas the first time, I wanted to slam my head into the window next to me.

At least I didn't have to drive. I wasn't sure I could have controlled my signature and still kept Jace's SUV on the road. All of the pain and frustration felt like it was worth it though when Jace first reported contact with another Awakened.

Under normal circumstances the best we could have done was all shrink down our signatures as much as possible and change directions in the hope of avoiding whoever was serving as the scout for the other side. Jace said that sometimes that kind of thing worked and the team that was trying to be inconspicuous managed to stay just far enough away from their enemies to skirt around them.

Sometimes it didn't work and the pursuers were able to stay in range of their targets. When that happened, things usually got ugly fast. If the balance of forces were close to the same then the pantheon that controlled the area typically tried to bring the interlopers to bay.

I asked him how that usually went down and his answer wasn't very reassuring. Apparently, back in the day, it had been common to try to lose a pursuing group by skirting into the edge of a third pantheon's territory in the hopes that the bigger group would decide against antagonizing their neighbors.

These days, now that cell phones made the coordination of widely dispersed groups possible in real time, that wasn't as valid a tactic because it was far too easy for the pursuers to just call the neighboring pantheon and set up an ambush. Apparently the chance to kill others of our kind was usually enough to bring even bitter enemies to a temporary cease fire.

I'd known that the Awakened culture was by-and-large poisonous, but I hadn't realized just how vicious the war really was. Jace and Kat had been so pleasant, and even Kyle had seemed very civilized. I hadn't realized just how desperate everyone was to bring down anyone who might someday be a threat. The most effective way to guarantee your survival was to make sure that you were the oldest, most knowledgeable, most memory-rich demigod around.

No wonder Byron had chosen to come to Jace and Kat. Kat was acting like a borderline psychopath where our new member was concerned, but I was starting to realize that she was a picture of restraint in comparison to most of our kind.

The briefing that I'd gotten in the hour or two before my family woke up hadn't exactly put me at ease about our trip, but Jace and even Kat had stressed several times that we now had an advantage that no other pantheon they'd ever heard about possessed.

I'd put on a plastic smile and tried to act reassured, but I wasn't—not until Jace called out that he'd just sensed someone up ahead of us and I reached for the image of a perfectly reflective sphere and pushed memories into the effect. Even as I forced the signature suppressor into existence, I was still terrified that something would go wrong. The list of potential problems had burned itself into my memory hours before.

None of the others could sense signatures while they were maintaining their own effects. That meant that they wouldn't know if my control started to slip, or if my effect had been improperly constructed in the first place.

Even if I did everything perfectly, there was still a chance that it wouldn't be enough. In order to be safe we had to make it out of range of whoever Jace had just sensed. If they were feeling particularly aggressive that wouldn't be as much of a problem because it would mean that they were already headed in our direction, thinking that we'd merely turned around and were fleeing, back in the direction we'd come from.

If they were by themselves—either an interloper like us, or just away from the rest of their pantheon—then they would probably shrink their signature down as far as they could, which would make it harder to find them at the same time it drastically reduced their sensing range. If that was the case, we'd be home free.

The more likely scenario though was that they were part of a pantheon and they would hold their position while their friends moved in to support them. That was bad because it meant that we had to cover twice as much distance before we would be out of their range.

Kat already had her eyes closed in an effort to retreat far enough inside herself to block out the discomfort of maintaining her signature suppression effect, but Jace looked back at me and managed a smile.

"It's going to be okay, Selene. Your dad has the radar detector going and we're doing twenty over the limit. It's not going to be a trip to Disneyland, but it will be endurable. We'll make it through to the other side of whatever territory this pantheon claims and be outside of their range by the time our signatures pop back into existence."

I looked back at Kat's SUV, the one with Ari, Sandra and Byron in it, and then gave Jace my best smile. He wasn't fooled any more than my dad was. Dad held himself back to just casting worried glances at me through the rear-view mirror, but Jace went ahead and verbalized the things we were all thinking.

"You're worried that Byron won't be able to maintain the suppression field around both him and Sandra."

"Yeah. I know he said that her signature was small enough to not add in a ton of extra strain, but I'm already starting to feel the effects of concealing just myself. If he can't keep it together then there's a good chance that none of us will make it out of here alive."

Jace reached back and held my hand. "It's going to be okay, Selene. Byron has been doing this longer than any of the rest of us. He has a better idea of his capabilities than we do. Besides, this isn't a normal relocation op.

"Usually Kat and I were hanging out in the wind, hoping that we could make it across hundreds of miles of territory without being seen, because we knew there weren't any reinforcements waiting for us at our destination. This time there are twice as many of us, and we're headed towards the Seelie Court's Utah location. We've been invited there, so if things take a turn for the worst we can still make a run for it—all we have to do is get into Salt Lake City and make one call and we'll have an escort waiting to scare off any pursuers."

"Yeah, I guess that's true. After seeing the Lady take down Fenrir I certainly wouldn't want to tangle with her—I'm probably just nervous about the fact that the phones are all working again. This would be a lot less scary if we didn't have to worry about the bad guys being able to call in reinforcements of their own."

Jace gave my hand another squeeze and then closed his eyes so he could concentrate on keeping his suppression effect up. I half expected for him to let go of my hand, but he didn't. In a perfect world, he would have climbed out of his seat so that he could come back and sit with me. In the real world, one that included Kat sitting next to me and my dad driving, Jace holding my hand from several feet away was probably as good as I was going to get.

I gave my dad a brave smile and then closed my eyes. Jace and Kat had been right, it was easier to focus on the effect without extra visual stimuli, but the good was simultaneously offset with bad. Without any other distractions there was nothing to dull the edge of the mounting discomfort the effect was causing me.

The headache started out as unpleasant and only got worse with each passing minute. The vibration seemed to penetrate deeper and deeper as we drove. Within a few minutes I started wondering if my head was going to shake completely loose.

Most Awakened with a flared signature could sense other Awakened with flared signatures out to a distance of seventy miles. If the person being hunted had their signature in a relaxed state that distance dropped down to around fifty miles. The radius of detection dropped all the way down to around thirty miles for an Awakened who was actively trying to compress their signature down as small as possible.

Jace's signature had been flared out when he'd detected the potential threat up ahead of us, which meant that we'd probably been no more than fifty miles away from whoever was up there. In order to be completely safe from someone who remained in the same spot we were going to need to cover the fifty miles between us and them and then an additional thirty miles.

Dad was driving fast, but that was still the better part of a full hour's worth of driving. The best I'd ever managed before this was twenty minutes and I'd wanted to cut my own throat by the end of that.

Byron had been confident that I'd have an easier time of it when our lives were on the line, but I was starting to realize that he hadn't been telling the full truth. Maintaining my effect wasn't any easier, I was just a whole heck of a lot more motivated.

ENDLESS

I forced my pain and discomfort off into one section of my mind, and sealed them up behind thick walls and a door that would have made the average bank vault jealous.

It worked for a while. The rest of the world faded out of existence and I only occasionally surfaced up far enough to hear my dad as he counted down the miles. The first twenty felt like torture. I thought I'd hit my limit on several occasions, but each time as the pain crested I told myself that I had to hold on for just a little bit longer, that this was about more than just me and what I was going through.

Around mile forty I realized that I'd been fooling myself for the first thirty miles. I'd thought I was being tortured, but that had been nothing compared to the new levels of agony I'd discovered in just the last few seconds.

I wanted to give up. I already had tears silently streaming out of the corners of my eyes, and I could hear my dad asking me if I was going to be okay, but I was doing everything I could to block out the sound of his voice. If I acknowledged my dad I was only one short step away from him telling me to stop trying, from telling me that it was okay to give into the desire to drop my effect and expose all of us to life-threatening danger.

It was getting harder and harder not to pay attention to his voice and then suddenly I realized that he wasn't asking me anything, he was telling us something.

"Jace, Ari is on the radio. She says that Byron is having a hard time keeping Sandra's signature suppressed. She's unconsciously fighting him. He's not sure how much longer he can keep his effect up. What do you want us to do?"

Dad had to repeat his question two more times and I had to squeeze Jace's hand several times before we got any kind of response. Even then, Jace sounded like he was at the bottom of a deep hole, barely able to hear us.

"How long has it been?"

"We just hit mile fifty-five. If the bad guys headed towards our last known position then we've got a good chance that you all can drop your effects and nobody will be the wiser..."

"Yeah, but if they just stayed where they were then we're basically sitting on their lap."

Dad was silent for a second. "It didn't sound to me like Byron has much of a choice."

"Okay, tell him to drop the suppression field. If he doesn't sense anyone then the rest of us will do the same. If there's someone else out there then we're setting ourselves up for a long chase, but there isn't anything to be done about it now."

Jace squeezed my hand. "Hold on, Selene. Just for another few minutes."

I tried to nod, but wasn't sure I managed to do anything more than just rock back and forth in my seat. Coming back to reality enough to listen to the conversation between Jace and my dad had made the pain worse. I'd found a place underneath the pain, a place full of white static, but the walls to that place were getting thinner and thinner. Dealing with the pain was taking something out of me, something important.

It felt like an eternity, but was probably only a few seconds later that Jace shook my shoulder.

"Drop the effect, Selene. There are two enemy signatures ten miles back from us. You need to clear your head so that you'll be ready to drop out of sight again before they catch up to us."

I shook my head. "I'm okay. Have Kat collect herself first—I can wait."

I wasn't actually sure of that, but I knew that Kat was more brittle right now than I was. With all of the other pressures on her, she might not bounce back if she got pushed too far trying to suppress her signature.

"That's what she said too. She wanted me to have you take a break first, but she was responsive and you weren't so I made her go first. She and Byron both got five minutes to pull themselves back together and now they and Sandra are all in hiding again. It's your turn."

It took several seconds for his words to register, and even then part of me was convinced that I was hallucinating exactly what I wanted to hear, that I was about to betray every single person who mattered to me. Maybe I would have stayed there stubbornly refusing to let my suppression field lapse until my ears and eyes started bleeding, if not for the fact that Jace was holding my hand.

I was capable of a lot of things. I fully believed that my mind could make me hear whatever it thought I needed to hear for the pain to go away, but nothing was capable of counterfeiting the way it felt when Jace was touching me. It had been my box of static that had kept me sane inside of my own little preview of hell, but it had been the feeling of Jace's hand on mine, the sense of peace that trickled from the contact, that had given me the strength to find that temporary sanctuary.

Jace's thumb caressed my hand again and I knew that was real. He wouldn't have been able to manage even that simple display of affection if he was buried in the same agony I was currently experiencing.

I let the suppression field fade and opened my eyes. The desire to flare my signature out was almost overpowering, but I resisted until Jace nodded at me.

"It's okay, flare it out. That will help you clear your mind more quickly."

It was like crawling out of a tiny box after being crammed inside for hours. It felt good, but it hurt all at the same time as mental muscles refused to stretch and relax. It only took me a second to orient myself and find the two Awakened Jace had warned me about.

"Wait, I can feel the two closer enemies, but there are also two more not very far behind them."

"Yeah, we all felt them too. That's bad news because it means there's a chance we'll end up fighting equal numbers."

"Yeah, except that fight won't be equal because I still don't know what I'm doing."

My dad gave me another concerned look, but Jace just flashed one of his trademark smiles. It was such a relief to see it that it took me a second to realize why it felt wrong. The smile wasn't different, but the situation wasn't one that called for happiness or levity.

"I wouldn't go quite that far, but I'll agree that an engagement isn't ideal right now. The good news is that everyone is either behind us or far enough away that we have a good chance of getting ahead of them before they make it to the interstate."

I double-checked everyone's position and the muscles in my neck and shoulders relaxed slightly as I realized he was right.

"Great, so we can just run then and we'll be fine?"

"Yeah, we could. The other option would be to try to lure the closest two Awakened into an ambush and take them out before they realized they were up against twice their own number."

I instinctively shied away from the idea, but the more I thought about it the more I could see the appeal to it. If we were really headed into a war, there was something to be said for taking out two of Kyle's people while they were cut off and unable to stand up to our superior numbers.

"Do we know for sure that whoever is out there is working with Kyle?"

Jace shook his head. "No. Kat and I haven't been back in the States for long enough to know the lay of the land after so long away. Back in the day this was the territory of a fairly combative pantheon."

"Combative good, or combative bad?"

Dad's question echoed my own. Jace shrugged. "We aren't that much different than normal people, Peter. The group that was here back before we left wasn't always good or bad either one. Mostly they were just driven by neutral emotions and very interested in preserving their territory. There's no telling if this is them or not, though."

"Then we need to run, Jace. Every fight I've been in so far has been terrifying. I'll do it again if that's what it takes to get us all away safely, but we can't afford to kill people we might end up needing in the fight against Kyle and the Unseelie fae."

Jace considered my words for a second before nodding. "That was my inclination too, but I didn't want to make a final decision without talking to you. If we decide to run it means that we're going to spend a lot more time suppressing our signatures. That isn't going to be any fun."

"I know, but that's still my vote. What did Kat and Byron say?"

Dad's chuckle was pretty humorless. "Kat wanted to ambush the two closest ones and then head after the remaining two if we thought we had any chance of catching up to them. Byron said that the group we were probably dealing with could go either way in the fight with Kyle, so he voted for avoiding them. It was a very…enthusiastic discussion."

I could only imagine. I should have thought to ask Byron very first thing about the pantheon that held the territory we were in, but then again it all still came down to a question of trust. I was mostly willing to trust Byron, so hearing his recommendation made me feel even better about my vote to make a run for it. Kat didn't trust him, so she wanted to do exactly the opposite thing he'd recommended.

Jace interrupted my thoughts. "I'll bet it was a lot more than just enthusiastic. I'm sorry you had to be caught in the middle of that. What did Ari and Sandra say? What's your vote, Peter?"

My dad shrugged. "Ari and Sandra seemed to mostly want to get somewhere safe. I can't blame them. Being in the kind of fight like the one you described between the three of you and Mephistoles sounds just as terrifying as Selene indicated. More so even for those of us who can't do anything to affect the outcome."

"Okay, noted. What about you?"

My dad looked at the rearview mirror again and met my eyes. "I want whatever is going to make my daughters safest in the long term. If that's running, then I'm all for it. If that means we need to set up an ambush and I need to try to take a tire iron to the back of somebody's head, then we should do that."

Jace sighed, and for the first time I realized just how much *he* was dreading being forced to throw a suppression field back up. It was easy to get lost in the fact that I didn't want to go back into that pain-filled state. I'd lost sight of the fact that Jace wasn't any more excited about it than I was.

"All right. We'll make a run for it, but we'll do it carefully. Peter, please stay close to the speed limit. Five or ten over is fine—the goal is not to stand out, so flow of traffic is best. Keep an eye out for anyone racing past us—that's likely to be our pursuers. If that happens it's okay, we just want to know so we can time our breaks. As long as we don't take a break when they are within a few hundred yards of us then we've got a good chance of making it out of here without any kind of confrontation."

Dad nodded. "I'll relay the plan to Ari so she's aware and can brief the others. It might be helpful though to mix up who takes a break together."

I could see that Dad was trying very hard not to say that he didn't want to be stuck in the middle of another yelling match between Kat and Byron, which was smart. Kat was probably in too deep to overhear anything we were saying, but there was no guarantee of that.

Jace gave Dad a sympathetic smile, but he likewise didn't mention the reason for the suggestion. "Okay, that's up to you then. Byron is likely to need a break first again unless Sandra figures out how to avoid fighting him, so when he needs a break just be sure to wake up Selene or me."

Jace turned toward me and reached for my hand again. "Are you ready to do this?"

I looked back at Bethany, who was still sleeping peacefully on the back seat, and then nodded. "Yeah, let's get on with it. The sooner we suppress our signatures the more likely it is that the bad guys won't be able to catch us."

"Assuming they're bad guys. Peter, wait until we both have our suppression fields up and then go ahead and slow down. That should cause the other guys to overshoot us because they'll expect us to continue on at the same speed."

I heard my dad's response, but it didn't register; I'd already envisioned the invisible sphere of a suppression field and forced it into existence. The break had definitely helped, but there wasn't anything magic about that. It was just like dropping down into a walk during the middle of a run. The slower pace was nice, it let you catch your breath and made you feel like you could pick the pace back up and run again when the time came, but the breaks were never long enough to let you maintain the pace you'd started out at.

The lactic acid might have mostly cleared out, but only mostly, and the fuel inside of the muscles was still depleted.

The first few minutes of having my signature suppressed weren't too bad, but I could feel the mental exhaustion building back up to where it had been before and the process seemed to be happening more quickly than before.

Sandra must have finally gotten her unconscious resistance to the suppression field under control—that or I was just doing a poorer job keeping track of time than I had the first time around—because the pain eventually exceeded what I'd been enduring just before Jace had told me I could take a break the first time around. I knew I was in trouble when I started losing my grip on the static-filled room inside my head where I'd taken refuge.

I started picking up bits and pieces of conversation between Dad and Ari. She was unhappy with our new, slower pace. She thought it was a mistake, that we should have continued on as fast as we could go, but Dad wasn't willing to overrule Jace.

Hearing their conversation was just the first sign that I was really struggling. At some point along the way, I felt Bethany land on my shoulder and ask my dad what was going on. By then the mental agony was starting to bleed through into physical agony in the rest of my body.

ENDLESS

Bethany weighed next to nothing, but even the feeling of my clothes rubbing against my skin was distressing and her few ounces of weight felt like an ice pick pressed against my shoulder.

I wanted to scream, but I was worried if I opened my mouth and gave into the urge that it would be the last straw.

A low keening filled the car, and it took me several seconds—time that felt like an eternity—to realize that the sound was coming from me.

"Sweetie, go ahead and take a break. It's what Jace would be telling you to do."

I shook my head violently and Bethany grabbed onto my hair like her life depended on it. She'd never had a problem being heard, and this time her mouth was only inches away from my ear.

"You have to take a break, Selene. If you push too far it can cause permanent damage. I know—I was there when Byron taught Jace how to suppress his signature."

I tried to remember if Byron had ever said anything about that to me, but I couldn't seem to think past the pain. The only thing I could hold inside my mind was the fact that Bethany and my dad had both given me permission to let go. They had given me permission and I hurt so badly that I wanted nothing more than that.

I dropped the suppression field with a gasp of relief as something inside my head clicked into place like a dislocated shoulder being reset.

My signature flared out without any conscious thought on my part and I could suddenly feel Awakened all around us.

Maybe Jace or Byron were capable of differentiating between different signatures—it had never come up in conversation—but I wasn't. I didn't know which of the signatures I could feel surrounding us were the two that had been close to us a few minutes before, and which ones were the two that had been moving in to support the original pair. All I knew was that the two that had grown to four during our last break had become six now.

My eyes popped open and I grabbed Kat and shook her with one hand while reaching for my dad's walkie-talkie with the other.

"Bethany! Get Jace up. Ari, you have to get Byron awake. They're too close—we're right on top of them."

Dad looked back at me with fear in his eyes, but I knew it wasn't fear of what was going to happen to him, it was fear of what was going to happen to Ari and me. I reached out again, flaring my signature even though there wasn't any need—not when the bad guys were this close—and tried to orient myself against the bundles of energy I could feel around us.

"Floor it, Dad. There's only one of them ahead of us, everyone else is behind us."

The engine on the big SUV howled as Dad pushed the accelerator all the way to the floor, and then I felt Jace and Kat both drop their suppression fields at the same time that Byron and Sandra popped into existence behind us.

We were closing on the closest Awakened at an incredible pace and I could only imagine what was going through their mind as they realized that they'd gone from being the hunter to the hunted. They'd thought that they were in control, that their pantheon had a three-to-one margin of superiority, and now they were cut off from their group by not two, but five of us.

They probably should have tried to outrun us, or failing that they should have pulled off to the side and tried to keep the other cars on the road between us and them until we'd flown past, hopefully too fast to permit anything more than a passing exchange of attacks. They chose neither course of action.

We were gaining too quickly—maybe at thirty or forty miles per hour. We were close enough that I finally had a sense of which car they were in. I pointed at a red Acura off to our right as Bethany landed on my shoulder.

"That one, Dad. Watch out, they might try to run us off the road."

Even as I yelled out the warning I realized that it was much more likely that the driver of the other car would choose a different way to try to kill us. My window was already unrolling, which good since I was pretty sure things were about to get dicey. I reached inside of myself, hoping to find a pool of happiness and rage that I could draw on, but worried that Bethany's warning hadn't come in time, that I'd somehow permanently damaged my ability to work effects.

I found my emotional reserve, and it was as powerful as ever—not surprising given just how many reasons there were to be mad. The wind blowing into the car and the sound of the wheels on the pavement were all the pulse I needed, and I amped my time sense up to five times normal before the window made it even a quarter of the way down.

There was a yelp from Bethany as the full force of the wind hit her and nearly threw her completely free of my shoulder. I reached up and grabbed her legs, securing her so she wouldn't be blown free of the car, and then I saw that the driver's side window on the other car was already down and a hand was slowly stretching out toward us.

There was the faintest sense of pressure, a change almost more imagined than felt, and then something inside of me reacted to it while my conscious mind was still trying to decide what it was I'd felt. Black pulses of energy like concentric rings of death shot towards our vehicle, but they were met by a rippling barrier just like the one I'd created the last time we'd been in a car chase.

I felt the barrier tremble from the force of the attack it had just intercepted, and only then realized it had been me who'd created the barrier. It was a shock—I had no more idea this time how I'd done it than I'd had the last time—but there wasn't time to question what I'd done. I made a throwing motion and my barrier shot forward and slammed into the Acura with enough force to crumple the frame.

A split second later two sun lances tore into the wreckage and created a shockwave of destruction that would have ruined the paint job on both of our vehicles if not for the shimmer of energy off to my left as Kat created a new barrier to shield all of us from the rain of destruction that Jace and Byron had just unleashed.

I looked forward to confirm that Jace was okay, and saw that he was already focused on the next task. He grabbed the walkie-talkie out of my hand and pressed the transmit button.

"Destroy the road behind us! It's the only way to stop them from following us."

I grabbed his arm and pulled the radio back towards me. "Try not to kill anyone, the rest of the drivers on the road with us haven't done anything."

"Acknowledged. Let me see what I can do."

As Dad rolled my window back up from his console, I turned and gently set Bethany down on my headrest. Byron stuck his hand out of the window and used a narrow beam of liquid golden light to start digging furrows in the road, first one lane and then the other. Once he had enough of a trench dug to slow down most of the cars following along behind us, he destroyed one entire lane of traffic for a distance of more than a hundred feet. I expected that to be the end of things, but a few seconds later he destroyed a big chunk of the other lane. The road was still travelable, but nobody was going to be driving very fast, not when they were going to have to switch between single lanes like that.

I sat back down in my seat and found Jace looking back at me. "Good work, Selene. If you hadn't put up that barrier there wouldn't have been anything left of us but twisted wreckage."

"It would be a lot more impressive if I hadn't been the one who dropped my suppression field early and lit up a metaphysical flashing neon sign pointing right to us. I don't understand why I was having such a hard time keeping it together."

Bethany flew over and hovered less than an inch in front of Jace's face. "It's a good thing I woke up when I did! Why on earth didn't you and Byron tell Selene that maintaining that effect could result in a loss of her ability to work effects? She was shaking and cold by the time I convinced her that she had to drop the effect. It's like you wanted her dead."

Jace looked like he'd been slapped. "I wanted nothing of the kind. Byron said that a person's signature becomes more dense with age, but is reset if they are killed and assume a new incarnation. He said that Sandra and Selene were the two who should have the least problem with a suppression field. He and I talked to Kat, but there didn't seem to be any point of bringing it up to Selene, since it would just be one more thing for her to worry about."

Kat grabbed the walkie-talkie and turned it off. "There you go. We finally have proof that he's lying. We need to come up with a plan for how we're going to get rid of him. My vote is for us to wait until just before we arrive at the Seelie Court. Tell him that we need to stop for fuel, and then once he's out of the car the three of us attack him all at once."

I started shaking my head even before she finished talking. "We don't have any proof that he was lying. Maybe there was something else going on. Heck, maybe I was doing the effect wrong. I'm not going to help assassinate him over nothing more than this."

Jace jumped in. "She's right, Kat. What you're talking about would be wrong, but if you're not able to see that anymore, then consider the fact that Byron knows things that we don't know. We can learn new effects from him, which makes him valuable. Throw in the fact that so far his intelligence about Kyle staging a massive takeover has been correct, and the last thing we should be considering is killing him."

Kat looked back and forth between Jace and me for several seconds, but in the end her gaze rested on my dad. She was scared, but she wasn't just scared for herself anymore. She was scared for him too.

"Fine. We'll do it your way, but when he turns on us I just hope we all survive so I can say I told you so."

Chapter 11

Our arrival in Salt Lake turned out to be anticlimactic. Byron's destruction of sections of the road had slowed down traffic behind us to the point that we easily outdistanced the bad guys, and we went back to traveling with one person flared out so they could serve as a lookout. We didn't sense anyone else until we were within a few miles of the city.

Jace kept telling me that the Seelie Court wouldn't allow Kyle's people to operate inside of their city with impunity, that the Court's outposts were always neutral locations where even feuding pantheons weren't allowed overt hostilities, but my stomach still tied itself into knots with every mile that passed, bringing us closer to whoever it was that we could all feel up ahead of us.

As we got closer we were able to sense three more Awakened off in the distance. Jace and Kat both agreed that one of the three was at the location of the entrance to the court. That probably meant that the Lady had stationed an Awakened at each of the four cardinal directions and then kept a fifth close at hand.

It wouldn't help in the slightest against members of the Unseelie Court, but it meant that she would have plenty of warning when it came to the other half of Kyle's forces. Any Awakened approaching the city would be sensed and her lieutenants would be able to dispatch a force to intercept. It made sense, but I still let out a scream as seven men and women in glittering armor dropped out of the sky, instantly surrounding both vehicles.

Dad locked up the brakes to avoid crashing into the tall, redheaded woman directly in front of us, and Ari managed to get the second SUV stopped without rear-ending us, but both collisions were avoided by the slimmest of margins. Bethany squealed as the fae warriors landed, but I wasn't sure if she'd been startled, or if she was just extremely excited to see others of her kind.

As surprised as she was, I was even more shocked. "Have things really gotten that bad, that they'll risk stopping us in plain view like this? I know the government is mostly concentrating on Kyle's terrorist attacks, but surely they'll notice something like this..."

Jace gave me an absentminded smile. "They're invisible to everyone else. You, Kat,

Bethany and I can see them because fae can't hide from us Awakened. Luckily they thought to make themselves visible to your dad or we'd be needing to replace yet another vehicle."

"So what do we do now? They are looking a little edgy."

"We all get out of the car, slowly and without making any threatening gestures, but go ahead and amp yourself up slightly. I recognize a couple of them, so it's almost certain that we're dealing with Seelie fae, but it never hurts to be prepared."

Kat grimaced. "Plus they may have revoked our invitation while we were traveling."

I frowned at Bethany. That probably wasn't fair—it wasn't like she was the one who had revoked our safe passage—but she was the closest proxy and the thought of having made that terrifying trip for no reason stoked my anger to new heights.

Jace frowned at Kat. "The Lady is one of the most honorable beings on the planet. She's never done anything like that before."

"Yeah, well, in case you haven't noticed, this isn't exactly the normal state of affairs. The Seelie Court has to be freaking out right now. They've always been fewer in number than the Unseelie Court. The only thing that's allowed them to stand them off for so long is the fact that the Unseelie fae spend most of their time looking for ways to stab each other in the back."

Jace reached for his door. "This conversation isn't productive. Everybody out."

I amped myself up to three times normal speed and wished that Jace had given me permission to grab one of the weapons from the hidden compartment under the back seat. The fae warriors were even more intimidating once we were standing outside and able to see just how tall they all were.

The last time I'd measured myself I'd been just under five ten, which was tall for a girl. I rarely had to look up to anyone unless they were in heels. These girls were all in flats and every single one of them was at least six foot tall and built like their lives depended on being in peak physical condition. The guys were even worse. They were at least six-two and their muscles had muscles. The Lady had gone into combat with Fenrir completely unarmed, but each of these warriors was decked out with at least one massive sword or ax.

They intimidated the hell out of me, but Jace walked up to the redhead and took our group in with a gesture as Kregor flew up behind him.

"I'm Jace. My companions and I are all expected. Kregor was told that the Lady was willing to see us."

The redhead nodded. "I'm Intravil. We were told to expect you. Park your vehicles and we will all walk to the nearest entrance."

Jace motioned Kat and me off to one side as he headed back to the SUV. A few minutes later both

SUVs were parked and Jace was asking about weapons. We were told that weapons were permitted. Kat, Jace and Byron all armed themselves with a variety of daggers—all small enough to conceal underneath their clothes—but I was pretty sure that was more for show than anything else.

I'd come to realize that Kat never went anywhere without some kind of weapon secreted on her person. Given the fact that we'd been heading through enemy territory, I was pretty sure that Jace and Byron were both packing too. I'd even considered carrying a knife, but ultimately had decided against it because I knew nothing about using short blades.

Amping yourself up to three or four times normal speed would do a lot to make up for those kinds of deficiencies, but I still had no business getting that close to someone who was trying to kill me. I needed a long sword—that or I needed to stay far enough back I could use a sun lance. The only problem was there was no way for me to walk around Salt Lake City with a massive sword strapped to my back.

I pulled a long, silver, two-handed blade out of the hidden compartment in Jace's SUV and then turned to Bethany, who'd returned to her normal spot on my shoulder. "Do you think that one of the Seelie warriors would be willing to carry this for me? If we get jumped by some of Fenrir's buddies I'm going to wish I had this, but

I don't know the first thing about making something this big disappear."

Bethany shrugged. I started to put the sword back in the compartment, but before I could finish Bethany zipped over to the leader. "My person is uneasy at the thought of running into one of our cousins without a real blade, but she's too new to have mastered the illusionary arts. I would carry it for her, but I'm not up to shifting something that heavy. Is there one of your people who would be willing to carry it for her?"

Intravil nodded a greeting, but there was something in her expression that I couldn't read. It was almost as though she'd been surprised at something Bethany had just said.

"You must be Bethany. The Lady has spoken of you—she is convinced that you're one of us, and her word has always been enough for me." She turned towards me and gave me a regal nod. "The Lady has also spoken highly of you, Selene. She said that you were instrumental in her most recent string of victories over Fenrir. If you would like, I would be more than happy to hold your weapon for you and conceal it from the eyes of the humans."

"Yes, please. I would really appreciate it."

I picked up the sword I'd laid claim to, and started towards Intravil as Jace strapped an ax and a sword crosswise across his back. Kat and Byron also got heavier blades out for themselves as I crossed the distance between Intravil and me.

ENDLESS

I set the sheathed weapon into her hand and then looked up and met her eyes for the first time. I was completely unprepared for what I saw there. From a distance her eyes had looked like anyone else's, but they weren't—not even close.

When I'd met the Lady I'd gotten an incredible sense of age from her. Intravil had the same sense of having seen more years than I could possibly understand, but there was something else there as well. The thing that looked out from behind Intravil's eyes was inhuman in ways that the Lady hadn't been.

Bethany was like the outspoken, second sister I'd never had. She had wings and a really odd perspective on things sometimes, but for all of that, I still just thought of her as an especially tiny person. Even the Lady hadn't struck me as being so obviously *other* as Intravil did now.

Even as my pulse sped up and my breathing got fast and shallow, I tried to remind myself that humanity wasn't necessarily everything people tried to claim it was.

Intravil not being human didn't necessarily mean that she was bad, but as I looked up into her eyes, I got the feeling that her definition of bad wasn't the same as mine. She looked at me like I was some kind of mildly interesting insect, like I didn't merit much consideration on my own. Despite her earlier acknowledgment of my part in helping the Lady defeat Fenrir, it was only Bethany's request on my behalf that made me worthy of her assistance.

"I will take good care of your weapon, little godling, and I will return it at your request."

I followed her gaze and realized that I hadn't let go of my sword. I still had my right hand clenched around it like my life depended on it. I mustered up an apologetic smile and forced my fingers to relax, one at a time.

It was like nothing else I'd ever experienced. My subconscious seemed to have realized just how alien Intravil was even before the rest of me had, and it was convinced that the tall, beautiful redhead was a potential threat.

I nodded my thanks and started to step backwards. The polite thing would have been to turn my back on her rather than acting like she was a coiled rattlesnake, but I just couldn't bring myself to let her get behind me—not as long as she was within striking distance.

Intravil reached out and wrapped her hand around my upper arm. The gesture had such a lazy confidence to it that it took me by surprise. I tried to tell myself that I could have dodged out of range if I'd actually been trying, but I wasn't so sure that was the truth. I was amped—not as far amped up as I'd been at some points already in my life, but amped up enough that most beings would have struggled to take me by surprise like that, but Intravil was apparently quite a ways up on the food chain.

"No need to back away, godling. Stay close to me so you'll have access to your weapon if something should happen."

There was a challenge in her eyes. She would hold my weapon regardless, but this was a chance to earn some of her respect, to show that I was something other than just another bug.

I forced my breathing to slow down and stepped forward. "Okay. Just let me know if I get too close and start tripping you up."

We shook out into a long line with Intravil and me at the front, Jace at the back with a massive fairy who had skin so black that he looked like he was made out of obsidian, and everyone else in the middle with one or more fae at their sides. Jace, Byron and Kat made their weapons disappear, and then we started moving.

The trip seemed to take forever. It wasn't just me either. I saw Intravil speed up and then force herself to slow back down at least a dozen times. Even on foot, she was used to moving a lot faster than this, but while we Awakened could have probably kept up with her, there was no way that Dad and Ari would have been able to sustain a pace any faster than the one we were already maintaining.

Ari was a runner—or at least friends with runners who took her out with them often enough that she had better than average en- durance—so I wasn't all that worried about her. My frequent glances back at the rest of our group confirmed that my dad was struggling. At first it wasn't as noticeable, but as the seconds slowly transformed into minutes his breathing grew more ragged.

My desire to show I wasn't actually terrified of Intravil kept me there at her side much longer than I would have stayed otherwise, but even that wasn't enough to make me turn a blind eye to my dad when his legs became so unsteady that it looked like he might collapse at any moment.

I slowed nearly to a stop as I moved to the left so that the fairy just behind us could pass me, but then Kat was at Dad's side, and a warm trickle of power washed over me as I caught the fringes of her effect. Kat grabbed Dad's upper arm and for a second I thought he was going to wave her off, but then Byron was on his other side and I felt another surge of power as the newest arrival to our pantheon amped my dad's circulatory and respiratory systems a little more.

My dad started to blush from embarrassment, but now that there were two of them bracketing him, each holding onto his arm to help support some of his weight, he seemed unwilling to make a big deal out of their help.

I turned back towards the front of our group and caught back up to Intravil within a few steps. The flawless Seelie warrior looked over at me as I regained my position at her side.

"You're father?"

"Yes, how did you know?"

She smiled at me, and there was something more to the expression than the cold indifference she'd displayed earlier.

"My gift is the ability to see such things. Your concern for him does you credit."

That was the last thing I'd expected to hear out of her and for a moment I couldn't come up with a response. "I didn't think that the fae would care about that kind of thing."

"We do. Only the most honorless of the Seelie Court would not feel some degree of respect and gratitude towards the individual who created us."

I half expected Intravil to be angry with me, but maybe there was a benefit to her not respecting me yet. As long as she didn't expect anything out of me it wasn't possible to offend her.

She gave me a chance to respond, but I didn't know what to say. In the end she just nodded to herself, seemingly satisfied with my response—or lack thereof—and snapped her fingers. I looked back just in time to see two of her people grab Ari's arms, supporting her similarly to how Kat and Byron were supporting my dad.

We ran the rest of the distance at a speed that would have been tough for even Olympic distance runners to match. I half expected the sight of us to cause bystanders to freak out, but there were surprisingly few people out and about on foot. People in cars had no real frame of reference for how fast we were going, so we made it all of the way to the nightclub that appeared to be our destination without any problem.

I didn't have to look twice at the bouncer in front of the club to realize that he was another Seelie warrior. He wasn't in armor and he didn't have any visible weapons, but he had the same perfect bone structure and tall, muscly build as the Seelie fae who were accompanying us. That was probably a good thing because Byron and my dad were the only two of us who looked old enough to make it into an establishment that served alcohol.

We were ushered into the club without any fuss, and Intravil led us through the press of barely-clothed, sweaty bodies without trying to communicate over the thumping music. A few minutes later, we found ourselves inside the suite of rooms that I was pretty sure belonged to the owner of the club.

If I hadn't seen the furnishings inside of Jace and Kat's house I would have stood there gawking at the sheer luxury of the owner's suite. The soundproofing was amazing. Out on the dance floor the music had been so loud I'd half expected my ears to start bleeding, but inside the owner's suite the heavy bass wasn't any louder than my own heartbeat.

ENDLESS

One entire side of the main sitting room was taken up with thick, tinted windows that looked out over the club floor. They allowed us to look out over the dance floor without being observed in return. A large hot tub took up one corner of the room, but I was more interested in the black leather sofas that dominated the center of the space. I'd made it through the run, but that didn't mean I wasn't feeling tired.

Intravil looked through the windows for a second and then turned and walked to the other side of the room and placed her hand on the massive floor-to-ceiling mirror mounted on the wall. For a second nothing happened, and then the mirror rippled and turned cloudy.

"It's ready—go ahead."

I looked over at Jace. Nobody had told me what to expect, but then again that wasn't entirely a surprise. There was so much I didn't know that he and Kat had to pick and choose what bits of information took priority. Generally that meant teaching me a new effect or weapons technique.

"It's okay. The Seelie Court exists outside of what we normally consider reality. Bethany told you that she's able to shift things into an in-between place. This is like that, only it's a lot bigger and accessible to other fae."

Dad and Ari hadn't had the benefit of finding out that Bethany could make piles of cash disappear, but they seemed to mostly be keeping up with the conversation. I looked up at Bethany and she shrugged.

"I don't know how it works either—this is something you only get access to when you've got way more power than I do. Really powerful fae like the Lady can carve out some sort of pocket dimension. Even the Lady is limited in the amount of space that she can bend to her will, but some of her most powerful lieutenants have lent their strength to the task as well. Between all of them they've created a home for our people, for the Seelie fae."

"But it's not accessible from just anywhere?"

"No. Only through special portals like this."

I nodded. "Which explains the guards. You wouldn't want to have a bunch of Unseelie fae raid the court."

Intravil picked up the explanation with a shake of her head. "The guards are here for other reasons. The Seelie Court is safe from any kind of intrusion. Only the portal wardens have the ability to open up a portal to our homeland."

Her response had been polite, but I could tell that she was getting impatient with the delay. I took a deep breath and then stepped forward into the mirror. I couldn't have said what I was expecting, but what I actually felt wasn't it.

The mirror felt like walking into a warm shower. Tingles of calm energy lapped up against my skin for a moment and then I was on the other side of the portal in what I could easily believe was a separate reality from the one I'd grown up in.

I was in a marble building, like something I would have imagined if told to visualize ancient Greek architecture. There was a breathtaking beauty to the tall, fluted columns and the polished floors.

The furniture was all slender golden rods that looked much too weak to support even my weight, let alone someone as heavy as the male warriors who'd accompanied us. The white silk cushions on the furniture looked like they would be hell to keep clean, but there was no arguing with the regal feel they gave the room.

There were large swaths of silk hanging from the roof, some white, some gold. But for them, the entire building would have been open to the outside. They were all down but for one, and I walked over to that edge of the room as Bethany came through the mirror behind me and landed on my shoulder.

"It's everything that Kregor told me it would be."

I tore my eyes away from the forest before us and looked at Bethany. "You've never been here before?"

"No. Kregor is always the one to run messages between Jace and the Lady. He told me it would feel like coming home—even the first time—but I didn't quite believe him until now."

I nodded, surprised that she'd managed to capture what I was feeling so perfectly. This felt like home, which was ludicrous given how different it was from my actual home, but there was no arguing with feelings.

The rest of our party trickled through the portal over the next few seconds. I'd half expected the entire group of Seelie warriors to accompany us all of the way to our meeting with the Lady, but only Intravil stepped through the mirror before it returned to its normal state.

She looked at the seven of us for several seconds before pointing at the mirror. "I am the only one who can activate the portal. I'm the one who brought you through, so you are my responsibility until you return to your plane or the Lady assumes responsibility for you. Follow along closely behind me or you'll get lost. Don't eat or drink anything. Our food would be unpleasant for Awakened and lethal for humans."

She handed me my weapon and then turned and exited the building without looking back, and we all hurried after her. The trip through the forest outside was unnerving. Don't get me wrong, the forest was beautiful. Most forests I'd seen in Colorado were hard to walk through because there was so much underbrush. This was nothing like that.

The trees were tall and widely spaced, and the only other plants growing underneath them were flowers and grass. I didn't see any insects, which meant that this was the kind of place where you could actually lie down on the grass for a nap and not have to worry about something crawling on you while you were asleep.

The forest *looked* perfect, but there was something odd playing at the edge of my mind as we walked. When I'd been little I'd had a tendency to get car-sick on long drives. Mom had told me repeatedly that my needing to hurl every time we traveled was a good thing because it meant I had a more sensitive sense of balance. She claimed that I was super in tune with my body and I got sick because my mind knew that what my eyes were seeing—the landscape rushing past us—didn't match up with what my inner ear was saying.

I'd always figured that she was just trying to make me feel better, but for once I was starting to think maybe she'd been onto something. We were walking at a fairly normal pace, but I kept getting the feeling that we were moving much faster than that. Ari was looking a little green around the gills too.

"We are here. Wait in exactly this spot while I announce you."

Intravil walked away without looking back, which was unnerving given that I'd just learned that she was our only ticket back home.

It was a good thing that we arrived when we did, or I probably would have lost my last meal. I was so busy trying to regain control of my stomach that it took me a while to realize that 'here' was another marble building, this one even bigger than the one we'd just left.

There was a sense of age to it that took my breath away. It was funny. Some part of me—my soul, presumably—was hundreds, maybe even thousands of years old, but this building still made me feel like some kind of insignificant insect. Maybe Intravil wasn't as off her rocker as I'd been thinking she was.

Intravil returned a few minutes later and led us into the building, which actually had separate rooms with real walls rather than just the large strips of fabric that I'd been able to see from the outside. The very center of the building turned out to be an enormous throne room, and the familiar figure of the Lady was waiting for us on the throne.

Somehow I'd been expecting her to look different this time. It was silly, but the first time I'd seen her had been back before I'd known that she was the most powerful Seelie warrior. Now that I knew she ruled the entire Seelie Court it only seemed fair for my perception of her to have changed—only it hadn't. She'd somehow looked regal even before I'd known who she was.

"You may all approach me."

Jace nodded and led the way. The rest of us followed in a loose clump that made it obvious we weren't entirely comfortable to be there. As we walked I took in our surroundings. The throne room was surprisingly Spartan. Then again, it didn't need much in the way of orna-mentation when it had nearly two score Seelie warriors standing around the perimeter of the room.

Intravil's people had been intimidating on levels only Fenrir had ever managed previously, but this group was something else entirely. Some of the guys were pushing seven feet in height and even the girls looked like they were nearly six-six. They were all built with the hard, defined muscles of gymnasts, and they were all wearing full-plate armor that had never been made by any human hands.

Each suit of armor was unique, and each was a work of art. The metal was all colored in astonishing, eye-catching hues that were the very definition of unearthly. One of the suits was black, and even that had a hauntingly beautiful iridescent sheen in the torchlight.

I'd been to a museum back in grade school and had a chance to see real armor. At the time, I'd been impressed with the way that the ancient blacksmiths had been able to form metal into such smooth, rounded shapes. I'd been astonished, even at a young age, by the narrow seams at the joints, but these suits made those look like time-worn relics.

The suits I was looking at now had joints too—they had to have joints in order to move—but there weren't any gaps. Instead, it was like there were articulating layers of metal that slid around in such a way that there was never any exposed flesh, no matter how the wearer moved. None of the suits I was looking at were sized for someone like me, and even if they had been, amping up my strength still might not have made me strong enough to move around inside of something that heavy, but I still found myself wishing that I could put one of them on.

A second later we all arrived to the edge of the small platform the throne was built on, and the time for sightseeing had passed.

"Thank you for seeing us, your majesty."

She inclined her head. "What brings you to my court, Jace?"

"As I'm sure you know, my brother Kyle has launched an offensive designed to take control over the entire world. Byron sought us out to report that his pantheon, a group of two dozen Awakened, was destroyed in a surprise attack. Kat and Selene were attacked by an Unseelie fairy in Denver and then chased by two Awakened as they fled the city."

"I'm aware of Kyle's plans. In fact, as I recall, the last time we encountered each other I was inclined to bring down Kyle's wards and end the threat he represented. Tell me, do you remember who convinced me not to follow my instincts on that occasion?"

My throat had gone dry. I wanted to hide behind Jace and the others, but I knew that wouldn't win me any points. The last few days had shown me that we desperately needed allies if we were going to survive what was coming, so it was time to take my lumps.

"It was me, your majesty. I was the one who said Kyle had good inside of him, that he could be saved."

"Yes, Selene, that was you. You told me to stay my hand, that you believed in him, and yet here we are just a few weeks later and not only does he have Excalibur, he also has a second artifact, the Brísingamen necklace. Combined, those two artifacts make him nearly the equal of any two of your kind."

I bowed my head, unsure what to say, but she wasn't done.

"Tell me, young one. Are you ready to acknowledge your mistake? Are you ready to admit that your words have led us all into ruin?"

I wanted to open up a hole in the ground and crawl inside, but something made me look up and meet her eyes. The Lady didn't have the same inhuman air that Intravil had displayed, but there was a force of presence there that demanded I give her what she wanted. I opened my mouth to do exactly that, but the words that came out weren't what I was expecting.

"I acknowledge that I was wrong about what Kyle was going to do, but I stand by my statement that it would be wrong to kill him before he'd done anything wrong."

"He had done things in the past that were wrong. He agreed with Mephistoles to not interfere while your pantheon was hunted."

"You knew that?"

The question burst out of me of its own accord, and for a moment I was convinced that I'd made a terrible mistake. The Lady's face went cold and distant.

"I know most of what happens in our shared world. Sometimes not until much after it's occurred, but sooner or later everything makes its way back to me."

"Yes, Kyle stood by and let Mephistoles and Sandra kill me, but that's not the same thing as murder. He told me that he didn't think there was anything he could have done to save me, but even if that wasn't the case, he at least partially atoned for that when he saved Kat, Ari and me from Fenrir. Kyle wasn't perfect, but killing him before he'd had a chance to do all of the terrible things that he's done over the last few days would have been nothing less than murder.

"I think that you're better than that. I know that I am."

For the briefest of moments I thought she was going to physically lash out at me. I felt tension slither through the room as my friends tensed up and the Seelie warriors around the perimeter of the room prepared to do battle.

"Leave us. I want everyone but Byron and Selene to leave. Not just the room, I want you all out of my home."

"We're at the highest state of readiness we've seen in the last thousand years, your highness. Is that prudent?"

The warrior who'd spoken looked like a male version of Intravil, just much bigger. He had the same perfectly straight red hair and unnaturally gray eyes.

"Wait in front of my house. If a call for help arrives you'll be placed to intercept the messenger and go to their aid. You'll have to do without me for a time if the worst comes to pass."

I thought he was going to protest again, and a new kind of tension filled the room. I'd thought that the weight of her gaze before had been tremendous, but it was nothing compared to what she leveled at him. Eventually the pressure became too much—even for him—and the Seelie warrior dropped his gaze and started towards the exit.

As soon as her people started moving, the Lady turned her attention back to me. It took several seconds for the fae to leave, and the Lady stared at me the entire time. I was so focused on not looking away that I didn't realize my friends had remained behind until Jace stepped up to my side.

"I want your promise that you're not going to hurt them."

"I told you to leave, godling."

"We aren't leaving until you promise that you aren't going to harm them."

Jace's voice was remarkably even, and hearing him stick up for us—for me—made me want to cry. I knew it had to have been hard for him to hear me defend Kyle, for him to be reminded of the faceoff outside of Kyle's wards only hours after I'd kissed his brother. Despite all of that, he was willing to stand up to one of the two or three most powerful beings in the world.

Maybe someone else would have attributed Jace's strength of will to having lived for so long, to having more than a hundred years of memories anchoring him, but I knew it was more than that. Jace was standing up to the Lady because it was the right thing to do and Jace was one of the few people out there who always did the right thing.

"Them, or Selene?"

It was a shrewd question. It gave both the Lady and Jace a chance to back down without losing face. It was shrewd, but it was also unworthy of her. She knew that Byron had only recently joined our pantheon. She knew that it would be easy for a lesser man to rationalize sacrificing Byron if that was what it took to get the rest of us out safely.

I turned and looked at my friends and family. Sandra was halfway to the door, but that wasn't much of a surprise. She didn't understand why she hated me so badly, but she did and it wasn't like she would be any good in a fight even if she did stay.

Dad and Ari hadn't moved though, and neither had Kat. All three of them stood behind us. They all looked terrified, but they hadn't moved.

Bethany currently stood on Kat's shoulder, almost as though she'd been forced backwards by the Lady's order and only managed to stop herself from leaving at the last moment. Despite that, she seemed to be psyching herself up to return to my shoulder. Even Kregor, who'd never said more than two or three words to me at one time, was waiting half a step behind Jace.

I already knew that Jace had stepped forward, risking the Lady's displeasure, but I was most surprised of all to see that Byron was facing the Lady without any trace of fear. It was possible that he'd stayed just because she'd ordered him to, but I didn't think so. He appeared ready to back Jace and me up—with his life if necessary.

"Them. They are both part of our pantheon and I'm not going to walk out of here until you've promised them safe passage back to the real world."

"You had that promise when I agreed to let you all visit me here in my home, Jace. That has always been the case."

"I know, but these aren't normal times."

"Even in my anger I would not violate those laws, godling. You have my promise that your pantheon is safe here. Now please leave us. I have things to discuss with these two."

Jace reached over and cupped the side of my face before nodding and turning around. At his nod they all left, everyone but Bethany, who returned to my side. The Lady cocked her head to one side and considered the tiny fairy who'd spent the last two decades looking for me.

"You need to go, little sister. I'll return Selene to you none the worse for wear in a few minutes."

I half expected Bethany to spout off something about holding the Lady to her promise, but apparently even Bethany had her limits, and she'd pushed the ruler of her people as far as she was willing to.

I wasn't sure what to expect when it was just the three of us, but when the Lady turned to Byron he didn't seem surprised by how things had developed.

"What is it that you want, Byron? Vengeance? Safety?"

"If I wanted safety then I wouldn't be here talking to you—we both know that."

The Lady actually smiled at his frank response. "Why then?"

"You know why I'm here. We are headed to a crossroads. If we don't all combine our efforts, Kyle will soon control everything."

"You're sure of that? Many of my strongest warriors are of the opinion that we are safe here. Unlike your Camelot, there will never be anyone strong enough to bring down our walls. We could easily retreat inside of these walls and let the Awakened and the Unseelie fight among themselves."

Byron sighed and looked back in the direction we'd come from. "That has the sound of an argument that has been dusted off thousands of times just over the last century."

"It probably sounds that way because it has. The Seelie fae have been fighting this war longer than any of you Awakened remember. I cannot count the number of times that it seemed our defeat was certain, but each time the other side started fighting with each other and we've always been able to snatch victory from the jaws of defeat."

Byron looked back at her and shook his head. "This isn't like those other times."

"How do you know?"

"Because during those other times Kyle wasn't leading the enemy."

That drew a small smile from her. "You're awfully sure for someone whose current incarnation is less than six hundred years old, someone whose memories can't extend back for more than two or three hundred years. I've learned over the last several thousand years that things move in cycles. Very little I see is actually new. Technology, yes, that changes, but people—especially the Awakened—remain the same."

"You're not any less practiced at misdirection than you were the last time we met. What you're saying may be true, but you and I both know that Jace and Kyle haven't been around long enough for the darker of the two miracle brothers to have been a threat the last time you faced an army. Things are different this time."

I got the feeling that the Lady was enjoying the discussion with Byron. It wasn't that she was failing to take the situation seriously. It was more like she'd...missed...talking to him. Like nobody else was willing to contradict her like he'd just done.

"You may be right about that one aspect of this situation, but that isn't going to be enough to convince many of my people. There is a growing pressure from my people to pull back inside the Court and seal the portals to the outside world. There is a strong belief that once we are no longer a threat, the Awakened and the Unseelie will turn on each other and then we'll be free to swoop in and pick up the pieces."

"Those people are wrong. Kyle is one of the best researchers to ever live. Just because no Awakened has ever managed to create a portal here doesn't mean that it's not possible. If you leave him free to expand his power unchecked he will someday open a rift into this place and you will be faced with a fight that you can't win. Cowering behind sealed portals isn't the answer!"

Between one heartbeat and the next, the Lady's hand shot forward and grabbed Byron by the neck. It shouldn't have been possible. I could tell by the way he was moving that he was amped up even more than I was. He should have been faster even than the most powerful fae, but he wasn't faster than her.

"Be careful, Byron. I've always allowed you a certain degree of latitude, but you are the last one who should be lecturing me about the danger of choosing a defensive strategy.

"You were to recruit and hole up inside of your precious Camelot until you were needed. If you'd held to your side of the agreement we wouldn't be in this mess. Rather than trying to scrape together an effective force from the dregs of your kind, I would have the single largest pantheon in the history of the world at my beck and call."

I wasn't sure what I should be doing. The two of them obviously had history together none of us had suspected. I had no way of knowing who was in the wrong, but I didn't feel like I could just stand there and let her kill him.

I loosened my sword in its sheath, but I couldn't quite bring myself to actually draw it and attack her. For one impossibly long second we all stood there frozen and then she released him with a push that sent him stumbling away from her.

"Almost, you make me forget myself, Byron. Nobody else could have sparked my anger like that."

"I did not violate our agreement. I went back to my pantheon and told them your terms. We agreed unanimously to accept your proposal and, as you know, I cast the foundational ward for what would someday become Camelot."

"Yes, and my people and I stepped up patrols in that area, buying your ward time to crystalize before it was challenged. Without my help your ward wouldn't have lasted a day."

"I know. We lit a bonfire that was visible from half a continent away at a time when we didn't have the strength that would have been required to stand off dozens of our kind eager to bring down our defenses and plunder the riches they assumed had to be hidden there.

"We owed you our very lives and every single member of my pantheon knew that, but once the wards were up and we began living inside of the bunker we'd built, the tensions inside that closed system quickly became unbearable. The majority took the view that while we'd agreed to serve as a strategic reserve for you, there had never been a definitive requirement to remain hidden away from the world altogether for hundreds of years."

The Lady sighed. "Your people reasoned that it was acceptable for them to leave Camelot and recruit others, therefore it was also permitted for them to live outside of Camelot."

"Yes—they felt that our discovery that it was possible to suppress our signatures by refusing to use our abilities gave us a chance to live outside in the world while still remaining hidden and able to intercede when you needed us."

"And you, Byron? What was your opinion?"

"I felt that we were not living up to the spirit of the law, but I was worried that allowing our group to splinter into smaller factions was an even larger danger. I'm sorry. Hindsight has proven that to have been the wrong decision."

My mind was whirling with new information. "Wait, the two of you worked together? What were you thinking taking so many of the good guys out of play like that? That's just asking for the bad guys to get the upper hand. Do you realize how much of the bad in the world can be traced directly to the two of you?"

Byron stepped toward me with a pleading look on his face. "You have to understand, Selene. The Seelie fae aren't wrong when they say that the Unseelie have always spent at least as much time fighting against each other as they do fighting against this court. We Awakened are no different.

"Someone like you or me is much more likely to die at the hands of someone like Mephistoles than at the hands of someone like Jace or Kat.

The same can't be said for them. Ultimately Mephistoles and Sandra were both defeated in large part because of Kyle's help. By pulling the good Awakened, the people who were able to work towards something other than just their own selfish hunger for power, out of the fight, we were preserving them. We were making sure that they wouldn't die and then return in an incarnation driven by negative emotions."

It was all suddenly clear to me, and I was shocked that I hadn't been able to see it before that. "You wanted them to kill each other off and then you would grab them when they came back better than they'd been the last time around."

"Yes, very much like what you're trying to accomplish with Sandra."

I turned to the Lady. "What did you get out of this?"

"What makes you think that I didn't just do it out of the goodness of my heart?"

"Call it a gut feeling."

Her smile wasn't the cold thing it had been earlier. "I'm the leader of the Seelie fae. Even when I believe in a cause I still have to make sure that my people benefit from any agreements I sign. Believe it or not, the idea of having a sizeable group of decent people like Byron who owed me a favor was very nearly enough all by itself."

"Very nearly is the same thing as just not good enough."

"Indeed it is. The truth is that the wards around Camelot were always going to be an incredible danger to my people. I knew when Byron first approached me that what he was proposing would create something that both sides would want for themselves. At that point there was no member of either court with even close to enough power to bring down that powerful of a ward—there still isn't."

Byron nodded. "But as long-term as the plans of the Awakened tend to be, that's nothing compared to the timeframe the courts both deal in. We both knew that eventually someone would become strong enough to bring down the ward I wanted to erect. If that was someone—preferably the Lady—from the Seelie Court then the good guys would have a real advantage."

"Assuming that they were able to hold off the Unseelie Court for long enough so she could drain them."

"Yes. Assuming that."

I looked back and forth between the two of them. "I don't know enough to understand what you're getting at. I can feel that the pieces all fit together somehow, but I'm still missing most of the important ones."

Byron cleared his throat. "Most Awakened don't ever pull their wards down. Even if they move on to another location, they tend to leave their wards up because that means they'll always have a safe spot to rest and recover in if they are on the run in that area. Of course there's never any guarantee that a ward will still be up when they get there, but most of us would rather know that there's a chance our sanctuaries will still be there when we need them."

"Wait, I thought all wards eventually got taken down by another Awakened or one of the fae who wants to drain them to increase their power. I thought that was the only way for them to come down."

"No, there's another way. Something about the creation of a ward results in more power being contained in them when they reach full maturity than was used to establish them in the first place."

"Doesn't that violate a bunch of physics laws?"

That earned me a smile, and I realized that I hadn't seen Byron smile very often. "Spoken like a true researcher. Yes, that *seems* to violate the laws of the world, which means that we don't understand the laws like we think we do. Under the right conditions, the person who created a ward can bring them down in a controlled discharge that releases all of that power back into the area around the location."

I had another of those moments when the world snapped into focus for me. "That power is easier for the fae to absorb, isn't it?"

The Lady nodded. "Yes, it is. In fact, that's the only real reason most of your kind ever bring down a ward. It's the ultimate reward for a fairy who's served them well. It can result in decades, or even centuries of growth in just a few hours."

I shook my head in astonishment. "There's our solution. Somebody teach me how to cast a ward right now so I can pull it back down and feed it to Bethany. Given what we're all headed into she needs every ounce of power I can spare. Even if it's not enough to allow her to fight and make a difference, it still could be enough to save her if she gets disembodied."

The Lady reached out and clasped my arm. "Your sentiment does you credit. Part of me would like to dismiss all of the rest of your kind as merciless monsters for not doing exactly as you propose, but that wouldn't be fair. The truth is, there are legitimate reasons why an Awakened would be reluctant to bring down a ward and feed it to one of my people. Wards are difficult to establish. The creation of the effect itself is difficult and it requires time for the ward to mature to the point where it can stand up to attacks.

"As Byron indicated, it's like creating a bonfire that all of your enemies can see. Building a sanctuary underground helps shield the ward from detection, but sanctuaries of that kind are not plentiful or cheap."

I nodded. "And given how dangerous traveling is, I guess I can see why some people would be reluctant. That's why you helped

Byron though, isn't it? He promised to bring the wards around Camelot down at some point and let you feed off of the energy. That way you win. It will put you well ahead of your enemies. It's the perfect plan."

"Very nearly. The biggest flaw is that it only works as long as Byron is still alive. If he were to die the wards would remain up until they were brought down by force, and it might not be me who brings them down."

She turned to Byron. "You know what I want. Our agreement would leave you with another sixty years before the wards would need to come down, but I want them down now—all of them. I need that power—my people need that power—if we're to have any chance of defeating the Unseelie Court."

For several long seconds Byron didn't respond. I wanted to yell at him that it was stupid to think of refusing. The Lady was right—we needed the power—but I could understand his worries. For all Byron had refused to let Kat run away and hide inside of Camelot for the next two or three hundred years, it was still hard to let it go.

He'd put the wards up knowing that they would have to come down eventually, but I suspected that he'd expected to be in a drastically different situation by then. He'd expected to have a large pantheon behind him, a group of people with hundreds of years of memories saved up, memories that they would gladly sacrifice in order to defend a new sanctuary for long enough that its wards would have time to mature.

He'd thought he was guaranteeing the future by entering into his agreement with the Lady, but now she was asking him to give all of that up at a time when he was even weaker than he'd been when they first entered into the agreement. That had to be hard.

The silence stretched out to the point where I was uncomfortable, but the Lady gave my arm a squeeze before I could intervene.

"Give him time, Selene. There is more at work here than you realize."

"More? What else can there be?"

"He's worried about giving me that much power. It was one thing to do that back when he was confident that he would have a powerful pantheon backing him up, but now it's not quite so easy to rationalize giving me a push that may very well make me strong enough to bring down any ward he could possibly cast. He's worried that the balance of power—so long tilted towards your kind—will now tip irrevocably towards my kind."

Byron nodded. "You don't understand what it's like, Selene. We're individually more powerful than all but the strongest of the fae. I've read histories that go back hundreds of years before my current incarnation. For the longest of times, the fae were nothing more than servants to the Awakened, but we've remained almost completely static for as long as history has been recorded.

"Occasionally someone will pioneer some new effect, or a new Awakened will surface, but our power isn't increasing at the same rate that theirs is. This is part of what is driving Kyle to do what he's doing. I can feel it in my bones. If I do this, there isn't any going back. The power I'll be unleashing will be absorbed by her and her most trusted advisors. If we win we'll be replaced as the masters of our world. The Lady will absorb additional power each time one of the Unseelie fae is vanquished, and by the end of the war she'll be unstoppable."

"And if we lose that power it won't be going anywhere, will it? It will mostly get absorbed by Fenrir and his ilk, leaving us forever outclassed in all of our future incarnations."

The Lady nodded. "I suppose it all comes down to a matter of trust."

Byron took a deep breath. "If I do this, then you pull out all the stops. This isn't just a war between you and the Unseelie Court. You won't be able to declare a victory until all of the Awakened on the other side are dead. Their journals will be preserved and given to us to study."

She cocked her head to one side. "Is that all?"

"No. You'll give us the artifacts you've been hiding so that we can use them against the other side in this war."

"I think that might be arranged as long as I had suitable guarantees that they would be returned to me once the war had been brought to a conclusion."

Byron shook his head. "No, they stay in circulation. They need to be studied and replicated. Those artifacts—more so even than the journals—are our heritage. They deserve to remain in our hands. No Awakened would ever agree to return them to you of their own free will."

"You seek to restore the balance of power that you fear you'd be destroying by giving me the power contained in those wards. Do you understand the damage that those artifacts could do in the wrong hands?"

That earned her a wry smile. "I guess it's just like you said earlier. It's all a matter of trust."

The two of them locked gazes, and the air almost seemed to crackle as the tension in the room continued to climb. Finally the Lady looked away, but I didn't get the feeling that she'd been defeated—more like she'd grown tired of the game.

"Leave us, Byron."

"There's to be no deal, then? I'll warn you that I'm not bluffing. I'm certain you could have our entire party killed if that is your wish, but that won't give you access to that power."

She shook her head. "I'm not going to have you killed. I understand your terms, but frankly they are not sufficient. Something else is going to have to be added into the pot in order for this deal to go forward, but it isn't something that's yours to offer. Leave us—Selene and I have much to discuss."

I could see a protest hovering on the tip of his tongue, could see how badly he wanted to be part of that discussion, but in the end he bowed his head in acknowledgment of the fact that she held most of the cards. He walked out of the room without saying anything else.

The Lady was silent for several seconds before turning back to me. "You must have questions for me, Selene. What would you like to know?"

"Why are you willing to answer questions now? I get the feeling that you're not usually this accommodating..."

"I'm not. Let's just say I recognize that it's impossible to negotiate in good faith with someone you don't trust. We don't have all of the time in the world, but it seems only right to give you a chance to get to know me a little."

I didn't even know where to start. She was about my height, which meant that she didn't loom over me like Intravil had, but that didn't make her any less intimidating.

"Why aren't you as tall as the rest of your people? Height seems to be a big deal. The younger fae are stuck being small, but everyone else seems to be racing to hit seven foot two."

"Height is a status symbol, but it's more than that. A bigger frame has an easier time exerting force than a small frame. My people chose bigger forms because it makes them more effective in a fight against something like Fenrir or the Minotaur."

"So your ultimate shape and form is under your control, but you haven't told me why you've chosen to be so short."

She gave me a guarded smile. "You are just as amazing as I was led to believe, Selene. If you'd just come right out and asked me who my creator was I would have refused to answer. Instead you work around the periphery of the issue."

"I can't take credit for that—I was just looking for a question that might give me an insight into you, one that wouldn't result in you picking me up by my throat and throwing me into the nearest wall. My asking that particular question was nothing more than dumb luck."

"It has been my experience that people attribute far too much to luck, Selene. Whether you know it or not, there is some part of you that sensed this was one of the best questions you could have asked me. I will answer, but you must promise to take this to your grave. You can't even write it down in one of your journals."

"Doesn't that kind of reduce the value of the information? I mean, if the name of your creator is really that important?"

"Yes, if you're trying to learn it in order to someday take advantage of me, then it gives the information an expiration date and reduces its usefulness. If, however, you just want to get to know me a little better and decide whether you can trust me, then it doesn't diminish my answer in the slightest."

I cocked my head to one side as I considered her response. She'd...relaxed...once it had been just Byron and I talking to her. It was almost like she'd been putting on a show, but once everyone else had left she finally felt like she could be herself.

This was that, but even more so. She was more at ease with me than I would have believed possible.

"Okay, I promise. You're right, there's no need for me to remember it forever."

"I picked this form as a form of homage to my creator, Selene. She was roughly this height and had similar coloring. I didn't copy her exactly because I am my own person, and because I didn't want to signal to all of my enemies where I'd come from, but I wanted to share that one link with her."

"She's gone now, I take it?"

"Yes, for many thousands of years now. She's an Awakened, so she's been reborn in a new incarnation—several actually—but the woman who sacrificed so much for me is long gone."

"You miss her?"

The Lady nodded. "Every day."

I was shocked. I didn't have any idea how knowing who her creator had been could be used to cause the Lady problems, but she'd just made it easier to connect the dots if that had been my intent. There couldn't be that many female Awakened out there, and if you excluded all of the redheads and blondes there would be a relatively small pool of candidates left.

"Why are you so reluctant to help us? It seems to me like we're on the same side here..."

That earned me a sigh. "I can see why you would think so, but the truth is that you Awakened have always been most afraid of other Awakened. I have a drastically different view of the world. Someone like Kyle is indeed a threat, but mostly that is because of the artifacts he's gathered and his abilities as a researcher."

"You're more worried about the fae, about the Unseelie Court."

"Yes. It speaks volumes to Byron's intelligence that he's keyed into the same worries that I myself have. He's worried about a day when Awakened are as far beneath even the weakest of the fae as humans currently are to you and him. He's a brilliant man, but he's also incredibly stupid not to have seen this ages ago.

"You and your pantheon think in terms of a war that can be won, of enemies who can be killed, who eventually come back, but come back as children who have lost all of their previous power and knowledge. I think in terms of a war that has been going on for thousands of years, of enemies who outnumber us, who rise again each time they fall, who come back with all of their knowledge and only slightly less power than they had before they were defeated.

"You worry about what Kyle will do to the world for the next few hundred years if he comes to power. I worry about the world a thousand years from now when it is ruled by immortal beings like Fenrir, beings who have nothing in common with the humans or the Awakened either one, beings who would have to be killed a hundred times before they would be in peril of truly dying."

My legs were shaking and tears threatened to fill my eyes. Every time I thought I had a handle on what we were up against, someone came along and showed me just how little I actually understood.

She was right. I loved my dad and Ari because I'd lived with them for more than seventeen years. Just as important, I'd lived among humans for my formative years and even now that I knew I wasn't really human I would still be living among them in the future.

They looked like me, acted like me and sounded like me. Even at my worst, I would feel a bond, a similarity between them and me. Even Kyle wasn't as inhuman and unconcerned with human life as Fenrir had been. Even Mephistoles still largely thought like the human he'd at one time thought himself to be.

Kyle and the Awakened he'd recruited to his cause might be the most pressing threat, but it was the Unseelie fae who were helping them who represented the greater long-term threat to the survival of humans and Awakened alike.

"What do you want from me? I think I finally understand. You're concerned you'll waste too much of your strength fighting against Kyle and the rest of the Awakened if you join in the battle, which would be disastrous later on, but you're equally worried that sitting the war out will just result in the Unseelie Court farming the rest of us for power. How is it that nobody other than Byron has seen this?"

"It's very easy to get caught up with smaller concerns and ignore the bigger concerns, the ones that you can't possibly impact working by yourself or even with a few friends, Selene. But Byron isn't the only one to have realized what we are eventually going to be up against. Even assuming that Byron is right and this is part of what is causing Kyle to make his play right now, the two of them weren't the first to realize that the true threat is the fact that it's always easier to be evil than it is to be good."

Her words weren't accusatory, but they still pierced me right to the core. The problem wasn't that it was easier for the *fae* to be bad than it was for the fae to be good. The problem was that most of the Awakened were themselves bad. Even if they weren't bad, too many of them let negative emotions fuel their effects.

Part of me wanted to point a finger of reproach at Kat, but I wasn't any better than her. She was fueled by a combination of anger and fear, but I wasn't sure that the sliver of happiness I injected into my workings was much better than the fear she'd defaulted to.

We were both still primarily working from so-called neutral emotions, emotions that still had the possibility of producing an Unseelie fae. I'd gotten lucky with Bethany, but I couldn't count on that always being the case.

I resolved then and there to work harder at increasing my reserves of happiness. If I didn't work on that now, there wasn't any guarantee that the next fairy I created would go down the path of light and goodness.

"Please. Just tell me what it is that you need me to do. How can I help? I'll get someone to teach me how to create wards and I'll put them up from sunup to sundown every day so that they are there to feed power to all of you once they've finished crystalizing."

The Lady reached forward and cupped the side of my face. It should have felt weird, but it didn't. It felt like the way my mom had touched me when words just wouldn't suffice.

"Your offer is one of the most selfless I've ever heard, but it's too late for that, Selene. Even very small wards will take weeks to fully mature to the point where the power released will be more than the power expended to create them. We don't have that kind of time. We're going to have to take the fight to Kyle and the dark court. It's the only way.

"In order to do that we need a symbol, someone who can convince the remaining Awakened—everyone who hasn't already allied with Kyle—to join our cause. We need someone who can stand toe to toe with Kyle and have a chance of surviving the confrontation."

"I don't understand. Why are you telling me this?"

"I wish I could let you spend the next hundred years here in my court, researching better ways of fighting our enemy, Selene, but you're going to have to be that symbol. Byron is right about the fact that our side is going to need an equalizer if we're going to survive. I believe the power from the wards around Camelot will go a long way towards evening the balance of power, but that's not going to be enough. Our enemies have at least two artifacts in their possession. We need someone to wield an offsetting power."

I could feel the edges of what she was trying to get at, but my mind seemed unwilling to put the final pieces together. I had to be reading the wrong message into what she was saying. I opened my mouth to ask her to explain, to beg her not to say what I feared she was about to say, but she beat me to the punch.

"The artifacts are dangerous. They each free the Awakened that holds them from the normal constraints, constraints that I believe are the only thing that has kept our shared world from being destroyed long ago. I refuse to trust just anyone with objects of such power."

"You can't mean me."

"That's exactly what I mean, Selene. I made a mistake when I gave Excalibur to Arthur. Not with regards to his character, he was all I could have hoped there, but with regards to letting that weapon out into the world. It has caused nothing but problems since he was killed. The net effect of the memories it preserves is small, but it serves as a dangerous symbol. You are the only other person I'm willing to entrust the one remaining artifact in my possession to."

I shook my head. "I'm the last person you should be giving that to. I don't know enough to protect it. Give it to Jace. He's good in ways that I'll never be good. Not only that, he can protect it."

"I'm sorry, Selene, but this is how things have to be. If we're to have a chance in the fight that is fast approaching us you'll have to be the one to wield the Scepter of Storms. Nobody else can be trusted with that kind of artifact."

The tears that had been threatening to make an appearance were back. Somehow the idea of beings like Fenrir taking over the entire world wasn't quite as scary as being the symbol that was supposed to stop them.

"This is crazy. You barely know me. You can't possibly be willing to give me an artifact based off of two conversations that collectively lasted less than half an hour."

"You're right. If that was all the interaction I'd had with you, I wouldn't be willing to propose this course of action."

Everything suddenly clicked into place. "You knew Genevieve. That's why you're willing to do this. You knew me in a past incarnation. This was about confirming that you could still trust me."

The Lady held out a hand and suddenly it was no longer empty. She was holding a long, golden rod that looked like it had more in common with the maces I'd seen knights wield in historical movies than with the scepters kings were supposed to have used.

"You're brighter than you give yourself credit for being, Selene. You're the one and only Awakened I trust will both use this addictive weapon for its intended purpose and then give it back to me—of your own free will—when the war is over. It has to be your decision though—Byron will never agree to bring the ward down otherwise. Will you do it?"

I was shaking as I reached for the scepter, but I reached for it nonetheless. I felt an odd jolt as my fingers touched it. It was a bit like an electrical shock, but it didn't hurt—it was more like having a dislocated shoulder popped back into place. I was so astonished at the artifact's reaction to me that it took me several seconds to realize that the Lady hadn't released the weapon yet.

"I wish this was the end of it. I wish I didn't have to include yet another provision, but Byron agreeing to bring down the wards around Camelot isn't enough for me to bring my entire court into the battle. In order to release this weapon into your keeping, Selene, I need you to promise me that you'll serve me for the next two hundred years."

I blinked, trying to understand. "Serve you how?"

"In any way I request. You will use your talents and abilities however I see fit, you will create any effects I require, and you will hold nothing back from me."

"Once we've won this war you want me to create wards, powerful ones that can later be brought down to feed you additional power. You want to speed up the process of becoming too strong for any group of Awakened to ever bring you down."

"Yes, among other things."

The implications were clear. I wouldn't have been able to understand the price she was asking of me even as recently as yesterday, but our conversation had done more than just provide me with hints as to who her creator might have been. It had painted a clear picture of a world where the fae were the most powerful force.

It was a world that still terrified me, and it was a world I would have to give up my last few years with my dad and Ari in order to bring about.

"No. I can't do it. I won't do it—I wouldn't even if I could."

She reached out and grabbed me by the shoulders. I half expected her to shake me, but she just held on, stopping me from running away.

"I wouldn't ask this if I didn't have to, Selene. It's necessary."

"And then what? Once I'm used up, with no more memory of my past than Sandra has of hers, I'll be released to do whatever I want in a world that you've remade into whatever image you believe is best? I thought you were crazy for being willing to trust me after just two conversations, but that's nothing compared to the insanity of expecting *me* to trust *you* based on nothing more than this."

"I know this is a lot to ask, Selene, but I promise you that no other fae on either side of this conflict has spent as much time with your kind as I have. None of my people have lived with humans like I've lived with humans. I don't forget anything, Selene—I can't. Out of all the fae who could end up ruling the world, I'm the most...human...option you're going to find."

What she was asking me to do was insane, but I looked into her eyes and I believed her. I couldn't explain it, but I did.

"Okay. I'll do it. Give me the scepter, convince your people to help us out, and I'll serve you for the next two hundred years."

Chapter 12

Five minutes later I was staring at an artifact I had no idea how to use, all by myself, with tears running down my face. I'd made the right decision—or at least I thought I had—but that didn't mean it was going to be an easy path to walk.

I couldn't have said for sure how long I sat there in the middle of the forest, but it couldn't have been more than five or ten minutes. It felt like I was there for hours, but Jace never would have left me by myself for that long.

As soon as the Lady had handed me the Scepter of Storms, I'd felt an uncontrollable need to get away. I'd expected her to think that I was trying to double-cross her, but she seemed to understand what I was going through. She showed me to a back door and I didn't even wait to hear her warnings about the danger of running off by myself. I disappeared into the acres and acres of trees at more than seven times normal speed.

I shouldn't have been able to do that. It wasn't like I'd never managed that powerful of a time amp before, but even now I still didn't know how I'd managed it the first time. The second time wasn't any more enlightening, but I was too emotional right then to wonder about how I'd managed to replicate something that I should still be years, or even decades, away from mastering.

I ran for several miles and then collapsed as I let my effects expire. Even as fast as I'd run, I still hadn't managed to outrun the Lady's words of caution. It was impossible for Awakened to travel through the forest without getting lost.

Luckily I had two friends who weren't about to let that stop them. After what seemed like forever Bethany showed up, leading Jace along behind her.

"Selene, what's going on?"

I held up the scepter. "I got it. She's agreed to help us out. Everything we wanted—almost everything, at least. I think she's bending one of Byron's terms, but I guess the two of them can hash that out once it becomes an issue. She gave me the Scepter of Storms, which she says is the last artifact still in her possession, and she'll rally the rest of the Seelie Court to go after Kyle and the rest."

Bethany looked torn, like she wasn't sure whether she was supposed to comfort me or if she would be better off giving Jace and me some privacy. Luckily Jace wasn't at all conflicted.

"Bethany, thank you for bringing me here. Could you give us a few moments? Don't go too far away, we'll need your help getting back, but Selene is going to need some time."

"Sure, I'll just be over there, far enough away that you'll have plenty of privacy, but close enough I'll be able to hear you if you yell."

Jace waited for a couple of seconds—just long enough for Bethany to be out of sight—and then knelt down and pulled me onto his lap.

"What's wrong, Selene?"

"What makes you think anything is wrong? I just told you that we got everything we needed. We finally have a chance of surviving this war."

Jace sighed. "I'm sorry I've been keeping you at arm's length for the last little while. I understand if you don't feel like you can trust me with whatever is going on, but I want to help if you'll let me."

Hearing that sent me into a fresh round of sobbing. It had to be hard for Jace to sit there like that—not trying to fix things or offer solutions to my problems—but he let me cry for several more minutes without saying anything.

"You're not the problem, Jace. I'm the problem. You have every reason in the world to hate me forever and yet you don't. Instead, you apologize for being distant and tell me that you want to help me out.

"I'm an idiot and I'm no good for you. Maybe that wasn't the case the last time around, but it's definitely the case this incarnation, even before everything that's happened today. You need to run away and forget about me. It would be the best thing for you."

"You're starting to scare me, Selene. What's going on?"

"The Lady gave me the scepter, but she wanted something in return. She wants a pet Awakened who will do whatever she wants for the next two hundred years. Once this war is over with, I'll be hers to use up until there is nothing left of the person I am right now."

Jace started shaking his head. The motion started out slow and shocky, but by the end the motion had become almost violent.

"No. That's unacceptable. We're fighting to stop exactly that kind of thing. Her making you her slave is no better than Kyle making you his. There's no difference."

"She didn't compel me, Jace. That's the only difference that matters. I agreed of my own free will."

"After she blackmailed you by threatening not to help us. Is there any difference between saying that you won't help someone who's going to die, and saying that you'll kill them?"

Strangely enough, my tears were almost completely gone by that point. Part of me didn't want to defend what the Lady had done, but the rest of me seemed determined to prove to Jace that she wasn't the villain here.

"I can't explain the difference, Jace. I'm no good with logic and debating. All I can tell you is the fact that I had a choice feels like it makes all of the difference in the world. It's true she backed me into a corner. I don't think I would have done that to her if our positions had been reversed, but I'm not even angry with her. She did what she felt like she had to do.

"I'm just sad that the price she's asking from me is going to mean that I'll lose everyone I care about. My dad, Ari, you and Kat—you'll all be gone. Dad and Ari will be dead for more than a hundred years by the time I'm done serving. You and Kat will still be alive, but I won't remember either of you and after two hundred years you won't remember me either. You'll have moved on."

"No, this isn't happening, Selene. This was your choice, but you're not the only one who can choose to serve. I'll help out. I have more than a hundred years of memories stored away inside of my head right now. She doesn't care about you, she wants the memories you're going to accrue over the next two hundred years.

"If I offer my hundred years' worth of memories and then help after that we'll both only have to serve for fifty years each. Maybe Kat and Byron will help out too. Kat could spare forty years without even noticing it was gone and Byron owes you for standing up to Kat. He's got at least a couple hundred years' worth saved away. There is no reason that you have to miss out on your time with your father and Ari."

I wanted to believe that he'd found the solution to my problem. There was no guarantee that Kat or Byron would be willing to help me out—not when the price of aiding me was going to be so steep—but even just having Jace help me would make a huge difference.

My dad wouldn't last another fifty years—not even with Kat doing everything she could to slow down the aging process—but Ari might. I'd still lose out on most of the time I could have had with her, but I would have something to look forward to.

I wanted it so badly, but in the end I knew it wasn't fair to Jace. I wasn't going to make him bail me out. Right or wrong, I was the one who'd made the decision to agree to the Lady's terms. I needed to be the one to pay that price.

"No, Jace, I won't let you do that. This is my battle. You need to stay strong. Kat and Ari and my dad are going to need you to keep them safe—I need to know that you're out there keeping them safe. I'm not stupid. Winning this war isn't going to mean that there won't be any more dangers out there waiting in the night.

"Winning this war is about stopping Kyle, about breaking up his alliance. Once that happens the biggest threat is over and the Lady will shift to a more cautious stance. She'll still hunt down rogue Awakened and Unseelie warriors, but that's going to take time. If you aren't there to protect the people I care the most about, then none of them will survive more than a few years."

I could see that he understood the picture I was painting, but he didn't want it to be true. He opened his mouth to argue with me, but I cut him off.

"No, Jace, this really is for the best. You're the best person I've ever met, and if anyone is capable of forgiving me for what I've done it's you, but you shouldn't have to—nobody should have to forgive something like that. I kept telling myself that the passage of time would help make all of this go away, but it won't—not really.

"I know what I'm volunteering for. Best-case scenario is that I'm an empty husk when she's done with me, but we both know it's much more likely that once I'm weakened I'll end up killed by some Unseelie warrior. That's okay though because it means I'll come back as someone else. I won't be the girl who was willing to cheat on you with your brother. Maybe then we'll be able to be together like we were meant to be."

Jace was shaking now. "Stop it, Selene. You can't talk like that. I'm not going to lose you again. I'm not going to spend the next two hundred years waiting for you and then watch you die at the end of all that."

"It's the only way for us to get past everything that's happened."

"No, it's not. I'm already past it. Let me burn up all of the memories I have stored away. When we're done with our fifty years of service I won't remember any of this. I'll just know that you are the beautiful woman who made getting out of bed worthwhile each morning."

I shook my head. "No, Jace, it wouldn't be right for you to pay that price just to get past what I've done. Besides, even that wouldn't solve our problem. You've written it down in your journals, what I did is never going away."

"It's gone. I'll rip that page out of my journal and never record it again. This can all be like it never happened, Selene. I want you and I'm willing to pay any price to make that happen."

"And what about Kat? She's not going to destroy any record of it having happened. What happens if we stumble upon one of Kyle's old journals two hundred years from now and you start wondering if I kept that from you? It's a short step from that to losing your trust in me. No, Jace, I don't want you to help. This can be my penance, this can be the way that I show how committed I am to you—to us."

I started to call out to Bethany, but Jace placed his hand over my mouth, cutting off my call before I'd managed to work myself up to any real volume.

"I can't stop you, Selene. I can't make you accept my help any more than I can make the Lady cut your sentence down in exchange for some of the memories I've squirreled away over the last century and a half, but if you're going to do this then I'm not going to let you walk away from me thinking that I don't love you just as much as I did before Kyle stole you away to his bunker."

Jace dropped his hand away from my mouth, but before I could say anything it was replaced with his mouth.

Kissing Jace was electrifying in ways nothing else in my life had ever been. The feeling of his mouth against mine, of his hands resting low on my hips, blew away all of the other concerns that had been right at the point of drowning me.

In that moment I wasn't the latest incarnation of an immortal demigod who was supposed to serve as a rallying symbol for the good Awakened and the Seelie warriors. I wasn't a crack researcher, I was just a girl, a girl who desperately loved Jace and who'd grown to crave his touch more than anything else.

I'd spent weeks tied in knots, wondering whether I'd be happier in the long run with Jace or with Kyle, and in the end it didn't matter because I couldn't participate in the atrocities that Kyle was so casually orchestrating. Kyle's lust for power outweighed all of the rest of the potential good I'd seen in him.

I still loved the fact that he'd been able to challenge me intellectually—probably in ways that Jace would never be able to. I loved the fact that I could unleash my anger and not worry about hurting his feelings. With Kyle I always knew that his anger was there eagerly waiting to slip its leash and crash against me with just as much force as mine crashed into him.

There was a freedom to the idea of being with Kyle that was undeniably tempting. I would never have to worry about being anything other than what I already was, but the attraction there went beyond all of that. Some part of me needed to…not break Kyle, but to gentle him.

Putting a saddle on any horse was an accomplishment, but when the horse was a powerful, independent-minded thoroughbred the accomplishment was all the more valuable. Maybe I finally understood at least part of what the girls in school had sometimes talked about. There was an appeal to the chase that I'd never understood until Kyle had entered the picture, and it was surprisingly strong.

I found myself angry that the option of dating Kyle had been taken away from me. It wasn't that I was mad because I still wanted to date him, I was mad because I'd never had the chance to decide on my own.

That meant that on some level my decision to date Jace—and only Jace—wouldn't be as valid, as powerful, as it should have been. I wanted the option of dating Kyle because I wanted to be able to turn away from Kyle and choose Jace with my entire heart.

Sometime in the last week I'd made that decision, but now I'd always have to worry that Jace would suspect I'd picked him only because I'd never had any other choice. That wasn't acceptable.

I leaned into Jace, pushing against him hard enough that he had to brace himself against the ground so that we didn't fall over. I ran both hands through his hair as I flicked my tongue inside of his mouth.

He gasped a little—unprepared for the strength of my response—and I used the distance he'd created between us to get at his right earlobe. I took it gently between my teeth and bit down with just enough pressure to drag another gasp out of him.

"I want you more than anything, Jace. As bad as all of the rest of this is going to be, it's the prospect of losing you that is the hardest to take."

He kissed me again, barely giving me a chance to get the words out, and then pulled the neckline of my shirt to one side so that he had clear access to the side of my neck.

"That is the one thing that you'll never have to worry about losing, Selene. I really shouldn't tell you this—I stop myself from coming right out and saying it at least a dozen times per day because I know it will make me less desirable, but I'm tired of fighting myself. I waited two hundred years for you once already.

"I'll do it all over again—I'll wait three hundred years if that's what it takes—in order to be with you again. I want you as my wife, want to know that you're mine and I'm yours. Nothing else is more important to me. Nothing will keep me from your side as long as that is where you want me."

As he spoke he worked his way down the side of my neck with his lips and I finally realized something I should have understood much sooner. He was right.

Everything I'd seen in the last seven years of watching guys and girls interact said that such an unguarded profession of love should have ruined everything between us. He'd just shifted all of the power in the relationship over to me, just handed me his heart with one hand and a knife with the other. It seemed impossible, but contrary to everything I would have expected, knowing that he was so completely devoted to me made me value him more rather than less.

Maybe that was the difference between being a girl and a woman. A girl wanted something—someone—precisely because they were capricious and hard to hold onto. She wanted it only as long as someone else wanted it too, valued it only as long as she wasn't sure she would be able to actually have it.

A woman though was capable of seeing the value behind true devotion. For the first time in my life I honestly didn't care about all of the things that motivated all of the girls my age. I'd always tried to tell myself that I was different, that I wasn't as shallow as they were, but I'd been lying to myself.

I'd still wanted all of the trappings of popularity. I'd been in love with the idea of having a boyfriend, of being gloriously, visibly in love. I'd been no better than Sandra, I just hadn't been attractive, popular or rich enough to make my dreams come true.

Even as Jace continued to rain kisses down into the hollow where my neck and shoulder joined together, part of me wanted to shrink away from him in shame at how shallow I'd been. Only I hadn't actually been just like Sandra. I'd wanted all of those things, but I'd been able to understand—on some level at least—that there was more to love than all of those showy things.

I couldn't have said for sure exactly how it happened, but I'd somehow moved past all of that. I wanted Jace precisely because I knew he would never leave me. I wasn't settling for him and I didn't value him less for his admission. Instead, I valued him all the more because I knew how amazing he was and I finally understood what it meant to be fully committed to someone. I finally understood just how hard that was, and I knew that only someone truly incredible—someone like Jace—could offer their heart to another person like that.

"I don't deserve you, Jace, but I will spend all of eternity trying to be worthy of you."

My words came out in a gasp as his mouth finally found that one spot, high on my chest, that always made me melt. He'd stayed well above the swimsuit line, but right then I would have let him do anything he wanted to me. My breathing was too ragged to do more than groan as he pulled back away from me.

"That is the one point we'll never agree on, Selene, but I will never stop trying to convince you that you're wrong, that you're worthy of me a thousand times over in a million different ways."

Looking into his amazing blue eyes, I finally managed to get my breathing back under control enough to be able to respond to him.

"You don't have to stop, Jace. It's just you and me."

He gave me a slow, lopsided smile. "That's exactly why I have to stop, Selene. We've never been together as anything other than man and wife and I'm not about to ruin hundreds of years of precedent."

"Still a believer, huh?"

"Absolutely. I can't believe that there's not anything else out there after this life. There has to be a purpose to all of this, has to be a higher power than just a bunch of Awakened and fae."

I leaned forward and nuzzled the side of his neck with my nose before kissing a soft trail up from his shoulder to his ear.

ENDLESS

"How does that work? You and I are never going to see any kind of afterlife if it's not possible for us to die permanently."

"I don't know how it works—not completely. I think that's why they call it faith. Maybe we're just sent back here again and again until we get things right."

Chapter 13

Everyone was waiting for us when we finally called for Bethany to come get us and lead us back to the rest of our group. I'd been expecting Dad, Ari, Kat, Byron and Kregor to be waiting, but I hadn't expected for the Lady to be patiently standing in front of her house, or for a group of more than forty Seelie warriors to be cooling their heels to one side of her.

My little breakdown had meant that a lot of people had been forced to sit on their hands, which dispelled most of the buzz I'd carried away from my make-out session with Jace.

"I'm really sorry—"

The Lady held up her hand. "You took what time you needed. It is not our place to question your needs, not when you'd just been handed such a burden."

The Scepter of Storms had been hidden to one side of me as we'd picked our way between the trees, and I could feel everyone's eyes zero in on it as the Lady spoke. The reaction from the fae was so slight as to be practically non-existent, but I still got the feeling that they didn't agree with her assessment that the artifact was a burden.

Kat's eyes were bright with desire as she looked at it, and I knew that she also saw nothing but the power she needed to make sure she never had to be afraid again. Dad and Ari looked confused, but I couldn't blame them for that—they knew even less about what was going on than I did.

Byron surprised me. I saw some of the same desire in his eyes that was so visible in Kat's, but for him the lust for power was more than offset by some level of understanding at what I'd had to give up in order to be handed such a powerful weapon. I could tell that he didn't know the details of my agreement with the Lady, but apparently he'd been in enough negotiations with her to realize that she never gave away anything for free.

"I have agreed to throw my full support behind Selene's cause. Byron and Jace were right to say that this isn't a war we can afford to sit out. This is another of the turning points. We must fight and win or we will fall to the dark court. It won't be tomorrow or even next year, but a loss to the forces that Kyle has assembled now will begin a pattern of losses of disembodiments that will eventually sap even the strongest of us."

A low murmur of protest ran through the assembled warriors, but she silenced them all with a look. "Some of you have sworn oaths of obedience to me. Others have not, but all of you have sworn to uphold the principles that the Seelie Court was founded upon. If you turn your backs on those principles you will never find refuge here again. I want a blood oath from each of you that you'll see this war through to its end."

The tension in the air was immediate and powerful. I was suddenly glad that we'd chosen to stop in a spot that left us well off to one side. For nearly a minute nobody spoke and then Intravil stepped forward.

"Are you sure that she's the one who should be wielding the scepter?"

"Yes."

"Very well."

Intravil unsheathed her sword and grounded it point-first in the dirt before running her right hand down the edge with enough pressure to draw blood. Ari looked like she was on the edge of losing her last meal, but it wasn't impacting me as much as I would have expected it to.

Maybe that was because I'd seen so much carnage over the last month since I'd found out that I was an Awakened. Maybe it was just because I was so mentally and emotionally exhausted from what I'd been through in the last two hours.

Both of those were possibilities, but I was pretty sure it had more to do with the hum of power I could feel arcing through the clearing. It was a bit like what I felt when Jace or Kat worked an effect around me. I didn't know the meaning of the ceremony, but one thing was clear to me—Intravil was discharging memories, which meant that the Seelie warriors were deadly serious about what was happening—they'd spent centuries building up their strength, and wouldn't expend energy like that without a good reason.

Intravil walked over and stood in front of the Lady, blood dripping down from her hand to the ground, which was now smoking and hissing all around the spot where the blood had impacted. After a couple of seconds Intravil made as though to pull away, but the Lady's hand shot out, grabbing her arm.

"This isn't a minor commitment you're making. Pay it the respect it deserves."

I thought for a second that Intravil was going to turn on the Lady, but before the younger warrior could move, the Lady released her and grabbed the bloody sword dangling from Intravil's other hand. While I was still trying to understand what was going on, the Lady sliced her own hand.

It wasn't a small wound, which was saying something given just how hard it was to hurt a fae. If the Lady had been a human she would have probably needed surgery, but she never even looked down at the wound. She just held her hand above Intravil's and let her blood drip down, some onto the ground and some onto Intravil's hand.

I'd thought the amount of power in the air after Intravil had cut herself had been impressive, but it was nothing compared to what I could feel now. The hum felt like it had taken up station inside of my head and was trying to split my skull in half.

I looked over and saw that Dad and Ari were less affected by what was going on, but Byron, Jace, Sandra and Kat had fallen to their knees. It didn't make sense that I would be able to endure something that was overcoming all of them. For a second I considered dropping to the ground as well, but something inside of me refused to display weakness. The Lady had said that we needed a symbol, that we needed someone to inspire the Awakened to fight on our side. It was just the five of us Awakened surrounded by fae, but I still knew I needed to be strong.

Maybe it was something to do with the Scepter of Storms—which I was still holding—maybe it was something else altogether. I wanted to understand, but even more important than understanding was following what was going on.

The flow of blood from Intravil had almost stopped by the time that the Lady had cut herself, but now it was back, a thin stream that was collecting in a small pool on the ground, mingling with the Lady's blood as bits of power, bits of memory buzzed unseen through the air.

Nearly a minute passed before the Lady finally nodded, apparently satisfied that Intravil had bled enough, but even then it was several seconds before Intravil closed her fist tight enough to stop the flow of blood. There was something challenging to the look she gave her superior, but she stepped away without a word, leaving the Lady holding the bloody sword that had already tasted the flesh of two of the fae before us.

The fae were already lining up, some eager, some resigned, but all apparently ready to take part in the ceremony unfolding before us. As each additional fae cut themselves on Intravil's sword the pressure in the air continued to increase. I'd expected that nothing would be worse than the torrent of power that had washed over me when the Lady had added her blood to the mix, but I was only partly right.

None of the others were able to match the sheer depth of the power she'd displayed, but something about their memories was more biting, harsher, harder to deal with. By the time we were through half of the fae, Jace and the others were no longer kneeling. He, Sandra and Byron had fallen to their backs, hands clasped against their heads, and the only thing stopping Kat from joining them was the fact that Dad had pulled her into his arms, cradling her like she was a child.

I'd still managed to stay on my feet, but my legs were shaking and I could feel the moment approaching when I would no longer be able to keep them from folding underneath me. It was a special kind of torture to be forced to stand there while fae after fae bled into the growing pool of blood at the Lady's feet, but it wasn't like anyone was asking us for anything—all we had to do was survive.

By the time the last of the towering figures was standing before the Lady, I'd fallen to my knees and the others were all unconscious. The last man, a platinum-haired specimen with skin that was alabaster-white, looked at me for several seconds before nodding and slicing his hand open.

The pressure to drop my head, to collapse the rest of the way to the ground had been intense, but somehow I'd managed to meet the eyes of each of the fae warriors. I thought I was home free until I felt Bethany launch herself from my shoulder and fly over to the Lady.

"You don't have to do this, little one. You have much more to lose if things go badly now. The rest of those present would be disembodied and lose much of their strength, but they would survive—you would not."

"I know, but that doesn't change the fact that this needs to happen. I can't go toe-to-toe with Kyle or Fenrir, but if I join in the oath I'll be of much more use than I am now."

The Lady nodded. "So be it. You may be the smallest here, but never let it be said that your courage was any less than the bravest in my court."

Bethany reached out with one hand as she hovered in place, steadying herself against the hilt of the sword, and then slid her hand along the edge of the sword and added two precious drops of her blood to the pool of blood—only as I watched it ceased to be a pool and instead turned into a red crystal that was more than a foot in diameter.

The Lady looked down at the crystal and nodded. "Very well, it is done. We're all bound to see this through or lose part of ourselves in the trying. So let it be done."

Chapter 14

Even after the ceremony—the blood oath—was over, I still didn't know for sure what it had all meant. Luckily, Intravil agreed to bring me up to speed as we traveled. Little did I know what she meant by 'travelling.'

Once the ceremony was finished, the Lady rallied her people and sent them out in a dozen different directions while she remained there at her house waiting for additional messengers to arrive. Our pantheon, which included—at least for me—my dad, Ari, Bethany, and Kregor, were sent back to Intravil's home and then through the portal and into the nightclub that I now realized she must own as well.

We waited there in her private suite for more than an hour while Intravil met with nearly a dozen fae, some with the classic, six-foot-plus build of experienced warriors, and some barely bigger than Kregor. Each of her people left the club like she'd set their feet on fire, and then she disappeared into her office with a man I was pretty sure was human.

Another hour passed without event. Intravil remained closeted with the guy I had to assume ran the club for her, and the rest of us were left with nothing to do but sit around and look out over the dance floor of the club. As frustrating as that was, we probably couldn't have gone anywhere even if we'd been given the go-ahead. I'd managed to walk back to Intravil's house under my own power, but it had been a close thing and Jace, Kat, Sandra and Byron had had to be carried the entire way. Dad had carried Kat, while two especially burly fae warriors had carried Jace and Byron and a slimmer female had carried Sandra.

It took nearly the entire two-hour wait before my friends were able to walk around under their own power, and even then they were pretty out of it. Bethany and Kregor had both volunteered to help run messages for Intravil, which meant that left just Ari, Dad and me to watch over the other four and worry about what was going on.

One of the servers from the club stopped by every twenty minutes to make sure that we were all okay and ask if we needed anything. Ari and I both ordered virgin daiquiris, but after the third one the novelty of free drinks started to wear off. I wanted answers, and some food—probably in that order.

I'd spent what felt like forever shifting the Scepter of Storms from one hand to another before I finally decided enough was enough and stood, fully intending to go knock on the door to Intravil's office and demand answers.

As luck would have it, she chose that moment to leave her office, but all I got out of her then was a quick "we've got to get everyone back through the portal" and then it was non-stop traffic through her living room.

The fae she'd sent out with messages came back with their numbers more than tripled and they were joined by the five Awakened we'd felt once we arrived in Salt Lake. I probably would have had a stroke when I felt the four from farther away start moving towards us, but by then I was pretty sure they were lookouts for our side. Of course it didn't hurt that the fifth Awakened, the one I'd been able to feel sitting less than fifty yards away from us the entire two hours we'd been waiting, chose that moment to walk through the door accompanied by two more of Intravil's people.

I got a long, hard glance which included several seconds during which the newcomer studied the scepter at my side, and then the Awakened, a tall black guy who, other than his height, was so average-looking that I was sure his appearance was intentional, disappeared through the portal.

Another hour passed during which everyone who arrived was ushered through the portal, and I was still no wiser regarding what was going on. It wasn't that Intravil and the others were necessarily trying to be secretive. They were speaking in English, but they might just as well have been speaking in code for all I understood. The terms and concepts they were discussing weren't things I was familiar with and while I knew some of the locations they were referring to, I had no idea why they were important.

Towards the end of the third hour, Bethany zipped back into the living room and disappeared through the portal for several seconds before returning with a blond fairy who was almost as wide as he was tall.

That was when I first noticed that I felt some kind of...kinship with some of the fae around me. It was hard to describe. I'd felt like I could trust Bethany almost from the first time we'd met, but now I felt much the same way with Intravil despite the fact that she was still one of the scariest...beings I'd ever come across.

Maybe that could be explained by the fact that I'd just spent the last several hours in her company—sort of—and that she'd been the one who'd taken us to see the Lady. I had a hard time believing that though because I wasn't usually very trusting—being picked on for years by someone everybody else thought was some kind of perfect angel did that to you.

As weird as that was, it was nothing compared to the crazy, almost irresistible urge I was feeling to trust the guy who was standing next to Intravil like he half expected to have to jump in front of a bullet for her.

I was still shaking my head, still struggling to understand what was going on when Bethany buzzed back through the portal and stopped off next to Intravil for a second before darting over to me.

"Come on, Selene. It's time for all of us to go through the portal."

"Wait, why? What was the point of coming here in the first place if we were just going to go back into the portal anyway?"

"You all got...a kind of overdose from being there while the blood oath was going on. You would have still recovered, but it would have taken three or four times as long if you'd stayed inside. By coming back to the normal world you were able to bleed all of that foreign energy off in time to be ready for what comes next."

I rolled my eyes at her. "Yeah, funny thing about that—nobody has bothered to tell me what comes next. You've been running around who knows where and everyone else seems to have a job to do, but the rest of us have been stuck here cooling our heels with no idea what's going on."

Bethany backed away from me as though buying herself room because she was afraid I was going to lose it. "Whoa. Settle down there, cowgirl. It's been an all-hands-on-deck kind of thing for the last little while. I'm sorry I didn't say anything before now, but it's not safe to talk out here where Kyle could be spying on us. We need to get back inside the Seelie Court where we're safe and then I'll tell you everything."

I frowned, but stood up and then helped Jace to his feet as well while Dad helped Kat and Ari helped Byron. I was turning back to help Sandra, but the new guy, the fairy who was roughly the size of a house, beat me over there.

We went through the portal one after another, and less than a minute later we were all on the other side and I was realizing that Bethany had been right. I could still feel the buzzing in the air that had started at the same time as the blood oath ceremony. It wasn't as bad now, but it was still going to give me a headache if I stayed here for very long.

"Okay, short stuff, what's going on?"

Bethany shook her head and motioned me off to one side as though she didn't fully trust the rest of the fae who were standing there with us. Jace and the others followed us over, which meant that the guy helping Sandra walk came along too, but Bethany didn't seem worried about him listening in.

"So here's the deal. You're the only Awakened who've ever witnessed a blood oath. Please don't tell anyone about what you saw—in fact, it would be awesome if you could leave it out of your journals."

We all looked at each other and, once I'd received nods from everyone, I turned back to Bethany.

"Agreed, now spill it."

"A blood oath is a way of binding a group of fae to a common purpose. It sounds like you could feel the memories that were being released, but what you didn't know is that the ceremony takes those memories and uses them to create a kind of living booby trap. If I were to go back on what I promised, if I failed to do my best to fight this war, then the power I donated to the ceremony will return to me and expend itself destroying many times that amount of my accumulated memories."

I blinked a couple of times, too shocked at first to get any words out. "So what, you've all made a suicide pact?"

"Not exactly, but sort of. It's like the Lady said. The rest of them donated more power than I did, but they had a lot more to start out with. They'll lose a lot, but they'll survive the loss unless they end up being disembodied a lot before that happens."

Jace was still shaking his head. "Why would the Lady ask her people to do that? More importantly, why would anyone agree to that?"

Bethany nodded in Byron's direction. "She did it because she needs to know for sure who she can trust. We're about to head off to Camelot and bring down the most powerful wards in the history of the world so we can feed that power into any fae who happen to be in the area. You have to remember that even the Lady can't be positive that all of the Seelie fae are really good guys.

"The portal wardens she's as sure of as she can be of anyone—if she wasn't then she never would have given them control over an access point into the court. It's been a long time since a new portal warden was added, so the odds are good that they are all loyal—that they are really Seelie—but for everyone else all bets are off.

"She's recalled most of the Seelie fae all over the world. What you all just saw in Salt Lake is happening in almost every Seelie outpost, but it's all a big diversion. While the biggest chunk of our people are headed directly towards Kyle and the Unseelie fae, her most trusted core—the portal wardens and the warriors who just took part in the blood oath—will be headed to Camelot where we'll all absorb every ounce of power in those wards.

"Sandra, Ari and Peter can all stay here where they are safe. The rest of us need to get moving or we'll be left behind."

Byron grimaced. "She won't leave us behind. I'm the only one who can bring down the wards."

Bethany nodded. "That's true, but I'm in constant communication with her—and with every other fae who added their blood to the oath stone. Saying that the Lady is getting antsy is an understatement. You'd have to invent an entirely new word to describe the urgency she's feeling."

A second later Intravil stepped through the portal and headed in our direction. "You're wasting time! You were all supposed to be halfway to the new portal by now." She pointed at the big guy who was helping Sandra. "You take her and the humans to where the food is being assembled. The rest of you come this way, we're running out of time to get to the portal."

I looked at Kat, Jace and Byron and shook my head. "They can't. It's all they can do to stand on their own—they aren't going to be able to walk to wherever the portal is."

She turned her unsettling eyes on me and nodded. "Yes, but help is nearly here."

Before I could ask her what she meant, a trio of impacts brought me around to see three of the warriors I recognized from the clearing earlier stepping away from their landing spots.

"Don't drop the scepter, Selene. You're going to need it."

Before I could ask Intravil what she meant, she wrapped an arm around my waist and threw herself forward with enough force that I thought for a second that everything below my hips had been left behind. It was the kind of impossible stunt you sometimes saw on cartoons or movies. We went from motionless to hurtling through the air in a blink of an eye, and I was convinced that we were going to crash into one of the pillars, but we shot between them and then her wings unfurled with a snap.

ENDLESS

Bethany's wings were clear like dragonfly wings despite being shaped differently. There was an iridescent sparkle to them that was amazing, but she had nothing on Intravil's wings.

They were shaped broader and shorter than Bethany's—more like a butterfly than a dragon-fly—but the really amazing thing was that they seemed to be nothing more than translucent planes of force. They were incredibly beautiful, and the way that they flexed in the wind was both amazing and a little scary.

Even more alarming though was the speed with which we were flying through the forest. As we'd headed through the first time, on the way to the Lady's home, I'd thought that the trees were very spread out, but now that we were screaming along at what I was pretty sure was more than a hundred miles per hour they felt like they were far too close together.

You don't need to worry, Selene. We aren't going to hit anything—I've done this thousands of times.

It took me a second to realize that she was speaking directly into my mind. It sounded exactly like she was whispering into my ear—except for the fact that even if she'd been yelling I still wouldn't have been able to hear her over the roar of the wind past my ears.

How are you doing that?

What, no protestations that this is impossible?

There was such a dry, understated feel to her humor that I couldn't help but smile.

In the last few weeks I've seen people run at more than forty miles per hour, been shot at by glowing bars of light, been attacked by a massive wolf straight out of Norse mythology, and met six-and-a-half-foot-tall people with wings who are much too good-looking to be anything other than fae. It feels a bit late to start screaming that none of this can be real.

Point taken. This is a side effect of the blood oath. All who are part of a blood oath are able to communicate directly, mind to mind. I suspect that is why the Lady chose to let you witness the cere-mony. It will make it much easier for you to stay abreast of events in crisis situations.

That makes sense—only she couldn't have known that was going to happen, since no human or Awakened has ever witnessed one of those ceremonies before, right?

Intravil was quiet for so long that I almost started worrying that whatever had made it so I could hear her thoughts had gone away. *There are no recorded instances of Awakened being able to participate in a blood oath ceremony. That has led most of my fellows to assume it has never happened before, but the Lady is much older than any of the rest of us. It is my suspicion that she's seen this happen before and just never mentioned it to any of us.*

Wait, I don't get it. I mean, I knew that she was the most powerful member of the Seelie Court, but I thought that was just because she was in the right places at the right times to gain power more quickly than the rest of you. Nobody said that she was older than the rest of you.

Nobody has told you, because very few know. You Awakened have long been the major power in the world, and we fae have had to carefully husband our few advantages. The fact that our memories extend back further than yours—further even than the written records you've maintained—is an advantage that we've used often.

I felt like someone had just peeled back another layer of the onion that had become my world. Back before Jace and Kat had found me it had seemed like the world was a solid place, a place where most things were exactly as they seemed. Now, it seemed like every truth I was told ended up just revealing more uncertainty.

I kept hoping that I would get used to the idea of never being quite sure what was real, but that wasn't the case. Instead, I was starting to cling ever more tightly to the few certainties I still had.

If that's the case, why tell me this now? Wouldn't it make a lot more sense to keep it a secret still? Although, I guess it might not end up mattering. Once the Lady is done with me I'm not going to remember having this conversation. All she has to do is make sure that she gets hold of any journals I write and your secrets will be safe still.

Intravil shook her head as she banked hard to one side to avoid another tree, this one more than twenty feet in diameter.

No, that would be foolish. The Lady wouldn't rely on such a fragile thread to maintain our secrets. It would be a small matter for you to tell your pantheon, and then containment of the information would become much more problematic.

Then why tell me?

I told you because she commanded it. She said I should...trust you. She thinks that if you promise not to say anything, or even write this down, that you'll keep your promise.

That pulled me up short for a couple of seconds. I pondered what she'd just said as Intravil spotted a break in the canopy above us and darted upwards with a quick downward thrust from her wings.

I guess she's right. If I promise not to say anything, I won't. I haven't actually promised anything though, so you're getting a little ahead of yourself.

Yes, but you'll promise now if you want to hear anything else.

That drew a frown out of me, but it wasn't like I had much of a choice. If I said no, I wouldn't have anything to share with Kat and Jace. If I said yes, then I'd have stuff to share but not be able to share it, which sucked, but at least then I'd know more about what was going on.

Okay, I promise. I'll keep your secrets.

Good. The truth is that the Lady is quite a bit older than any of the rest of us.

How is that possible?

Intravil shrugged as she made towards another hole in the canopy that was still miles away from us.

None of us know and so far she isn't saying. All I can tell you is that she was there when I was created, and she hasn't changed visibly since my first memory, so she had to be, at the very least, several hundred years old. She's never told me anything important about the time from before she and I met.

How is that possible, Intravil? For her to be the oldest, that would either mean that she was the very first fae to be created or that all of the rest of the fae from before her time were destroyed.

Yes, that's exactly what it means.

You don't think that she was created significantly before the rest of your kind, do you?

There was a long pause as Intravil dove into the clearing that she'd identified a few seconds earlier.

No, I don't.

I thought it took a lot to kill fae permanently. That isn't the kind of thing that could just happen by accident, is it?

No, it couldn't. If I'm right, somebody—some Awakened—was actively hunting us down to make sure that we would never become a threat.

Chapter 15

The Lady was waiting for us in the clearing, along with more than twenty Seelie warriors. As the rest of Intravil's people landed over the next few seconds I received several more shocks.

Jace, Kat and Byron were all unable to hear me. In fact, it appeared that being present for the blood oath ceremony hadn't had any kind of effect on them at all. It was one more indication that there was something different about me.

Intravil had promised to bring me up to speed on everything while we were traveling, but the trip hadn't actually taken very long. I wasn't sure if she'd been expecting that we'd make the trip on foot, or if her view of what I needed to know was dramatically different than my own. She was so different than me, it was hard to know for sure what was going on in her head, but I was pretty sure that she hadn't purposefully lied to me.

Luckily, the Lady took a few seconds to pull me off to one side and let me know that Ari, Sandra and my dad were all safe, and that she'd arranged to have regular shipments of food brought through one of the few portals she was leaving active. Apparently the prohibition on eating and drinking inside of the Seelie Court was because any food or drink that remained there for very long eventually took on other properties and began emitting a kind of energy that wasn't good for humans to eat.

"So it would kill them?"

"No, Selene. It wouldn't kill them, but it would change them. They would no longer be human or Awakened either one. They would be something in between your kind and my kind. There are some benefits—longer life for humans is the main one—but they would never be able to leave the court again. They would became prisoners here more effectively than if we bound them in chains."

There wasn't much I could say to that. I was ashamed to admit—even to myself—that my first thought was that if Dad and Ari both ate something that had been contaminated by fae energy it would mean they might still be alive when I got done with my two hundred years of service.

Talk about selfish. I resolved to make sure that they were both back in the real world before telling them about my agreement. It was possible that my dad would choose to eat something here just in the hopes of living long enough to make sure that the Lady eventually released me as she'd promised, but that wouldn't be fair to him. I didn't want him to make that choice out of concern for me and then end up resenting me because of it.

I couldn't imagine spending centuries here. Bethany was a pretty good sort of person, and even the Lady seemed remarkably human for a being who was several thousand years old, but the rest of the fae—the ones who spent most of their time here—were a lot more like Intravil than they were like Bethany. It would be like being forced to move to another planet, one where the aliens didn't particularly have much use for you.

"Thank you for making sure that they'll be taken care of. What happens next?"

"The portal wardens have all been added into the blood oath by now and all but a few of them are headed this direction. I've detached a few of my most trusted lieutenants to lead an assault on one of the Unseelie Court's main portals in Poland, but it is primarily meant to distract our enemies so that they don't realize that our true focus is on the wards around Camelot."

"So we'll go in with your most trusted people, your most deadly warriors, and you'll all walk away with the power you'll need to be able to win the war."

"Yes, that's the plan."

"What about the rest of the Awakened? There were five of them in Salt Lake. How many are you bringing along on this mission, and how are you going to go about gathering up the rest of the ones who haven't picked sides yet?"

The Lady smiled and the expression looked almost maternal. "Intravil is unique among my portal wardens. I would have expected for her to have the hardest time relating to your kind, but somehow she's managed to gather the largest contingent of Awakened to protect her portal out of all of my people. We have a few more Awakened who we can count on to work with us and not leak to Kyle's people. They will be joining the assault."

"Because they won't be any good here?"

"Exactly. Some of my people wanted me to send your pantheon—everyone but Byron—to participate in the assault as well, but I didn't want to let you out of my sight this early. It will take you time to become experienced in using the scepter, and until you are, it is risky to send you anywhere that might result in you being captured. I don't want Kyle getting his hands on yet another artifact.

"I could have sent Jace and Kat off and kept you and Byron here with me, but I knew that you would feel better knowing that the two of them were nearby. Besides, I know that the two of them will do everything they can to keep you safe and the scepter away from Kyle."

My stomach started to unknot and I managed a smile of my own. "Thank you—that means a lot."

"Of course. As for the other Awakened who might be willing to join our fight, I've had my people reach out to them. There are a few we can just call directly, but most of the Awakened who were more open about their locations are already dead. Helena wasn't the only location that Kyle and the Unseelie court hit. The ones we still believe are alive will have to be contacted through other means."

"What kind of other means?"

"Classified ads, code words left on message services, and dead drops in out-of-the-way locations among other things. It will take some time before we'll know for sure how many of them survived and are willing to take up arms against Kyle."

"How long?"

"I don't know, Selene. I've delegated the contacts to the fae who have the best relationships with the individual Awakened. They are mostly younger and not in a position to help out with the war in other ways."

"Do each of the Awakened have one or more fae who…monitor…them?"

"Yes—at least all of the Awakened who aren't completely ruled by negative emotions. Sometimes they monitor them directly, sometimes at a distance. Sometimes they even monitor them indirectly by way of a contact with their pantheon."

"Kregor. Kregor is the one that you've been using to keep an eye on Kat and Jace."

"Indeed, and you as well during your last incarnation."

"I guess it makes sense—Jace is his creator, so he has a reason to be around us."

Some of my bitterness must have leaked into my voice. The Lady sighed. "He isn't trying to manipulate you, Selene, and I know that he would never betray Jace. It's as I said before, all fae—all light fae—feel a certain debt of gratitude toward their creator. He's just trying to watch out for you and make sure that you don't get blindsided by something that could be avoided."

I nodded, but this time I wasn't as convinced. Byron was right. They hadn't been able to drop off the grid until they'd managed to distance themselves from whoever was keeping an eye on them. The Lady seemed to mean well, but it was obvious to me that the system was far from perfect.

She had leaks in her organization, fae who claimed to be loyal members of her court, but who were actually working for someone else, either the Unseelie fae or for one of the Awakened. Her intelligence network had probably saved many lives, but it was equally true that it had probably resulted in several unnecessary deaths.

"Kregor didn't join in the blood oath. Does that mean he's not as loyal as you think he is?"

I'm not sure what kind of response I expected, but the slow shrug I got was unsatisfying. "There is no way to be sure, Selene. Fae as young as Kregor aren't expected to join in. If Kregor were to do that and we were to fail, it would be likely that he would be destroyed. My suspicion is that he was just scared."

"But you don't know for sure."

"We aren't any different than humans in that regard. We can err and get people killed, either out of malice or simply by not thinking. The real question is whether you believe that Jace could have created him while burning a negative or even neutral emotion. As long as Jace was burning a positive emotion then Kregor's failings won't be driven by malice."

"Don't you know?"

"No. Jace believes that Kregor is Seelie, and Kregor has never done anything to make me doubt his allegiance, but I have no way of knowing for sure. He was created several incarnations ago, and Jace is basing his belief on journals that it is entirely possible Kregor modified at some point."

I sighed. "I'm starting to understand what we're up against. At least I know that Bethany is Seelie."

"Do you, Selene?"

"Yes, she's only growing when I use positive emotions."

The look I got wasn't exactly pitying, but it wasn't far off from that. "Really? I take it that you only ever burn positive emotions, and that you've been observing her for a long enough period of time to know for sure that she's growing like you expect her to?"

"No. No, none of that is true. I don't have any idea, do I? Even her joining in the blood oath is no guarantee—she could just be playing a much longer game."

"*Now* you know what I'm up against, Selene." The Lady gave me a sad smile and then turned and walked back over to the gathering of her people.

A few minutes later, we were apparently all there at the rendezvous location because the Lady reached forward and put her hand on a tall, freestanding mirror in the center of the clearing. As the first of the Seelie warriors went through the mirror, Bethany flew over and landed on my shoulder.

"How are you holding up, Selene?"

I tried to put my doubts out of my mind, but now that they'd taken root I knew I wasn't going to be able to get rid of them.

"I'm okay. It's a lot to take in. I don't know why I keep thinking that I'm starting to get a handle on what's really going on in this new world that Kat and Jace thrust me into. Every time that happens, something else comes along to turn everything upside down—you'd think that eventually I'd learn."

"Don't worry, that's what you've got me for."

Right, except now I was realizing that I couldn't trust her, not like I needed to be able to. If Awakened like Jace couldn't be sure that their companions were Seelie, then how was I supposed to know? There was only one answer. I needed to work harder to change my default emotion. I needed to get to the point where every single effect I worked was powered only by happiness, and then I needed to survive long enough to make sure that she was actually growing once I cut off all of the neutral emotions.

Given that we were about to head into a massive war, that was already a tall order, but that was just the beginning. Once I knew what Bethany was—Seelie or Unseelie—I needed to find a way to leave myself a message, one that couldn't be changed or counterfeited, one that I would recognize, but which nobody else would.

How was that even possible? I could tell the Lady, but even that wasn't any kind of guarantee. Even assuming that I trusted the Lady, all that would mean was that in my next incarnation the Lady would be able to tell me that I'd told her Bethany was light.

That information was only good if I was really working for the right side when I told her that Bethany was one of the good guys. Was I really that confident that I could never be anything but good?

"A penny for your thoughts?"

I shook myself and forced a cheerful smile out onto my face. "I'm just worried about what comes next. I'm not ready to end up in some kind of massive war."

"Don't worry about that, Selene. You just keep your head down and focus on mastering that scepter. The older fae tend not to address me mind to mind, but speaking that way takes more effort than doing it the old-fashioned way, so there is plenty of actual talking going on. I've picked up some bits and pieces over the last few hours. The Scepter of Storms is a big deal. That's why Intravil agreed to back the Lady's play this time. Those two don't usually see eye to eye on much, but apparently Intravil figures that the Lady wouldn't break out the scepter if she didn't think this was our only hope."

"Right, the scepter." I looked down at the long, golden rod and tapped the big, bulbous head with my free hand. "I guess I should just be grateful that I haven't dropped it so far. I probably would have on the flight over here if Intravil hadn't kept one hand on it the entire time. I'm such an idiot. I was asking about everything else under the sun when I should have been finding out how to use this overgrown stick."

Bethany started to answer, but then grimaced. "It sounds like we're being summoned. I just got a message from the Lady and she wants us over at the portal right now."

"She couldn't just call us over?"

"I guess she figures it would ruin her image to yell at us."

"So instead she yells directly into your mind?"

"That's about the size of it. Just be glad that it's tougher to talk to your mind than it is to talk to the mind of another fae or you'd probably be getting the same treatment."

I nodded, but somehow I wasn't convinced. I didn't have a good reason to think that the Lady was going to treat me better than she treated Bethany, but I still got the feeling that she wouldn't have been yelling at me—even if it had been easier to talk to me mind to mind.

I hurried over to the portal, Bethany on my shoulder, and went to step through the portal, but the Lady stopped me with a hand on my arm.

"This isn't like the other portal you've used. My entire court knows that there is a portal out here, but up until now nobody has been able to figure out where it goes because I've never told them. You're going to want to take a deep breath and hold it as you step through. Things are going to be a little disorienting this time around so try not to gasp in surprise or you're going to get water in your lungs."

I nodded reflexively—I still didn't understand what she was saying—and held my breath as I stepped through the large, freestanding mirror.

Disorienting didn't even begin to cover things. I was under water, which I'd been expecting even if I hadn't understood how that was supposed to happen. What I hadn't been expecting was the way that gravity would suddenly go crazy. It was all I could do to keep from puking as gravity was suddenly pulling me forward.

The water was warm, which was a good sign—it meant that I couldn't be at the bottom of the ocean or anything crazy like that—but I still started freaking out, flailing around in a vain effort to spin myself around so that I'd be able to see the surface of the pond.

It wasn't working. For a second I thought that I'd forgotten how to swim, but then I realized that the problem wasn't my swimming, it was the fact that I still had a death grip on the Scepter of Storms, which was pulling me straight to the bottom of the pool.

I was more than a little surprised that I'd managed to hold onto the scepter while panicking like that, but apparently even my subconscious was fully onboard with the idea that the scepter was more important than anything else I'd ever put my hands on. I had an instant in which to consider letting go so that I'd be buoyant enough to ascend, and then a strong pair of hands grabbed me and I was being pulled through the water with powerful, sure strokes.

I surfaced a second later and sputtered until the Seelie warrior who'd grabbed me got me over far enough that I was able to touch the sandy bottom of the pond. I looked around and saw two more warriors standing out in the middle of the water. Neither of them was wearing armor either, which answered the question of whether their armor was removable or if it was just something they manifested as part of their natural form.

"Holy cow! I could have drowned. I know she told me to hold my breath, but that still wasn't what I was expecting."

Intravil grabbed my free hand and helped me up onto the shore next to her. "It was a surprise for all of us. This portal is nothing less than genius. We all suspected that this one might be the Lady's, but there was argument as to whether anyone—even someone as powerful as her—could maintain three separate portals."

"I guess that argument was just settled rather spectacularly."

"Indeed it was. She also just settled all of the wagers regarding where the portal exited. None of us realized that you could use a naturally reflective surface like this to create a portal. Apparently the sheer size of the top of the pond means that there's no way to control where exactly you end up when you come through, so it took longer for our swimmers to get to you than it did for most of the others."

"I guess I should just be glad that you thought to have somebody get ready to catch me. When the Lady warned me about there being water on this side of the portal, I probably should have thought to worry about the thirty pounds of solid metal I was carrying, but it never even crossed my mind. I could have drowned—right after I lost my lunch. I'm glad the portal from your club wasn't this bad—I don't think I could take this kind of transition more than once a day."

"Transitioning back over from this side to the other will be even worse if we have to do it quickly. It will be a lot harder to avoid falling over going that way, which means piling through quickly one right after the other would be a disaster."

I nodded, hoping that we wouldn't have to wage some kind of fighting retreat on our way back here, but most of my attention was focused on taking in our surroundings.

We were in some kind of desert, but not a sandy, Sahara kind of desert—it was rockier than that. The fae who had gone through the portal before me were arranged in a circle around the pond, all on the highest bit of ground in their immediate area, and all looking outward in an effort to make sure that nothing surprised us.

Everyone was dripping wet, but unlike me the Seelie warriors all still managed to not look like drowned rats—they still looked majestic and perfect.

Apparently the Lady wanted to make sure that we poor Awakened had plenty of time to get through the portal because she waited until then to send Jace through. Between the ax in his hand, the sword strapped to his back, and the knives I knew he had concealed in various spots on his person, Jace was carrying around at least as much weight as I was, but he handled the transition better than I did.

He came through the portal amped up enough that he had more time to orient himself before he started sinking, and he had the strength required to mostly fight his increased density. He still might not have made it over to shallow water before he ran out of air, but one of the fae who'd grabbed me fished Jace out within a few seconds of his arrival.

Kat came through the portal into shallow water, which was probably even more disorienting than what I'd experienced because it meant she'd actually hit the bottom as she came through, but at least it meant that she was able to stand right up once she figured out what had happened.

Byron also had to be towed out, and then Bethany followed through a few seconds later. I'd been surprised that the Lady had held her back—I hadn't even felt her leave my shoulder in the instant before I'd stepped through, but it had been a smart move. As desperately as I'd been thrashing around I could have seriously hurt her without meaning to.

"Where are we?"

Intravil smiled. It was a hungry, disturbing expression. "We're in New Mexico, less than ten minutes' flight from the outer edge around Camelot. The Lady didn't just draw the location for this portal out of a hat. She located it far enough away that nobody from the Helena pantheon was likely to find it, and yet still close enough that she would be right in their back yard."

She was right, this portal hadn't come about by chance. It made me wonder how many other portals the Lady had secreted in strategic, out-of-the-way spots that nobody else knew about. I was hoping a lot because that would mean that she was even more powerful than anyone had realized. We were going to need all the help we could get.

A split second later the Lady came through the portal, shimmering into existence between one heartbeat and the next under the surface of the water. It didn't look like she was carrying any kind of weapon underneath her clothes, not based on how easily she rose to the surface of the water and swam over to us.

Once she was on solid ground, she walked over to a massive boulder and easily shifted it to one side. I hurried over in time to see her pull a long, white sword out of a hollow in the ground.

"Let's go. Every moment might end up mattering."

Intravil wrapped one arm around me and grabbed hold of the end of the Scepter of Storms again as she threw herself into the air, but this time I managed to amp up my strength before we left the ground. That meant her help wasn't strictly necessary, but I wasn't about to complain. I'd look pretty stupid if we had to circle back around to pick up the scepter.

I half expected Intravil to speak to me again using the link that had been established via the blood oath, but after nearly a minute had passed without any sense of mental contact between us, I tried to initiate it.

I practically gave myself an aneurism pushing my thoughts in her direction, but nothing happened so I tapped on her hand to get her attention.

Yes?

I need to know how to use this hunk of metal. Is that something you can help me with?

There was a pause for several seconds, but I didn't initially realize that Intravil had just gone directly to the one person who might know.

Hello, Selene. Intravil said that you needed help using the scepter?

Wow, I hadn't expected to be talking to the Lady mind-to-mind like that. She wasn't yelling at me or anything, but I still got an impression of restrained power that was only a couple steps away from blowing my mind into pieces.

Yes. I'm sorry if now isn't a good time, I was just thinking that I should probably figure out how to use it as soon as possible. There's no way of knowing when we'll end up fighting Kyle and the rest, and if I wait until then it might be too late.

Now is as good a time as any, but the truth is that I don't know how to use it. No fae has ever been able to use any artifact. It seems the derived memories that we absorb from you Awakened are so different as to preclude our being able to activate artifacts.

I should have realized that. If the Lady had been able to use the Scepter of Storms herself there wouldn't have been any reason for her to give it to me. Still, I must have some reason for thinking that artifacts could be used by more than just us Awakened. It took me several seconds of thought before I was able to zero in on the reason I'd been thinking that.

I thought that artifacts didn't require someone to burn memories—that's supposed to be why they are so awesome.

Indeed, that is how most of your kind think they work. The average Awakened has never possessed even one artifact in any of their incarnations. They see an enemy wreak unimaginable destruction without ever seeming to run low on emotional reserves and assume that the artifacts are completely self-contained, but the truth is that all artifacts require at least a small amount of memory to be consumed before they will work.

I pondered that answer. *So they work kind of like amplifiers, amplifiers that are so effective that from the outside it looks like the user doesn't actually have to sacrifice any of their memories to get them going. How do you know all of this?*

The silence stretched out for so long I was almost worried she'd just broken off contact altogether as a way of avoiding my question.

Many thousands of years ago one of your kind explained a surprising amount about the known artifacts to me. I know roughly how they function as a result.

How is that even possible? I thought that nobody knew how they worked.

There was a hint of resignation in the Lady's voice now, like she wished she'd never let slip that she knew how the Scepter functioned.

This individual actually created at least one artifact, and was uniquely positioned to make educated guesses about how the rest of the known artifacts at that time worked.

I wanted to pursue that line of questioning. There was so much I didn't know about artifacts, and yet they were one of the main drivers of the conflict between the different pantheons.

Everyone seemed to believe that getting their hands on an artifact—or even better, getting their hands on journals detailing how to make new artifacts—would change their existences forever. The Lady obviously knew more than she was telling me, but I was growing more and more certain that pushing her on this issue would be a very bad idea.

Maybe Kyle had been onto something when it came to his belief that the fae—Seelie and Unseelie alike—were actively trying to take artifacts out of circulation. The Lady had apparently been the one to give Arthur Excalibur, so at one time she'd been willing to hand out artifacts to the Awakened she trusted—and she'd done it again by giving me the Scepter of Storms—but she'd been pretty clear earlier that she thought she'd made a huge mistake with Excalibur.

Are there any hints at all that you can give me with regards to making this thing work? I understand that you've never used it yourself, but any little tidbit of information could make the difference between me being able or unable to help out during the next engagement.

The Lady was flying less than thirty feet away from Intravil and me, effortlessly gliding on wings that had an ethereal white glow to them. She'd spent the entire conversation up until then apparently focused on where we were headed, but now she looked over at me for several long seconds before nodding.

I don't have very much to give you to go on, but I suppose it's pointless to hold anything back now that you have the actual artifact. More than that, it would be negotiating in bad faith to refuse to tell you what I know.

I was glad she'd pointed that out. I'd been secretly thinking much the same thing, but I hadn't been anywhere near ready to bring it up. It was a good thing that the blood oath hadn't given her the ability to read my mind.

You're going to need to open yourself up to the scepter. I know it's not much, but it's all I have to give you.

Thank you. You're right, that isn't much to go on, but it's a ton better than nothing.

I would have spent the rest of the flight trying to 'open myself' to the scepter, but I'd finally realized that the wards around Camelot were the cause of the sense of pressure I'd been feeling from the first moment we'd arrived in New Mexico. It felt like my brain was being jammed up against the back of my skull in an attempt to get as far away from the wards as possible.

I didn't remember feeling anything like that when I'd been inside of Kyle's bunker, but maybe that had been because I'd been inside the wards rather than outside of them. It was also possible that we'd left too quickly for me to notice the sense of pressure back then, but I suspected that it had more to do with the fact that Kyle's wards had been orders of magnitude less powerful than what we were approaching now.

It didn't leave much room for opening myself up to anything. A minute later we landed and Byron hurried over to me, taking my hand as he led me to what looked like a solid rock wall, but which turned out to be a cleverly concealed door.

"Hold still. I'll key the outside ward to you so that you'll be able to think rather than wanting to just rock back and forth on the ground."

He was right—it only took a second for him to make the wards safe for me to go through, and then the sense of pressure all but vanished. I could still feel the outer ward, I could still sense its incredible power, but it wasn't uncomfortable anymore.

Jace and Kat stumbled over and Byron added both of them to the list of people who could walk through this ward without being instantly vaporized.

"You're safe to walk through now if you want to, but I'd suggest you stay on the outside still. There's another ward a few dozen yards inside there and it's almost as strong. I'd key all of them to you, but I don't think our friends are going to want to wait around for that—besides, it feels kind of pointless to spend the time and effort given that we're here to bring all of the wards down anyway."

Jace nodded. "Understood. Thanks for doing that though—we were going to be absolutely useless here otherwise."

I looked around at the Seelie warriors and realized that none of them seemed to be suffering any ill effects from being so close to the crackling field of energy. Nobody seemed overly eager to get close enough that an accidental slip could result in them being disembodied, but other than that they were all acting normal—or at least as normal as a bunch of powerful fae ever acted.

"I guess they don't have to worry about having the wards keyed to them if they don't want to travel through them?"

Byron shook his head. "Nope. They can't sense the wards as easily as we can, which is pretty useful at times like this."

He looked around at the gathered fae and then, at a nod from the Lady, took a deep breath and stuck his hand into the ward all the way up to his elbow.

"I guess it's time to get this show on the road."

The first discharge of energy took me completely by surprise. I'd seen sun lances that were powerful enough to destroy armored cars, but that had been nothing compared to this.

It was like standing at ground zero for a lightning strike. My hair started to float upwards and then everything took on a blue tint as the first arc of energy lashed out from the surface of the ward. Jace, Kat and I had stayed in place, standing just a few feet away from Byron, and it wasn't until that instant that I thought about the fact that all of that energy was going to have to pass through us on its way out to the waiting fae.

That first jagged, cerulean bolt of lightning went right through me—right through my chest and out my back. I screamed in surprise, but it didn't actually hurt. It was a warm breeze that went through me like I was nothing more than a thin piece of material.

I turned my head just in time to see the energy arc towards the ground and then abruptly change direction and slam into the Lady, outlining her with a brilliant corona. Her expression didn't give anything away, but I had to assume that it didn't hurt her because she just nodded to Byron.

"Bleed the energy out faster—the rest of my people won't be able to grab any until you reach the limit of my ability to absorb it. Ramp it up slowly so that we don't waste any of it, but ramp it up."

Byron's eyes took on the distant gaze of someone who was trying to do a complicated math problem in his head, but the arcs of power started to increase in frequency.

It only took a few seconds before there were nearly always at least three or four discharges of energy leaving the ward at the same time. The rest of the fae stepped closer to the ward and I watched as the bolts started hitting them as well.

Once the power coming off of the ward exceeded the Lady's ability to soak it up, the arcs started splitting, forking into jagged blue tongues that hit multiple fae at once. I saw Bethany absorb a finger of power that was no bigger around than a paperclip and realized that the group as a whole must be pretty close to their maximum if she was starting to get in on the action. My hypothesis was confirmed an instant later when, for the first time, a discharge of power hit the ground rather than being soaked up by one of the fae.

"That's it, Byron! Hold it right there if you can—that's as fast as they can take it without wasting any of it."

He nodded in response to my yell, but it was obvious that he'd reached a point where it was becoming difficult to hold back the tide of power that wanted to leave the wards. Jace grabbed my arm and pulled both Kat and me back more than a dozen feet.

"He's at the tipping point. There's enough energy being discharged from the wards that he's going to start struggling to keep it all from going at once. I've seen it happen before, but never with something this big. We're not going to want to be too close if he loses control."

The alarm that I'd felt when the first arc of power bored through my chest was back. "Wait, nobody said anything about this being dangerous. Is he going to get hurt if he loses control?"

Jace shrugged, but the normally casual gesture betrayed his concern. "I don't know. It's not usually a problem. It's rare that anyone brings down a ward like this, and usually when they do the fairy who is sucking down the power is more than equal to the task of absorbing everything, even if it all comes down at once. The energy is keyed to all of us, so it shouldn't hurt us, but it's still theoretically possible that our bodies could get overloaded if enough power—even keyed power—were to be shoved through us."

The lightning coming off of the ward was growing despite Byron's best efforts. The blue glow given off by the bolts lit him up with a harsh light that made him look a lot older than he'd looked even just a few seconds earlier. Every wrinkle and bead of sweat stood out in stark relief, and I could feel the burden on him growing by the second.

The Lady was at the center of a continuous discharge of power that was so bright I couldn't look directly at it, but that was the case for all of the fae. They were all wrapped in jagged, erratic bolts that differed only in the amount of light that was being given off.

"Selene, don't look directly at it! It's like looking at an arc welder—it will blind you if given enough time."

I let my eyes rest on Bethany—now almost a full inch taller than she'd been a few minutes before—and then forced myself to look away as I realized that she might already be past the point where she could only absorb my memories, and only then if they were powered by the emotion that had originally created her.

Part of me was happy for her. I still wanted to believe that she was really on my side, that she was fully Seelie, but mostly I was just worried about the fact that I'd missed my chance to prove where her allegiance actually rested.

Kat was obsessively scanning our surroundings. She caught my gaze and motioned outwards with her chin. "You need to be amped up and watching for threats. This is as critical a time as we're going to see today. While their full attention is focused on absorbing all of that power, our winged friends are all the next best thing to completely vulnerable."

I nodded, and did my best to follow her orders, but I couldn't stop myself from stealing glances at the wards out of the corners of my eyes. There wasn't as much of the power hitting the ground now as I'd expected there to be.

There was still a lot of it being wasted, but judging by what I was feeling there was more than twice as much power shooting out of the wards as there'd been when I'd told Byron he'd hit the sweet spot. That should have meant that just as much power was now striking the ground as there was being absorbed, but that definitely wasn't the case. It took me a second to understand what was going on.

ENDLESS

The tendril of energy feeding into Bethany was as big around as a pencil, and it looked like all of the rest of the fae were likewise absorbing more as well. They'd all apparently absorbed enough power that their strength was growing and thereby increasing the amount they could each absorb.

Nobody had given me a clear idea how long it was supposed to take to bring down the outer ward around Camelot—probably because nobody had any experience with a ward this powerful—but we'd been there for nearly five minutes by that point. I was feeling pretty good. Byron had managed not to lose control of the energy and discharge it all at once and the fae were getting noticeably stronger.

Everything was going perfectly right up until I felt the first hostile signature approach. I turned towards Jace, but he didn't need my warning. Neither did Kat, but she looked like she was about to have a heart attack.

"What do we do, Jace?"

There was a second of relative silence as Jace flared his signature, and then he kicked a nearby rock with enough force to shatter unaugmented bones.

"There are eight of them."

"That's too many—even three would probably be too many right now given that we need to defend the Lady and her warriors. We need a plan!"

Jace turned back to Byron, shielding his eyes against the brilliant blue light with one hand. "Byron! Bring it all down at once. We've got hostiles incoming and we're going to lose half of the fae if they get here while everyone is still overwhelmed trying to absorb all of that power."

Kat grabbed Jace's arm. "We're never going to get another shot at this. Once that ward is down it's down for good—all of that extra power will just be wasted."

"I know, but Byron is obviously in too far to back out now—it would rip him apart to try to cut the flow off. It's all he can do to keep it from just grounding out all at once. Better to consolidate the gains we've got so far than risk having the Lady and all of her most powerful warriors disembodied by a few Awakened."

Kat looked doubtful, but she nodded—only it didn't matter because nothing had changed on Byron's end.

"Byron, can you hear me?"

Kat and I lent our voices to Jace, but it didn't seem to make any difference. Byron was too consumed with trying to regulate the tide of power breaking over our companions to register any kind of external stimulus. Jace tried to push forward and physically shake him, but he only made it a few feet before his steps faltered. Translucent ripples of force sprang into place around Jace as he created a barrier effect, but even that wasn't enough to buy him more than another four or five steps.

Jace retreated back to my side, shaking his head. "It's no good. It's like trying to walk into a tornado."

I scrambled for a solution, but by then it was too late. I'd been focused on the eight signatures I could feel quickly approaching us, and completely overlooked the fact that it was unlikely Kyle would have sent out that many Awakened all by themselves.

The tide of dark shapes that came racing over the hills wasn't moving as quickly as the Seelie fae could have flown, but they were moving much faster than any natural creature could have, and given the way that the rocky hills had shielded them from view, they were still on us almost before my overworked mind could register their presence.

I thought we were all dead. They outnumbered our side by more than three to one, and the Lady's warriors were all still frozen in place as they dealt with the raging torrent of energy being directed their way.

That was exactly what would have happened, but as the Unseelie fae closed to within a few yards of us they started absorbing the power coming off the wards, and suddenly our people were moving around—sluggishly, but they were moving again.

Jace was already surging forward as the first set of lightning bolts hit our enemies, and Kat was only a couple of steps behind him. By the time I realized that we had a brief window of opportunity and got myself moving in the same direction, Jace had reached the closest Unseelie fae and lashed out with a titanic blow from his ax.

The fastest Unseelie fae had largely been the smaller, weaker members of the horde. When you combined that with the fact that they were also moving sluggishly now that they were caught up in the maelstrom of energy, they were easy targets.

Jace tore through the three closest enemy fae. He dropped them to the ground with three strikes and took no damage in return. Kat reached her first target as Jace disemboweled his third enemy, and her sword took something that looked like a centaur across the chest in what I was sure was a fatal wound even for a fae.

I stepped towards a snake dog that looked an awfully lot like the thing that had ambushed us in Denver, and lashed out with the Scepter of Storms. Under normal circumstances, amping myself to three or four times normal speed was barely enough to allow me to stay half a step ahead of even a moderately powerful fae. Luckily, this wasn't anything like any of the other fights I'd been up against.

The snake dog was moving like it was drunk. It was all it could do to even begin to dodge my blow, and it was child's play for me to adjust the arc of my swing so that my weapon took it across the head. The results weren't as gruesome as what Jace and Kat were doing with their edged weapons, but the thing that fell to the ground less than a second later didn't look much like it had before I'd hit it.

I was pretty sure I was going to be sick later, but right then there wasn't time for any of that—I was just glad that the much-vaunted Scepter of Storms was still effective as a plain, old-fashioned blunt instrument.

More of the Unseelie fae were arriving every second, but even with the new arrivals it hadn't been enough to make it so our people were moving like normal. All the fae, both good and bad, were moving like they'd forgotten how to make their limbs respond to their desires, and each Unseelie fae we put down was one less fae to help absorb the energy still pouring off of Byron's ward, but there was nothing to do but kill the bad guys as quickly as we could while they were still unable to resist us.

Right now Jace, Kat and I were the next best thing to unstoppable, but once the eight approaching Awakened arrived the balance of power would flip back to the other direction. Our only prayer of winning was if we could manage to kill so many of the Unseelie that the Seelie warriors could help hold off Kyle and the rest, but even that was a faint hope as long as everyone was still distracted by the lightshow Byron was putting on.

I lost track of how many fae Jace and Kat killed—it was all I could do to keep track of who I was fighting. We split up—not the best idea for when we ended up facing the incoming Awakened, but absolutely the best option for killing as many Unseelie fae as possible before that happened.

I killed something that was part woman and part bird, and then caved in the chest of a woman who had the bottom half of a snake. It was at that point that I realized the bigger, slower, stronger members of the Unseelie Court had arrived.

The Lady and her warriors were fighting back now. They had their weapons out and were doing their best to defend themselves, but it was like watching a bunch of knights from some kind of historical movie flailing away at each other. Nobody was moving very fast, all of them were off balance, and the blows that were landing mostly seemed to be wasted against our side's armor or the other side's unnatural vitality.

It was painful to watch in comparison to the time that I'd seen the Lady disembody Fenrir, but it was the only thing saving Kat, Jace and me. We were four-hundred-pound tigers rampaging through a pack of stray dogs, but even tigers could be taken down by enough dogs.

I slammed my scepter into the leg of something that had the body of a man but the head of a jackal, and was rewarded with a sharp crack as his limb folded up under him. I would have taken advantage of his sudden lack of mobility to crush his skull, but something that I was pretty sure was a manticore threw itself at me, and it was all I could do to whirl back out of the way without losing my head in the process.

I was fast and strong, but there were just so many of them. I slammed the haft of my weapon down into the leg of a woman who looked normal other than the white, iridescent scales covering her body, but it was nothing more than a flesh wound—I couldn't generate enough force to break her femur because I immediately had to reverse my weapon and use it to check something that looked like a six-foot-long, wingless dragon.

As the Unseelie fae pressed harder and harder I was forced to move faster and faster myself, and I felt my technique starting to slip. The biggest advantage of amping up my time sense had always been that it provided me with plenty of time to figure out how I was going to move, but now there was so much going on that I was having a hard time processing it.

I was having to make tricky judgment calls regarding who was moving the fastest and which blow was going to land first as I retreated back away from what felt like a constantly moving wall of fanged, clawed flesh. My movements became more sporadic and jerky as I was forced to wait until the last possible second before moving.

Part of me wanted to forget trying to land blows of my own, to just retreat backwards as fast as I could, but I knew that would only be delaying the inevitable. Running away wasn't going to save me—I had to kill the fae in front of me or I'd end up dead myself.

The stress on my body—and my shoes—was intense. I was managing only weak, ineffectual blows—little more than I could have done under normal circumstances without amping my strength—but I still held out hope that one of them would make a mistake. I cut sharply to my left at the last second, trying to dodge a blow from the big brother to the wingless dragon from before, and I felt my right shoe give way completely.

My skin was amped up enough that I couldn't even feel the rocks underneath my feet, but my bare foot didn't provide as much traction as my shoe had. I went down to one knee as my leg went out from underneath me. I was as good as dead, but that didn't stop me from reaching for my anger and the heat I would need to tap into a peak memory that might have a chance of producing a sun lance capable of stopping the monster that was about to end me.

Between one second and the next, a shining form interposed itself between me and my attackers. Intravil never even had a chance. Even the Lady probably couldn't have withstood that blow, but Intravil never even flinched as the dragon tore her nearly in half.

I heard screaming as I lunged forward and slammed the thick end of my scepter into one of my opponent's front legs. It wasn't until I felt the bones in that leg break that I realized the screaming was coming from me.

It was a mistake. I'd hurt the dragon—which was easily as heavy as Fenrir had been the last time I'd seen him—but it wasn't a fatal blow, and the fae to either side of him shot forward, fully intending on swamping me under...only as Intravil hit the ground there were suddenly half a dozen other figures between me and my enemies, and the one in the center was the shining, slender form of the Lady.

The energy being bled off of the ward hadn't gotten any smaller—if anything it had continued to grow as Byron lost control of what he'd started. Everyone was still moving like frat boys on the tail end of their second keg, but they were there, fighting, and they'd bought me the time I needed to recover.

I tried to slip between the Lady and the warrior on her right, but she checked me with her elbow without even looking back at me. I'd seen her hit Fenrir and shatter ribs that I couldn't have broken if I'd hit him with a garbage truck. She could have easily snapped my neck, but instead the blow was just enough to send me spinning away from the battle a split second before one of the Unseelie fae would have taken my head off.

I caught glimpses of the fight as I tried to regain my balance. Jace and Kat had left behind a trail of Unseelie bodies that dwarfed anything I'd managed to do, but that was hardly surprising given that I didn't know the first thing about fighting with my current weapon. I was relying on my speed and strength to carry the day against slower, disoriented opponents rather than any native ability.

I'd done well, better than I would have believed possible, but Kat was unchained fury and Jace was a model of efficiency. Kat landed two blows for each of Jace's strikes, and every one of her blows drew blood, but each of Jace's attacks was targeted precisely to end his opponent's ability to fight. They didn't always kill, but after each stroke of his ax he was able to move on knowing that even the ones who survived wouldn't last for much longer.

It was a shrewd tactic. A dead fairy was in no position to continue to absorb the maelstrom of energy surrounding us, but an injured, dying fairy was still apparently able to absorb at least some of the power being bled off into the air and ground.

The carnage left behind by my two friends was nothing less than unimaginable, but it hadn't been enough. Our side was still outnumbered by more than thirty percent, and it was starting to show. I didn't see any sign of Fenrir—maybe he didn't trust Kyle after their last encounter—but the dragon had the Lady more than occupied and I could see a horned figure that could only be the Minotaur making his bloody way through our lines, cutting down some of the best fighters the Seelie court had to offer.

The Lady had saved me, but in doing so she'd lost the battle. She and the warriors closest to her were holding their own against the dragon and his allies, but it meant that the odds against the rest of our people were even worse and they were falling at too quick a rate.

Apparently I wasn't the only one to realize how dire our situation had gotten; Jace had adjusted his course and was cutting his way towards the Minotaur. I'd seen Kyle go up against Fenrir and survive, but he'd had the advantage of Excalibur and an actual time-bending effect that had allowed him to move and fight at twice the speed he otherwise could have managed by mere time amping.

Jace was good—maybe even Kyle's match, I didn't know for sure—but everything I'd heard indicated that the Minotaur was every bit as powerful as Fenrir. Without the advantages that Kyle had been operating under, I wasn't sure that Jace could win—even with the distraction of all of the energy flying around us.

There was only one answer. I planted—ruining my one remaining shoe—and then threw myself over the top of the Lady. She and the dragon were locked in what looked like a ponderous, slow-motion exchange of blows, and it was the easiest thing in the world to clear both of them and land just behind the dragon. I spun in place and hit the dragon with every ounce of strength my amped-up frame was capable of generating.

If I'd had any questions regarding whether or not the Scepter of Storms was more than just another mundane weapon, they were answered in that moment. I hit the dragon with so much force that I felt the shock of contact even through the sensation-deadening layer of my augmented skin, which split open in several spots across my palms as my overworked body failed to keep up with the demands I was placing on it.

Any normal weapon that size would have bent under that impact, but my scepter simply transmitted a portion of the blow back up through my hands, arms and shoulders as it shattered the dragon's spine. I wasn't close enough for a blow to its head to be a possibility, but paralyzing it halfway down the length of its body would be more than enough to leave it a sitting duck for the Lady to deal with.

I didn't waste any time hitting it again. Instead, I used the momentum imparted to me as my weapon bounced back away from the dragon and slammed the Scepter of Storms into the next Unseelie fae in line with enough force to pick it up and launch it several dozen feet through the air.

ENDLESS

A flicker of movement, barely visible out of the corner of my eye, caused me to throw myself forward, and I just managed to avoid what looked like a giant jaguar as it sailed through the space I'd just been occupying. The Lady's sword licked out, striking with a casual grace and speed that was only possible because she was at least an order of magnitude stronger than I was—even while I was amped up. Her strike cut completely through the jaguar, and then I was running towards Jace with everything I had left inside me.

The ground blurred underneath me as I dodged the corpses of fallen fae, but all of my attention was on Jace. He and the Minotaur had already exchanged several blows. The Minotaur was limping, but Jace's left arm was hanging limply at his side, obviously broken.

Jace was trying to retreat, trying to buy himself enough time to work a healing effect, but his opponent knew better than to give him enough room to do that. Jace dropped his ax and clawed desperately for the sword he'd strapped to his back so many hours before.

I understood what he was doing—the sword was a much better option for fighting with one arm. He needed a weapon that he could stab with, something that wouldn't leave him completely vulnerable with every swing, but it was the wrong move. Jace should have been faster than the Minotaur, but his shoes had disintegrated somewhere along the way. Even worse, the

Minotaur had dropped down to all fours in an effort to get more traction and when he threw himself forward he did so with limbs powered with the kind of strength that flowed through Fenrir or the Lady's bodies, strength that no mere Awakened could possibly hope to match.

I screamed again—a combination of useless warning and rage. I wanted to look away, to spare myself the sight of what I knew was coming next, but some iron core inside of me refused to miss out on Jace's last moments. If I couldn't do anything else for him, at least I could do that.

The Minotaur shot forward like a bullet out of a gun. He'd dropped his massive bronze ax in order to make it so he would be able to generate the maximum possible speed, but he didn't need it—not when his head was topped by a pair of razor-sharp black horns. Jace tried to compensate for his error in dropping his ax. He planted his left foot and threw himself to the side, but it was too late.

The tip of one of the horns pierced Jace's chest, and part of me wanted to throw up, but there wasn't time for that. I was still too far away to stop what I knew was going to happen next, but that didn't stop me from trying.

There was less than a dozen yards between Jace and I now, but the Minotaur had landed and I saw massive muscles in its arms and legs flex as it started to whip its head to one side in an explosive motion that would finish Jace off.

ENDLESS

My anger was already stoked as high as it could go, but it felt brittle, like it was barely strong enough to keep my current effects up and running. I would have tried to work some kind of effect regardless, counting on the fact that peak memories required less in the way of emotional reserves to burn them, but none of my effects were capable of stopping what was about to happen.

Right then the tsunami of energy pouring off of the ward to my left surged to impossible levels. The light it gave off as it discharged into the ground and the surviving fae from both sides was beyond blinding, but I welcomed it because I knew there was no way that even the Minotaur was going to be able to move while that much power was beating against him.

Despite the fact that I couldn't see anything, I never even slowed down. I barreled forward with nothing but my memory of what I'd seen a split second before to guide me. The Scepter of Storms had been up even with my eyes, but as I took what I thought was the last step separating me from my target, I spun my weapon backwards in a single revolution that brought it upwards with every ounce of force I had left. I'd dropped my weight as the head of the scepter passed behind me, and then as it started upwards, I rose up onto my toes and I prayed that I would be able to hit the Minotaur as I intended.

The impact of my scepter hitting something should have been the most welcome thing I'd ever experienced, but I was instantly overcome by a fear that I'd missed the Minotaur and hit Jace instead. I needed to be able to see, needed to know what I'd done. An unaccustomed weight settled on my shoulder a second later, startling me, and I reflexively reached for my anger, but rather than any of the effects I'd ever used before, something else burst out of my forehead in an invisible stream of destroyed memories.

I blinked, and then suddenly realized that I could see again. Bethany was on my shoulder, screaming something into my ear, but there was something else—something more important than Bethany—that I needed to take care of.

I turned the other direction and saw Jace, motionless on the ground in a pool of blood. More importantly, I saw the Minotaur rolling to a stop several dozen yards away from us. His shoulder was an unusable mess, crushed by my attack, but he'd just proved that he didn't need a weapon to be dangerous. He'd been bad enough back when he'd been surrounded by discharging energy. I had no chance of victory and I knew it, but I couldn't just give up—not when Jace's life was at stake.

I lowered the head of my weapon down onto Jace's chest and another stream of memories burst out of me as I worked an effect that I shouldn't have had the emotional reserves to force into reality. I heard a gasp from below me as Jace sucked in his first breath in several seconds, but by that time I'd already started moving forward.

I couldn't have explained it, but I'd somehow known that he was going to be okay as soon as the artifact touched him. All that was left was making sure that he had time to get away, time to run to safety.

The sounds of battle were thick around me as fae, Seelie and Unseelie, tried to destroy each other. I suspected that we were still outnumbered, but there wasn't time to look around and confirm one way or another.

The Minotaur pulled himself back onto his feet and shook his head as though disoriented. "That was well done, godling. It's been a very long time since someone hit me that hard."

"That? That's nothing, I'm just getting warmed up."

He shot forward, moving with the kind of speed that was only possible for an Awakened or the most powerful of fae. He wasn't as nimble as Fenrir, but if anything he was faster. That was okay though, I'd had a chance to take his measure while he was fighting Jace, and he was down one limb, which meant he wasn't as fast as he should have been.

He dropped his head as he came in, fully intending on goring me, but that also meant that he had to move his head slightly to one side so that he could connect with something other than his forehead. I waited until the last possible second and then committed, spinning to the side as I lashed out with my scepter.

I connected with the base of the horn closest to me, shattering it with a resounding crack that would have made me sick if I hadn't been so completely overcome by bloodlust. I'd succeeded in depriving him of half his natural weaponry, but the force of my blow changed his course and he barreled into me, leading with his damaged shoulder.

It was a glancing blow, but we both still cried out in pain—me because I felt one of my amped-up ribs crack, and him because his joint was already a mass of agony. The collision knocked me to the ground.

I landed within arm's reach of him and he would have had me right then if not for the fact that Jace appeared above both of us and stabbed downward. Jace didn't succeed in landing the killing blow he'd been hoping for, but he did send our enemy rolling away, and that saved me.

I half expected Jace to charge forward while the Minotaur was off balance and still rolling across the ground, but instead he reached down, grabbing me by the arm. He pulled a shriek out of me that was part pain and part surprise as he yanked me to my feet, and then I felt a rush of energy shoot out of him.

His barrier effect materialized into existence behind us just in time to save us from being run over by several dozen Unseelie fae who were retreating back to the Minotaur in the hopes that he would be able to save them from the Lady and her warriors.

The Lady herself glided by less than a second behind the stampeding fae, running her hand along the edge of Jace's barrier without actually stopping to look at us.

"Get her far enough back that she's out of danger. We need her accessing the scepter's true powers rather than brawling with it like it is no different than any other hunk of metal."

Jace dropped the barrier and half led, half dragged me back over in the direction of Byron. Something about healing him—or possibly it had been the collision with the Minotaur—had sent me into shock. It was like I was trying to function through a layer of gauze. None of my thoughts could make it out to where they were actionable.

Kat met up with us at the same time as we reached Byron, and helped Jace pull me into the hidden doorway that Byron had revealed when we'd first arrived. One thought finally broke free of its restraints, and I tried to turn around, tried to get back outside where I had a chance of making a difference in the fight.

"It's too late, Selene. They're here. We have to get behind the next ward or we're all dead."

I didn't understand. I tried to pull away and Kat slapped me. Everything came back to me all at once. She was right. I could feel them out there, the eight Awakened that I'd somehow managed to forget about during the last few seconds. They weren't just close, they were right on top of us.

It was amazing that I could still feel them around the pressure from the second ward, the one that had been revealed once Byron finally brought the outer ward down. Maybe that was part of why I'd had such a hard time getting my mind to work.

I turned, making my way into the tunnel under my own power, and Kat let go of me to grab Byron, who was conscious, but obviously having a hard time getting his body and mind to respond to him. He was the last person I would have expected Kat to go back into danger for, but she didn't even flinch as she darted back out of the tunnel and grabbed his arm. She pulled him into the tunnel, dragging all hundred and eighty pounds of him along behind her with an ease that was only possible because of how far up she'd amped up her strength.

She beat the sun lance that would have otherwise killed both of them, but the rock fragments that went flying as the attack hit the mountainside cut into her and Byron both.

Byron shook his head and then struggled to his feet and started leading us deeper into the tunnel as Jace conjured a soft ball of light. "Thanks for getting me out of there, Kat."

Kat sent out half a dozen sun lances, carving away thousands of pounds of rock, and then suddenly the mouth of the tunnel was collapsing with an unimaginable roar as we all sprinted deeper into the darkness so that we wouldn't be caught up in the rubble.

"I didn't have a choice. We need you alive to get us inside the next ward, or none of us are going to make it past the next hour."

Kat was right—the rock between us and the other Awakened wasn't going to save us. I could feel effects snapping into existence on the other side of the debris, hissing, angry expenditures of power that were stronger than anything I could hope to manage in my current state.

Byron led us past several corridors without responding to Kat's dig. It seemed almost like he was counting the passages, which didn't put me at ease regarding his knowledge of our surroundings.

Jace seemed to share at least a little of my concern. "What are all these passages?"

"They lead to other entrances mostly. The space between the first and second wards has several tunnels that run around the entire perimeter of Camelot. We knew once we created the outer ward that there wouldn't be any way to hide the fact that something important was sitting out here, but we wanted to make sure that we had plenty of options when it came to getting in and out of the outer ward without being seen."

Kat was all but pushing Byron on ahead of her. "How much further are we talking? Those guys back there have to be pretty close to breaking through by now and unless you're ready to hold them off all by yourself, none of us have the reserves to even make some kind of fighting retreat."

"We're almost there. Just be patient for a few more seconds."

Jace was suddenly paying a lot more attention to the tunnels we were passing. "How well disguised are all of those other doors, Byron?"

"Pretty well. They were all created so that in order to open them you have to cross the plane of the ward. They probably could have been blown open with the right combination of high explosives, but even the few that were found were never attacked directly because the other side knew there was no point. There wasn't any way to get past the ward."

Jace's knuckles went white on the hilt of his sword. "We've got to move faster than this. Somebody could already be in here with us. If the locations of some doors are common knowledge at the Unseelie Court then they could have come inside as soon as you brought the outer ward down."

We were close to the ward now—I could feel it beating on me with very nearly the same amount of pressure as I'd experienced when I'd been standing only inches away from the first ward. That was good because it meant that we should be just about to our destination.

Byron darted down a side corridor, counted his steps, and then turned and put his hand against a section of the wall with enough force that it should have shattered every bone in his hand. Instead a square of rock moved back, exposing seams in the wall that were so tiny I hadn't been able to see them even when I'd been looking right at them.

Byron grabbed Kat's hand as he turned a lever buried deep inside of the wall, well past the plane of the second ward. "I'm keying the ward to you now."

The entire section of wall that we'd been facing was sliding back out of the way now. Watching it with my time sense still turned up to three and a half times normal meant that it seemed to take forever for the doorway to open enough that a person would be able to walk through it, but I knew it was actually moving quickly for something so large.

I felt something out at the very edge of my range, and flared my signature in an attempt to extend my range. I gasped at what I found, and Bethany grabbed ahold of my ear to stop me from accidentally throwing her off of me as I stumbled into the wall.

"What is it, Selene?"

"The Awakened from behind us have split up. Two of them are still back there trying to get inside, but there's another one already in here with us. It's hard to tell for sure with all of this rock between them and us, but I think they're close."

Jace looked like he wanted to swear. "You're right. They are really close—maybe less than a hundred yards. I'm such an idiot. I should have been flaring my signature this entire time to get enough range to actually know what we were up against. Hurry, Byron! We're out of time."

At that point everything happened so fast that even my amped time sense almost wasn't able to keep up. Byron smiled in relief as the metaphysical tumblers all lined up, and then he pulled on Kat's arm, sending her into the doorway now that it was safe for her to pass through the ward.

A flicker of motion, barely visible out of the corner of one eye, brought me around just in time to see Fenrir come charging out of the darkness. The ward beckoned just inches away, but it still wasn't keyed to Jace, Bethany or me. I screamed—not that it did any good—and shoved Byron, sending him into the ward at the same time that I took off in the other direction, Jace less than a foot behind me and Bethany holding onto my hair for dear life.

As we sprinted down the hallway with Fenrir lumbering along behind us I took solace in the fact that Byron and Kat had made it to safety—hopefully they would be smart enough to stay behind the ward. Even as I thought that, part of me was rooting for them to come back out and attack Fenrir, but I knew that would be stupid.

We were in long halls that were barely wide enough for Fenrir to run through, which would have been great if not for the fact that he was something like two tons of iron-hard flesh that was the next best thing to impossible to stop.

I no longer had enough emotional reserves to power even a peak-memory attack, and even if Jace was in better shape than I was, he wasn't going to be able to get off two such attacks before Fenrir ran him over, and I was nearly positive Fenrir couldn't be felled with a single strike.

My augmentations started flickering as I reached the point where my reserves were too depleted even to maintain the effects I already had up. As long as we were both amped up and charging in a straight line there was a good chance that we would be able to stay ahead of Fenrir, but if we had to change directions then his four points of contact with the ground would give him the advantage.

We were racing against the clock, which would have been bad enough all by itself, but we were also racing directly towards the other Awakened I'd sensed just seconds before. I was pretty sure that we were screwed no matter what, but Jace apparently wasn't willing to give up on our chances yet.

I felt a tingling surge of power and realized that he'd burned a peak memory. I wanted to yell at him not to stop, but before I could get the words out past my gasps for more air, I realized that his footsteps had never faltered.

He'd attacked blindly, throwing a sun lance back behind him without looking back to ensure that he would be able to hit. It actually wasn't a terrible idea given just how little room there was for Fenrir to dodge, but Jace had done the unexpected and aimed his attack not at Fenrir, but at the ceiling.

I felt the rumble of crashing rock as the top of the tunnel started caving in, and I started to slow down. I was desperate for a chance to let my lungs and circulatory system catch up with the ruinous demands I'd put on them, but Jace didn't let me.

"There's no time, Selene. I probably only slowed Fenrir down slightly, and even if I stopped him completely, we still have a hostile up ahead to worry about. We need to take a turn up here soon or we'll definitely run into whoever is up there."

I nodded weakly, too out of breath to manage anything more than that, and forced my body to pick the pace back up. Within a few steps, I could hear Fenrir working himself free of the rubble that I'd been so hopeful would disembody him.

Bethany seemed to sense my concern because she turned around so that she could report on his progress.

"His back legs are trapped, but not for much longer—it doesn't look like he's broken anything."

We ran down the tunnel for several more seconds, and every spare bit of attention I had was focused on trying to figure out where exactly the other Awakened was. Jace was right—we needed a cross tunnel soon or we weren't going to have any kind of chance of avoiding another fight.

"He's free, guys, and he looks pretty pissed."

I wanted to tell Bethany to fly ahead of us and scout for a way around whoever was up there waiting for us, but I knew that would be a suicide mission. Bethany might have absorbed the equivalent of several centuries' worth of power outside of the ward today, but she was still no match for any Awakened.

The tunnel we were in abruptly opened up into a massive space, and a surge of relief flashed through me right up until the point where I saw Kyle standing off to the side of the cavern.

Chapter 16

None of us were particularly surprised at the sun lance that shot away from Kyle a split second after we exited the tunnel. I wasn't even really all that surprised by the diameter of the beam or the intensity of the golden light it emitted.

Kyle was the bearer of not one, but at least two artifacts. His necklace gave him the emotional reserves of two Awakened, and Excalibur made it so that he didn't consume memories as quickly as the rest of us.

I could have managed a similar attack if I'd been willing to burn another peak memory. Jace probably could have bettered Kyle's attack by using a peak memory, but neither of us could possibly hope to produce anything even close using only baseline memories.

I fully expected to die in that instant. I'd been living on borrowed time ever since Fenrir had attacked Kat, Ari and me the first time, thrown into one life-threatening situation after another, and it only seemed right that all of the violence was about to catch up with me. Once I realized that it was Kyle who'd been waiting to ambush us, the only thing that really surprised me was the fact that his devastating, unstoppable attack was directed not at Jace, Bethany and me, but rather at the ceiling of the tunnel we'd just left.

The ceiling came down with a thunderous crash that made Kat's earlier effort look like child's play. Initially the dust was so thick that I couldn't even see my hand two inches away from my face, but then a strong wind kicked up and before I knew it we were no longer coughing.

Kyle hadn't moved from where he'd been standing when he'd caused the cave in, which was a testament to just how convinced he was that he completely outclassed both of us. Unfortunately—right now at least—he wasn't wrong.

"You should have stayed holed up in Cold Springs. You would have been safe there."

The idea that we would be safer behind the puny, still-maturing wards at Jace and Kat's house than we would be with the Lady and the entire Seelie court was crazy. I started to shake my head, and then suddenly it all made sense.

"You were going to let us sit out the war."

"Yes. Achieving that goal got harder after Byron made it all of the way across country and ended up at your doorstep, but I still managed to convince Fenrir and the others that there was no reason to go looking for a fight with the four of you. That's no longer possible, now that you're actively helping her."

Jace shifted me around behind him, shielding me with his own body. I was touched; it was incredibly gallant and completely useless. Bethany was shifting around like she wanted to say something, but I reached up with my free hand and gently patted her legs, hoping that would keep her quiet.

"So what now, brother? You'll just kill us and take the Scepter of Storms?"

"I made myself a promise, Jace. I'm not going to kill Selene—not unless she gives me no other choice—but I've made no such promise where you are concerned."

Kyle brought his hands up as though planning on lashing out with some kind of long-distance attack, but I darted around in front of Jace, denying Kyle a target.

"Don't do that. I'm not going to let you kill him."

I could feel the anger beating at me, anger that was as familiar as my own pulse. Kyle looked at me, and for once I could tell exactly what he was thinking. He was angry, but also oddly pleased. My standing aside and letting him kill Jace would have simplified his life in dozens of ways, but he preferred me to be the proud, unbending woman he'd known for so many centuries. If I'd cowered and simpered he would have lost respect for me, and I was suddenly aware just how important that respect was.

"Step aside, Selene. He's not worth risking your life."

"No. If you try to kill him then we'll fight you—all three of us."

I could see just how little my threats worried Kyle, but before I could open my mouth and say anything else he nodded.

"Very well. I was going to let you keep the scepter—it's obvious that you don't know the first thing about using it—but instead I'll give you a choice. Jace or the artifact. You can't leave here with both."

There it was. He was giving me 'options,' but I wasn't going to let him dictate my choices like that. I had no choice but to refuse both, but even as I prepared to tell him he was going to have to kill all three of us, I wondered if I was making a mistake.

I didn't want Jace to die, but Jace's death was a single—short-term—problem. In twenty years or so he'd be back and we could pick up where we'd left off. Letting Kyle get his hands on yet another artifact, on the other hand, would affect people all over the world. The Lady had seemed confident that we couldn't win without the Scepter of Storms—otherwise she never would have agreed to place it in my custody. If I handed it over to Kyle then I was guaranteeing the destruction of anyone who even thought about trying to resist Kyle.

I would do almost anything to keep the scepter out of Kyle's hand, but it was the almost part of that statement that was the problem. If I had the chance to trade Jace's life for the scepter, then not doing so was putting his life above the lives of billions of other people. Maybe I was making the wrong decision, but that didn't change the fact that it was the only decision I could make and still be me.

"That's not a choice, Kyle. If that's your position, then I guess we're going to see how much oomph Jace and I have left."

Even as I said it, I reached inside to check my emotional reserves. It was a reflexive, pointless action. I'd just checked them a few seconds before and they'd been guttering—ready to give way at any moment. I'd checked them knowing that nothing could have changed in such a short period of time...only something had changed.

The deep, calm pool of happiness that I found waiting for me felt limitless. It took me a second to realize what I was feeling. I was happy because I was about to prove to Kyle, Jace and the rest of the world that I valued Jace more than anything or anyone else. It was irrevocable proof that I really had chosen Jace.

It was like the last seventeen years of my life had all been aimed at enabling this one moment, and I suddenly realized that this was the depth of emotion that would be required to create a fairy. I'd been astonished at what I'd felt while fighting Sandra to a standstill, but that was nothing compared to this. My only regret was that I didn't have more years of experience—more raw fuel—to throw into the fight I was about to be sucked into.

Even as I had that thought, I realized that I was wrong. I had one other regret, but it was a regret that I could still do something about.

"Bethany, when the fight starts I want you to make a run for it. Don't stay around here and try to help Jace and me. You have to get away."

"No, Selene. I'm still small, but I'm bigger than I was, and much stronger than you would expect for my size. I can help!"

"The best thing you can do to help us would be to hide away somewhere safe for the next seventeen years. Once Jace and I are old enough to be identified you can bring us together and tell both of us that I picked Jace again, that I'll always pick Jace."

I'd only thought that the anger coming off of Kyle had been intense. It was nothing compared to what I was seeing in his eyes now, but that was okay. Giving Bethany that order had been the last missing piece. The pond of happiness, deeper than anything I'd ever encountered before, was now an ocean.

I couldn't survive this fight, but I could make sure that Kyle didn't get away. He was angry, but his anger couldn't possibly be as strong as my happiness—if it had been, he wouldn't have been able to stop himself from lunging forward and snapping my neck.

Kyle's necklace made his emotions twice as strong as mine under normal circumstances, but this was anything but normal. I instinctively knew that I could power effects that would erase years of my life in an instant. Kyle had more years of experience to throw into the fight, but that just meant that I was going to have to kill him in the first second or two of the conflict.

As he and I locked gazes, I realized that the pain in my face was coming from the huge smile that refused to leave me. Kyle looked at my expression and I realized that he knew just how strong my emotions were in that instant. He looked into my eyes, and he saw his death—both of our deaths—and he was the one to flinch first.

"Fine. You can both leave—I can't stop you, not without breaking my promise to myself. If you keep moving the direction you were headed, there is a vehicle just a hundred yards or so down the corridor. You can use that to get back to Colorado. I'll head back outside and lead the fight against whatever dregs from the Seelie Court are still alive. It may not make much of a difference, but you'll have half an hour's head start."

For the briefest of instants, I considered demanding that he hand over both the Brísingamen necklace and Excalibur, but I instinctively knew that he would never agree to that. Going back to what he'd been before—friendless, weak—was a fate worse than death to Kyle. He would fight me if I made that the condition for all of us walking away from this cavern alive, and while there was a good chance that I could kill him, there was no guarantee that Jace and Bethany would survive that confrontation.

Besides, I suddenly very much wanted to live.

Jace and I edged across the room while Kyle backed into the tunnel behind him. A few seconds later, he'd vanished into the darkness. Jace, Bethany and I were safely alone in the tunnels.

Chapter 17

Kyle hadn't been lying about the vehicle. I wasn't exactly sure if that was a surprise or not. He could have easily backed down and left us to wander the tunnels in confusion until he could come back with help. All he'd needed to do was stall, but instead he'd given us a chance to escape.

As difficult as it was to believe, I was pretty sure that he'd let us go at least partly because he really hadn't wanted to hurt me. That wasn't the only reason—I'd seen the fear in his eyes, seen the fact that he wasn't ready to die and lose all of the years of research and preparation he'd put in to get this far—but it was a significant part of why he'd done what he'd done.

That was hard to wrap my mind around, and not just because everything he was doing was going to eventually hurt me. I was struggling to keep two opposite ideas in my head at the same time. Kyle was the villain of this piece. He was unquestionably evil—the terrorist attacks he'd ordered were plenty good enough proof of that—but he was also gallant and he had a stubborn kind of integrity that I couldn't help but admire.

The only thing I was sure of at this point was that no matter what else happened I wasn't going to ever pick Kyle over Jace.

The 'vehicle' turned out to be a brand-new jeep with the kind of massive tires and lift kit that made off-road vehicles able to navigate terrain that should have been impassable for anything motorized. In short, it was the perfect vehicle for making the drive back to civilization.

Jace climbed into the driver's seat as Bethany and I climbed into the passenger seat, and then the jeep roared to life and we were tearing down the wide tunnel where it had been housed. The little ball of light that Jace had conjured when we'd first entered the tunnels had provided all the light I could have realistically asked for, but there was just something more reassuring about the halogen headlights of a motorized vehicle.

Maybe that would change once I knew how to create that particular effect myself, but for now the headlights felt more reliable, more permanent. That was something I needed after all of the fighting and death from the last few hours.

Less than a minute into our drive, we saw a touchpad on the wall. Jace slowed down enough that I could press it, and a loud groan signaled that the exterior door had started to raise itself.

I would have waited for it to finish opening, but once again Jace's superior experience saved the day. He floored the jeep, tearing down the tunnel towards the bar of sunlight, and timed our exit perfectly. I reflexively ducked down in my seat, worried the bottom of the door would tear the top of the jeep right off of the body, but we squeaked out with inches to spare, and were moving at more than forty miles per hour as we exited the mountain. It was a good thing because a familiar-looking pooka was waiting for us.

I thought for a second that Jace was going to ram it, which would have been a disaster given just how dense a fairy that size could make themselves, but Jace cut the wheel over hard at the last second. I half expected the jeep to roll—we did go briefly up onto two wheels—but Jace managed to keep the vehicle under control, and as we passed the Unseelie fae I realized that I had my scepter in my hands.

I'd reflexively amped up my strength and time sense when I saw the pooka, and it was the easiest thing in the world to clamp down on my seat with my left hand while my right swung the Scepter of Storms with enough force to shatter the pooka's neck.

We left Camelot behind in a cloud of dust, and I let myself believe for a little while that we'd made a clean escape. I should have known better than that. The trail that led back to the freeway was in good shape considering the fact that Byron and the others hadn't used it very often, but it was still not the kind of surface that would allow a vehicle to travel at highway speeds.

Jace did a remarkable job of nursing as much speed out of the jeep as could be expected under the circumstances, but it still took what seemed like forever to get to a paved road where he could really open the vehicle up.

About that point I found myself wishing that Byron had stowed away something faster. It wasn't a fair wish—a sports car wouldn't have made it a hundred yards on the trail we'd just finished driving, but now that we were on a real road our top speed was still uncomfortably less than what Bethany could manage if she were to take to the air.

Granted, most of the Unseelie fae chose to abandon the winged shapes they were born with—trading them out for forms that were stronger and able to take a lot more damage—but there would still be some Unseelie fae with wings serving as scouts. Jace tried to reassure me, but I wasn't positive that he was quite as confident as he was trying to let on.

I asked Bethany how fast someone like that was able to move, but she didn't know, and nobody was responding to her efforts to establish mind-to-mind communication with them. That was another bad sign. Bethany had absorbed a tremendous amount of information in just the few hours since the blood oath had taken place, but there was still way too much that she didn't know.

Our best guess was that they were either all disembodied or so busy fighting that they were keeping her out so as to make sure that she didn't distract them at a critical time.

Of course that didn't explain her inability to get hold of the fae the Lady had sent with the diversionary force, but Bethany thought that might have something to do with the sheer distance between us and them. Either way, it meant that we were on our own—at least for a little while.

We'd been on the road for nearly twenty minutes before I saw the first flicker of motion up high in the sky that told me we weren't out of the woods. The first speck became two and then three as more of the Unseelie scouts found us.

They maintained their distance for quite a while. A few minutes after we'd been spotted, one of the three scouts peeled back off—probably to go summon reinforcements. Jace kept telling me that we would be fine—that something as big as Fenrir could never manage a sustained pace in excess of ninety miles per hour—but by that time I could see the holes in his argument.

We couldn't sustain that kind of speed either, not in the long term. We could go without food and water, we could even swap out who was driving and avoid having to stop for rest, but we were eventually going to have to stop for gas.

As long as we had a big enough lead, a five-minute stop to refuel didn't have to be the end of the world, but there was no guarantee that we would be far enough away from all of them at that point to make it back onto the road before they caught up. The really big guns would be further back, but now that I'd lost the focus that had allowed me to connect to the vast ocean of happiness earlier, we weren't in any state to fight off even a weak group of fae.

Jace tried to get me to take a nap, but every time I closed my eyes I saw visions of us being attacked by swarms of smaller flying fae. They wouldn't even have to kill us, they could simply pin us down until something bigger caught up with us.

That would have been bad enough, but if I were in their shoes that wouldn't be the only option I would have been pursuing. The Unseelie Court might be drastically different than what I'd seen after stepping through the portal in Intravil's club, but it was also located in the in-between space. That meant that they had a network of portals too, a network that even Jace and Bethany knew only a little about, a network that could easily move dozens of fae hundreds of miles instantly.

The guys who were flying—or running—along behind us were a threat because they meant that we couldn't go to ground and disappear while we rested and replenished our emotional reserves, but the real threats were all of the fae who had taken off at a run towards the closest portal back to their court.

It wasn't going to take a rocket scientist to figure out where we were headed. Kyle knew exactly where Jace's house was, which meant that the odds were really good that there was going to be an unfriendly welcoming committee waiting for us when we arrived in Cold Springs.

The best thing we could have been doing was coming up with a plan that had a chance of saving the three of us, but nobody seemed to be willing to broach the subject. Apparently we were all hoping that something would change on the mind-to-mind communication front with Bethany and the rest of the blood-oathed fae.

It turned out that it was only possible to sustain feelings of pure terror for so long. I was still scared, but somewhere along the way scared became the new normal, and I felt myself finally start to drift off.

Given the level of exertion I'd put myself through over the last few hours, I expected to fall asleep instantly once the adrenaline stopped flowing into my system, but instead my mind remained mostly alert as my body slowly started to shut down.

It was peaceful—calming even—but as good as that felt, I knew that was the wrong thing to be feeling. I was right on the edge of falling asleep when I decided that I had to start talking to Jace and Bethany about our options if we arrived in Cold Springs and found a group of Unseelie warriors waiting for us. I tried to claw my way back to full consciousness, but it was like there was a slender but impossibly strong cord holding me there.

The harder I flailed, the less progress I made. It made no sense, but in the end—after an indeterminate amount of time—I finally became so mentally exhausted that I couldn't keep fighting. I gave up and let myself sink.

I expected to fall asleep, but instead I entered another state of consciousness, one where I could feel another...presence...inside of my head. It was the scariest thing I'd ever experienced. Even having someone else's voice inside of my head had been a light, surface kind of intrusion. This was something alien swimming inside the lowest levels of my mind, something big, something powerful.

I expected whatever it was to lash out at me. I could tell it was powerful enough to shatter my mind and leave me nothing more than an empty shell, but it didn't do anything. It just sat there, nearly motionless, as though waiting for something.

I cautiously reached out to whatever it was, and found that it welcomed contact with me. It...hungered...for something that only someone like me could give it. It took me several seconds to realize that it wanted direction, wanted me to command it.

Asking it what I was supposed to do—how I was supposed to order it around—felt stupid, but I was fresh out of other ideas. I reached out and silently questioned it and then gasped in surprise as it showed me a sea of blue sparks that was like nothing else I'd ever seen.

Some of the sparks were brighter than others, and there were sections of the vista that were more densely packed than others, but everywhere I looked, sparks surrounded me. They weren't motionless either. I was moving through them—fast enough for me to be able to register the movement after only a couple of seconds' worth of observation—but it was more than that. The sparks seemed to be moving on their own as well, swaying in relation to each other. It was almost like trying to watch a single molecule of water as it traveled through the ocean.

Each spark rose and fell in relation to the others, swirling around in slow motion. I almost felt like I should be getting motion-sick. The human mind wasn't meant to register that much movement at once—at least not in that level of detail—but something about the presence sharing my mind seemed to be buffering me from all of that.

I got the sense that there was more there, just beneath the level I could see, almost like each of the sparks was orbiting around a different center, but I didn't try to drill down to that—I was almost positive that even the visitor inside of my mind wasn't going to be able to shield me from the consequences if I tried to do that.

I reached out to cup one of the sparks with my hand, unsure if it would hurt to touch it, but I didn't actually have a hand in this place. There wasn't anything visible extending out from me to the spark that had caught my eye, but I could still feel some kind of sensation as whatever I was sending out in to the world slid past other sparks. It was like I'd grown another arm, one that my puny Awakened brain hadn't ever been meant to control, but which still somehow served at my command.

As I touched the spark I felt a tingling and the presence inside my mind woke up. I hadn't realized that it was sleeping—that it had been operating at only a fraction of its capability—but that was exactly what I was feeling now. Something took control of my mental arms, and the flash of panic that raced through me was undeniable, but the presence sensed my concern and calmed me—suppressing the emotions that it didn't want me to feel.

That should have scared me even more, but apparently that wasn't one of the permitted feelings. I was forced to watch as my arms swept through the shimmering universe around me, gathering the sparks into a denser cloud up above me.

The light from the sparks grew more intense as they got closer together. It was more than just a function of the density of the sparks, it was as though they were drawing energy from me—only I didn't feel tired. I was nothing more than a conduit running between the presence and the sparks.

It was beautiful in ways that I hadn't expected. I wanted nothing more than to stay there watching the sparks forever, but something was demanding my attention.

At first I thought that it was the presence, but it had moved beyond asking me for anything. It just took what it wanted—like it was doing now as it swept even more sparks upwards, packing them in around the dense, swirling mass we'd already created.

It felt like I was at the bottom of an impossibly deep hole, but I could hear something ever so faintly.

"Selene! Did you hear me? You've got to wake up. I can't drive and fend them off at the same time."

That probably wouldn't have been enough to pull me back from my new surroundings all by itself, but now that I'd registered the words, I was also able to recognize other sensations. Someone was shaking me—hard enough that I was probably going to have bruises.

I felt a flash of annoyance, and realized for the first time that the presence inside my head was letting me regain some of the control it had taken away from me. The voice had been joined by another—a higher-pitched voice—and now someone was pulling on my hair.

I know the voices, but it was surprisingly difficult to put names to them. Jace...Bethany. Remembering my companions brought me back far enough to open my eyes. I expected that to snap me completely out of the odd, spark-filled world I'd been experiencing, but that was only partly true.

I was back in the real world, but the sparks were still there, layered over the top of everything else. There was a moment of vertigo as my perspective shifted. Before I'd opened my eyes, I'd somehow been both infinitely closer and impossibly far away from the sparks. Now they were closer to me, but smaller—so small that they were nothing more than a soft blue glow that seemed to permeate everything.

"What's going on?"

I looked over at Jace, noticing how amazing his eyes looked with an electric blue overlay, and then followed his arm as he pointed at a group of six moving objects that had gotten close enough to be more than just distant dots.

"Unseelie scouts. They apparently decided to try to take us now rather than waiting for reinforcements. Do you have any emotional reserves left? Can you knock them out of the air?"

I opened my mouth to tell Jace that I didn't have anything left, and realized that my invisible arms were still there, still moving around—almost completely independent from my will. More importantly, I could still feel the presence inside my mind.

It wanted me to do something. There was a lot that it was allowed to do without me—without my approval—but there was something that it needed me for, some kind of imperative that it couldn't fulfill without me.

It was focused on the approaching fae. It wanted me to reach out and touch them. Without understanding why, I reached my hand towards the closest fae. My invisible arm had to lengthen to have any chance of touching any of our enemies. It did, but the growth in my forearm was nothing compared to the growth between my shoulder and elbow.

Even with the presence inside of my mind suppressing most of my natural responses to things, it was enough to make my skin crawl. I'd never been meant to control an appendage that was so mercurial, and my mind—even with an assist from the presence—was having a hard time making the limb function well enough to actually touch the closest fae.

It was like trying to pick up an egg with a spoon that was more than ten feet long, but then all of a sudden something snapped into place inside of my mind and it became easier—still hard, but easier. I touched the fae, but nothing happened until my elbow brushed against the impossibly bright swirling mix of sparks high over our head.

A split second later a burst of lightning shot down out of the clear sky and vaporized the fae I'd been touching.

I was in shock. If it had been solely up to me I would have sat there with my jaw halfway to my knees, but the presence was still at least partially in control. I wanted the fae gone, wanted us to be safe again, and apparently that was enough for it to fulfill the requirements of whatever safety mechanism ruled it.

My elbow didn't move away from the mass of energy, but my hand swept through the remaining fae like I was batting at flies. They were closer now—either they hadn't yet realized that I'd just killed their companion or they figured their best defense was to get close enough that I wouldn't be able to hit them without risking hitting our Jeep as well.

It didn't matter. In less than two seconds, I'd touched all five of them with my insubstantial limbs and a series of blinding blue bolts struck them from the sky. The thunder was so close it shook our car, one impossibly long rumble that I felt all the way down to my toes.

Bethany tugged on my hair again and I looked over at her.

"What just happened, Selene?"

I looked down at the shining rod that had yet to leave my hand in the hours since the Lady had given it to me.

"I just figured out how to use the Scepter of Storms."

Chapter 18

We debated the best course of action for nearly an hour. All three of us felt like we should turn around and try to drive off Kyle and the Unseelie fae, but none of us really wanted to go back there. Maybe things would have been different if Bethany or I had been able to get hold of the Lady or one of her people, but we couldn't. That meant we had no idea what we might be headed back into.

The scepter had just proved itself adept at destroying weaker fae, but there was no way to know how it would do against someone like Fenrir—not without actually getting close enough to strike him with a bolt or two—and that was incredibly risky.

If the scepter was capable of taking him out with one or two strikes, then we'd be home free. That would mean that we could drive right up to Camelot and destroy fae as fast as they showed themselves. That could change everything. If we could destroy the bulk of the Unseelie fae, then the Lady and the rest would be well placed to kill them again as soon as they were able to reform their physical bodies.

If, on the other hand, we drove right into the center of Kyle and all of his forces and found out that taking out even something the size of the pooka I'd killed required dozens of lightning bolts, we'd be screwed. I couldn't amp myself, which meant that I'd be tons slower when it came to launching attacks, and Jace would be completely useless. If we got in too deep and got surrounded by bigger fae it was entirely possible that we'd get killed and Kyle would end up with the Scepter of Storms.

Not going back meant that there was a good chance the Lady and the others who'd accompanied us out to Camelot would be killed several more times as Kyle and the others farmed them for the memories released each time they were killed. That would have terrible implications for the war, but in the end, all three of us decided that was the best way to go. We needed time to recover our emotional reserves before we went back into battle.

The rest of the trip back to Colorado went smoothly. We stopped twice for fuel, and each time stayed at the gas station just long enough to fill up the tank before racing back to the interstate.

ENDLESS

Jace was beyond exhausted by the time we pulled into the garage, and I wasn't much better off, but we couldn't afford to swap out, not as long as there was a chance that I'd end up behind the driver's seat when we got jumped by whoever Kyle had sent on ahead to ambush us. I spent the entire trip at least partially immersed in the blue-tinted vista that being linked with the scepter brought on.

Having another presence in my mind—something that was supposed to be nothing more than an inanimate tool, but which was feeling more and more alive by the hour—didn't become any less unnerving, but I forced myself not to push it away. The last thing I could afford to do right then was lose my connection with the one thing that gave us a chance of surviving the war.

Arriving at the house was a huge relief. Incredibly, nobody had come through and destroyed our wards, which meant that they were a little stronger than when we'd left. They still weren't going to stop anyone who really wanted to push them over, but that put them one day closer to reaching maturity and crystalizing.

Jace and I argued for nearly a minute over who would keep watch while the other slept. Bethany finally told us both to go to bed while she kept watch. It was a calculated risk. Bethany couldn't sense the approach of other Awakened, which meant that she couldn't do anything to head them off before they hit the wards, but in the end we decided she was right.

It wasn't a matter of *if* someone was going to hit the wards, it was a matter of *when*. Given that, it was most important that Jace and I get back up to fighting strength as quickly as possible.

That meant that we might lose the outer set of wards, but the odds were good that Bethany would be able to make it down to the vault in the basement before anyone could stop her. That ward was good enough to hold even Kyle out for at least a few hours, which would buy us time to attempt a breakout.

The scepter probably wouldn't be much use that far underground, but if we both went after him at the same time there was a decent chance we'd be able to drive him off and make it back up to where the scepter could work its magic—assuming I could figure out how to use it again.

Jace and I both headed down to the vault, and I didn't realize just how much tension I'd been carrying until we stepped inside the innermost ward and were well and truly safe. I'd known that I was worried—fleeing for your life tended to do that—but I hadn't realized just how much it had been affecting me.

I debated showering, but only for half a second—I was just too tired. Jace made noises like I should take his bed and he would go take

Kat's bed, but I just pulled him down onto the bed with me without saying anything.

He didn't fight. Both of us were too tired to do anything other than sleep—even assuming that was a boundary we'd been interested in crossing. All we really wanted was the comfort of knowing that we were more than eighty feet underground with a powerful ward between us and whatever nastiness was crawling around outside the house.

I woke up to an empty bed and the smell of French toast teasing my nose. I stumbled out of bed, surprised to find out that I'd slept for more than four hours. That wasn't quite a record since I'd made my transition to full Awakened, but it was pretty close. Apparently the fighting combined with using the scepter had taken more out of me than I'd realized.

Jace looked up at me with a smile as I dragged myself into the kitchen. "How are you feeling?"

"Like death warmed over, but I think some breakfast might get me back to feeling like normal."

"Are you thinking that you'll have to club the bread a few times in order to get it to an edible state?"

I looked down and realized that my scepter was still in my hand. I didn't remember picking it up when I'd climbed out of bed.

"Wow, I didn't even realize I was carrying it. I guess I'm still a little nervous that we're going to get attacked. That or maybe that it's going to disappear if I put it down for more than a couple seconds. I'm surprised I was able to let go of it long enough to fall asleep last night."

"I'm not sure you did. When I got out of bed this morning you were cuddled up next to it."

That made a cold wind blow through me. I did a cautious survey of the inside of my mind and confirmed what I'd been worried about. The presence was back.

I wasn't sure whether I was more concerned that it was still there, or that I was becoming so used to it that I hadn't even realized it was there when I woke up. I wanted to ask Jace what he thought about what was happening to me, but I just forced a smile onto my face.

"Do you think that there's time for me to jump through the shower before the food is done?"

"The food is just about finished, but it will keep. I'll stick plates over everything and put it inside the microwave so that it all stays warm."

I wanted a shower in the worst way, but even more than that, I wanted time to myself, time to pull myself together and figure out what I was going to do about the permanent visitor inside of my mind. Even so, hearing that Jace was going to have to wait for me stopped me before I could take a second step towards the bedroom.

He sent a reassuring smile my way. "It's really okay, Selene. Go ahead. I'll just finish up here, make sure that nothing will get cold while you're cleaning up, and then I'll run up to your room and grab you some clothes."

I'd forgotten about that. The two bedrooms down in the emergency shelter under the house were fully stocked with clothes for Jace and Kat, but there hadn't been time—or space—in which to move clothes for the rest of us. I nodded numbly as a tide of emotion started to crash over me, and hurried into the other room before I could start bawling.

I stripped out of the dirty clothes that had carried me through some of the most terrifying fighting of my life, and made it into the shower and got the water turned on in time for it to drown out my sobs, but it was a close thing.

I'd left the Scepter of Storms leaning against the wall, but it had required a concentrated effort on my part, and that just added to the overwhelming nature of my predicament. The last thing I needed was to be addicted to an artifact that was supposed to be inanimate, but which was proving to have an agenda of its own.

Once I got started crying, I knew that I wouldn't be stopping anytime soon. That was bad because I had a very limited amount of time before Jace would start worrying about me. I wanted to just slide down the wall and curl up into a ball at the bottom of the shower, but I forced myself to get started lathering up. I couldn't afford to break down completely—not if I wanted to keep Jace in the dark about what was going on.

There was plenty of hot water, and I kept turning it up, but no matter how hot the stream coming out of the shower head got, my insides still refused to warm up. I was pink all over and my skin was starting to smart, but I still felt like I was freezing to death.

I'd gotten a lot better at compartmentalizing stuff over the last few weeks. I managed to get the shampoo rinsed out of my hair before it happened. I was sitting there—water running down the back of my head—mostly back under control for the first time since I'd realized that I'd spent the night with a death grip on my scepter, and then I felt it reenter my mind.

Somehow I'd thought that I was safe as long as I wasn't in contact with it. I'd felt the beginnings of some kind of addiction, but I'd been thinking that the real battle was going to be stopping myself from constantly touching it. I hadn't realized that we were linked tightly enough now for it to invade me from several feet away.

I completely lost it. I couldn't have explained all of the reasons why my world felt like it was coming down around me. I *was* scared of what was going to happen now that I was linked to the scepter. The Lady had warned me about this when she'd given me the last artifact available to our side, but she'd been more cryptic even than normal, and I'd completely failed to understand what she'd been hinting at. The question of just exactly what price this particular artifact was going to extract from me was terrifying enough all by itself, but it wasn't the only thing bothering me.

I lost track of time for a few minutes and somehow ended up sobbing, curled up naked at the bottom of the shower while hot water pelted me. The only thing that brought me back to myself enough to register what was going on was the sound of Jace knocking on the bathroom door.

"Selene, are you okay? I went upstairs to get you some clean clothes. I was going to just leave them outside of the door, but it sounds like you're crying."

I tried to muster up an answer, but all that came out was more sobs, and a second later the door to the bathroom clicked open.

"I'm coming in, Selene."

That did the trick. I was still crying, still a complete wreck, but I was also scared to death of having Jace see me like that.

"No, stay out. I'm still not dressed. Everything is fine."

"You don't sound fine."

"Just put the clothes on the counter and close the door—I'll be out momentarily—I'm fine."

I wasn't fine, but I knew that I had to be convincing. Jace stood there, silent and motionless, for several seconds before I heard my clothes rustle followed by the click of the door closing.

I still wanted to fall apart, but I forced myself to turn off the water. I was shaking too badly to towel myself off very well, and I could feel what little control I had left starting to crack again.

I grabbed my underwear and pulled it up over my wet, quivering legs as tears continued to stream down my face. It was a small victory, but it was enough to strengthen me to the point where I could dig my bra out of the pile of clothes and get it pulled into place.

By then I could feel my control starting to come back to me, but all that did was make me careless. I was reaching for a towel again so I could take another try at drying my hair when it happened. My bare leg brushed up against the Scepter of Storms and the invasion of the artifact trying to batter its way deeper inside of my head completely undid me.

I screamed in pain and collapsed to the floor. The pain disappeared as soon as I broke contact with the scepter, but the fear and worry was going to take a lot more than that to go away.

Jace was through the door a split second later. "What's going on?"

I tried to tell him once again that I was fine, but it would have been a lie. I couldn't even get to my feet on my own. Jace wrapped a towel around me and then picked me up, cradling me in his arms.

"We've got to get you out of there and dried off. I don't like the way you're shivering—you can't afford to get sick right now."

ENDLESS

He carried me out into the bedroom and set me down on the edge of the bed before heading back into the bathroom for more towels. My towel was too wet to fight the chill inside of me, but he just wrapped more layers around me and pulled me into his arms, rocking me back and forth.

"Whatever it is that has you worried is going to be okay. I'm going to make sure of it."

"You can't say that. You can't protect me from this—nobody can. I can feel it inside of my head. Even when I'm not touching it, it's still there, drawing me towards it."

Jace shifted me around so that I had to meet his gaze. "Are you talking about the scepter? What do you mean it's inside of your head?"

"The Lady warned me about it, but she only told me part of what was going to happen. Maybe she didn't know all of it—who knows how long it's been since one of us used it last. It's inside of my head, Jace. It's not like a magic wand or something that I can just point at the bad guys and strike them down.

"That's why it didn't work for me while we were back at Camelot. I couldn't use it until I linked with it, and that couldn't happen until I relaxed enough for it to get inside of my head. It happened while we were in the car when I was starting to fall asleep, and now it's controlling me.

"I let go of it before I went to sleep last night. I distinctly remember setting it down on the floor next to the bed. I wanted it close enough that I could grab it if Bethany came zipping down to tell us that someone was attacking the wards, but I didn't want it touching me."

"Why didn't you want it touching you, Selene?"

Jace was asking because he wanted to hear it from me, but I could tell that he already knew.

"Because I didn't want it inside my head, Jace. It wants to be used. It likes nothing better than to call lightning down from the sky and kill things—kill people. It would lay waste to everything around it if it could, but it can't access the lightning without me. I'm like some kind of massive, cosmic safety—which would be fine except for the fact that I can feel it pulling at me all of the time now. Sometimes it's quiet, sometimes it's loud, but it's always there, telling me to tap into all of the energy sitting out there waiting to be used."

"So we'll make sure that you never touch it again, Selene. We'll lock it away in a pit some-where with a ward that makes the one around Camelot look like child's play. If that doesn't work then we'll have Bethany shift it out of this plane and promise never to give it to you again."

I slowly shook my head. "It doesn't work like that, Jace. Even if what you're suggesting would get it out of my head, I still couldn't do it. If I don't use the scepter then people are going to die. My dad, Ari, Kat, you. All of the people I care most about are in the line of fire right now and if I don't stop Kyle and his allies then they'll all die—along with four or five billion other people. I can't let that happen."

"It doesn't have to be that way, Selene. The weight of this entire war doesn't have to rest on your shoulders. You can give me the scepter and I'll go out there and stop Kyle and the rest."

"It won't work, Jace, and you know it. You've got decades of experience at this kind of thing. You're hell on wheels with that ax of yours, and more than capable of killing most fae all by yourself once you're amped up. I, on the other hand, am the next best thing to useless.

"Giving you the scepter would just take me out of the fight at a time when we need everyone to be at their best. I have to wield the scepter because that's the only way I can make a difference."

Jace's arms tightened around me. "You're not useless; if that thing works like advertised, whoever isn't using it will just be along to watch the light show."

"Thanks for trying, Jace, but this is the way it's going to have to be. The Lady cautioned me against letting anyone else assume this particular burden. She made it sound like it *might* destroy me, but that it *would* destroy anyone else who tried to carry it. I'm not going to be responsible for that."

"Maybe she's wrong. We'll never know until we try…"

"No. I made a promise. It scares me to death, just like the thought of being the one who's responsible for stopping Fenrir and the rest, but I'm not going to back down now—not when there are so many people depending on me."

Jace had looked worried before, but now he looked positively anguished. "What can I do, Selene? I want to help you. This isn't a fair thing for anyone to ask you—you're not even eighteen yet."

"It's okay—I've got an old soul. I'll make it through to the other side as long as I know you'll be there waiting for me."

Neither of us spoke for several seconds, and for the first time since before he'd pulled me out of the shower I felt the overwhelming attraction that was always a part of any interaction with Jace. A few seconds before I'd been shaking because I was so cold, but now I was shaking for a different reason entirely. This had nothing to do with the cold, and everything to do with being in Jace's arms.

I was sure that my desire was plain on my face, but I was unable to force myself to look away. I looked up at him, at the perfect jawline, soulful eyes and wavy blond hair, and I was pleased to see that his lips were slightly parted and his breathing had sped up.

We sat there with me on his lap—in my underwear with nothing more than towels draped around me—for a single frozen moment, and then his face moved down towards me. I met him halfway, and the feeling of our lips meeting sent pleasant tingles of electricity humming through me.

We'd nearly died—not just once, but several times—and I could feel that the urgency building between the two of us was partly because of that, but there was so much more to it. For Jace this was—in some ways at least—a continuation of a marriage that had lasted for hundreds of years, a marriage that he still remembered the majority of—a marriage that had included a lot more than just kissing.

I couldn't even begin to understand everything that had passed between the two of us during that much time, but despite that, the sheer amount of things that happened in just the last few weeks had left me feeling like we'd already traveled an impossible distance together. Him finding me, me starting to fall for Kyle, all of the things we'd said and done since then, and all the things that had remained unsaid.

It was all building, a pressure that demanded release, and despite the fact that part of me wanted this to happen, I was too scared to let things move forward without making sure I understood what it all meant. Jace's hands were tangled up in my hair, gently pulling me into him, but I pushed against his chest with my free hand.

"Jace. We need to talk."

He shook his head. "No, we don't, Selene. If there was anything left that needed to be worked out it was resolved inside of those tunnels. You made your choice—put me ahead of the welfare of everyone else you cared about. It was the wrong choice, but that doesn't mean that I don't appreciate it. You don't have anything to apologize for."

I thought I was all cried out—that there wasn't anything left inside of me—but his words drew more tears out of me. I leaned back into him and kissed him softly as I cried tears of joy.

"That's all I needed to hear, Jace. I just needed to know that there was still a chance for us to be together. I'll use that stupid scepter for however long it takes to kill Kyle and the others, and I'll stop it from taking me over. I will find a way to come through this so that we can be together."

Our kisses got even fiercer. It was like we were trying to keep the future at bay with the heat of our need for each other. It was a dangerous game to be playing, and I knew it. I was still wearing almost nothing, and even Jace's control had limits, but I was afraid if I stopped that it would break the moment and we'd have to go back to breakfast and trying to figure out how to stop Kyle if the Lady and her court had been destroyed.

Jace pulled me tighter against him, and I could feel the hard planes of his body as though we were separated by nothing more than tissue paper rather than thick, fluffy towels. I'd never been this hyper-aware of the nerve endings running through my skin before.

The towels were softer than any clothes I'd ever worn, there was a sensual feel to them rubbing against my body as we moved against each other, and the very real possibility that they would slip at any moment and expose all of the flesh that I'd been working so hard to keep covered up earlier only added to the rush of kissing Jace.

Jace's hands were on my shoulders now, only inches from the top of one of the towels, and I knew that almost any other guy would have done something to send the towel cascading down to my lap, but he resisted the desire, moaning as I kissed him.

My hands were under his shirt now, and it was my turn to groan at the ache that was building inside of me. The angle was terrible, but I couldn't get enough of his skin. His abs were like slabs of polished marble and it was all I could do to return the favor he was showing me and resist the urge to tear his shirt off.

Jace's hands dropped down to my waist—probably to distance himself from the temptation—but I didn't make things any easier for him. I leaned in and gently nipped at his right earlobe, and I couldn't tell if the tremors were coming from him or from me anymore.

I shifted around to the other side, fully intending on biting his other ear, but a stray lock of my own hair got in the way. I reached up to move it out of the way, and my towel started to slip.

The smart thing would have been to pull back as I made a desperate grab for the quickly falling fabric, but I was overcome by recklessness. Instead of doing the smart thing, I threw myself forward, slamming my body into Jace and trapping the towel between the two of us as he fell backwards onto the bed with me on top of him.

His hands were on the bare skin of my back, and I could feel cool air caressing my legs. I could feel Jace's surprise at our current position, but that lasted only the barest fraction of a second before his mouth moved down low on my neck, and then I was beyond anything even remotely like conscious thought.

He traced a trail of soft kisses forward toward my collarbone, and I gasped as the sensation threatened to consume me. I pulled myself forward, arching my back slightly in order to give him better access to my neck and clavicle, but then his arms clamped down around me, pulling my face back down to him for a single long kiss before he pulled back.

"We need to stop now, Selene. Trust me when I say that I want to keep going, but that wouldn't be fair to either of us."

"You have the self-control of a saint. I thought you were waiting before because you didn't want to let things get too far before telling me about Kyle..."

Even as the words tumbled out of my mouth I realized only an idiot would mention a brother she'd kissed just a few weeks earlier to the guy she'd just finished making out with—especially if she was still hoping to convince said guy to resume the making out—but Jace just gave me a slow, lopsided smile.

"That was part of it, but that wasn't the only reason. I wanted you to have a chance to make your own choice—and you've had that now—but there's more to it than that."

"Is it because you think I still have feelings for—"

He silenced me with a shake of his head. "Of course you have feelings for Kyle. I don't expect those to go away instantly—in fact they may never go away. Even when we were together before, you still had feelings for Kyle. The important thing is that you've picked me, and I know you're not the type of girl to go back on that kind of decision—not when you know what you're getting yourself into."

"Why then?"

Jace sighed. "I could tell you that I'm worried that you're racing into stuff precisely because you feel like you need to prove something to me—"

"That's totally not the case! I..."

I wanted to keep going, to tell him that what I was feeling right then wasn't driven by any kind of external circumstances, but I couldn't go on—not under the weight of his knowing stare.

"Okay, you might have a point—a very small one, but one all the same. That's not a reason for us to stop though—if you're going to worry about stuff like that, you'd be a lot better off worrying about the fact that I'm scared out of my mind there might not ever be another chance—we might not make it through the next twenty-four hours."

"Actually, that was going to be my second point. I could come up with at least another half dozen reasons for us to wait, but the truth is it all comes down to the fact that doing this right now would be wrong. After all of this is over and the world goes back to whatever passes as normal for people like us, I'm going to ask you to marry me. Sex can wait until then."

It hadn't escaped my notice that he'd just proposed—sort of. I wanted to yell 'yes' and tear his clothes off, but he wasn't wrong to be worried that I was rushing into something that I probably wouldn't have done under other circumstances.

That was a fear that went both ways though. I didn't want to make a big deal out of his stated intentions, not when it was possible that his feelings would change after we defeated Kyle and the rest. In the end, I just tried for the truth.

"So you want to marry me, and I want to marry you. There's no reason to wait, Jace. What difference are a marriage certificate and vows said in front of a clergyman going to make? I'm not going to be any less committed to you six months from now, and I don't want to wait and miss this chance. Despite the brave front you're trying to put on, we both know that the odds against both of us making it through this war alive and sane are pretty steep."

Jace leaned forward and kissed the bottom of my neck again, and I felt my eyes start to roll back into my head. I thought for a second that I'd convinced him, but then he pulled back and brushed a lock of hair out of my eyes.

"That's pretty amazing, right?"

"You don't need to ask that—it's obvious it's mind-blowing. All you have to do is pay attention to the fact that I forget to breathe every time you do it to me."

"Yeah, I'll be honest, I kind of like the way you do that. Your heart skips beats too, sometimes."

I pulled one hand away from my towel for just long enough to try to shove him back down onto the bed, but it was like pushing against a tree.

"How much of the intensity you feel is because you're being kissed by me, and how much of it is because we're skirting around the edges of things that we shouldn't be doing?"

I opened my mouth to tell him that it was all him, and then realized that I couldn't answer truth-fully—not without admitting that he might be onto something.

"So you're saying that something being 'wrong' adds extra spice to it? So the only reason that we can't do this is because we were both raised to think that we shouldn't be doing it?"

Jace gave me another smile, but this one had an edge of sadness to it. "No. I think that God has given us laws for a reason, and this would be a bad idea regardless of whatever we believe or don't believe, but I know that you don't share my feelings, so I picked an argument that you could relate to."

We sat there in silence for a while before I shrugged. "Did that ever change? Were you always the man of faith while I was agnostic?"

"No. You came to believe in a higher power of some kind. Our beliefs weren't exactly the same, but they were close enough—it just took you a long time. You've never been particularly big on faith."

I sighed and nodded. "Okay, you win. I don't want to do something now that's going to ruin things later on. Making out with you is already mind-blowing and I'd hate to spend the next hundred years wishing that every time was as amazing as the first time. You know, you could have just told me that you didn't want to go against your beliefs."

Jace leaned forward and kissed my forehead. "I considered it, but there were two problems with that idea. I'm actually surprised that you didn't see them immediately for yourself, oh crack researcher."

"Oh, yeah? Well, since I'm feeling particularly stupid today, how about you just tell me what they are?"

"The easiest one is the fact that you're incredibly persistent. You would have meant to back off, but the simple fact that you don't share my beliefs would have meant that part of you would have continued pushing at the edges of what I was willing to do."

I wanted to disagree with him, but the truth was that he was right. He'd told me before now that he wanted to wait to have sex until after marriage, but that hadn't stopped me from throwing myself at him just now. Part of me kind of felt like I should go crawl under a bridge somewhere. It was a pretty slimy thing to be doing, so I deserved for him to be condemning me, but his expression didn't look condemning at all.

"Okay, that makes sense. You're right, I haven't been very supportive of your beliefs—not like I should have been. What you did was smart because you put it in terms that make me feel like I've got skin in the game too. What was the other reason?"

"Despite all of my beliefs, you make me want to cross lines that I would never even think of crossing with anyone else, Selene. I'm ashamed to admit it—it makes me feel like some kind of fair-weather believer—but where you are concerned, I'm not as in control of myself as I should be. I guess at the end of the day, the reason I just gave you—wanting to make sure that our second and third, and thousandth time is as amazing as the first—is a bigger driver for me right now than anything else. Unlike you, I truly *know* just how happy we could be. I've already experienced just how amazing we can be together and I don't want to do anything to jeopardize that."

Chapter 19

Paradise would have been staying there behind our wards with Jace forever. Even better would have been if I'd been able to just lie back down on the bed and let him hold me until the sun eventually flickered out.

Reality didn't permit anything of the sort. After a few minutes in each other's arms, I decided that I'd better go get dressed—we were playing with fire, and despite the conversation we'd just had, I wanted him to uncover me just as badly as he wanted to do it.

We were partway through breakfast when I felt a second alien presence inside my mind—this time it was the Lady. I wasn't sure whether I was more relieved that she was still alive and able to communicate, or more angry that she'd left the three of us cooling our heels for so long.

She didn't give me a chance to express either emotion to her though, so it didn't end up mattering. She brought me up to speed in quick bursts of information that scooted right up to the edge of what I was capable of absorbing.

The fighting at Camelot had continued on for hours, and even now it was flaring up from time to time as one or more of the fallen fae managed to reassemble their forms and both sides rushed into the area—one to disembody them and the other in an attempt at giving them enough cover to make a run for it.

Neither side seemed to want to go head-to-head again right now. The carnage that we'd experienced while Byron had been bringing down the ward was apparently like nothing that had ever been experienced before in however many thousands of years the Lady had existed.

Rather than charging back in at each other like they'd done last time, both sides had spent the last few hours looking for vulnerabilities in the other's holdings all over the world. I would have expected Kyle to focus on trying to defend his holdings, that or on attacking the Seelie Court's few remaining active outposts, but he'd instead opted to resume wholesale terrorist attacks on major cities around the world.

When I heard that, I was suddenly very glad that neither of us had turned on the television or the radio yet. It made a sick kind of sense really. He knew that we cared about all of the innocent people he was hurting, so he was using them against us. We couldn't possibly be strong enough everywhere to make sure that he couldn't hurt people, and trying to stop his efforts would just spread us out and make us vulnerable to being ambushed by his forces.

We'd lost a couple of Awakened before the Lady finally pulled back and let him have his way with all of the juicy civilian targets out there. In hindsight, I could see that it was the right decision, but I wasn't sure I could have done it.

The Lady told me that in the last six hours there had been unexplained explosions in DC, New York, Boston, Chicago, Salt Lake City, and LA. That would have been bad enough all by itself, but I got the feeling that her list wasn't comprehensive.

I knew enough by now to know that there had been attacks in other countries. Kyle thought on a global level, and having rival countries blaming each other for all of the damage and destruction would only increase the chaos and further his aims.

It went without saying that without a strong force of Awakened and Seelie Court fae out there in the world actively trying to defend all of those civilians, there wouldn't be anything to stop Kyle from killing as many people as he wanted to kill. Only it turned out that Kyle wanted people around to rule over after all of the fighting was done. The Lady had called his bluff and he'd backed down.

People were still dying—some from additional attacks, some from secondary effects that had been caused by the initial attacks—but the rate of terrorist incidents had dropped off steeply over the last hour before she'd called me. The reduction in incidents was at least partially because the Lady had kill teams out—one or two Awakened backed by a score or more of the finest Seelie warriors she could spare—looking for the Awakened who were behind the attacks.

They'd managed to kill six Awakened so far at the price of an equal number of disembodiments on our side, but I didn't need her to tell me that those losses wouldn't have been enough to stop Kyle if he'd really wanted to step up the attacks.

The Lady ordered me to get Jace and Bethany headed to Salt Lake City again, and then left my mind. I tried to get hold of her again, but it was no use.

Jace and I finished eating, and then I headed upstairs to take a turn watching out for bad guys while Bethany zipped outside to a nearby field of wildflowers. Twenty minutes later, Jace finished double-checking the supplies he wanted to bring along with us, and once he'd hauled everything up to his Viper the three of us left his house, the Scepter of Storms wrapped in a towel and clenched tightly in my right hand.

With the top up and the windows closed, there wasn't anything to stop Bethany from getting some sleep, and she dropped off within minutes of the house disappearing behind us. That left Jace and me free to talk about anything we wanted, but the conversation predictably ended up focusing on the war.

I'd told him only the bare essentials back at the house—just that we were supposed to meet the Lady's people at Intravil's club again. It only took a few minutes to relay everything I knew, and that was even with me splitting my attention between talking and monitoring our surroundings for the signatures of other Awakened.

I gave him a little while to digest everything I'd told him, playing with the radio until it became too depressing, and then turned it off and started asking him what it all meant.

"I'm not sure, Selene. It's like the Lady said—there's never been an all-out war like this before. Even if she's wrong—or lying—and this isn't the first time that both courts have gone at each other with the gloves completely off, it happened so long ago that none of the journals I've been able to get my hands on have even hinted at the conflict."

"So how does it normally work—for the smaller fights that you do know about?"

"With the fae, it's usually about the memories that they can absorb by disembodying each other. The real powers—the Lady, Fenrir, the Dragon, and the Minotaur—all are pretty careful not to cross paths. Their biggest value has historically been as a deterrent, so none of them have been especially eager to find out who's really the toughest."

"Because once it was established that they would lose against that particular fae they would always have to run away. Why did the Lady agree to come fight Fenrir when he had Kyle and me bottled up inside of Kyle's wards? That doesn't sound like the kind of thing she's usually known for."

"You're not wrong. I had Bethany and Kregor approach her from the angle of this being the best chance she was ever going to get to feel Fenrir out. With Kat and I backing her up—and the possibility of an assist from you—she really wasn't at very much risk of losing.

"I still didn't expect her to come though because once the other side knows that she's left home and therefore can't just step through any of the Seelie Court's many portals, the Unseelie court tends to start acting up. Even the weaker players tend to get more adventurous when they know that she can't materialize more or less on top of them and ruin their fun."

That gelled with what I remembered from the encounter between her and Fenrir. I turned the information over inside of my head for a minute or two.

"So what you're saying is that we have no idea why she would have done that?"

"Not exactly. I can't tell you for sure, but the obvious answer is that she wanted a shot at

Fenrir. It could have been that she figured things would be quiet for long enough for her to disembody him once or twice and steal some of the power he's spent so long accumulating. It's also possible that she cared less about increasing her own power and just wanted to try to bring Fenrir down enough that some of her lieutenants would have a chance against him."

"Wait, that sounds important. What do you mean by that?"

"It's harder to say for sure who's the next most powerful Seelie fae after the Lady. The Seelie don't tend to get monstrously big like the Unseelie do. The Unseelie probably have at least a rough idea of the relative ranking of most of the top-tier warriors on the other side, but I'm not really on speaking terms with any of them, and the Seelie tend to be pretty quiet about stuff like that. Kregor can tell you chapter and verse about who's who among the weaker Seelie fae, but that's not the kind of thing that the Lady or her closest advisors tend to share with the newer arrivals in her court.

"So as a result, none of us Awakened really know how close any of the Lady's lieutenants are to being able to step into her shoes, but the smart money says that there has to be at least one or two of them who are approaching her level of power. If that's true, then Fenrir being knocked down a few pegs could possibly make it so that one or two of the Lady's strongest warriors could have had a chance at taking him down without her help."

"Which would mean that they could farm him for energy and gain even more strength."

Jace nodded as he shifted lanes to put more space between us and a pair of burnt-out cars that had been pushed off to the side of the road.

"Yeah, in theory. Of course, Fenrir showed up at Camelot looking just as mean and tough as ever, so if that was what the Lady was hoping for it sounds like she failed. Of course, it's possible that she killed him once or twice and then called for help, but once she was gone whoever she brought in wasn't able to pin him down the next time he re-manifested.

"Actually, that's less likely given that he's Unseelie and doesn't have any wings. On second thought, he probably just disembodied one or both of them."

My head was spinning again. "So what happens in circumstances like that? You've got one or more powerful fae who've been disembodied, and someone else has absorbed some of their power..."

"There are a lot of different variables, but it always has the chance of turning into a hotspot because it means that whoever disembodied them knows roughly where they will materialize when they finish reassembling themselves. If there is enough power at stake and the fae who survived the fight thinks that they have a chance of winning the next one, they will often stay around and try to do it again. Sometimes they are successful, sometimes they lose the next fight, and sometimes the loser of the first fight manages to get away."

I rubbed my temples with my free hand—the hand that wasn't holding onto the Scepter of Storms. "I'm beginning to see what you mean about lots of variables."

Jace chuckled, which made me smile despite the gravity of our situation. "We're just getting started. Sometimes the winner of the first fight isn't sure they can win the second one so they run back to their friends and bring back reinforcements. Sometimes the group gets back in time and kills the first fae, but other times they walk into a gigantic trap because the disembodied fae has powerful friends who knew where he was headed and got worried when he was gone for so long."

I nodded, finally beginning to see the ramifications of a fae being disembodied. "So I'll bet that occasionally fae from one side let themselves be disembodied so that they can set a trap for a much bigger group."

"Yep. That doesn't happen very often though because nobody can guarantee that the winner from the first fight will go back for reinforcements. Honestly, what happens more often is that someone really powerful will let themselves be beaten as a way of luring a big group out of position to defend some asset. If the ploy works, then it's worth the cost of losing a little bit of power."

"And if it doesn't?"

"If it doesn't, then the fae who was beaten the first time usually just farms the original victor until either they get most of their lost power back or someone even more dangerous comes along. That can take a long time though—weaker fae require a lot more time to come back from being disembodied than someone like the Lady does."

"So there's a time element to everything as well. That must mean that when the stakes are really high everyone has to act quickly or they miss out on the chance to go after the fae who's just been disembodied."

"Yeah. There have been some really terrible decisions made over the years because one side or the other wanted to farm someone powerful who'd either had a bad string of luck or was purposefully trying to lure the other side into making a mistake."

"So what you're telling me is that it's all a gigantic game of chess, and each time somebody falls there are ripples that flow through the entire fae community as everyone tries to adjust to wring the most advantage they can out of the situation without getting themselves killed in the process."

"Yeah. It's a lot bloodier than chess, but that's about how it works. The opening fights in this particular war probably have smoke pouring out of the Lady's ears. I'm with you in wishing that she'd gotten back to us sooner, but I'm not necessarily surprised. Both sides have to be jockeying for position, and given that our side is heavily outnumbered, things are even worse than normal."

"About that. Given that our side is so much smaller than the other guys, what's to stop them from just bringing the Seelie fae down one by one, and then setting up camp in the location where they were killed with two or three times as many people and making sure that they always get disembodied instantly as soon as they manifest a new form?"

"Nothing really. It's been tried a million times, but our side tends to have wings, which means that we're a lot faster than the Unseelie Court. Usually when something like that happens the Lady's warriors just take to the air and put themselves out of reach of the big hitters. It's tough still. When a fae re-manifests they don't come back in exactly the same place as where they were disembodied, but there isn't that much variation to where they reappear, and the Unseelie fae are still plenty fast on the ground."

I could practically feel my mind stretching, but it wasn't the unpleasant sensation I'd generally associated with school. This was all stuff that I'd presumably mastered at some point in the past, which meant that I didn't have to doubt my ability to learn it, but it was more than that. This was stuff that could very well keep me alive. It was astonishing how much motivation that provided.

"So if having wings is such an advantage for us, how come the other side doesn't keep their wings as they get bigger? If they were as fast as us, there wouldn't be anything stopping them from farming the Seelie warriors until they managed to destroy them."

"Yeah, more variables. Wings are useful in a certain set of circumstances, but there are reasons to pick a completely earthbound form like Fenrir has done. It takes a lot more power to increase your strength without a corresponding increase in weight. The same thing goes for making your body more resistant to damage. It can still be done, but there is a noticeable difference between the raw combat potential if you stack up a Seelie warrior and an Unseelie warrior both of whom have absorbed the same amount of power."

I nodded. "So it's all about what you're aiming for. The Unseelie Court is a much more brutal place with a lot more infighting, so they go the route that will give them the best chance of surviving. The Lady, on the other hand, favors a quicker, more mobile army, so her people all keep their wings."

"Yeah. The Seelie Court has its own share of heated disagreements, and it's not unknown for things to come to blows from time to time, but at least there the fae don't have to worry about someone from their own court disembodying them again and again in order to absorb their power. Really, when you get right down to it, the Unseelie Court is more like a prison than anything else. Everyone at the bottom of the pyramid has to ally themselves with someone bigger or they have no chance of surviving.

"It goes like that all the way to the top where you have Fenrir, the Minotaur, and the Dragon, all of whom are desperately looking for some kind of advantage against the other two. When you get right down to it, it's always been more like a four-way war than two sides really going at each other with everything they have. That's probably the most amazing thing Kyle has managed to accomplish in the last few weeks. We've all been worried about the possibility that the Unseelie Court would rally behind a single figure, but I'm not sure any of us really believed it.

"It's a bad precedent. We can't just win this war by the skin of our teeth. We need to beat the other side convincingly. We need to disembody them enough times that even Fenrir and the other two are weaker than most of the Lady's lieutenants or they'll just come back after us again in a decade or two. Once they get used to working together, all the mobility and discipline in the world won't be enough to offset their superior numbers."

Chapter 20

We made it to Salt Lake City without any problems, but there were a couple of times that I felt solitary signatures out there a few dozen miles away from us. Normally, where you sensed one Awakened there was bound to be more, but it seemed like all of the pantheons we'd come up against on our first trip had relocated—probably because they'd been recruited by one of the courts.

The only Awakened left were the singletons who were either too weak to offer any kind of value to a pantheon, or who were so bad that nobody else was willing to work with them. It was very reassuring to feel the signatures I spotted move away from us for a change, but it was still a relief when we spotted the club.

It was closed—either because of the hour or because Intravil had shut it down once she knew that she was going to be leaving it unattended. The doors were all locked, and the windows were all barred, which was somewhat ironic considering that nothing short of a bank vault was going to keep someone like Fenrir out.

Then again, maybe that was the point. Locks wouldn't stop the Unseelie fae from breaking in, but it would at least make it obvious that the club—and therefore the security of the portal—had been compromised.

We pulled up to the underground parking garage and Jace pressed the call button while Bethany anxiously danced from side to side on my shoulder.

A couple of seconds later, a voice asked us our names and then told us to look into the cameras that were mounted prominently all around the entrance to the garage. We all smiled prettily for whoever was watching us, and then the heavy steel doors opened and we were allowed inside.

Apparently looking like a known ally to the Seelie Court was enough to get us inside the parking facility, but it didn't buy us any more than that. A group of six Seelie warriors were waiting for us as we got out of the Viper, but once they'd had a chance to look us over, one of them asked if we needed any help with packing our things into the club.

Bethany brought me up to speed while I trailed along behind everyone else, the scepter in one hand and a bag containing changes of clothes and toiletries in the other.

"The cameras can be fooled. They don't put much stock in them. Really they were just buying time for the security group to get down here. They let us in because they figured they could handle us if we turned out to be someone other than who we said we were."

"I'm not sure if that's reassuring or terrifying."

Bethany gave me a big smile. "I think that's kind of the point. Welcome to the professional paranoia inherent to fighting people who can make themselves look like anyone they want."

Intravil was waiting for us inside of her private suite. She looked me over, confirming that I still had the scepter, and then ushered us through the portal without any of the pleasantries I'd learned to expect from seventeen years of dealing with humans.

I tried to thank her for saving my life back outside of Camelot the day before, but she cut me off with a curt gesture and I could feel Bethany tugging on my ear as though to tell me not to go there. It was frustrating—I wanted to acknowledge that she'd sacrificed some of her hard-won power on my behalf, but now apparently wasn't the time.

Once we were on the other side of the portal, we found Dad, Ari, and Sandra waiting for us. Dad swept me up into a hug that made my ribs creak, and then let me go so that I could give Ari a hug.

"I'm so glad that you're okay. Nobody is telling us anything. I don't know what I was expecting, but it wasn't this. We've been basically abandoned here. They left us with a pile of food that all had dates on it and told us not to eat anything after it had been here more than five days. Since then we're lucky if someone checks in with us once a day. How are Kat and Byron? They aren't—"

I shook my head quickly. "They're both okay—at least they were when we last saw them. We got separated, but they made it inside the wards that surround Camelot before we got chased away, so there's every reason to believe that they're still fine."

"What about the wards? Did Byron manage to bring them down?"

I'd spent almost my entire life with Ari. For a brief time after my memories had crystalized, I'd probably remembered a time before she'd been born, but that had been lost somewhere during the fight with Mephistoles and Sandra. Now I couldn't remember a time when Ari hadn't been around. I'd seen her in almost every circumstance and I couldn't remember a time when she'd been so subdued.

"Yes. Byron managed to bring down the outer ward, but things didn't exactly go as expected. We had a couple of minutes where our side got to siphon off as much energy as they could absorb, but then something like a third of the

Unseelie Court showed up and started leeching off the energy feed."

Sandra frowned. "So we didn't actually come out at all ahead?"

Jace shrugged. "It's hard to say for sure. The Lady and some of her most powerful warriors got some time to themselves, and they're extremely powerful, so they absorbed quite a bit of energy while that was going on.

"Once the bad guys showed up the pendulum probably swung the other way—simply because there were so many of them, but with all of that power discharging into every fae within a hundred feet, they were all in sort of a state of shock. Kat, Selene and I took advantage of that to disembody a bunch of them. We were making progress reversing any gains they might have gotten, but then Kyle's Awakened buddies showed up."

I was glad that Jace was so willing to take point on most of the interactions with Sandra. I knew it wasn't fair to dislike her—she might have some of the same tendencies and flaws as the version that had killed me at the end of my last incarnation, but she wasn't that same person any more than she was the same person who'd stabbed my dad when ordered to by Mephistoles.

My dad seemed to have forgiven her—I should be able to do the same, but I was having a harder time doing that than I'd expected. I was starting to see why it was so rare for someone to be recruited into another pantheon after being completely drained of memories—not that it was common for total memory loss to happen in the first place. It took extremely strong emotions to achieve that, emotions so strong that you could make the case that in order to feel them you had to be—temporarily at least—a little insane.

I forced a smile on my face instead of the scowl that wanted to hang out there and picked up the thread of the conversation.

"By that time, Kat, Jace and I were all pretty much depleted. We got cut off from the Lady and all of her people, so we retreated back into the tunnels inside of the mountain and Kat collapsed the entrance.

"We were hoping to get inside the second ward before anyone made it inside there with us, but Byron only managed to get the wards keyed to Kat before Fenrir jumped us. Jace, Bethany and I were lucky to make it out alive.

"From there we headed home and spent a few hours inside the wards in the basement recuperating and catching up on our sleep. At that point, the Lady got hold of me and ordered us to Salt Lake, presumably so that we could join back up with everyone."

Dad shook his head. "Judging by what we've seen so far, there isn't anyone here to join up with."

Intravil stepped through the portal just in time to catch the very end of what Dad had just said.

"That is not correct. Up until recently, there hasn't been anyone significant here to join up with, but that is changing as we speak. The Lady's forces have been harassing Kyle's people—specifically the Awakened he has managed to recruit. In the hours since you last talked with her, we've managed to kill another eight Awakened at the price of ten disembodiments."

I interrupted her before she could continue. "Wait, that's a terrible loss ratio. Why are you continuing to attack like that when you're losing more people than you're taking out? I mean, I know that not all of the fae who were disembodied are going to get stuck somewhere, surrounded and unable to escape, but surely some of them are…"

Intravil gave me a look that seemed to say that I was being insensitive. "Things are proceeding according to plan and the Lady has assured me that our losses so far—even if the disembodied prove unable to escape—are still well within tolerances. The most recent operations have been carefully planned so that our people would be able to rendezvous at the few remaining operational portals. They are arriving as we speak. It's past time to move if we're to remain on schedule."

The old me—the one who thought she was just another normal teenage girl—would have just shut up and obeyed. Even the newer me who'd been in five or six real fights in the last four weeks probably wouldn't have gotten in Intravil's face under normal circumstances, but I could feel a pressure building inside me, a pressure that had been growing so gradually that I hadn't noticed it, a pressure that I was only then realizing came from the weapon in my right hand.

"No. I'm through being herded around without so much as a please or thank you. You let us in on the plan—right now—or you can call up the Lady by way of the blood oath and tell her that she needs someone else to bear the scepter."

Intravil looked like she was more than ready to squash me like the insect she thought I was, but the threat was far less effective when delivered by someone who seemed to be moving in slow motion. I hadn't even realized that I'd amped myself, but I had.

Maybe I wasn't a match for Intravil all by myself, but I wasn't all by myself right now. I had a powerful artifact at my side, one that was begging to be used and which seemed to be whispering to me that we were more than capable of taking *any* fae down.

Before that moment, I hadn't been sure that there was anything capable of forcing me to touch the scepter with my bare skin again, but my family being in danger did the trick. I slid the towel out of the way and touched the cool metal of the artifact with one finger.

I still hadn't taken any visible action that could be construed as being threatening, but the scepter had already assumed control of my mental arms and was busy gathering up a dense cloud of shimmering blue sparks around me. I wasn't just a defenseless human anymore. I was more than that—more even than the Awakened I'd spent the last few weeks trying to become.

We stared at each other for several seconds before Intravil finally blinked. "The Lady's plan hinges around the destruction of as many of the enemy Awakened as possible. If they are dead then they can't serve as a source of replacement power for the dark court."

"Wait—you don't mean just in the normal way, do you? You're not just talking about the absorption that happens during fights. You're talking about Fenrir and the others chaining them up somewhere and forcing them to work effects until their memories are completely spent."

Intravil nodded. "It is a possibility. The Awakened who've joined themselves to the dark court have done so because they believe that Kyle will be able to play the various factions inside the court against each other. Barring that, they believe that collectively they are a strong enough force the Unseelie fae won't dare turn on any one of them. As the war progresses and they are killed off, there will come a point where that will no longer be the case."

"So you're just going to speed that process along? Doesn't that seem counterproductive?"

"Every Awakened who dies now is one less Awakened who will have the chance to spend the next several days or weeks funneling power into the dark court with their every action. At this point, we have very few good options available to us. This is one of the least bad ones."

I half expected Jace to jump in. I could see the wheels turning inside of his head. My dad probably didn't understand a third of what was being said, but he looked like he wanted to say something. I wasn't about to let him make himself a target of Intravil's anger.

I would have spoken up for no other reason, but the truth was that what I said next needed to be said.

"This isn't just some kind of spur-of-the-moment decision, is it? You guys have been planning something like this for a long time. You knew if things got really nasty between you and the Unseelie Court that one of the first things you would do would be to put down as many Awakened as you could."

"Just be glad that you didn't throw your lot in with Kyle, and that the light court—at least while it is ruled by the Lady—is above such actions."

"Don't hold back, Intravil. Go ahead and let the other shoe drop. I can tell there's something else that you've been holding back from me."

She gave me a condescending nod. "There is a secondary reason to eliminate the Awakened—even at unfavorable rates of exchange—at this point. We're about to head back to Camelot and have Byron begin bringing down the second ward."

"That's crazy! We'll just end up in the same position we were in yesterday. Kyle and his people will sense the energy being discharged and hurry over to attack."

She looked at me like I was a particularly stupid child. "That is exactly what we're counting on. The fact that the Lady created a portal so close to Camelot means that we can deploy our surviving Awakened to the location more quickly than Kyle can move his people around. We've mousetrapped the other side.

"If they do nothing then we will absorb all of the power from the second ward and grow even stronger. If they attack, then they will do so into a storm of energy that will rival the one that we all experienced yesterday."

Jace nodded and picked up the explanation. "They'll be fighting sluggishly again, just like yesterday. The Lady is setting this up to be a fight where the side with the most Awakened will win. If we can kill Kyle and the rest—and do it quickly enough—then we'll be free to tear through the Unseelie warriors much like we did last time. Only instead of just three of us, there will be many more times that."

"Indeed. We won't benefit from the energy release of their disembodiments—at least not the initial time, but if you godlings are able to carry your end of the battle, we'll have defeated the bulk of the enemy forces, gained a tremendous amount of power from the second ward, and be able to disembody the Unseelie fae again and again as they reassemble their forms."

I finally understood, and I was stunned at the audacity of the plan. The Lady had taken what was supposed to be a long, drawn-out war and forced it into a single battle, one that we had a decent chance of winning.

"For the first time, you'll be the ones with superior numbers and because you're so much faster and more agile, it's very unlikely that any of them will be able to escape once they start rematerializing. Not given that they'll be coming back at different times. Fine, I'm impressed. Let me say goodbye to my dad, Ari, and Sandra and then Jace and I will follow you to the portal."

Intravil shook her head as four of her people stepped forward, one for each member of my pantheon.

"You misunderstand. Our advantage isn't sufficient to allow any able-bodied warriors to sit this fight out. Under normal circumstances your father, sister, and Sandra would be useless against the dark court, but these aren't normal circumstances. They will be coming with us and fighting in the battle."

Chapter 21

I'd been ready to throw down against Intravil right then and there. Maybe I wasn't the biggest, baddest Awakened out there, but I wasn't going to let her force my dad and sister into a fight that they were completely unprepared for.

The Scepter of Storms was still humming away in the back of my mind, and the field of sparks floating over us was even brighter than it had been a few moments before when I'd stared her down the first time. Things would have come to blows if not for the fact that my dad and Jace both interposed themselves in front of me, making it so that there was no way to get at her without risking them getting injured.

The two of them picked me up—one on each arm—and towed me back far enough away to be out of earshot.

"I know how you must feel, Selene, but now isn't the time to be throwing yourself at Intravil."

"Do you, Jace? Do you really? Your parents have been dead for centuries, and you and Kyle have been at each other's throats for at least the last two hundred years. She's threatening my family."

"Yes, I know exactly what you're feeling because she's also threatening the single most important person in my life. You. I know that it's hard, but you need to calm down. There is a reason she waited to tell us this until we were here in the Lady's realm. We're trapped here unless the Lady or one of the portal wardens let us leave."

He knew me better than anyone else—better even than my dad. I could see where he was going, but he kept talking, making sure that there was no doubt what we were up against.

"Just the Seelie warriors here right now outnumber us. I saw what you did with the scepter, so maybe you could beat them. Maybe you could even fight off all of the other fae and Awakened currently converging on this place so that they can head over to the portal leading into Camelot, but even if you can, so what? All that will mean is that we'll be stuck here with a very limited supply of food and water, no possible escape, and we'll have contributed to the failure of the Lady's plan and, in doing so, handed Kyle control over the entire world."

He was right to keep going. Every word he uttered made it more clear that I couldn't afford to buck orders right now, but they also awakened a white-hot fury that exceeded anything else I'd ever felt. I wanted to kill Intravil, not just disembody her—I wanted her dead. The Lady was only marginally lower on my crap list, but it had been Intravil who had lured us here where we had to choose between obedience and a slow and lingering death.

"Fine, we'll go along until all of us are back in the real world, and then I'll drop her and all of her people. Dad, Ari and Sandra can all make a break for it, and you and I will go on to Camelot and help fight off Kyle and the others."

Apparently it was my dad's turn to talk. "I'm not going anywhere, Selene. I think it's a good idea to get your sister and Sandra to safety, but from what I understand, this is quite possibly the only time in my entire life when I'll have a chance at taking down these Unseelie fae. I'm staying. Give me a weapon and point me at the bad guys."

"Dad, you don't understand. Maybe you're right—maybe you would be able to make a huge difference in the second half of the fight after Kyle and all the rest of his Awakened are dead and it's just a matter of attacking fae who are drunk off of all the power they've absorbed. The problem is going to be getting to the second half of the battle. Kyle's people aren't going to hesitate to kill you and they won't be sluggish—they won't even have to get within arm's reach of you to kill you. You're not ready for this."

Dad shrugged. "Maybe, but the way I see it, the question just boils down to whether I'm willing to send you out there into danger while I run off to somewhere safe. Maybe I'll die out there, but maybe I'll be able to save you from one of those monsters before I do. You're apparently the one with the best chance at swinging the battle in our direction and saving the world. It would almost be worth dying just so that I could say that I helped save the world. It's definitely worth it if I might have a chance to save you."

I didn't even begin to know what to say to that. My dad was wrong, but he was also an adult. I couldn't force him to do anything—at least not without risking alienating him forever, and having my dad alive but never willing to forgive me was nearly as bad as having him die.

Jace stepped forward and whispered into my ear. "He's worried about you, but he's also worried about Kat. Let him stay. I'll amp him up. It means that I won't be able to attack anyone from a distance, but if your artifact is as scary as I think it is, I won't need to. You're more than capable of that—what you really need is a couple of people who are willing to watch your back and deal with anything that gets too close for you to hit it with a bolt of lightning. Trust me when I say that Kat and I will take good care of him and your sister both."

The implication was that there weren't enough of us to also amp up Sandra as well—not if I was going to be focused on raining lightning bolts down on our enemies' heads. It was tempting to leave things there, to trust Kat and Jace to keep my dad and Ari safe and just chalk Sandra up as a loss, but I knew that wouldn't be okay. I took a deep breath and then walked back over to Intravil.

"Fine. I get the stakes that we're up against, but the only way I'm doing this is if you agree to find someone to keep an eye on Sandra. If I had my way, none of those three would be out there—they aren't ready for this kind of fight yet—but if you can find someone to amp Sandra up then Kat and Jace can take care of the other two."

Intravil shook her head. "You're in no position to be making demands."

I reached out to the Lady, seeking her mind in the darkness that surrounded me, but came away with nothing. I turned to Bethany, who was once again on my shoulder. "Can you get through to the Lady? The only way we're going to make progress fast enough to make her deadline is if she gets involved."

Bethany nodded, and a second later I felt a familiar presence inside of my mind.

You're causing problems again, I see. Intravil has been keeping me up to speed on your discussion.

So does that mean that you're in agreement with her?

ENDLESS

There was a moment of silence and then the Lady gave off the mental equivalent of a shrug. *I could be convinced either way. You both have valid points. Your family and Sandra are not prepared for what we're asking of them, but we don't have any choice but to field the biggest force we can.*

So hire a bunch of big bruisers. Intravil's club must have bouncers—pay them to come fight.

She sighed. *I'm trying very hard to avoid having this conflict spill over into the human world any more than it already has. Money is a very poor motivator. It can work in the short term, but in the long term it always fails. Once someone has money, they either want more—in which case you eventually can't meet their demands—or they decide that they have everything they need and you lose your power over them.*

If we lose that won't matter, but if we win, I'd prefer not to have our existence be common knowledge. We are vastly more powerful than any small group of humans, but we are not inde-structible. Given enough incentive and time, they would eventually find ways to exterminate us.

It was sounding like she already had her mind made up, but there didn't seem to be any point in mentioning that. Instead, I played my last card.

Look, I know you're worried about having yet another of your people operating at less than full strength, but if you don't do this then you're not going to be able to trust me—which means that you aren't going to be able to trust Jace or Kat. Heck, you may not even be able to trust Byron.

I don't take kindly to being blackmailed, Selene.

I could feel the cold in her words, could feel her stepping back, but I dove into the connection, stopping her from severing it.

So don't think of it as blackmail. I can use the scepter, and you want me to be able to focus fully on that. If you take care of my family—even the one I don't particularly like—then I'll be able to deliver lightning wherever it is most needed on the field. That could make all the difference in this fight and you know it or you wouldn't have given me the last artifact in your possession.

I had her, I could feel it, but she was quiet for so long that I almost thought I'd been wrong.

You've accessed the artifact, but you're still fighting it.

How can you know that?

I know it because I know you. If you really want to make a difference in this fight—a big enough one to justify losing the offensive abilities of three Awakened—then you're going to have to stop fighting. You'll have to stop holding the presence at arm's length and let it become a part of you.

I thought you didn't know how this worked. I didn't even bother trying to hide the venom in my thoughts. She'd lied to me, and done so in a way that meant I'd been ill prepared for the reality of using the scepter. If I hadn't managed to link when I had, Jace and I could have been killed. It would have been totally unnecessary and it would have been her fault.

Yes, I lied to you. I lied to you because it was the only way to make sure that you would be able to form the link rather than fighting it off. My question remains, Selene. Are you willing to subsume yourself in the link? If not then there is no guarantee that you'll be able to tap into the scepter deeply enough to make a difference in this fight.

The implication was that unpleasant things were going to happen if I refused her demands, but I'd gone into the conversation knowing that was the case. It was getting harder and harder to tell the good guys and the bad guys apart.

Fine. You've got your deal. I'll let the artifact completely inside of my mind and we'll all just have to hope that I can still keep enough of a grip on who I am to stop myself from killing everyone on both sides.

That won't be a problem. If you lose control of the link I'll kill you myself.

I wasn't sure if she meant that to be comforting, or threatening. Even more concerning was the fact that I was going to be stuck serving her for the next two hundred years. That prospect had been bad enough when I'd been sure that she was one of the good guys.

Chapter 22

If I'd had my choice I would have run all of the way to the portal where everyone was assembling—or at least had someone other than Intravil carrying me. I was disappointed on both counts. Once I finished my conversation with the Lady, Intravil stepped forward and wrapped one arm around my waist and launched the two of us into the air.

I knew the flight to the portal wasn't going to take long. That was a good thing considering just how uncomfortable I was around her now. It had been bad enough just when I'd been convinced she didn't think the way I did. Now that I knew she was perfectly fine with the idea of sacrificing my family, my skin practically crawled when she touched me.

Unfortunately, a short flight meant that I didn't have much time to say what needed to be said. I tapped her arm to get her attention and then waited for her to initiate contact.

ENDLESS

More demands?

No. Look, I don't particularly like you, and you don't really like me, but that just means that you had that much less of a reason to throw yourself in front of me. If it wasn't for you, I'd be dead right now.

Yes. Yes, you would.

Apparently she wasn't inclined to make this any easier for me. I was tempted to just blow off the rest of what I'd been planning on saying, but I knew that wouldn't be right. If I didn't take this opportunity I might not get another one.

I just wanted to say thank you. I know that what you did came at a cost for you. I don't think that means you like me or anything. I know you were just doing it because you figured that I was a key part of the Lady's plan, but I'm still grateful. So...thanks.

It took her such a long time to respond that I actually thought that she'd cut off our mind-to-mind link without bothering to tell me that we were done talking. It would have been incredibly rude, but I'd already established that she didn't function by the same set of rules as I did.

Just as my mind turned to other things—to the battle I was just about to be thrown into the middle of—Intravil finally responded.

I didn't expect that out of you. That couldn't have been easy to say—not after I was so willing to force your hand where your dad and sister were concerned.

I shrugged, confident that she could feel the gesture even through all of the layers of armor.

You didn't exactly make it any easier, but right is right and wrong is wrong. The right thing to do when someone pays that kind of price for you is to recognize it. I'd offer to try to make things right, to let you...tag along while I work effects, but I'm sworn to the Lady for the next two hundred years. By the time she's done with me I'm not going to remember any of this so I won't be in a position to make good on that kind of promise.

I heard undertones of what felt like humor in her response. *It's just as well—I'm long past the point of being able to spend decades following someone around in the hopes of scavenging bits of power like that.*

After a long pause she continued. *You know, you're different than I expected. I was purposefully trying to make it harder for you to thank me.*

Why would you do that?

Because the best way to test someone's character is to make it hard for them to do the right thing. Anyone will do the right thing when it's in their best interest to do so, and most will do it when it's easy. Only a few people ever do the right thing when it's difficult and against their best interest.

Does that mean I passed?

I'd responded flippantly, frustrated that Intravil was talking about right and wrong after helping to condemn my family to near certain death, but she seemed to take the question as being legitimate.

Yes, I think that you did.

We passed the rest of the flight in silence—mental and otherwise—and before I knew it we were at the freestanding mirror that led back to Camelot.

There was already a line of people, fae and Awakened, waiting in single file to go through, but apparently being the wielder of the Scepter of Storms meant that I got cutting privileges. The second time through the portal was still disorienting, but I was more prepared for it this time, and I came through close to the edge of the pond.

I stood up and immediately turned back toward the center of the pond, anxious to make sure that my dad and Ari were going to be okay, but a gentle hand on my shoulder pushed me towards dry land.

"The more people we have in the water, the more likely it is that someone will get hurt as they come through. I have people tasked with making sure that everyone makes it out of the water unharmed—you need to watch the horizon and prepare in case we have visitors."

It was hard not to respond to the Lady with something snarky after everything that had happened, but I forced a smile to my face and trudged over to the shore.

Half an hour later everyone was through and I could feel several Awakened ranging around the fringes of my normal range. I considered flaring my signature out to establish exactly how many people were out there, but we'd been given strict instructions before going through the portal.

Jace was supposed to keep his signature suppressed. Ideally I would have been doing the same, but there was no way that I could do that and be ready to repel threats with the scepter at the same time. Since I couldn't suppress my signature completely I—and all of the rest of the Awakened—were supposed to keep our signatures shrunk down as small as we could keep them.

The Lady supposedly had Seelie warriors ranging out several miles from the location of the portal so that the bad guys wouldn't be able to sense us, but based on what I could feel even with my signature shrunk down, it wasn't working. If I could sense them, then they could sense me.

It would have been nice to let my signature expand back out to its normal volume, but I didn't give into the temptation. I was under orders, and it was always possible that the signatures I was sensing weren't just moving around because they were trying to get closer—they might be running away from a flight of Seelie warriors right now. Under these circumstances, keeping them too busy to report back on what they'd learned was just as good as taking them out permanently.

ENDLESS

The fae all lined up behind the non-fae, which included my dad and Ari, both of who were wielding long spears. Sandra was standing nearby turning a narrow sword over in her hands like she was hoping that she'd remember how to use it between now and when the fighting started.

A couple of seconds later we were all in the air and the warm wind from our passage was rapidly drying our clothes. This time I was being flown around by no less than the Lady herself. I figured she was worried about losing her secret weapon to some kind of fluke attack.

It became apparent as we landed that everyone else had received a much more in-depth briefing than our pantheon had. Almost as soon as their feet touched the ground, the rest of the Awakened began blasting large sections of the mountainside away. It took me a second to realize why the Lady had ordered that particular action. She didn't want this battle to take place inside of the tunnels that Byron and the others had cut into the mountain so many decades earlier.

That was exactly the kind of fight that most suited the Unseelie fae. We needed to be close enough to absorb the energy bleed from the wards, but we also needed a nice, open space where everyone would be able to maneuver once the fighting got started.

While the other Awakened went to work opening up a giant bowl in the solid rock before us, the Lady sent Jace in one of the tunnels off to the side with instructions on how to find one of the entrances to the second ward.

I was suddenly glad that I hadn't been one of the people who'd been tasked with mapping out the tunnels while monsters like Fenrir roamed through them. Knowing how to get to one of the cross tunnels that led to the second ward was all well and good, but that didn't necessarily mean that Kat and Byron were waiting by that particular egress.

This plan could go sideways pretty soon if we couldn't get through to our friends before the bad guys started showing up. It was one more thing to worry about, and I'd been fretting over it for nearly five minutes before I realized what I was doing. I was obsessing about the stuff that I couldn't control as a way of avoiding thinking about the stuff I could control—stuff that I didn't want to be my responsibility.

I shouldn't be there freaking out about Kat and Byron—not when there was every chance that I was going to need to use the Scepter of Storms at some point in the next few minutes. I was shaking from fear as I did it, but I closed my eyes and reached out to the sea of tiny blue sparks all around me.

The sparks were denser than I'd expected them to be, but apparently my artifact had been on edge too. It had been quietly gathering up the energy we would need for when the storm started.

I thought back to when I'd killed the flying fae that had been trailing us, and tried to compare this swirling, heaving storm of electricity to the field I'd generated that time. It was more—definitely more—but it was hard to tell how much more. I was considering just leaving well enough alone for now when the Lady stepped up behind me.

"You're going to have to do better than that. You haven't gathered up nearly enough energy yet."

"How can you tell? Can you see it too?"

"The field of sparks? No, but I don't need to be able to see them. When you get fully integrated with the scepter everyone will be able to see the effects."

She turned and walked away before I could ask her what she meant, but I opened my eyes in time to see that she leveled a significant look at my dad and Ari before she left. If using the artifact had been merely a matter of tapping into my anger, I would have been good and ready after that, but it wasn't.

Bethany had been flitting around the area, taking in the activities of the Awakened who were still boring into the mountain, but now she returned and landed on my shoulder.

"Don't let her get inside of your head, Selene. You just do what you need to do—the rest of us will take care of everything else."

"I thought she was supposed to be one of the good guys."

Bethany shrugged. "She is, but she's also a general and a queen. She has to make some tough decisions. Don't worry though, nobody has ever seen her do anything really terrible—usually when she's giving someone a really bad time it all ends up being for their own good."

"Somehow that's less reassuring now that I know that she's the oldest fae. It just means that the last really nasty thing she did was so bad that nobody survived to remember it."

Conscious of the fact that I had a finite amount of time to deepen the link to the point where it needed to be, I reached out to the pulse of the world and channeled a sliver of anger to amp my time sense up.

I took a deep breath and started trying to lower the barrier between the portion of my mind where the scepter had taken up residence, and the rest of me. It was even harder than I'd expected it to be.

My artifact sensed what I was trying to do, and threw its weight up against my barrier, but all that did was trigger an involuntary reflex to strengthen the barrier.

What are you doing? That's just making things worse.

The only response I got from the presence was even stronger efforts to bring down my shield. I should have known better than to try talking to it. It either didn't understand, or it was just playing dumb and working harder to get at the core of my identity. Neither option was particularly appealing.

I sent a surge of disapproval roaring through the barrier, and for the first time the presence seemed to take notice of something other than its desire to kill or its need to fully integrate with me. It backed off—not completely, but enough that it was more like having someone leaning against the doorway to my mind rather than having someone throwing themselves against it.

I tried again to bring the wall between us down, but all I managed was to thin it down to where I got a better sense of what was waiting for me on the other side. That just scared me even more. What I'd been thinking of as a presence was really more like half a presence.

It wasn't balanced enough to be considered fully self-aware. It was more like a virus. It was all of the questionable virtues taken to the point of being vices, and it desperately needed a host in order to realize its full potential.

Bile rose in my throat at the thought of becoming the host for something so rapacious. I sat there frozen in amped-up time, seconds passing as minutes, and no matter how hard I tried I couldn't bring down that wall. If asked, I would have said that it was outside of my control, but the truth was that I couldn't bring myself to *want* the barrier to come down. Until I actually wanted that to happen, no force in the world was going to be able to manage that particular task.

Someone stepped up behind me again, and I initially thought it was the Lady. I started to bristle, and then realized that whoever was behind me was much too tall to be her.

It was Jace. "We've found them, Selene. The Lady must have had someone make contact with them while we were gone. They were waiting for us. Byron is starting the process of bringing down the second ward. We would wait and give you more of a chance to figure this out, but the advance scouts say that there's a group of Unseelie fae and Awakened on the way.

"We expected that, but not one this big. Kyle didn't take the bait. He must have realized that everything else was just smoke and mirrors. He knows that this is where the war is going to be settled."

I tried to respond, but something about my efforts to integrate with the scepter must have been more successful than I'd realized. I was strangely disconnected from my body. I could hear Jace, but it was like listening to someone underwater. I tried to disconnect and swim back up far enough to respond, but it was no good. The scepter wasn't willing to give up any of the ground it had gained.

Jace waited for a few seconds, seconds that felt like forever to me, and then leaned forward and kissed my temple.

"I'll do everything I can to keep Ari safe and Kat will do the same for your dad. No matter what happens, I don't want you to beat yourself up about any of this. Us winning or losing shouldn't be your sole burden to carry."

Jace slipped away while I was still trying to respond, and then I realized that he'd left because of the yelling. It was everywhere, the chaotic screams of people who'd thought they were ready for what was coming, but who'd never realized just how badly they were outnumbered.

My eyes snapped open, and I thought for a second that I'd regained a measure of control, but that wasn't the case. The scepter had just finally realized what was going on and it didn't want to fight blind.

The first of the energy arcs from the ward started discharging into the fae gathered around me as I finally located the opposing force. Kyle had learned from the last battle. He'd somehow convinced everyone to stay together and the Awakened were in the front of the host.

The scepter was demanding that I allow it to begin hurling lightning bolts. It didn't care where or at whom—its desire was for destruction in all its forms. For a second I couldn't remember why it was important that I confined the destruction just to the approaching figures, but then it came back to me. The closer figures weren't just targets, those were my friends and family.

I reached out with invisible hands and connected the sky above us with one of the figures in the center of the approaching line. The bolt of lightning that ripped out of the sky was a cascade of tiny blue sparks that merged into a single brilliant river. It left a jagged afterimage on my physical eyes, but that didn't matter; I could still distinguish friend from foe.

I expected the bolt of lightning to vaporize the Awakened that I'd targeted. It was at least as powerful as the ones that I'd used to disembody the Unseelie fae, but as robust as even a weak fae was, that was nothing compared to someone who was able to wield the stuff of miracles.

My attack drove its target to their knees, but whoever it was managed to erect a barrier effect at the last second that was up to the task of deflecting the worst of the energies away into the ground. I needed more energy.

The fae and Awakened both were moving at impossible speeds, but I put that out of my mind and reached for the energy in the sky once again. This time I didn't settle for a brief, glancing connection. I sank my elbow deep into the firmament and then closed my fist around the same Awakened I'd hit once already.

This time the bolt of energy lit up the landscape with a flash that was easily as bright as the sun. I blinked away the spots in front of my eyes, but that wasn't necessary—my link with the scepter had shown me a man-shaped group of sparks shattered into a million fragments, all of which disappeared before they finished clearing the blast site.

ENDLESS

I'd succeeded. The bad guys were down one demigod, but the energies that the scepter had spent the last hour assembling were largely depleted after just two strikes. I desperately tried to scoop additional sparks into the fading maelstrom in the sky, but for every spark that went bobbing towards the pool of energy I was trying to replenish, it seemed as though three more swirled away from my hands.

My efforts weren't going to be enough. They weren't working fast enough, not given how fast that group was moving towards us. I needed more, and for the first time, I really wanted the wall down.

This was about more than just me. I could already see the first of the long-range attacks starting to flicker out from Awakened on both sides. Something had to change—right now—or every single person I cared about was going to die.

The barrier was still there, separating me from the scepter's presence inside of my mind, but this time I was the one that crashed into it. It came down like it had been crafted out of nothing more than tissue paper, as though it had never been there in the first place.

The scepter's presence clicked into place inside of my mind and suddenly I wasn't just me anymore. I'd been hoping that combining with the artifact would be something like putting on armor. I hadn't been that far off. I could feel the presence layered over what I'd come to think of as me, but there was more to it than that.

Tendrils of that armor—of that alien presence—had burrowed deep into my psyche. It was like putting on a set of plate armor and then being trapped inside of it as it grew roots, roots that extended all of the way from the front plate to the back plate.

The roots had forced themselves into my flesh and I had no idea whether it would be possible to cut them free at a later date, but that wasn't as important as the fact that my mental arms had expanded more than ten-fold.

Now when I scooped sparks into the reservoir of energy I was trying to maintain in the sky, they all went exactly where I wanted them to go. Even more important, my mental arms moved with the speed of thought and reached further than my natural eyes were capable of seeing.

I was still moving at more than four times normal speed, and I spent nearly eight whole seconds scooping sparks from everywhere I could reach. There was no way to deplete the world around me—I could see new sparks rushing in to fill the absence I was creating—but the results were still astonishing.

I watched with my physical eyes as the boiling, expanding sea of energy was mirrored by black storm clouds that stretched on for dozens of miles in every direction. I finally understood what it was that the Lady had been looking for. This was the physical manifestation of someone who was fully linked with the scepter.

With one hand I continued to amass greater amounts of energy, but the other set about using what I'd already gathered. Lightning bolts started splitting the sky, vast blue flashes that each lasted for what felt like a full second to me.

Each time I launched another attack, one of the enemy Awakened died. There were more of them than I'd realized—far more than the Lady had been expecting—but I wasn't the only one killing them now. The other Awakened who'd chosen to ally themselves with the Seelie Court had joined in the fight for real now, and enemy Awakened were dropping in pairs.

A tiny corner of my mind was shocked that I was wielding as much power as more than two score Awakened, that it took all of them to keep up with the rate I was destroying our enemies, but mostly I was just reveling in the sensation of lightning racing along my mental limbs.

The scepter still couldn't talk—linking with me had changed it in ways that I still didn't understand, but it hadn't gained the power of speech yet. Then again, it didn't need it. I could feel its enjoyment, and the emotion screamed that this was what we'd been made to do.

It was getting harder to find the enemy Awakened. We'd picked off most of the ones in the vanguard and the others were mixed in with the dark mass of Unseelie fae headed towards us. That was concerning to the Awakened part of me, but the artifact—the part that was more and more in control of what was happening—was less concerned about that. It was just happy to kill our enemies. Awakened, fae, humans, it didn't matter, they all died the same.

I picked out a tall, horned figure and reached more deeply into the energy above me. I didn't just brush against the Minotaur with one hand. I grabbed hold of him and exulted in the white-hot charge that connected the sky and ground.

The charges I'd used to kill the Awakened had been nearly an order of magnitude bigger than what I'd used to kill the flying fae, but this was nearly another order of magnitude bigger than that. The arc of blue power that struck the Minotaur was nearly as big around as he was, but it didn't vaporize him like I'd been expecting it to.

It drove him to the ground and left smoke rising from his fur in irregular patches, but that wasn't good enough—not for the artifact, and not for me. I was still raining lightning down on him with my left hand, but I shoved that elbow even deeper into the maelstrom and then sent the other one up to join it.

With both hands wrapped around the Minotaur, the point of impact where the two bolts hit him was nothing less than blinding. I'd closed my eyes in an effort to protect them, but the brilliance of the river of sparks was so intense that it was too much even for my second sight. I turned my head away for several seconds and then let go of him and examined what was left of one of the three most powerful Unseelie fae in existence.

I still hadn't managed to vaporize his body, but what was left was definitely dead—or at least as close to dead as he was going to get without a few hundred more disembodiments. It was a success—if you could call draining the pool of energy above me almost empty to kill a single enemy a success.

It begged the question of how we'd ever managed to kill any of the top-tier fae, but all I could figure was that electricity was kind of a blunt force. It couldn't reach in, carving a tiny path to the vital organs. It had to blast the target's entire body and overwhelm their electrical resistance before it could destroy organs and kill.

All of that flickered through my mind as I reached for more power, pulling it in from more than a hundred miles away in bolts of lightning that flickered between the clouds. I knew that I needed to get back on the offensive, but I was still having a hard time picking out the Awakened from the mass of fae. Even worse, the approaching host had gotten close enough while I'd been frying the Minotaur that they were now enveloped inside of the energy bleeding off of the wards.

I'd been hoping to get another round of lightning bolts off, but it wasn't going to happen, not without risking taking out people from my own side. There was nothing to do but enter the battle and fight the bad guys hand-to-hand. Something made me drag my feet though.

My ability to destroy the approaching Awakened was the thing that was supposed to swing the battle in our favor. Now that I couldn't do that anymore, there wasn't any guarantee we could win. I needed another option, a better way to kill than just wading in and slamming people in the head with the scepter.

As I stood there, desperately looking for a course of action that would save my dad and Ari, something changed in the sky above me. The maelstrom of sparks had become a whirlpool, and the circular motion was pulling in power independent of anything I was doing.

Someone broke through the slowly moving line of Seelie warriors in front of me, and just the fact that they took a swipe at one of the armored figures told me everything I needed to know. Jace and Kat were both engaged with opponents of their own.

I started forward at a run, fully intending on crushing the life from his body before he could make it to Ari or my dad. I was still a dozen yards away from him when a bolt of lightning shot down and wrapped itself around the head of my scepter before racing off and blowing the approaching Awakened into nothing more than smoke and vapor.

It wasn't something that I'd consciously done. Apparently, the scepter had gotten to the point where I just needed to classify someone as a threat in order for it to take them out on its own.

The discharge of energy out of the firmament hadn't stopped. To my second sight it looked like the sky had turned into a terrible blue tornado that touched down in one spot and one spot only. The ball of power surrounding my weapon had grown in size and intensity both. I kept expecting it to electrocute me, but as scary as that was, it was nothing compared to the idea that the scepter had assumed such control over our ability.

I should have been cowering on the ground, desperately trying to shut it all down, but instead I sprinted forward, fighting to get out into a more target-rich environment. The Seelie warriors closest to me had formed a shining wall of flesh and armor in an attempt to keep me safe while I rained destruction down on our enemies, but we were way beyond that now.

They'd closed ranks, plugging the hole that had been left by the Awakened I'd just killed, so I simply threw myself into the air, sailing over their heads with my weapon raised above me.

I seemed to hang there in the air motionless for several long seconds. It was beyond any time amp I'd ever experienced. This was something else, something that came from the scepter, but that didn't matter. All that mattered was the fact that I had plenty of time to look around and pick out enemies.

I hit the ground in a flurry of light and heat as bolts of electricity shot out and skewered half a dozen Unseelie fae and an Awakened who'd been just about to shove a sword into the Lady's back.

I'd traveled so far from the girl I'd been just a few months ago. Learning to burn my memories and amp my body in ways that I never would have believed possible had been exhilarating. I'd felt superhuman dozens of times before this, but this was the first time that I'd ever felt truly godlike.

I tore through the three closest Unseelie fae with three quick strokes of my weapon while it electrocuted a dozen more. I moved forward out of necessity. I'd cleared an area around me more than two dozen yards in diameter. Jace, Ari, Dad and Kat all hurried along after me, and various Seelie warriors were still moving drunkenly in my vicinity, but none of the enemy figures I'd been able to identify so far still lived.

The battle was as good as ours. The energy from the ward was hitting a crescendo, a buzzing, tingling storm that appeared to rival the destructive bolts coming from the scepter. All of the fae were the next best thing to incapacitated from the effort of harnessing the power being released into the air, and Kyle's Awakened were now dropping like flies.

ENDLESS

It was just a matter of time. I would easily carve my way through anyone who tried to stand against me. That was good, that was what I'd started the battle wanting, but somewhere along the way that had changed.

I wanted an opponent who was worthy of me, one who had the ability to give me a run for my money. It was impossible—had been ever since the artifact in my hand had been created—but that didn't stop it from desiring exactly that.

The forest of bodies before me shifted and then I saw what I was looking for. The big, wingless dragon that had given the Lady so much trouble during the last fight shot towards me on an even dozen legs. I threw myself to the side, surprised that it was moving so quickly despite the energy being released from the ward.

Even as I got out of the way, my weapon discharged a single, continuous bolt of electricity into my enemy. The smell of burning flesh assaulted my nose as I reversed direction and slammed the scepter into the Dragon's side, shattering one of the attachment points for its many legs.

The crunch of broken bones was immensely satisfying, but I knew that the real damage was being done by the lightning bolt. That was an attack that would have already killed a lesser opponent several times over, but the Dragon simply roared in pain and whipped its tail toward me. It wasn't going to go down for anything less than what I'd done to the Minotaur.

I leaped over the tail as it whipped by me in slow motion, and destroyed another leg in the harsh, flickering light of the energy sizzling from my weapon. I'd never enjoyed a battle so much.

Under normal circumstances I never would have survived against such a powerful opponent for more than a few seconds, but some combination of the enhanced time sense from the scepter and the unrelenting hiss of the lightning was tipping things in my direction.

We battled for what felt like hours as I dodged blow after blow and slowly destroyed the legs that provided the fae with its mobility. At one point I heard my dad yelling for me as he approached, but I ordered him back.

The old me would have done so out of concern for him; the new me did it because I didn't want anyone to rob me of the satisfaction of destroying one of the four most powerful fae all by myself. The glow from the energy being unleashed from the wards had combined with the light coming off of my weapon to make it impossible to see. I was fighting with my eyes closed, depending on my second sight and the dragon-shaped group of sparks it revealed to keep me out of trouble as I darted in to land another blow.

ENDLESS

I was unstoppable, a titan in a war being waged by insects, and then between one heartbeat and the next, the second ward came down and everyone around me sped up until I was only barely faster than them. My mind was still functioning faster than it ever had before, but my body was chained by gravity and slowed by the very air around me. The bonds hadn't been noticeable when everyone else was moving so slowly, but they were terrible indeed now.

I dodged another attack from the Dragon, and then at the last moment I heard something massive running towards me. I spun around just in time to see Fenrir barrel into me, completely undeterred by the bolts of lightning coming off of my scepter.

I was dead—I knew it. There wasn't any way to avoid Fenrir, not when he was moving that quickly, not when I was already committed to moving away from the Dragon. It was only a matter of time. Then suddenly something no bigger than me slammed into Fenrir from the other direction.

No person that small should have been able to redirect more than two tons of raging wolf. No human—or Awakened—could have possibly generated enough force to even inconvenience a fae as powerful as Fenrir, but this wasn't a human, it was the Lady.

She hit with the force of a wrecking ball. It was the kind of impossible collision that made the earth around the point of impact shake, and she was almost successful. She hit Fenrir hard enough to send him careening, but not quite enough for him to completely miss me.

Fenrir hit me with what should have been a glancing blow, but with his preternatural bulk behind it, the impact was anything but minor. I probably should have lost my arm altogether—I would have if not for the fact that my bones, muscles and ligaments were amped up to many times their normal strength.

As it was, all three major bones in my arm shattered. The pain was excruciating, but I hardly even noticed it over the despair I felt as the Scepter of Storms went cartwheeling away from me.

For a moment there I'd been convinced that the Lady had saved me, but it turned out she'd only delayed my execution. She would doubtlessly keep Fenrir occupied, but that still left the Dragon—weakened and slower than normal, but more than a match for me in my current state.

I felt something settle on my left shoulder. It was Bethany. A tiny part of me wondered at the ability of the mind to take in minutiae even in life-and-death situations. Before now, she'd always landed on my right shoulder. I spared a fraction of a second to be grateful that she'd avoided my damaged shoulder, but mostly I was focused on trying to reconnect with the scepter.

I'd been able to feel it hovering in the back of my mind before the link had finished integrating. It only made sense that I would still be able to do so. I reached out for it and tried to summon a blast of electricity of sufficient strength to drive the Dragon away.

I could still feel the scepter skittering around the edges of my being, but now that it was no longer physically touching me, I couldn't bend it to my will. The lightning feeding into the weapon from the sky was already starting to fade away, discharging harmlessly into the ground.

"Save yourself, Bethany. Get out of here—go tell Ari and the others to get out of range. They aren't a match for something like this."

I threw myself backwards, trying to buy myself a few extra seconds of life, and happened to look over at Bethany a split second before I hit the ground. She was bigger than she'd been before—not as big as Kregor, but well on her way. That would have been a shock all by itself, but I was even more surprised to see a silvery, crystal sword materialize in her hand.

The sword wasn't sized for her, it was sized for me—and it landed in my left hand as I hit the ground. My fingers reflexively gripped it before it could go sliding away, and in that moment my entire world changed.

The attack that burst from the end of the sword looked like a sun lance, but it wasn't. There were differences that I couldn't even begin to explain, not the least of which was the fact that it was easily twice as big as anything I'd ever managed before—even when using a peak memory. The attack tore through the Dragon lengthwise, completely vaporizing the first four-fifths of the monstrous fae before it finally expended the last of its energy.

I looked around and saw an involuntary pause in the fighting around me as everyone realized what I'd done. I saw fear in the eyes of Kyle's people and questions in the eyes of everyone on my side.

I wanted to answer their unvoiced questions as badly as they wanted them answered, but I didn't have any idea what had happened. The pause in the fighting had been so brief that I wouldn't have even been able to register it if not for the fact that I'd been amped so far up. Now that everyone was moving again—unrestrained by the energies that had been coming off of the second ward—I suddenly felt much too slow.

I tapped into a wellspring of joy that hadn't been there before I'd grabbed hold of Bethany's sword—a wellspring that was much vaster than anything else I'd ever experienced—and between one blink and the next, everyone slowed down.

In the next breath a warm pulse of power ran down my right arm, and I'd already shifted the sword over to my dominant arm before I realized that I didn't know how to do either of the things that I'd just experienced. It was all I could do to amp myself up—I had no idea how to layer on additional speed and strength effects while maintaining the first set, and I still didn't know how to work healing effects.

I was moving at something in excess of ten times normal speed—fast enough that even the fastest fae felt like they were moving at half speed. That should have made me all but invulnerable—it would have against just one or two opponents—but the shock of my having killed the Dragon seemed to have worn off.

Every Unseelie fae within a hundred yards seemed to be rushing me at the same time. I knew that wasn't actually the case—the Seelie warriors around me were stepping into the path of that avalanche of darkness, but we were still heavily outnumbered and I'd suddenly become the priority target.

I stepped forward to meet my enemies, and never even considered going back for my scepter. The Scepter of Storms had been an impressive weapon when wielded by someone with more than four times my normal strength, but it was nothing compared to the glowing, crystalline sword that Bethany had given me.

Where before I'd crushed limbs and caved in skulls, knocking massive bodies to one side, now I simply sheared through everything that came at me. I'd hoped to be able to continue to advance, gaining as much ground as possible with which to retreat later on, but that proved an impossibility.

I waged a fighting retreat, slicing nightmarish creatures in half whenever possible, settling for cutting off limbs on the rare occasion when I couldn't reach something more critical, and it wasn't until a dozen of the Unseelie Court's finest had fallen to the edge of my blade that I realized I was fighting with a skill and deadliness that I'd never acquired during my seventeen years of life in this incarnation.

I fought as though a master swordswoman had possessed me. The press of bodies was so thick that I still would have been over-whelmed if I'd been using a normal weapon, but the crystal sword dropped body after body without ever getting caught on ribs—its only failing was that it didn't do anything about the momentum that the fae were carrying into our exchanges.

It wouldn't do me any good to kill an enemy and then be crushed by what was left of him, and so I continued to fall back. It wasn't until I felt the ground underneath me begin to slope upwards that I realized the Unseelie warriors had nearly succeeded in trapping me against the edge of the bowl that the other Awakened had carved out of the mountain.

The real me, the one who had been so scared of linking with the Scepter of Storms, had no idea what to do in this situation. I could see the Lady leading a charge on one side of the river of snarling forms, backed up by Intravil and other familiar faces, but for all of her awesome strength and speed she didn't seem to be making any more headway than Jace and Kat were on the other side of the mass of enemy fae.

They weren't going to arrive in time and I didn't know what to do...only somehow I did. My free hand came up and black filaments no bigger around than a single strand of my hair shot out of my palm. Every thread hit an enemy fae, and cut through the exact center of their chests as though they were made out of nothing more than smoke. Each time a thread pierced an enemy, it split into two more threads.

Not every thread hit a new enemy, but many of them did, and a split second later the space around me was enveloped in shiny black threads that had multiplied so many times it looked like someone had woven a tapestry between all of the figures around me, a tapestry that was impossibly fine, and which hung perfectly suspended in the air by the bodies that had been incorporated into its design.

As each dark fae had been struck, they had stopped moving—frozen in place into perfect stillness. Some of the bigger fae had required more than one filament to stop them from continuing forward, but there had been plenty of threads to spare.

My entire corner of the battle was covered in the black threads, with only a few islands on the fringes where someone from my side had been hemmed in by the filaments without actually coming into contact with them. I felt the threads pulsing with something simultaneously familiar and alien, something that wanted to pour into me, but which I instinctively knew I needed to keep at arm's length. I reached out and pushed against that force, sending it crashing through the filaments, and between one heartbeat and the next every fae in that interlocked network dropped to the ground as though their strings had been cut.

I'd been standing slightly higher than my enemies—high enough that I'd believed that I'd been able to see everything, but I'd been wrong. As the fae collapsed in front of me, I saw a flash of movement dart forward out from behind the thickest concentration of falling bodies.

I was still moving at more than ten times normal speed, but that still wasn't enough—not when Kyle was racing toward me at somewhere in the range of twelve or thirteen times normal speed. He streaked across the ground like a silver-tinged bullet, barrier effect shredding the tattered, already dissolving black threads, and the sight of him took my breath away.

Numbers spun through my mind like a high-speed ticker tape, so fast that I couldn't identify individual equations, but I somehow knew that it was an analysis of how much power Kyle was burning to maintain such a powerful barrier effect while still moving at such amazing speed.

It was the kind of display that would have been completely impossible without the necklace he'd taken off of Mephistoles' body, but even with that artifact most Awakened still couldn't have managed it. It was a display of efficiency and emotional strength that only the most learned Awakened could possibly understand.

Someone like Jace or Kat would have dismissed it as a product of Kyle owning two artifacts, but I knew better. Only someone who truly understood the universe around us could possibly work with such efficiency. The Brísingamen necklace amplified someone's emotions, but it could only work with what the Awakened in question was capable of sustaining on their own.

Kyle wasn't just angry, his fury had reached another realm completely. It was the kind of emotion that was capable of creating a new fae, a peak that only few Awakened ever achieved in any given incarnation.

The old me was terrified to know that all of that emotion was combined with such incredible knowledge. It was figuratively shaking in our boots to know that those two powerful attributes had been married with two of the most powerful artifacts ever created.

The rest of me simply reacted.

I amped up my time sense and all of the supporting systems to something equal or maybe even a little better than what Kyle was sustaining, and then I started throwing dark bolts of energy that seemed to compress the air as they passed through it.

The ticker tape was back and it was still moving much too fast for me to focus on any one piece of information, but once again I was able to derive an overall impression of what the numbers and equations meant.

Kyle's energy and emotional expenditure bordered on the impossible, but he'd come at it from the most efficient way possible. He'd created his time amp as one single effect and then done exactly the same thing as he'd amped up the rest of his systems individually.

I'd gone about things in the opposite manner. I hadn't had any choice—not once I'd realized that Kyle was shooting towards me at more than twelve times normal speed—but that meant that each of my effects had been less efficient than they otherwise would have been.

Just in amping my speed, strength, circulatory and respiratory systems to thirteen or fourteen times normal speed by way of three separate layers of effects, I'd already expended more energy and emotional reserve than Kyle had in creating all of his effects.

When you added in the black bolts that I was hurling at him, the answer was a number that didn't make sense. It was too large—much too large to have been generated by just me, even when I'd been at the peak of my abilities.

Kyle changed direction again and again, working his way towards me like a field runner. The combined output of his effects was beyond impressive, but he was apparently at the limit of his abilities. He was committed to closing far enough that he would be able to use his sword—there simply wasn't anything left over with which to throw any kind of distance attack at me and he didn't dare drop his barrier effect.

My attacks continued to chip away at his barrier. All I needed was one good strike at the center of his field, but he was denying me that with a skill that hadn't been gained in any laboratory.

I came close on four separate occasions, and then he was within arm's reach of me and it was too late for any of that. His sword swept across his body with a smoothness and speed that I shouldn't have been able to avoid, but I didn't even try. My sword crashed into Excalibur with a shock that I felt all the way from my wrists up to my shoulders.

His eyes went wide, but I wasn't sure if it was because I'd managed to intercept his blow or if he'd expected my sword to snap from the force of his blow. I didn't have time to dwell on it, but I'd been equally shocked that my weapon hadn't sheared through his with the same ease that it had sliced through powerful fae bodies.

His weapon swung around again and darted in towards me in a straight thrust, but I managed to turn it to one side at the last second and lash out with a kick to his knee. It was a blow that would have destroyed the knee of any lesser opponent, but his soft-tissue augmentation held and he simply fell back to force the next exchange to take place at a distance that favored him.

I was in trouble. I'd somehow acquired skills beyond anything I remembered learning, but they weren't the equal of his—at least not while I was still second-guessing them. He was better than me and he was going to cut me to pieces within the next pass or two unless I managed to come up with a better plan.

I retreated, sword a blur as I battered away attack after attack, but I didn't manage to buy myself enough room to launch any kind of distance attack. He followed me and never let up in the slightest.

Jace and Kat were jockeying for position less than a dozen yards away from us, but they couldn't risk any kind of distance attack while the two of us were moving so quickly and they were both obviously too worn out from keeping Ari and my dad amped up to face Kyle sword-to-sword.

Dad and Ari were both moving slowly now, their augmentations dropped so that Kat and Jace could marshal their strength. Ari just looked scared, her eyes darting from side to side as though expecting one of the Unseelie fae to kill her, but my dad was headed in my direction as though intent on trying to get a blow in on Kyle.

I wanted to yell and warn him off, but Kyle's circulatory amp seemed to be better than mine. I was already gasping for oxygen, lungs working against air that seemed to have the consistency of silly putty, and I didn't have any breath to spare. More importantly, I was worried about drawing any attention to my dad.

I was a demigod, but that didn't stop me from praying to whatever else might be out there. I prayed that Kat or Jace would see my dad and stop him before he got close enough for Kyle to notice him, but they were both too focused on Kyle and me.

Dad took another step and he was suddenly even with Jace—less than a dozen yards away from Kyle and me, but lacking the augmentations that would have allowed him to flee if Kyle turned on him.

Kyle sprang forward with a speed that exceeded anything he'd yet displayed, and then as I threw myself backwards to avoid his thrust, he reversed course and covered the distance between him and my dad in two lightning-fast bounds.

I was already moving forward again by the time he took his first step, but it was too little, too late. Jace and Kat both flashed into motion, but they were simply too slow. They weren't going to save my dad—not as depleted as they were—all they were going to do was make sure that they were the next to feel Kyle's blade.

A flicker of motion off to the side was my only clue that another player had entered the field. Byron was moving at something approaching twenty times normal speed. The computer in the back of my mind ran the numbers. He had to be burning a peak memory—that or he was an even more talented researcher than I'd been led to believe. He was coming into the fight fresh and he was fast, but Kyle saw him at the last moment, and Kyle apparently was the superior swordsman.

Excalibur took Byron low on the right side of his chest, and the shock from the pain instantly dropped him out of amped status. Kyle casually punched my dad in the chest hard enough that I heard ribs shatter, and then he turned around and stabbed me in the stomach.

This time I saw the blow coming, but I was too committed to avoid it. All I could do was drive my blade home in him at the same time.

Neither of us managed a clean, killing stroke. We'd both stood up on our tiptoes at the last second to make sure that the other person missed our heart. I wondered if Kyle had been the one to teach me that in some past incarnation, and then Kyle and I locked eyes and there wasn't any room for idle speculation.

I felt his attack, insubstantial but still deadly, and responded out of reflex without consciously understanding what was happening. I felt the pressure of his thoughts trying to bore into my brain and I pushed back against him, searching for a soft spot even as my hand locked down around the wrist holding his sword.

He'd already done the same and just like that our physical bodies mirrored what was going on inside of our minds. We were frozen in place, intertwined in ways that meant that the slightest loss of control could result in our death.

I reached into the depths of my memory searching for an answer as to what was going on, and was surprised when the answer floated to the surface. We were both performing a kind of anti-healing on each other. It was a deadly, painful way to die, one that was only possible when the subject was within arm's reach, and a large part of me was shocked that Kyle would choose to violate his promise in such a terrible way.

He pressed against the arteries inside of my head, trying to rupture the walls, and I strengthened the blood vessels at the same time that I tried to constrict his airway. It was a complex, lightning fast dance that was the equal of anything I'd seen so far on the battlefield. We moved around inside each other's bodies in an intricate battle where the slightest delay in shoring up some vital system would be just as lethal as shoring up something that wasn't under attack.

I wasn't Jace. I'd never put in the decades of study required to master the effects that dealt with the body on the levels that we were manipulating. Apparently Kyle had, but somehow all of that knowledge was at my fingertips too.

We were like two draft horses who'd been tasked to pull a heavy load in opposite directions. We ramped up our power in a smooth, continuous curve that quickly surpassed anything that either of us should have been able to manage.

The computer running in the back of my mind was flashing up numbers that were well in excess of anything I'd ever seen before. From the outside it looked like it all happened in an instant, but to me—still running at more than a dozen times normal speed—it seemed to take forever for us both to finally hit our maximum output.

It was a battle that I couldn't win. I had less than two decades of memories to offer up against the centuries that he'd lived. I'd gotten lucky somehow in my fight against Sandra, a fight that should have left me wiped as clean as her, but I couldn't count on that happening again.

Years vanished in fractions of a second as memories sprayed out of my forehead in an invisible stream that felt like it should have forced me over backwards. I felt Kyle's anger beating down on me as he amped up his strength further in an effort to break free of my grip on his wrist.

I compensated for his increased strength as I tried to savage his nervous system, nearly managing to force all of his neurotransmitters to fire off simultaneously before he thwarted me. I kept expecting him to overpower me, but we were just too evenly matched for that.

The rest of the world started to fall away from around me, but before it completely disappeared I heard Jace yelling that it wasn't safe to separate us, and felt Bethany land on my shoulder.

ENDLESS

Jace was right. I was relying on the pressure Kyle was exerting against my systems to prop them up even as I kept him from pushing them too far. Locked together as we were, it would have been child's play for Jace or Kat either one to kill Kyle with a single stroke of their sword, but the sudden collapse of all of his efforts at once would probably kill me as well. We were locked into a battle that would only end when one of us ran out of power or made a fatal mistake.

The battle felt like it had lasted forever, but the computer in the back of my mind disputed that conclusion. It was certain that we'd been locked together for only slightly more than a minute, but even that felt wrong. A full minute of this should have drained me several times over.

I retreated inside of myself, trying to hold off Kyle with most of my efforts while still figuring out what was happening. For the first time I was able to sense the specific memories that were being consumed as I worked my effects.

I remembered sitting in a darkened room with the sword that was now buried in Kyle's chest resting across my knees. I wasn't alone. Bethany was there, less than an inch tall, and wide-eyed.

"You're going to have to keep this a secret from everyone. It's got a lot in common with a ward. It needs time to mature—to crystalize and reach its full potential. As much as I would like to take it into battle with me tomorrow, I can't. Do you understand?"

"No, but I'll do it for you anyway. I owe you my very existence…"

"Don't talk like that, Bethany. You aren't my slave. You don't owe me anything. I ask you to do this because it's the right thing to do—because you are the very definition of Seelie."

She took a deep breath and nodded. "How will I know when enough time has passed?"

I shook my head. "I don't know. All of my research for the last hundred years has been pointing towards this artifact in one way or another, but now that I've created it we are in uncharted territory. It may only take a few years, or it may take decades—centuries even."

"I don't understand. If there isn't any way for me to tell when it's ready to be used, how will I know when the time is right?"

"You'll know the time is right because you won't have any other choice but to give it to me. It will be the right time because I will have won your heart and you won't be able to bear seeing me cut down."

The memory slipped away from me before I could finish analyzing it. There were so many layers of significance there that I knew would be forever lost to me, but rather than fixating on that, my mind turned to the question of how I'd known with such certainty that Bethany was a Seelie fairy.

As soon as the question crossed my mind I was pulled into another memory, one where I was sitting on the floor with a crystal as large as my palm cradled between my hands. The images played through my mind and I was able to watch the crystal as it elongated and took the shape of a sword—of my sword.

The emotion I was feeling as it happened was one of pure joy, a joy that I'd been skirting around for weeks without ever understanding. It wasn't the happiness of a soft bed and a warm meal, it was the joy of creation, a happiness that was unlike anything else. I'd been feeling the strongest of positive emotions when I'd created Bethany. She couldn't be anything other than Seelie fae.

The outer layers of my mind were still focused on the battle with Kyle. Somewhere out there I was still fighting him, desperately trying to stop his heart or send his other organs into a cascading failure. It was an important fight, a fight that I was only barely managing to stay abreast with, but no matter how hard I tried, I couldn't tear myself away from the images in my head, the images being consumed in the battle.

Someone else touched my shoulders, a heavier hand, and the memories streaming out of my mind changed. I caught flashes of me walking down a long hall with Intravil at my side. She was still cold, still distant, but there was more humanity in her eyes.

Another pair of hands wrapped themselves around my upper arms, and suddenly I was sitting on a riverbank in a jungle somewhere. I wasn't wearing much, just some crudely cured animal skins, and as I reached down for water a crashing from behind me brought me around to find a massive feline creature flying toward me.

The fangs and claws were only feet away from me, and I knew in that moment that I was going to die. That knowledge tore something free inside of me and a bolt of blinding light shot from my hand. What was left of the creature was blasted back into the forest and I knew that my life would never be the same again.

Time stuttered forward and I was running through the jungle, unarmed but unafraid of anything that might be out there stalking me. I crashed into a clearing and sprinted towards a squat stone pyramid only to have the ground underneath me give way before I could take my third step.

My head hit a rock and I lost consciousness. When I woke, I was tied to a post facing Byron...facing my father. He was the reason I'd come. The others, the ones who walked on two legs like us, had captured him. They feared me, feared what I was capable of, and their answer to the fear was to sacrifice both my dad and me to whatever strange powers they believed in.

I'd thought time was my only enemy, thought that merely arriving soon enough would guarantee my victory, but I'd been overconfident. Byron looked at me, desperation in his eyes as he struggled against his bonds, but there was nothing either of us could do about the priest who approached me with an obsidian knife held high. I reached for my sun fire, but the blow to my head had left my thoughts muddled and my powers useless.

I closed my eyes, preparing for death, and then I heard a crack as Byron ripped his post from the ground in a feat of strength that was beyond anything I'd ever seen before. The others attacked him, but the ropes around him snapped and they were as children before his strength.

He saved my life, but just as important, he saved me from the unending loneliness I'd been able to see stretching out before me. I wasn't the only one of my kind any more.

Time stuttered forward again and I was once again standing at the edge of a river, a mountain at my back. I was surrounded by people, but more alone than ever. I hadn't wanted to become a goddess. All I'd wanted was to be safe, to be left alone to expand the boundaries of my ability.

The others hadn't been willing to let that happen. They'd pursued my father and me for years. Eventually we'd found another group, one in the middle of a war, and we'd been taken in.

We'd tried to keep a low profile, but that had gone out the window the first time one of the others had attacked us in broad daylight in the middle of the village. I'd killed him with my sun fire and from that moment we'd been forced to become gods to be worshiped or demons to be feared.

All efforts at peaceful negotiation had failed, and our people couldn't leave—not with the others behind us and the new enemies before us. For decades we fought a defensive war to hold the fertile valley that made life something other than just a cold drudgery.

Our people gave us the best gifts they knew how to give, crude though they were, but all of the gifts in the world couldn't make up for the fact that we were forced to kill for them at every turn. Our enemies were possessed of a savage cunning and the kind of determination possible only when religious zeal was married with greed.

We had something they wanted, and they came at us in an unending stream. My father and I killed them by the dozens, but eventually one of them got lucky and I was once again all alone.

I was inconsolable for months. I led war bands into the territory of our enemies and I killed them by the scores, but eventually I realized that no matter how many of them I killed it wouldn't bring my father back, wouldn't fill the hole inside of me.

Somewhere along the way I realized that I was losing my memories more quickly than I was creating new ones. I was just one person, and even a god—this god at least—had limits. I eventually hit on the solution to our problem, but it took another decade before I was able to work out how to make it happen, a decade in which my people were harried from all sides, a decade in which men died in battle and their wives and children rarely survived to see the next sunrise after their defeat.

Looking back over that time, I expected to feel anger or hatred as I contemplated the possibility of destroying the new enemies, the ones who'd killed my father and ravaged my people. I didn't though. I felt a sense of satisfaction and joy that my power would finally be used to create something, to carve a permanent change of the face of our land.

It was time. I reached deep down inside of me and tapped into the joy for once rather than the anger I usually used, and it was a vast power, a force stronger even than the river before me. I reached toward the mountain at my back and pushed it over, damming the river a mile or two upstream from where I stood, sealing the pass that our enemies used to reach our land, and flooding their home.

When it was all over my memories were measured in months rather than decades, but my people were safe. The others were still a threat, but we could deal with just one enemy.

A few hours later I met her for the first time.

She was no longer than my thumb, physically weak, but loyal and unyielding. She was a companion who was just as different in her own way from my people as I was. Even better, she didn't seem to age, and as time went on, she grew.

It was a slow process, one that resulted in just the tiniest of gains after even the passage of decades, but it was measurable. I was getting very good at measuring things. With her as our scout, my warriors and I had chased the others back several days' journey.

We still experienced occasional harassing attacks, but by and large my people were finally safe, and I'd turned my attention back to understanding how I was able to do so many things that others weren't able to match.

Back in the present, I felt a growing sense of pressure pulling at me as Kyle redoubled his efforts to kill me, and I temporarily lost the thread of memory I'd been following. I shored up my defenses, pushing him far enough back that I could return part of my attention to my past, and returned to the memories that were finally answering some of my questions.

I was sitting in an open-air room at the top of a stone temple, a room that was still crude, but which was luxurious in comparison to the way my people lived. Normally the stone floors were packed with functionaries, but tonight things were different. It was just me and my fairy companion—a three-foot-tall woman who I finally recognized as the Lady.

"Are you sure about this? You don't even know if something like this is possible. I don't want to lose you for no reason."

I reached over and rested a hand on her shoulder. "I don't want to be lost any more than you want me to be lost, but I have to do something. I never thought that the others would eventually ally themselves with another of my kind. I should have rooted them out decades ago and turned everything on that side of our border into a desolate wasteland, but it's too late now."

She shook her head. "No, it's not. Let's go, just you and me. We'll leave behind the army so we can travel more quickly and we'll go drop a mountain on their favorite pass."

"We've talked about that. The conditions aren't right for that. I couldn't manage to drop anything that big, not in a way that would accomplish what we're after."

"Fine, we'll come up with another plan. If we sneak into their capital we can probably assassinate both of them and get back out before their guards can respond."

"I don't think we can. They always seem to be a step ahead of us. No matter what precautions I take, they know exactly where I'm going to be. They always manage to make sure that one of them is there to foil any attack I lead, and while I'm tied up saving our army at that location, the other one rampages through our defenses somewhere else. I don't know how they are doing it, but I'm becoming convinced that they can sense me from a long distance away."

That stopped her. She was small, but she was already decades old, and she'd seen more combat than any of my generals—rarely on the front lines, but from her vantage point in the sky she usually had a better idea of how things were developing than I did. The information she relayed to me, and then from me to my commanders, had been a major component in our success so far in keeping the others from completely overrunning our defenses.

"How long have you suspected that?"

"I'm not sure. There was just something in the back of my mind that kept telling me that nobody could have such a fantastic string of luck. It wasn't until the battle last month that I realized what was going on."

"That's why you sent the reserves around their flanks like that. You know that the others wouldn't be expecting you to operate our people that far away from you."

"I didn't *know*—I still don't know for certain that they can sense me—but it's starting to look like my theory is correct."

"In that case, I'll have to go after them myself. They can't sense me."

"No, I'm not going to let you throw your life away, you're too important for that."

She shook her head, lip stuck out in something dangerously close to a pout. "I'm not important and you know it. I should have gone after them years ago. I may not be big enough to drive a spear into their chests, but there are a lot of other ways to kill someone. I could poison their food, or barring that, stab them in their sleep with their own knife. They can see me, but the rest of their people can't."

I took a firmer grasp on her arm, making sure that she wouldn't be able to fly away. "Their army outnumbers ours by nearly three to one. Your ability to pass messages is the only thing that has allowed us to survive so far."

"Not true."

"Fine. It's not the only thing, but it's one of our few advantages. Don't get too caught up with the idea that they can sense me. I made that mistake for a while, but the truth is that even if I learn how to replicate whatever it is they're doing, it still won't change the fundamental balance of power. There are two of them and just one of me. I've got an edge in that my research has made me more effective than either of them is individually, but at the end of the day they are gaining memories twice as fast as I am.

"That is why I have to proceed with the creation of the weapon. I have to find a way to change the balance of power—and soon—or nothing else will matter. This weapon has the potential of making it so my powers are more efficient. If I'm successful it could mean that I'll be able to face the two of them on equal footing."

"What if you're wrong? What if you waste all of those memories in an attempt to create this...artifact...and at the end of it all you're left without a weapon, without any memory of how to fight, and without any idea who I am?"

I pulled her to me and hugged her, careful not to put pressure on the delicate wings growing out of her back. "It's a risk, but it's one I have to run. Just know that no matter what happens I'm incredibly proud of you."

She tried to shake her head, tried to deny my words, but I didn't let her. "You're something unique. I'm still learning what it is I can do, but I can't shake the feeling that eventually I'll reach the end of my capabilities. You, on the other hand, show every sign of being able to get stronger and stronger. Not only that, you don't age, so there's every reason to think that eventually you might end up as the single most powerful being to have ever lived.

Our people call me a god, but that was disproved when my father was killed. I'm powerful, but I'm not a god. You, though, you just might be the next best thing to a true god, and if that's the case I'm glad that you're you—a truly good and caring individual—rather than someone like those two monsters currently leading the others."

The memory stuttered again, but I got the sense that hours passed. When I finally collapsed down onto the floor a familiar-looking sword was buried to the hilt in the stone floor of the temple. I finally understood how the Lady had come into possession of Excalibur—I must have given it to her.

The years skipped forward in flashes. I saw more fighting than anyone should be forced to endure. The Lady was taller now—either a product of having been nearby during the creation of Excalibur or because of the constant expenditure of power by all three of the Awakened involved in the war—but we were always outnumbered, always on the run.

In the end, her fears proved to be valid. It took almost a decade, but by the end of it all I barely remembered my own name. The two Awakened at the head of the other army killed me and then razed the beautiful city that my people had spent unimaginable hours creating.

I died with a set of memories that were measured only in days rather than centuries, but I died happy. I'd managed to give Excalibur to the Lady, and she'd hidden it away in the in-between, the place that only she could access.

Flashes of other lives followed. In one the Lady found me and gave me my old journals—the ones that had survived the fighting. I spent decades learning how to read them again, decades during which I managed to keep my abilities secret, but the journals proved to be insufficient.

There was a terrifying arms race going on. Our kind—the demigods—had started out with just my father and I in a past incarnation, but by this point there seemed to be Awakened at the head of every developing civilization. There were scores of us, and they all spent most of their time discovering better ways to kill each other.

I died deep inside a cave, hunted for days by a pair of Awakened in the hopes that I knew something that would help them fight off the threat on their western border.

The lives flashed by one after another, mostly in bits and pieces. The clearest stretches were the ones when the Lady was nearby, often without my knowledge. I was too young and naive to understand what was going on, but it was apparent to me now—viewing history in flashes that covered years.

The war between the Awakened was bad, but the unseen one between the fae was every bit as terrible. The fae were slow to be born. It was a rare Awakened who survived long enough to amass sufficient memories to fuel the birth of another fairy, and Awakened who found themselves in circumstances where they were able to sustain the necessary emotion were even rarer.

The Lady started out with an incredible advantage. She'd been fortunate to see both the creation of an artifact and more than a century and a half of sustained warfare. She was bigger than the first few fae she found, and quickly figured out how to feed off of their deaths. She never attacked first, but she nearly always won in the end.

ENDLESS

The entire earth spun towards darkness, an endless cycle of war and destruction as Awakened banded together to pull down their strongest neighbors before then turning on each other. I should have caught only the events that took place in my part of the world, but instead I seemed to be picking up things from all over—even other continents.

I saw the rise of Atlantis, saw a pantheon of twelve Awakened unite to create something good and beautiful. I was one of them, still young, but more than willing to throw myself into the task before us. Kat was there too—a lighter, happier Kat—as was my father, the man who would someday come to be known as Byron in a different time and place, a different life.

We didn't recognize each other, didn't share any link beyond what we'd developed during that incarnation in Atlantis, but that link was enough. He became my mentor, my father in everything but name. He was the leader of us all, the man who united us into a force that managed to hold off the barbarians at our gates for more than two centuries.

The last hundred and fifty years was a constant picture of death and destruction, but through all of it he kept me separated from the bulk of the fighting. He told me—told us all—that it was because I was an even more gifted researcher than him, that we needed me to be doing what I did best if we were to have a chance of winning the war.

I did my best. I created dozens of new ways to kill and nearly an equal number of ways to heal the injured. Kat used my discoveries to patch up our soldiers and feed them back into the meat grinder again and again until there wasn't anything left to patch up.

Each time the pressure from Kyle's attack in the present shifted and demanded my attention, I staved him off. Each time I was pulled partway out of the flow of memories, I told myself that the things I was reliving were nothing more than an echo of the past, but it didn't help. It all felt so real.

I watched as a failed experiment resulted in the creation of another fairy—once again a female. She started out small, but she was the only one of her kind in a city that teemed with the energy of expended effects. I watched her grow over a very short period of time, watched her throw herself into the hottest parts of the battle, the spots where my pantheon used their abilities to fight other Awakened, other pantheons.

I watched her accompany Byron and the others on daring missions where they cut off the head of the enemy armies, killing the generals and Awakened who were attacking us. Time and time again the other members of my pantheon seemed on the verge of total victory, but no sooner had we defeated one enemy than another rose in its place.

Our success had painted a huge target on our fair city, and by the end of the war we started seeing Awakened we'd defeated and killed reborn to fight us again.

In the end, I once again wagered everything on a single throw of the dice—ignorant of the ways in which history was repeating itself. This time my research had gone down other paths, but once again, my fairy familiar stood at my side as I embarked on an act of creation that was beyond the imagining of most of my kind.

When I finished with the shapeless lump of metal I'd started with, it was more than just recognizable, its form was burned into my mind, both in the past and in the future. I created the second artifact of my existence, and then I carried the Scepter of Storms into battle and slew entire armies by myself.

It was addicting, and there was so little of me left to fight off the scepter's influence. This time I'd created something that could function on its own, something that didn't require my memories to wield it, but I'd misjudged the effect it would have on someone who was little more than a child by then.

My fairy companion—Intravil—wasn't much help. She'd grown up in a different environment than the Lady. They'd both seen the horrors of war, but things had become even more horrible as our ability to kill had improved. Intravil didn't look at life and death the same way that the Lady had. She was still good, still created from predominantly positive emotions, but she saw nothing wrong with my using the scepter to destroy our enemies and then pursue them back to the lands from whence they came.

My mind recoiled from what I did after that. I rarely used my abilities during that time—relying on the power of the scepter—but when I did, my fueling emotion was an anger that was so strong it was nearly unhinged.

It was the destruction of Atlantis that finally brought me back to myself. I'd been too successful. My campaign to eradicate all of the civilizations that had threatened us brought Awakened we hadn't even known about into an alliance powerful enough to destroy Byron and the others in my absence.

Somehow the Lady found me and convinced me to entrust the scepter into her care. I died a short time later, hunted by the tattered remnants of the armies I'd shattered with bolts of lightning.

Things grew even darker after that. Human sacrifice abounded and being born an Awakened was a delayed death sentence. Once our powers awakened we never aged, but few of us lasted more than a few decades.

I skipped forward thousands of years, years where I seemed not to have any memories. The only flashes from that time period seemed to be fragments of memory seen through the Lady's eyes or occasionally through Intravil's.

I came back to myself partway through an incarnation, came back to concern in Kyle's eyes as he helped me out of bed. I relived the times in London that I'd read about in the journal in Kyle's bunker. I experienced the decades before that, and I found out that I was every bit as happy as my journal had led me to believe I'd been.

I felt the pain of our escape from London, and watched as Jace continued to hold himself in the background of my life as I tried to rebuild my relationship with Kyle, tried to connect with what was left of the man he'd been.

It all flashed through my mind in an instant, and then my eyes opened and met Kyle's back in the real world, the world where we each had a sword in our chest, and a battle between the Seelie and Unseelie Courts raged around us.

The pressure inside of my head had been matched with pain in my chest and a tingle in my arm. I'd allowed myself to become too distracted. He had the upper hand, but I finally understood something that I'd never fully understood before. Not in a dozen incarnations or ten thousand years.

Strong emotions could come about from circumstance. Fear, anger, joy, they could all be transitory things that washed through us and changed us for a time, but circumstance wasn't the key to the emotions that brought real power.

Real power came about by investment. Emotions capable of altering the landscape of the world, of creating artifacts or birthing new fae only occurred when someone had dedicated unimaginable resources towards an end.

The sword in my hands wasn't Bethany's, it was mine—the final of three artifacts that I'd created. I wasn't the only Awakened to have ever created an artifact, but by all indications I was one of the most successful. Each time it had been the result of decades or even a century of research, research that had been powered by concern for my friends and family, concern for the people I'd loved the most.

Each time I'd been convinced that my creating an artifact would be the key to saving the people who were most important to me, and each time I'd tapped into the joy that thought had brought to me.

The last time I'd known I wasn't going to survive to see the next sunset, but I'd still known that I'd succeeded, that I'd managed to create something that was going to eventually allow me to protect everyone I cared about.

It was going to take time to delve back through my memories and understand what the crystal sword did, but for now I knew it somehow connected me to past lives, and that it allowed me to tap into the emotions I'd felt when I'd created it.

Each time I'd touched that vast, powerful reservoir of emotion I'd been convinced that nothing could be stronger, but I'd been wrong. Kyle's rage at being thwarted in his centuries-long campaign to make sure that he could take control of the world was the equal of what I'd felt twenty years ago. It might even be slightly stronger.

It wasn't, however, as strong as the joy I felt at knowing that after thousands of years of effort I'd finally achieved what I set out to do. All of the people I'd ever cared about—all of the fae and Awakened who I'd sacrificed so much for—were here now with me and I finally had the power to protect them.

That was a joy that dwarfed anything I'd ever felt across ten thousand years of life. I reached down into that pool of emotion and began slowly pushing Kyle out of my body. The stream of memories leaving through my forehead was a torrent that should have drained me a dozen times over in just a few seconds, but my memories also seemed to be vast and limitless in ways that I didn't understand.

I freed myself from Kyle's attacks with an ease that shouldn't have been possible, and I watched fear blossom in his eyes. I pushed against the arteries leaving his heart, and felt him desperately trying to keep them from tearing.

His efforts weren't equal to the worst that I could do. I could have easily killed him then and there, but I held back. I pushed him right to the edge of his capacity, and I watched the light in his eyes go out. I watched his eyes turn from the shuttered, cynical windows of someone who'd seen far too much of the worst the world had to offer, to the innocent, bright eyes of a child.

I watched centuries of experience vanish and didn't relax my attack until he dropped to my feet, unconscious. I reached out to Bethany and Intravil—mind to mind—and asked them to watch over Kyle. I felt their shock over the fact that they couldn't block my thoughts anymore, but that was unimportant.

They acknowledged my request, and that was all the assurance I needed to pull Excalibur from my chest, healing myself at the same time that I pulled my latest creation from Kyle's chest and healed him without even touching him. I stepped away from Kyle and with a thought brought the war to a halt. Every Awakened fighting a metal-clad fae was instantly incinerated, and then a series of silver, spinning disks materialized at various points in the battlefield and cut the surviving dark fae to pieces.

It was only after every single threat had been neutralized that I finally let myself collapse.

Epilogue

I woke in a strange and wonderful bedroom. It reminded me a little of Kyle's bunker. It had the same lack of windows and the same extra-bright lighting aimed at making the room feel bright and airy.

As soon as Bethany realized I was awake, she shot out of the room like her wings were on fire. A few seconds later the tastefully-furnished room was filled with bodies. Dad and Ari were there—both looking more than a little shell-shocked as a result of the battle—as were Jace, Kat, Byron, Bethany, Intravil, and the Lady.

All of the people—nearly all of the people—I'd ever cared about were there with me. It wasn't quite perfect, but the fact that all of the rest of them would eventually be reborn into new incar-nations meant that it would eventually be perfect.

I looked around the room and smiled at Byron first. "I assume I have you to thank for the accommodations?"

"Yes. We're down to just one ward around Camelot now, but it's still stronger than anything else within a thousand miles. It seemed prudent to get you and that sword somewhere safe while you were unable to defend yourself. The Seelie Court—aided by the few surviving Awakened—is busy mopping up outside. They seem to have things under control, but nobody wanted to take any risks—not with a weapon that apparently puts all other artifacts to shame."

The Lady nodded gravely. "You've handed us the opportunity we've been waiting thousands of years for. With nearly the entire Unseelie Court disembodied at one time there is nothing to stop us from destroying them again and again each time they manifest a new form. It will be a task that will take years, but with our superior mobility, there will be very few of them who escape."

She had questions, I could see that, but she seemed willing to let me decide what was answered and when. After thousands of years, we'd returned to the state we'd been in during my first incarnation. I was once again the one with the most answers. The most surprising part of all of that was the fact that she was perfectly happy for the table to be flipped around.

I had so much that I wanted to tell all of them, but there was something else that was even more important. I checked that my new sword was still safely at my side, and then cleared my throat. "What about Kyle? Is he here too, or did you decide to leave him on the other side of the wards?"

Byron frowned. "I wanted to leave him out there, but Jace insisted he be brought inside. We have a work room that includes a smaller ward. It wouldn't be enough to keep him contained in his heyday, but now that his memories are all gone and we've secured both Excalibur and the necklace, it will do."

"Could you please take me to him?"

Nobody was particularly happy about that request, but after a second Byron nodded and led the way out of the bedroom. Everyone had reasons to dislike Kyle, but it was the flash of disappointment on Jace's face that was the hardest to bear.

He'd convinced Byron to offer Kyle sanctuary, but I could see now that he'd done so only because he'd known it was what I would have wanted.

Kyle was still asleep when we arrived, which defeated the purpose of going to him, but at least I could make sure that he didn't wake up locked in a magical prison. I thought for a moment that Byron was going to refuse to pull Kyle out, but I reached back into memories from times when my word had been law, and wrapped myself in the same kind of surety.

Once Kyle was resting comfortably in the bed I'd occupied only minutes before, I turned back to everyone else.

"Some of us have suspected for a while now that things went differently than everyone expected during the end of my last incarnation. Bethany knew what happened, but she did an amazing job keeping everything quiet."

"It was your last request. I couldn't do less than my best for you. It was the only way that I would get you back—the real you."

I could see the confusion on everyone else's face—everyone but Jace. He'd obviously understood more than he'd let on about what he'd found in my research journals. Not all, but enough to put many of the pieces together once the reality of my sword was staring him in the face.

"I was killed by Sandra and Mephistoles—just like everyone thought—but I spent the night before creating an artifact, creating this sword. It's not an accident that it's made of crystal—that's the only structure I could find that had a chance of storing our memories. This artifact is a composite of most of the memories I burned up during the process of creating it, but it's also much more.

"It also serves as a kind of magnet for all memories—especially for memories from my past incarnations. It connects me to those memories in ways that I still need to explore, but for now it's enough to say that I can experience some of my past lives and it also serves as an emotional reservoir."

Kat let out a low whistle. "That's how you were able to wipe Kyle clean. You weren't just burning memories from this incarnation, you were burning memories from thousands of years ago."

"Yes. That's also the reason for all of the other things that have been happening that we couldn't understand. I've been linked to this sword to some degree even while Bethany had it hidden away in the in-between. That's why I defaulted to happiness instead of anger, it's why my memories crystalized back through my entire life rather than just from the point of awakening forward. It's even the reason that I was able to pick up effects so quickly and the explanation for my being able to outlast Sandra in our fight. I should have lost more memories than I actually ended up losing."

"Why did you let Sandra kill you at the end of your last incarnation?"

Jace had asked the question, but I could see that he knew at least part of the answer already.

"The artifact needed time to mature and finish stabilizing."

"Now that it's stabilized, how much do you remember?"

"A lot. My earliest incarnations are very spotty, but I seem to be able to access any memories that are a part of a fae I'm actually in physical contact with. I remembered big portions of my first incarnation because the Lady was touching me while I was fighting Kyle."

I gave them a second to digest that particular piece of information. It was so obvious in a lot of ways, but none of us had seen it. Up until now, only the Lady had known that I was her creator. She'd no doubt known that I'd created Intravil, but even that knowledge had probably been hidden from all but a few people.

"There's more. It turns out that Byron was my original father in that first incarnation, and I created Intravil during a failed experiment during the time of Atlantis."

Kat looked like her jaw had come completely unhinged. "How are you remembering that now? You aren't touching either of them…"

"Once I access the memories that make them up, I created a duplicate of those memories. As time goes on, I'll regain everything that was ever lost—either because my sword will draw it to me, or because I come into contact with the fae who've absorbed those memories. For now though, the clearest memories—other than the stuff I got from the Lady and Intravil—are from my last incarnation. There are holes there—probably stuff that Kregor absorbed—but otherwise it seems to be pretty complete."

Jace flinched. He knew. He'd suspected, but now he knew that I remembered my time with

Kyle with near-perfect clarity. I wished that there was a way not to hurt Jace, but I wasn't doing him any favors by hiding the extent of the changes my sword had worked on me.

It was bad enough that Jace knew I'd just spent what felt like years swimming back down memory lane—through a time when I'd been happily married to Kyle—but I could see that everyone else was starting to clue in too.

The Lady was the first to clear her throat. "Fenrir, the Minotaur and the Dragon aren't scheduled to rematerialize for a while still, but it's not a perfect science. It would probably be best if Intravil and I were out there ready to assist in case we get an unexpected surge of people reappearing."

I grabbed her arm, stopping her before she could leave. It was the kind of action that I never would have considered before this, but the balance of power had shifted back to something much more like our early days together.

I had a well of emotions and memories that was the next best thing to limitless. There was still a chance that she would eventually become more powerful than me, but that day was centuries in the distance.

As things stood now, even working two-hundred years' worth of effects to satisfy my debt to her wouldn't even be a sacrifice because I would know that those memories would eventually all make their way back to me.

"Were you ever going to tell me?"

"I don't know. I provided you with hints, but it was safer for you if nobody suspected that I had a weak spot where you were concerned. I've tried to tell you over more incarnations than most people can imagine, but you became so different after that first incarnation. You were darker—driven by anger more than anything else. I kept hoping each time you died that you would come back the way I remembered you from the first time around, but time and time again you didn't.

"I'd nearly given up hope by the time I saw you outside of Kyle's bunker. You were still driven mostly by anger, but for the first time in forever, there was an undertone of joy there. I could sense it in the energy I absorbed during the fight with Fenrir."

I nodded in understanding of all of the things she wasn't saying. Nobody else could possibly understand the lonely vigil she'd experienced. I would probably be hailed as a hero for having turned the course of this battle and saving billions of people, but it had been the Lady who had laid much of the ground-work for our victory.

She'd fought an unending war against the dark fae even before the Unseelie Court had existed, and she'd done it primarily because I—in my first incarnation—had asked her to. It was a kind of loyalty that defied understanding or definition.

"Thank you for trusting me with the Scepter of Storms. I know how hard that must have been for you."

"It wasn't as hard as you think. I'd seen you relinquish it before—I knew that you would give it back to me again when the time was right."

One by one, the rest of my friends and family filed out of the room. Ari went quietly, but I could see the questions in my dad's eyes as Kat led him out. I gave him my most reassuring smile, hoping that it would help him see that he was always going to be my father, that nothing I'd remembered had changed that.

Byron might have been my first father, but that didn't take anything away from the man who had spent the last seventeen years caring for me, the man who'd pressed on even after Mom had died. I owed a great debt to him, a debt that I was going to do my best to repay in the time I had left with him.

It wasn't surprising to me that Byron lingered on after most of the others had left. "I'm not sure what to say. The idea that I might have had a family in past incarnations isn't exactly a shock, but I never thought that any of them might have been Awakened. I never thought that I might be standing face to face with someone who could tell me how it all started. Where do we go from here?"

"We take it a day at a time. It's going to take some time, but I'll do my best to fill you in on the high points. I don't know anything at all about several of your incarnations, but in the two I know best, you were a great man, one I was proud to know."

"I only wish that I'd continued that legacy this time around. I nearly cost us everything with my vain quest to sidestep the violence I saw coming for me centuries ago."

I reached up and wrapped my arms around him. "There is a thread of shared experience that runs through our various incarnations, Byron. It's slender—so thin that most of the time we never even suspect it might be there, but it is. After what you've been through in some of your previous lives, I don't blame you for wanting a break from war.

"It doesn't make you any less of a great man. There is a reason that the Lady agreed to assist you. She broke thousands of years of neutrality to help you create Camelot. I think that she recognized you from my stories. I think that she wanted to help the man I'd told her about, the man who made me what I was."

Byron's eyes were suspiciously bright as he turned to leave the room, but he managed to make it out without crying, and then it was just Jace, Kyle and me. The same way it had been for more than four centuries.

"You remember what it was like to be with him, don't you? You remember just how happy the two of you were…"

"Yes."

I wasn't sure how to proceed, but it didn't end up mattering. Jace didn't give me a chance to say anything else.

"I won't stand in your way, Selene. This is the perfect opportunity for the two of you. He's lost all of his memories, and now rather than just reading about what you had with him, you experienced it again. I don't need you to paint a picture for me. If I'd had any doubts, the way that you've made sure he was taken care of over the last few minutes would have laid them to rest."

Jace turned to go, but I grabbed his arm. "You're not wrong about what I saw while I was reliving all of that. Kyle and I were desperately happy. I spent most of those centuries so happy I could barely see straight. More importantly, I understand how Kyle's obsession took root. He considered all of the rest of us his responsibility.

"When he lost everything, that sense of responsibility was combined with a sense of powerlessness that would have warped some of the strongest men to have ever lived. I know what we did wrong last time. I know how to bring him back and have him be like the old Kyle, the one that you and I both knew and loved."

Jace flinched with every word, but it needed to be said. He needed to hear all of it. Someone else would have lashed out at me, but not Jace. He wanted to—needed to—but something inside of him knew it was wrong, and Jace was better at listening to that guiding voice than almost anyone else I knew.

I took a deep breath and continued. "I want to bring the old Kyle back—I'm committed to it—and not just because we'll need his help. I've watched this play out before, Jace. Any time a group of people get together and try to create something better, the rest of the world comes together to try to destroy that creation. Sometimes it takes time—hundreds of years even—but eventually it happens.

"We've won a tremendous battle, but there are still Awakened out there who didn't join either side, Awakened who were too dangerous even for Kyle to bend to his will. We have to have his help—now rather than twenty years from now—if we are going to have a chance of surviving what's coming."

Jace was shaking now. "You don't have to justify yourself to me, Selene."

"Yes I do. I know it's going to be hard for you to have him around like that while we are together, but it needs to be done."

Surprise flashed through his eyes, and I saw a flare of hope—incredibly strong but quickly suppressed.

"I saw how happy Kyle and I were, Jace, but I also saw the relationship that you and I had. You weren't just what I needed at the time, you were what I needed. I loved Kyle, but I loved you just as much, and the only thing that kept our relationship from being perfect was the fact that you always thought that I picked you because I didn't have any other choice.

"This is me making sure that you know I have a choice. I could bring Kyle back, and I *will* bring Kyle back, but it's you I want to spend the rest of this incarnation with—and all future incarnations. This isn't just until death do us part, Jace. If I die I'll eventually come back into contact with my sword and relive this moment and every other moment leading up to this one.

"It's funny considering that we can't ever be destroyed, but I never really believed in forever until now. I believe in forever, and I choose you—forever."

Author's Note

I hope that you've enjoyed Endless. I always envisioned The Awakening as a trilogy, but I would be lying if I told all of you that I couldn't see other directions for The Awakening to continue. I don't have any plans right now to write a fourth book in The Awakening Series, but it's hard to say what the future will bring, so don't be surprised if at some point we all visit, Selene, Jace, Kat, Bethany and the Lady to see what happens next. The only thing I can guarantee is that none of you will be able to guess what the good guys will be up against next.

Acknowledgements

The Awakening was a labor of love that consumed a significant chunk of my life, but despite everything I put into these books, they never would have been possible without the help of an amazing group of people.

The first round of thanks needs to be expressed to my tireless editors, RJ Locksley and Amy Jirsa-Smith. I don't really believe in perfect books, but without these two ladies, Endless (and the rest of The Awakening books) would have been even further away from perfection than they already are. Thank you both for your assistance cleaning up so many of the mistakes my fingers put into the original manuscript.

My team of advance readers continue to be much better and more amazing than I deserve. A big thanks to Jenine, Janelle, Mei, Heather, Merissa, Mimi, Mark, Mom, Dad, Shalese, Matthew, Lachele and Kim. Thank you one and all!

With the launch of The Awakening I also added a special group of readers to my launch team. You are too numerous to list out here, but please know how much I appreciate all of you!

Finally, I most definitely couldn't have done this without my wife, Katie. She was the one who convinced me it was time for us to try this crazy writing thing full-time and not only has she been my first reader for nearly a decade, she's created a breathtaking array of stunning covers to go along with my words. Thank you, Katie!

About the Author

Dean Murray is a prolific author with dozens of titles across multiple pen names and more than half a million copies of his work currently in circulation.

Dean started reading seriously in the second grade due to a competition and has spent most of the subsequent three decades lost in other people's worlds.

Things worsened, or improved depending on your point of view, when he first started experimenting with writing while finishing up his accounting degree. These days Dean has a wonderful wife and two lovely daughters to keep him rather more grounded, but the idea of bringing others along with him as he meets interesting new people in universes nobody else has ever seen tends to drag him back to his computer on a fairly regular basis.

Keep up to speed on Dean's latest projects at deanwrites.com.

Stone Heart

Dani's new home isn't just another stopover in a long chain of places she'll never see again, it's the home of both Caine and Jerek, two guys like nobody she's ever met before. One represents the best friend she's been hungering for, and the other represents something much more.

It should be the perfect recipe for a fairytale, but Caine and Jerek live in a dark, shadowy world and one of them is hiding secrets that will change everything, secrets that relate directly to Dani.

The Society

People need to be monitored, or they'll repeat the mistakes of the Desolation, a centuries-old war that killed billions of people and destroyed civilization.

Skye is part of the Society, the hi-tech, nanite-endowed group responsible for making sure that the millions of surviving people—grubbers—are confined to the ancient, decaying cities where they can be watched to ensure they aren't redeveloping the weapons technology that came so close to extinguishing life on the planet.

When the Society's monitoring programs pick up troubling developments in one of the grubber cities, Skye is ordered in to deal with the man responsible, but what—and who—she finds once she arrives will change everything.

Broken

Adri Paige's arrival in Sanctuary thrusts her into a dangerous, shadowy world most people don't believe exists, and places her in the middle of a war between darkly handsome Alec Graves and charismatic Brandon Worthingfield that threatens to consume the entire town.

On the surface, both Alec and Brandon are nothing more than average high-school guys, but as Adri is pulled ever more deeply into their conflict she realizes that one of them wants to kill her. Adri needs to decide who to trust before her time runs out once and for all.

The Greater Darkness:
(Writing as Eldon Murphy)

Something powerful is stirring in the darkness. Something so ancient that even creatures who've been alive for hundreds of years have long since discounted this new threat as nothing more than myth.

Normal humans will be caught in the crossfire, but then that's always the way of things. Geoffrey has no memory of his past life or any idea how to survive in the violent, dangerous world in which he's trapped. Despite his best efforts, he's about to find himself in the middle of a conflict that threatens to sweep away everything, and everyone he's been fighting so hard to protect.

Frozen Prospects

The invitation to join the secretive Guadel should have been the fulfillment of dreams Va'del didn't even realize he had. When his sponsors are killed in an ambush a short time later, he instead finds his probationary status revoked, and becomes a pawn between various factions inside the Guadel ruling body.

Jain's never known any life but that of a Guadel in training. She'd thought herself reconciled to the idea of a loveless marriage for the good of her people, but meeting Va'del changes everything. Their growing attraction flies against hundreds of years of precedent, but as wide-spread attacks threaten their world, the Guadel have no choice but to use even Jain and Va'del in their fight for survival.